I0552706

THE VERY
BEST OF
TRUE
EXPERIENCE
VOLUME I

On Newsstands Now:

TRUE STORY
and
TRUE CONFESSIONS
Magazines

True Story and *True Confessions* are the world's largest and best-selling women's romance magazines. They offer true-to-life stories to which women can relate.

Since 1919, the iconic *True Story* has been an extraordinary publication. The magazine gets its inspiration from the hearts and minds of women, and touches on those things in life that a woman holds close to her heart, like love, loss, family and friendship.

True Confessions, a cherished classic first published in 1922, looks into women's souls and reveals their deepest secrets.

To subscribe, please visit our website:
www.TrueRenditionsLLC.com or call **(212) 922-9244**

To find the TRUES at your local store, please visit:
www.WheresMyMagazine.com

THE VERY BEST OF TRUE EXPERIENCE

VOLUME I

From the Editors
Of *True Story* And
True Confessions

Published by True Renditions, LLC

True Renditions, LLC
105 E. 34th Street, Suite 141
New York, NY 10016

Copyright @ 2013 by True Renditions, LLC

All rights reserved. No part of this book may be reproduced or transmitted in any form or by any electronic means, without the written permission of the publisher, except where permitted by law.

ISBN: 978-1-938877-57-5

Visit us on the web at www.truerenditionsllc.com.

Contents

It was a strange marriage and an
even stranger honeymoon. My husband seemed
charming and attentive at first, but, at no time,
not even a moment, was I able to forget that it
could all disappear in an instant, because. . . .

I PAID A MAN
TO MARRY ME!

It wasn't *my* fault that I wasn't good looking like the rest of my family. It didn't keep me from the same romantic dreams and ambitions as Ruth and Katherine, my sisters, who had married well, if not brilliantly, and were perfectly happy, with husbands and children

Then, one day, I faced the truth: Even with all my father's money, I couldn't get a husband. What was the matter with me? I tried to take an inventory—average hair, a respectable figure, and yet, a manner that was diffident—an inability, apparently, to feel at ease when everyone around was happy and relaxed. I knew that those traits might have been counted as liabilities. On the other hand, as Katherine often said, I had style. I knew how to wear clothes well, and I was intelligent. I knew that I could give a deep and lasting devotion to the man I loved, and I believed that I would be able to make a man happy.

Surely, those are assets, I repeated over and over again. Many men didn't ask for more than that. And then, I did have my father's money. . . .

That was where my inevitable downfall began. I believed that money could buy something that only character should bring. I believed that a man could be bought.

Later, I wondered how anyone could have been so deluded, and yet I knew, as we all know, that the world is full of frightened and unhappy women who hold to that belief as tenaciously as they do to their religions. And none of them can ever learn through the experiences of people like me. They can learn only through sorrow.

It was on my twenty-fifth birthday that I decided I was going to marry before another birthday came around. Twenty-five! I thought. Katherine had married at twenty-one and Ruth at eighteen. What was the matter with me?

What was the matter with me, indeed, was that I actually believed that it was of any consequence how long one waited for the right man.

But I'd thought it most important then. I had been helplessly blinded by the emptiness of my life.

My unhappiness was elemental, as deep as any woman's who wants to be loved. I didn't know how long I would have drifted in that state of wretchedness if I had not met my father on the street one day, walking with a strange young man. The very fact that he was with a stranger made me look at him with a special interest.

"Harriet," Father said, "this is a young man I hope we're going to see a lot of. This is Douglas Kern. His father and I were business associates, a long time ago."

"Yes, Miss Flanders," Douglas Kern said, taking my hand. "As soon as my father died, the first person I thought of was your father. I knew that he could give me just the advice I needed."

"Has he?" I asked. I wasn't sure how well I kept the eagerness out of my voice, for his good looks, his friendliness, and his animation had set my heart to beating wildly.

"I'll say he has! He's introduced me to Mr. O'Rourke, and it looks as though I am going to make a fine connection." He smiled broadly and I couldn't help smiling in return.

"I'm so glad," I told him. "Then we surely will see you often. Don't forget!"

"How could I?" he answered gallantly. I felt a sudden tremendous wave of excitement.

"I can help get you settled," I said, smiling, as I took Father's arm.

As Father and I walked up the street, I asked him about Douglas Kern.

"I don't know anything about the boy," Father said gruffly. "His dad was a clever businessman—maybe the boy takes after him. Anyway, I'm glad to help."

I squeezed Father's arm. "You're always glad to help, aren't you?" I asked. "There never was a father like you."

"There never were many daughters like you, dear," he said. "I guess I ought to know."

My eyes filled with tears. Dear Father. Ever since Mother had died, he had lavished all his love on me. I knew that he sensed my unhappiness, although he never mentioned it. I felt that one of the greatest happinesses that would come to him would be for him to see me contentedly married.

Things happened very swiftly after that. I still don't remember all that took place, which is remarkable, as it were my ambitions that were being realized.

Douglas began coming to the house—cheerful, handsome, full of a zest that seemed the very height of romance to me. Almost without my knowing it, I had an escort—an escort that any girl would have been proud to be seen with. He danced well, and he played bridge, golf, and tennis well. In other words, he had everything that spelled popularity with the set of which I longed to be a part. It grew to be, "Harriet, will you bring that nice Mr. Kern up for cocktails tomorrow?" Or, "Harriet, you seem to be the only one who can persuade Douglas Kern to come to the barbecue next week." I was in heaven. Everything that I'd always wanted seemed almost within my reach. I remember that I actually pinched myself once to make quite sure that I was not asleep.

Douglas's success with Mr. O'Rourke, a rich real estate speculator, sounded like a success story. Mr. O'Rourke was apparently so struck by his ability that, very soon, he put him in charge of the investment department of the business.

"A secretary and everything, Harriet!" Douglas told me enthusiastically. "What do you think of that, for a poor boy who didn't have anything?"

"And, is your secretary a blonde?" I teased him, my heart overflowing with joy for his success.

"Actually, she has brown hair," he answered succinctly. "She used to be my dad's secretary. I sent for her when I heard that Mr. O'Rourke had ordered a secretary for me. She understands the funny Kern ways."

"Oh, I think it's wonderful, Douglas!" I exclaimed, and suddenly my throat got very tight.

What is this going to mean to me? I wanted to ask. Douglas had been at the house so often—and, whom had he come to see, if not me? There was no one else to see, except Father. Douglas was mine—I knew it! He couldn't help but be mine. I would die if I were wrong. I knew that I loved him for himself—for his personality and charm, his good looks, and his gentle ways. I could not, at that moment, have seen anything wrong with him if I had tried to.

He was talking excitedly, striding up and down the room. "I've got big plans, Harriet. No small-time dreams for me. I can do it, you know. I can be a big shot!"

"Yes, I know, Douglas," I answered, almost as excited as he was.

For Douglas, there was the promise of dizzy heights of business success—for me, the promise of success as a woman who was married, secure, and loved. I couldn't put it into words. I didn't dare. I merely looked at him, and perhaps, he caught some of my thoughts. He grabbed my hands and swung me around.

"We're a good team, Harriet. I don't think anyone could beat us!" he told me happily.

What had he meant? My heart beat wildly, but he said nothing

3

more, and presently, let my hands fall. Yet I knew—somehow I knew—that it wasn't the end. It was only the beginning.

He sat down abruptly, opposite me. "Harriet," he said, "tell me about your old man. Does he like me? Does he think that I've got what it takes?"

I laughed. "I'm sure he does, Douglas. He has great respect for Mr. O'Rourke's judgment, and if he says that you're good, my father believes him. But, why do you want to know?"

"I admire your father," he said earnestly. "A man so rich and successful. It would mean a lot if I felt that a man like him thought the sky was my limit." A deep frown settled between his eyes. He was silent for a minute, and then he looked up at me, and there was a cold—almost ruthless—look in his eyes. "Do you think he believes that the sky's my limit?"

How could I answer for Father? My father, who had never discussed business with me? Yet, Douglas was forcing me to answer!

"I think that he'd allow a man like you the sky for a limit," was all I said.

It seemed to satisfy him. He stood up and threw out his broad, strong shoulders. "You'll both see," he promised.

My thoughts were so full of Douglas! Vera Longworth had just called and demanded that I bring him to the big annual dance at the club. I spoke about him to Father that night as we were having dinner alone.

"Don't you think that Douglas is coming along fast?" I asked. And I felt the sudden awful shiver of fear that he would not answer as I desired.

"Yes, he certainly seems to be," Father answered gruffly. "His own father understood all the shortcuts to success, too. I guess he must have learned plenty of lessons."

"Father!" I exclaimed. "You sound as though Douglas weren't honest."

"I don't know anything about the boy," my father answered. "But I know enough about business to know that quick success is seldom just luck."

I couldn't go on with my dinner—I was suddenly sick at heart.

"You mean to tell me that you distrust Douglas?" I asked.

"No, I don't mean that," he told me. "I'm just too old, and sick, to be carried away by illusions."

"Father!" I cried in dismay. "What do you mean? Has the doctor told you anything—"

"No, dear, nothing new. The old machinery is bound to run down someday." He patted my hand. "I haven't any ambitions anymore—they're all behind me. All but one—to see you happy."

4

I leaned over and kissed him. "I know that. You've been the most wonderful father anyone could have."

"Tell me," he shot out as though he'd just had a new idea. "Are you in love with Douglas?"

I felt the color flood my face, and for some unaccountable reason, I fumbled for words.

"Yes, I guess I am," I answered finally, not able to say anything more to express my full need for Douglas.

"Hmm," Father said. "I see!" Then, after a moment, he went on. "I guess you're old enough to know your own mind. I just want you to be happy."

And, oh, I was so happy the next night! All my dreams had come true. I couldn't imagine anything more in the world to want. Douglas had asked me to marry him! The moon and the stars seemed to hang motionless. All the sounds of the country seemed to be waiting, listening, as there, on that country lane, he'd put his arm around me and begged for my answer.

I was in such ecstasy that I wasn't able to say a word. It seemed as though the flood of happiness that swept over me had drowned my voice. Finally, I said yes—that was all—and buried my head against his shoulder.

He shouted out happily and, holding me by the shoulders, kissed me again and again. "The sky's the limit, Harriet!" he cried. "You and I—the sky's the limit!"

"Yes, my darling—" I murmured as he clasped me tenderly in his arms. Everything I wanted was given to me in that one moment.

It hurt my pride a little to have my engagement treated like a source of surprise and wonder. I could almost hear some of my friends saying, "Well, who would have thought it? Harriet Flanders has landed Douglas Kern! Why, he could have had anyone!"

He could have had anyone, but he wanted me! my heart sang over and over.

Ruth was outspokenly pleased. Katherine took me in her arms and kissed me.

"You know how happy I am, honey, if you're happy," she murmured.

Only Father seemed reticent. At no time did he express his approval though, by the same token, he said nothing to discourage me. He knew of the parties that were given for us. He was always friendly and jovial with Douglas, who was in and out of the house as often as he could be, but I knew that he was dissatisfied. That subtle attitude of his was the only thing that made me hesitate about naming the day for the marriage. Douglas kept prodding me. "We'll have to decide where we're going to live," he would say. One day he suggested a new idea.

"Unless you think we could stay with your dad for awhile?"

"Do you want to do that?" I asked, hoping—praying—that he would feel the need of our own home as much as I did.

"Well—we haven't a lot of money yet. We have to keep up appearances. I don't know whether we could afford the sort of place we should have, with my position."

"Your position isn't any better than Percy Grant's," I couldn't help saying, "and they don't pay much rent for their house."

He grinned and took me in his arms. "Honey, my position is going to get better all the time. In a year, you won't be able to say that."

I kissed him happily, my heart swelling with pride. "I'll do whatever you want to, darling."

"Talk to your dad, then," he coaxed. "Maybe he'll—" He didn't try to finish the sentence.

I talked to Father that evening. He was looking pale and his manner was listless, but I felt a good deal of the reason for that lay in the fact that we hadn't been entirely honest with each other. I sat at his feet and, holding his hand, told him about Douglas's and my conversation that afternoon. He didn't make any comment for some time, and then he interrupted abruptly.

"You're sure this marriage is going to be everything you've hoped for?" he asked.

I squeezed his hand. "Quite sure, Father. Are you sure that you're not just worried about losing your youngest daughter?"

"My youngest daughter deserves all the happiness that she can get," he answered. "That's all I'm thinking of. I just want to be sure she's getting it."

I was silent for a minute, struggling with my words. "The truth is that you don't quite like Douglas. Isn't that it? Why?" I asked finally.

It seemed to me that the minutes were hours before he replied. "Personally, I have nothing against the boy. He's jolly and full of fun and has brains. It's just that I've heard little things about him, things that one can't track down—hints that he's pretty sharp and not very scrupulous."

I felt such hot anger then that, for a moment, I almost hated my father. My voice was very cold when I responded.

"I don't believe it. People are always jealous of a young man who knows what he wants."

"Maybe they are," Father answered gently. "But perhaps it's not always jealousy. Maybe they realize that unscrupulousness in business may mean unscrupulousness in the home, and can cause the wife great suffering."

"No! No!" I cried. "I won't listen to this. It's not like you to make

6

a lot out of rumors and hearsay. Why, Douglas has made every young man in this town look silly. I'll bet he's the most talked-about person in town! And I'm proud of him!"

I hardly knew what I was saying. Father put his arms around me and pressed my head against his shoulder.

"You're sure you don't want Douglas just because you see your sisters and your friends married—and because there is a ridiculous idea that young women are a failure if they haven't got husbands?"

I couldn't even listen to his words. They touched such a tender spot in me that I burst into wild crying.

"There, there," he said, stroking my hair. "I'm sorry, Harriet. I had no business saying that. Every girl has a right to a husband—and a right to make her own choice. I wish you'd just let me satisfy myself that everything that Douglas does is on the level. Just let it be a whim."

"Absolutely not!" I insisted as I wept. "I'd feel like a traitor. How could you ask such a thing? Make him tell you himself, if you're so afraid that he's dishonest."

Father's answer was gentle and calm. "You're the one who's marrying him, Harriet. It's up to you to decide what to do."

"Then I want to marry him as soon as possible," I whispered, still sobbing. "Waiting is tempting fate."

I realized much later that his patience had been wonderful. My words must have hurt him terribly, but he'd given me no indication of it.

"There is only one thing I want," he said, "and that is to feel that, married or not, you are independent. I'll arrange tomorrow to transfer forty thousand dollars in stocks and cash to your name. You'd get it when I died, anyway, and I'll feel better if I know that you have it. But keep it for yourself, child—for you, and your children."

I couldn't say anything. At last, I roused myself and kissed him. "Thank you, Father."

As I lay in bed, the thought went through my head: I'll tell Douglas the first thing tomorrow. Now we can have our own house!

From that day on, everything seemed to go swimmingly. Father, apparently, had resolved to see the best side of the marriage, and Douglas was jubilant. He agreed enthusiastically to the suggestion of buying of a house, and insisted that he be allowed to go over all the items of the settlement.

"Maybe I can double some of those stocks!" he exclaimed eagerly.

"No!" I said, with unexpected sharpness. "If Father couldn't get everything there was out of them, no one else could. I want to leave them exactly the way they came from him." I could see that Douglas was annoyed. "You think everything you touch will turn to gold," I teased him.

"Why not?" he answered promptly—harshly. I didn't answer, but I was determined that I would be my father's daughter in that one thing—I'd look after my own money.

A week before the ceremony, Father gave a huge party for us. Lanterns were strung in the trees, lights played on the fountain that stood in the midst of the garden, and an orchestra played for the dancing, which took place not only in the house, but on a terrace that had been built over the lawn.

Douglas was as excited as a child. I knew that he loved parties and all the conviviality of friends, and I was terribly proud of him that night. He looked so handsome in his evening clothes.

Just as the guests were beginning to arrive, he turned to me. "I entirely forgot to tell you, honey, that I asked Lana Foster, my secretary, to come tonight. You've never met her, and she's young and likes a good time. It seemed kind of mean to leave her out."

"Of course, darling," I answered. "I'm sorry that I didn't think of it myself."

When she appeared, Douglas went over promptly to speak to her and bring her over for me to meet. She was an extraordinarily pretty girl. Her voice was low and cultivated, and I took her hand impulsively.

"I'm so glad you've come," I said. "You look lovely. And, you must promise to have a good time."

I told Douglas to introduce her, and I saw her frequently, floating about in the arms of one man after another, apparently having a wonderful time. Then, I forgot about her completely.

It was my evening, and I made the most of it. It was the kind of evening that I had dreamed about all my life. What more could a girl want? Every time I looked at Douglas, my heart turned over. All those wonderful people had come to celebrate my happiness and know that I had as much right as they, to the kind of happiness that I desired. I received many compliments on the party and many wishes for my happiness. When Douglas and I danced together, I knew that many people were talking about us and that a few of them were genuinely pleased with my bliss.

The evening passed swiftly. Champagne flowed as only Father could make it flow, and the music got better and sweeter as the evening went on. I was floating on the very heights of joy.

I'll never know how long my happiness would have lasted if I had not stepped out onto the terrace for a moment to cool off. I sat in the dark silence for a minute, listening to the music, and looking at the stars. I was thinking that, in a week's time, I would be Douglas's wife. Suddenly, I was aware that others were sitting near me. I heard a man's voice protesting and a woman's voice weeping. It wasn't curiosity that made me listen—it was really solicitude for my guests. I could not hear their words, but I did realize, after a moment, that the man was Douglas!

At first, I thought very little about it. I would probably have slipped away had I not heard the voices growing louder and the girl's sudden cry.

"Douglas!" she said, as though she were suffering. I didn't hear their words and I did not know who the girl was, but I could tell by the inflection of Douglas's voice that he was speaking with great passion.

Suddenly, I felt cold all over. An icy hand seemed to hold me rigid, and I would have given a year of my life not to have come into the garden at that time. What did it mean? Was something happening that could touch my happiness? Was Douglas guilty of something that I did not know about? Try as I might, I couldn't make Father's words leave my mind

Eventually, my fright and apprehension made me slip through the bushes and run into the house. I flew upstairs to my room and, in the darkness, flung myself on the bed, trying to fight the insidious and gripping terror. I wasn't sure how long I lay there—torn by every conceivable, nameless fear—but after awhile, I heard a knock at the door. Douglas stood in the light of the hallway.

"Honey," he said softly, "the maid told me that you had come up here. What's the matter?"

"It's all right." I tried to speak naturally. "I'm coming downstairs."

He crossed to the bed and sat down, taking me in his arms. I wanted to hold him as tight as I could and force him to dispel my fears, but I did not dare let myself go. He held me very tightly for a moment.

"I wish you'd tell me, honey," he whispered. "We shouldn't keep anything from each other."

I knew that what he'd said was true. With a sudden panic, I wondered if there were anything wrong with a relationship that prevented me from speaking frankly to him. I tried to speak, but I couldn't. I gave up at last, puzzled and disturbed, and tried to powder my nose in the dark so that Douglas would not see my tearstained face. When I went downstairs, all the joy had gone out of my party

I was hysterical, I told myself the next day. My subconscious had taken in more of Father's old wives' tale than I had realized. I loved and trusted Douglas. I furtively smoothed the folds of my wedding gown which had just been hung in my closet. That gown was my badge of happiness—my passport to a new life!

I hid my face in its folds for a moment and the smooth softness seemed to calm me. Everything was going to be all right.

How was I to guess that I would have a caller that day—and what that would mean to me? Even when the maid announced that Miss Foster wanted to see me, I thought that she had just come to say what a nice time she had had the night before.

She seemed to me to be even more attractive in the daytime than she'd been at night, and I welcomed her in as friendly a manner as I knew how.

"Sit down," I said. "I really shouldn't be so nice to you because you were quite the belle of the ball last night. But, I'm glad. You certainly were an asset to the party."

She seemed nervous as she sat down and smiled only briefly.

"Where are you living in town? If I had only—" And then she interrupted me.

"Please—please!" she said nervously. "Don't be so friendly. I haven't come here as a friend."

"What do you mean?" I asked, sitting down weakly in a chair.

She hesitated for only a moment, and then began to speak resolutely. "Douglas and I—you mustn't marry him! He's belonged to me for three years. I can't let him go!"

I thought afterward of how strangely expected those words had been. It was almost as though I had been waiting for them. And yet, I hadn't known what to say. Her soft, low voice had gone on remorselessly. "He's terribly weak—and terribly ambitious. Between the two—" She shrugged her shoulders. My face must have been as pale as death, for she cried out solicitously. "Please, don't look like that! Isn't it better to face these things?"

"No," I said hoarsely, fear tugging at me frantically. "No—it's not better. I don't care how long you've had him. All I know is that he's mine now and I intend to keep him!"

"How can you expect him to be faithful to both of us?" she asked.

"I don't!" I almost shouted. "His wife will be enough for him. Oh, I hate you! You came here last night and started this. You were with him in the garden, weren't you?"

"Yes," she admitted.

"Why hasn't he married you, if you love each other so much?" My voice rose wildly. "Why is he marrying me when he could have you—if he wanted you?"

She answered in a low, clear voice. "I told you that he is very ambitious. The fact is—you have money."

It was as though she had put a knife in me. For a moment, the pain was so great that I could hardly think. All the agonies of frustration and despair that I had felt before I met Douglas hurtled back at me and I wanted to scream and scream in an effort to drive them away.

"I'm terribly sorry," she said, almost kindly. "I had to say it. You must understand the situation."

"Tell me one thing," I demanded, rigid with an effort to control myself. "Did Douglas send you here? Did he know that you were coming?"

"No, he didn't," she confessed.

"Then—get out! Get out as fast as you can. And, I don't ever want to see you again!" I had gotten to my feet and stood with my hands clenched in front of me. "Get out," I said again, almost in a whisper.

"I understand," she told me as she stood up. "But be sure of what you're doing—if you marry Douglas."

"If I marry Douglas?" My breath caught on the words. As the door closed behind her, I gave way to hysterical weeping, and only the cold compresses of Darla, the maid who'd heard me, were able to quiet me.

Of course, as Lana Foster knew, I was not able to free my mind of her words. They ran through my head until I thought I would go mad. I couldn't think of, or feel, anything except the terrible implications of what she had said. Would I have to buy my man, after all?

The humiliation was almost as hard to face as the defeated sense of love—for I truly loved Douglas. Could I go through a ceremony with him and have Lana's words buried deep in my heart and mind? No, there was only one thing to do—find out if what she'd said was the truth.

Women who have suffered the same agony—and, I don't pretend that I was the only one—know how fateful that decision was. Would I have the courage to send him away if I discovered that what Lana had said was true? In all honesty, I didn't know.

He came to see me that night. He was as full of plans as ever—talking, telling me things, and leaving me no chance to say anything about myself. At last, I asked him to come out on the terrace with me as I had something very important to say. My heart seemed to be choking me, and I couldn't say anything for a moment. Then, I recited my little speech as hurriedly and calmly as I could.

"Douglas, I feel I must tell you. Things have been happening. Father—" I almost could not go on. "Father has had to cut my settlement in half."

It had been said. I couldn't take back those words. I could never fool myself again. I had burned all my bridges.

To my horror, I felt him stiffen. He said nothing at all. "Well," he said at length, and his voice was tight and hard. "Well, that's—not so good."

"What do you mean, Douglas?" I asked, still hoping—hoping that I would hear a lover speak.

"Either you're double-crossing me—or your father's a skinflint!" I'd never heard such venom in a voice. "Nothing's happened to his money, I know. Which is it?"

All life seemed to drain out of me. My voice was a whisper. "You have no right to say that, Douglas. You know that that's a lie."

"A lie! Why should it be?" he demanded furiously. "You led me to believe one thing and now—a few days before our wedding—you tell me something that can't be true."

"Then, that's all that marrying me means to you?" I got the words out with a supreme effort.

He hesitated for a moment. Then, he answered me, and his voice was harsh and low. "Yes."

I backed up against the wall of the house and tried to steady myself. I saw him glance at me, and after a moment, he came toward me. I didn't know what was going through his head, but I suspected that he felt that he had overplayed his hand. There might be something, still, in a girl with half of forty thousand dollars. Oh, could any thought be more bitter than that?

"I'm sorry, Harriet," he said, taking one of my cold hands. "Maybe I shouldn't have spoken that way. But, after all, you know me pretty well by now. I'm going places and I can't be sentimental about it. Whoever helps me can come along. Otherwise—I haven't time."

"What about Lana Foster? Can she come along, too?" I asked.

He dropped my hand as though it had burned him. "What do you know about Lana Foster?" he demanded.

"I heard you in the garden last night," I said, content with half the truth rather than the scene that I knew would ensue if I told him Lana had been to see me.

"Lana's a nice kid. She's pretty. But it's nothing serious, Harriet. Get that into your head." He seemed fiercely determined to make me understand.

"I don't know anything about that," I said stiffly. "All I know is that you brought her here to town."

He didn't answer. Finally, he tried to take my hand again. "I'm sorry, Harriet. But it's better to be frank. I'm not going to marry you unless you have the forty thousand dollars—because I need it."

It was blackmail, and I knew it. He was blackmailing my marriage! Which was more important—to have honor and self-respect and no husband, or to go through with a marriage that would be a farce? I couldn't answer it then, and no one realized the shame of not being able to answer it, better than I.

"I see," I whispered.

"I like you, Harriet. I like you a lot. I probably love you as much as I'd love any woman, but love isn't enough for me and it never will

12

be. What about it?" His tone was cold and brisk, almost businesslike.

"I'll tell you later." I had to get into the house or I was afraid I would break down right then and there. "Come back tomorrow night."

"Okay," he snapped.

So, that's the end, I thought to myself. There goes the romance. There goes Harriet Flanders's husband, home, and happiness.

I didn't sleep much that night. A troop of nightmares passed before my opened eyes.

I couldn't fight it—anything but to give up my new prestige in the eyes of those that I knew. I barely considered my self-respect. It had ceased to have even any arguing value. I couldn't measure how far I had sunk. It seemed to be the nadir.

The next evening, I told Douglas in a small, strained voice that I had pleaded with Father and he had agreed not to cut the settlement. As a sort of nod to my own dignity, I added an amendment to the original arrangement.

"He doesn't trust you, though. He wants me to handle the money myself."

He looked at me silently, and I knew what has going through his head: Harriet will be wax in my hands. Then, he smiled. "That's good. I'm glad. I'll try to make you happy, Harriet. You're a fine girl."

You're a fine girl. The memory of his words rang over and over above the organ music and the sound of the minister's voice. In my opinion, he might as well have said, "You've given me the money, and all you get out of it is the knowledge that your husband doesn't love you." As I came down the aisle after the service on Douglas's arm, trying to smile at all the guests who were crowded in the pews, I realized that I had betrayed every decent instinct that a woman could have.

The reception was an agony. But, I smiled, shook hands, accepted congratulatory kisses, cut the wedding cake, accepted the bridal toast, and finally, went upstairs to change into my traveling clothes. Had there ever been a honeymoon like mine was going to be? Whom had I to blame but myself?

When the door to my room was suddenly flung open and Lana Foster stood there, pale and wild looking, I really felt no surprise. What she represented was all a part of the picture.

"So, you did it!" she said. "Maybe you think that you'll get away with it—but you won't! You'll be sorry! I'll curse your marriage!"

One of the maids had caught hold of her arm by then and was trying to pull her toward the door. She shook the maid off.

"I'm going. I have nothing more to say, except that you don't have to worry about me anymore. I wouldn't stay in the same town with you two. I'm clearing out today. And you may have him—and all your grief—without my interference!"

"I'm sorry, Miss Harriet—" the maid began, but I stopped her with a gesture.

"Help me with my hat, please," I said. "I mustn't keep my husband waiting."

I can't even begin to describe the weeks that followed. They were no better and no worse than I'd expected. I was deeply grateful that we had our own home, for then I could keep the real situation from Father and my sisters. I believed that Katherine sensed some of it; but she said nothing about it—and when we were out together, Douglas was gallant and attentive to me. He was pleasant at home, too. It was merely that never for a moment, day or night, was I allowed to forget the sword that hung over my head.

In spite of the fact that I ostensibly controlled my money, Douglas got every cent of it that he wanted. I didn't have the heart to fight him. His ambitions were beyond all reason as soon as he knew that forty thousand dollars was practically within his hand. He left his company and started out as an investment broker on his own. I was sure that he was as slick and smart as any man, but he was a born gambler. To take risks seemed to him the highest kind of business judgment. He had no respect for men who "plodded along," as he called it, and were satisfied with a small profit at regular intervals.

"What if I do lose money? I can always make it up again!" was his motto.

Father must have known something about what was happening because Mr. Pedersen, the president of the bank, was a close friend of his. But, he never said anything to me. He seemed only to grow paler and thinner before my eyes. Within six months, Douglas forced me to go to Father and ask for some more money. I argued and pleaded with him, but he was adamant.

"Either you go to see your father, or I leave," he told me. "I've got to have the money or everything I've been building up will go to ruin. Which is it?"

After he had said those words over and over again, a significant number of times, my brain seemed to be numb. I agreed to speak to my father.

It was the hardest thing that I had ever done. His judgment of Douglas's character had been so extravagantly fulfilled that I felt I should go to him on my knees. But, he was very understanding. He took me in his arms and when I started to cry, he dried my tears with his big handkerchief.

"I'll bolster up his credit if that's what he wants. Money isn't worth breaking your heart over, Harriet."

"It's just—" I tried to say through my sobs, "it's just that I've—"

14

He hugged me. "Never mind, my dear. I know. Happiness isn't always where we think it is."

Douglas wasn't any too pleased to have credit, rather than money, but I suppose he realized that it was the best he could do. Once, I'd suggested that he give up the insane idea of having his own business. I knew that any number of men would have been only too glad to have him with them, if he acted right away, before he got a bad name. But, he'd sworn at me violently.

"Don't be a fool! I'm too good to work for any man."

That was only one of our quarrels. They took place at all times, over the months that passed. Every time anything went wrong he threw up to me the fact that he didn't love me, but that I had made him marry me, anyway. I knew that his new secretary had taken Lana's place—in every sense of the word.

Anyone had a right to ask why I'd stayed with him. The only answer that I could give is that my pride had still paralyzed me, in spite of the fact that our quarrels had become public property. And, beyond that, I still—incredible as it may have seemed—loved some old dream about him. I'd always hoped and believed that he would change—that a miracle would happen.

It was that deep-seated belief that made me decide to have a child. It was another of those blind impulses that left me no time to think of what a terrible thing I might be doing to the child. I tried to reassure myself that Douglas liked children and that surely, he would see the need of preserving our child's happiness.

The baby was a boy and we named him Duncan, for my father. Father adored him, and Douglas seemed like a different man when he was holding the baby or looking at him in his crib. I almost allowed myself to believe that there was a chance for us. I realized, all too soon, that I had cheated myself again and, on top of that, given Douglas a weapon which could hurt me more than anything he had used in the past.

In spite of his unquestionable love for Duncan, he used him deliberately and cold-bloodedly as a whip to extort more money from my father. He threatened to leave me and take Duncan with him if I didn't get what he needed and, in my fear, I didn't allow myself to regard his threat as merely that—a desperate attempt to manipulate me.

Father finally told me that he had no more money to give me. His stocks had been wiped out by a bad market and Douglas held taken advantage of the credit that had been extended to him to such a point that he had put Father in a deplorable hole that seemed to be closing in on him. He told me that Douglas's affairs were hanging by a thread and only a lucky gamble would keep him from outright failure.

Duncan, at three years old, was the only real and true thing to me in those days. The morning I heard that Father had died in his sleep, I held little Duncan in my arms for hours, not heeding his squirming and cries. I had to have him close—I had to say his name over and over again, as though in some way, it would bring my father back to me.

Douglas was so nervous that I thought he would drive us all mad. He kept demanding to know how soon the will would be read, and when the time came, he paced up and down the room.

The will was very brief. It had been drawn up a bare month earlier. Father's estate had dwindled to the point where there was little beyond the house, the automobile, and small annuities for Ruth, Katherine, and me. The others knew who was to blame for the situation and didn't spare Douglas anything. I kept silent. What was there to say? The little annuity would barely keep Duncan and me if anything happened to Douglas. I didn't know, then, how soon it would have to be put to the test.

The reading of the will meant the end of Douglas's enterprises. His credit was gone and the enormous liabilities he had created for himself were enough to send him to prison. He had juggled funds and shortchanged everyone, it seemed.

But that humiliation did not come. Douglas was allowed to turn the business over to a receiver, but of course, he could not salvage a thing for himself.

His reaction to what had happened was not surprising. He had balanced himself for so long on a precarious, shifting sense of values that he had burned out all his stamina and had nothing to sustain him. The doctor ordered him to bed to prevent a complete nervous breakdown. Practically overnight, we were swept away from a standard of comfortable living to virtual want. The annuity was all that stood between us and destitution.

I should have been inured to shock by then, but I found that I wasn't. Yet, as long as I could protect my son, I didn't care about Douglas and myself. When I found that my husband's doctor bills were cutting down Duncan's share, though, I felt the need for action. I talked to the doctor and he confirmed me in my suspicions.

"It's more mental than physical, Mrs. Kern," he told me. "If he'd get out and find a job, it would do wonders for him."

That night, I spoke to Douglas. I tried to make him see the need of immediate action, but he seemed to shrivel before my eyes.

"I can't!" he almost wailed. "I'm a sick man. I can't, and I won't! I'll never again be bossed by anyone again. When I'm well again, someone'll back me, and then you'll see."

I turned away wearily. What was the use? There were no more illusions to be torn from my eyes.

16

The next morning, I set out to find a job.

It was lucky that Father had had so many loyal friends. I had no training of any kind, but it wasn't long before I got a job in the hat department of our largest department store. Mr. Proctor, the personnel manager, made it very clear that it was because I was Duncan Flanders's daughter that I was getting the job. In time, I came to look forward to my hours there as my real life. The time I spent at home, with Douglas, was merely an interlude. Katherine had offered to keep the baby for me during the day, so I had no fear of any harm coming to him.

At night, I was tired. I would have given anything to be able to be someplace with Duncan alone. But, the fact was, Douglas was insatiable. He seemed to store up all his grievances, all his wild ideas, all his fantastic plannings, to hurtle at me when I sat down after dinner. If I did not respond as he thought I should, he would fly into a tantrum and curse me as though I were the commonest thing in the world. Sometimes I grew frightened. His mind seemed to have been affected.

If it hadn't been for Duncan, I might almost have felt sorry for Douglas. I knew that he had a good brain and undoubted capacity, all of which had been diverted into the wrong channels. But, his tantrums increased. One rainy night, Theo Wilde—the buyer of my department—brought me home in his car, and Douglas flew into a rage and accused me of unfaithfulness. I knew then I would have to leave him.

I had not been unfaithful to him, not even in my thoughts. Theo Wilde was an amusing and charming man, and I'd found that I had much in common with him. Suddenly, after Douglas's explosion, I questioned in all bitterness why I should be faithful, and why I had not met Theo Wilde a few years before. Then, I hid my face. The only brutally honest thing that Douglas had ever charged me with was the fact that I had compelled him to marry me. I was lying in the bed that I had made for myself.

But I believed that, for Duncan's sake, I should be free. I wouldn't ask anything for myself, but I knew in my heart that Duncan must be brought up in a normal and healthy atmosphere. It took all my courage to tell Douglas what I had decided.

"You'll have to learn to care for yourself," I finished after I'd had my say. 'You're young and have plenty of ability. You'd be the first to condemn a man—under ordinary circumstances—who'd allowed his wife to support him. Duncan is my first consideration. He's nearly four now, and old enough to realize that we live like savages."

"You can't leave me!" he screamed. "I'm a sick man. That's desertion."

"You're not too sick to go out and get drunk," I reminded him sharply.

"I'd die if I didn't have some fun!" he cried. "Nobody will give me a job. They see that I'm sick. Anyway, Duncan is my child as well as yours!"

"He's my child," I said coldly. "You can never take him from me."

I had never been so sure of anything in my life. I did not listen to anything else he said. That night, I decided to make my plans. I couldn't leave Duncan indefinitely with my sister, and yet I felt I couldn't take care of him until I was settled in my new life. Like a bolt from the blue, I suddenly remembered our maid's mother, a fine woman who lived a few miles out in the country. I was confident that she would take care of Duncan for a few dollars a week.

The next day, I spoke to the maid and she said she would arrange it. I didn't tell her that I was leaving Douglas. I merely said that Duncan needed a change.

That night, Douglas went out and, while he was gone, I packed my things. I had already taken a room near the store and I moved my suitcases there during the evening. I looked about the house. No woman could have had less sentimental ties. There was not a thing there that I would miss. What a terrible and sad commentary on my marriage!

All the next day, I lived in terror that Douglas would appear in the store and make a scene, but I was spared that. He called me up during the day and when I answered, all he said was, "So you're still there!" and hung up.

My nervous tension was so great that every time I picked up a hat, my hands shook like an old woman's. Every now and then, I had to sit down and wait for a spell of weakness to pass. I'd had no idea that I would feel such a reaction. It seemed as though all the agony of the past years was draining out of me and at the same time, taking some essential strength from me.

Theo Wilde noticed that I was upset and insisted that I have lunch with him. He didn't ask me any questions. He told me how good my work was and that he would be able to manage a raise for me after the first of the year.

My gratitude made me want to weep. What a kind, wonderful man! All that evening, I sat alone in my little room, my hands folded in my lap, doing nothing. What peace! What utter serenity!

For two weeks, I heard from Douglas only three times. That both surprised and relieved me. Once he asked where Duncan was, and another time, he asked for money. He made no move to see me. His tone seemed humble—almost broken. He'd called me "honey" when he'd called me the last time. It had touched something deep down that had never been destroyed. But, I still had no regrets about leaving him.

One Saturday, I'd planned to visit Duncan the next day. I'd just been going out to buy him a toy before dinner when I'd seen Kathleen's car drive up. Katherine ran into the house. I remember that I held onto the side of the window, an unaccountable terror gripping me.

Katherine came to see me often—why should I have been so frightened?

She must have been shocked by my expression when she pushed open the door, for she ran to me and put her arms around me.

"Steady, Harriet," she cautioned. "It's all right. Come and sit down." She held me as she led me to the couch and sat down beside me.

"What is it?" I whispered. "What's happened to Duncan?"

"There's been an accident, Harriet. There now, you mustn't go to pieces! Duncan and Douglas are in the hospital."

"Douglas!" I almost screamed the name.

"Yes. It happened on Old Country Road. He must have gone to your maid's mother's for Duncan."

I was standing up then, fumbling with my hands, and trying to pull on my gloves. "Take me to Duncan immediately! I can't stay away another second!" I exclaimed.

"That's why I came," Katherine answered calmly. "They don't know the extent of the injuries, but Douglas was able to talk, and blamed the whole thing on himself."

"Yes, of course it was his fault," I cried fiercely. "He's taken everything from me. Now he wants to take Duncan!"

Katherine tried to soothe me, but all I could do was to tell her to drive more quickly. My terror was so great that I couldn't move.

When we reached the hospital, I jumped out first and ran through the open door.

"My baby!" I cried, clutching the head nurse by the arm.

She gripped me tightly by the shoulder. "I'm so sorry. We did everything we could. He died from the loss of blood."

"Douglas?" I asked, trembling—begging.

"No—the little boy," she told me softly.

I have no recollection of the next few days. Katherine told me later that they thought I was going to die. When I was able to be up and around, I wondered over and over why I had not died. I saw no purpose in living. Katherine said that Douglas wanted to see me, but I refused. I truly thought that I would kill him if I saw him. I couldn't work, although Theo Wilde told me that he would hold my job for me. All I could do was to think and dream of Duncan, and to store up a reservoir of hatred against the man who had taken him from me.

Hatred makes any woman old and ugly. It's a poison that destroys every normal thought. Kindness and consideration were wasted on me. Ruth finally told me that she didn't know what to do with me. She told me that I'd have to work it out in some way—myself. Katherine was the only one who stuck by me. In her brisk, candid way she tried to restore me to life. Where consideration failed, though, the brutal truth won out.

"Harriet," she said, "I wish you'd look at yourself. You don't even look human. I'd like you to see Douglas, too. Oh, now, don't jump up! I've never been very fond of Douglas, but he's suffering, too. And Harriet—" She paused and took a long drink of the cocktail she held in her hand. "You must never forget that you married Douglas for better or worse—and you knew it. What you did was a moral crime. Douglas told me—he doesn't defend himself. His side isn't a very pretty picture, but you both knew what you were doing—and apparently, you had a price to pay. One can't fool with life."

I looked at her, stunned. You can't fool with life, I thought. Was that what it amounted to? Of course, it was—that's why I'd felt no real shock at her words. Horror, yes, that such a thing could be true, but no disavowal of it.

"Katherine—" I stumbled over my words. "Katherine, I've done something so terrible! I did it to Duncan. I brought a child into the world who had neither a father nor a mother—just parents. I tried to use him to remedy something that was already rotten. Oh, Katherine, this is a terrible punishment—but I deserve it!"

I think my sister realized that my words had shaken me out of my hatred, and that the tears that followed were one of the best things that could have happened to me. After a while, she left me alone and presently, she came back with tea.

"Drink this," she said. "It's going to mean a new start, Harriet, but you've got your feet on the first rung of the ladder."

When I went home that night, I felt weak and drained—but it was as though everything had been emptied from me to ready me for a new life.

"You can't fool with life!" I whispered. I decided that I'd take my punishment like a woman and not cringe.

I went back to my job the following Monday and before the week was out, I had agreed to see Douglas. I knew that I had to do it if I was going to be genuinely honest with myself.

Douglas was thin and worn. He had none of that hard, bright glitter of confidence. But he had something else—humility.

"Harriet," he said. "Please forgive me. I'm trying."

"I know you are, Douglas," I answered gently. "So am I—trying."

We left it at that. Nothing has gone beyond that for six months, but Douglas, I know, is trying to make amends. And, so am I. He has a job—a job that would have been humiliating for him a year ago, but one which he seems to enjoy. I have no impulse anymore to divorce Douglas. I have a feeling that some day—some way—when we've worked out our punishment, who knows what the future will hold? And if we do decide to give our marriage another try, we'll be together because we both want to be.

THE END

SHE'S ONLY 4—
AND PSYCHIC!
My sweet little girl knows things
a child never should

My favorite time of day has always been twilight. I love the feel of the day wrapping up, the snug feeling I get when I see the lights coming on in the neighborhood, and hear the almost-audible sigh of the world slowing down for another day.

It was just that time of day when little Kaleigh Miller, a three-year-old friend of our daughter, Alexandra, was kidnapped. After that, it seemed as though there would never be a safe place in the world again. I remember glancing at the clock as I fixed dinner. Steve, my husband, would be coming home from a three-day stint as a fireman for the national park near where we lived. I'd missed him when he was gone, and I was looking forward to spending four days with him when he came home. I couldn't wait to see him.

My thirteen-year-old daughter, Melissa, was in her room upstairs. Supposedly, she was studying, but I could hear the sounds coming from her television set—as usual, she was watching the all-music channel she loved so much. Alexandra, my four-year-old, was curled up on the floor of the den playing with her dollhouse.

Just then, Steve walked in the door. The girls came flying in to hug their dad and tell him all their news. I stood back, smiling, until he turned to me and took me in his arms.

"I missed you," he murmured. He always said that to me, and I always loved hearing it.

"Me too, you," I whispered back to him.

Melissa, who was going through a trying period of being negative and contrary, broke the happy homecoming spell as we sat down to dinner. "Ugh, roast beef! I'm starving, but there is no way that I'm eating red meat."

Steve and I looked at each other and rolled our eyes. We had agreed that we had to be patient with Melissa, but she challenged our patience more than once in a day's time. I realized, and so did Steve, whom she adored, that she was a normal teenager—her hormones were raging.

Melissa was growing taller but she still didn't have much of a figure. We knew that she liked boys but, unlike some of her friends, she wasn't getting any attention from them yet, and it angered and bewildered her. Unfortunately, she took out a lot of her anger and moodiness on Alexandra. It was sad and unfair, because Alexandra absolutely worshipped her sister.

"Well, you can fill up on the veggies and bread," Steve said. "I'm starving, too, and I'll have some of that delicious roast beef."

Melissa sat down and started to fill her plate with food. She glanced at her dad quickly. She adored him so much that, despite her moodiness, she was obviously anxious for his approval. "I got an 'A' on my math test," she announced.

"I had a dream about a math monster," Alexandra said, obviously trying to keep the conversation upbeat.

"You are the monster," Melissa snapped. Finally, though, she smiled, and that made Alexandra beam with happiness. "You don't even know what math is."

"Yes, I do," Alexandra countered. "It's a bad man."

We all laughed then and Alexandra laughed with us. Sometimes it hurt her feelings when we were amused by the things that she imagined, because they were so real to her. Still, she was such a loving child, and so crazy about everything in the world that she knew, that it was hard not to find her endearing. Nothing detracted her from her flights of fancy—mixing fiction and real life together.

"Why don't we have a swimming pool?" Melissa demanded out of nowhere.

Both Steve and I groaned. Melissa was forever campaigning for a pool, but it was about the last thing on the list for Steve and me. We had enough money, but sometimes just barely enough and we were trying to save for a bigger house—and maybe one more child.

"How about a nice, cold shower?" Steve teased. "That ought to do more for you than splashing around in a heated pool."

"I am so sure," Melissa told him in her sarcastic, put-upon voice.

We finished dinner without too many more arguments and, after the kitchen was cleaned, the girls headed upstairs to their rooms. Alexandra loved to watch the two TV shows that she was allowed each night with her doll, Samantha. Melissa loved to talk on the phone, play her music, and pretend, sometimes, to do her homework.

I was in heaven as I sat snuggled next to Steve on the couch. I loved the precious and scarce time he and I had alone together. I started touching his body, feeling myself stir with desire for him.

He kissed me on the forehead. "Don't distract me," he whispered. "The kids are still awake, and it won't do you any good."

"Just wait till I get you upstairs," I murmured seductively, nibbling his earlobe.

It was at that moment that we heard an announcement on the news about a breaking news story. We both sat up a little straighter. There was always something a little chilling about the sound of the serious words "breaking news" on television.

"I hope it isn't a big fire," Steve said. "I'm beat. I don't want to be called back to work."

It wasn't a fire, though. We watched in horror as a pretty, somber-faced reporter stated that a three-year-old child had allegedly been kidnapped from a gas station near our home.

"The details of the story are as yet unavailable, along with name of the victim," the woman said. "What we do know is that the child was with her father, who was at the counter paying for gas. He thought his daughter was at his side, but when he turned around, she was gone. A search by the father and several store employees, as well as some patrons in the store, failed to locate the missing child. Stay tuned for more developments in the story as they develop."

"Oh, my God!" I exclaimed. "What a terrible tragedy! Maybe she just wandered away outside and got lost."

"I hope so," Steve said. "What kind of animal would kidnap a child?"

We sat silently for a few moments until Steve turned to me again. "I wonder if it's the gas station we go to all the time."

I felt a slight shock of fear go through me. "I don't know," I answered. "There are so many of those places around that it could be anywhere."

"I'm going to drive over there and see if it's the one," he told me as he stood up.

"No," I protested. "Don't go. I'm scared."

"You'll be okay," he said reassuringly, bending down to kiss my forehead. "I'll only be gone a few minutes. I'm really curious. I guess it's the fireman in me. I want to know where the action is, and see if I can help."

"But, honey, nothing is on fire," I reminded him, pulling on his hand to coax him back to the sofa.

"I want to go," he insisted. "I'll be right back."

I knew my husband well enough to know that there was no way I could talk him out of going. He did have a real concern for public safety.

I went upstairs to check on my girls after Steve had left the house. I didn't mention anything about what I had heard on the news to either of them. I just wanted to look at my kids and make sure that they were safe.

I knocked on Melissa's door. "I'm busy!" she shouted. "Go away."

I opened the door, anyway, and walked in. She was sitting at her computer, apparently chatting with one of her online friends. She loved sending emails, and she loved the teen chat rooms. I was careful to monitor what sites she logged onto on the computer. And, I'd warned her over and over about talking to strangers who might be preying on young girls.

"I know, Mom. I know," she'd always say, shaking her head in exasperation.

"That's a nice way to greet your mom," I tried to joke as I entered the room.

She looked at me angrily for a moment. Then, her eyes softened. "Sorry, Mom. That was rude of me. I'm just in the middle of some really good stuff with Ashley about a girl in our school that we both hate."

"Well, that sounds like a wonderful way to spend your time," I said sarcastically, but I gave her a hug, anyway. "I'll disappear. I just wanted to have a glimpse of your sweet face."

"Ugh," she groaned. "Sweet and full of zits. I am so hideous."

"Oh, please, not that again," I told her with an exaggerated sigh. "You know you're a beauty. And I am not saying that just because I'm your mom."

"You're weird," Melissa teased, smiling with pleasure at my remarks.

"I guess so," I said, doing a little jig for her. She rolled her eyes at as I left her room.

I knocked on Alexandra's door next. "Mom, Dad, is it you?" she called out excitedly.

"It's only one of us, and that's me. I hope I'll do," I told her as I walked in.

Alexandra smiled and held out her arms to me. She was in bed reading, or trying to read, one of her beloved books. She had taught herself to recognize a lot of the words in books and she loved to be read aloud to so that she could recognize even more. She was crazy about fairy tales. She loved stories about imaginary worlds where princes and poor girls found one another and lived happily ever after.

My youngest daughter had an imagination that wouldn't quit. One day when she was smaller, she was standing at the kitchen window looking out while I was cooking.

"Mom," she said dreamily. "When I grow up, I don't want to live in a house."

"Why not?" I asked, thinking for just an instant that she wasn't happy at home.

"I want to be a cloud," she announced with certainty.

"What a lovely idea," I told her.

Steve and I had warned Melissa time and again not to make fun of her sister and her imaginary world and friends.

"She freaks me out sometimes," Melissa complained. "She talks to people who aren't there."

"Well, they're there for her," I scolded. "And it doesn't do you, or anyone else, any harm to let her fantasize. When you were her age, you thought you were adopted. Do you remember that?"

Melissa blushed. "I remember. I thought I was really the pastor's little girl, because he was so handsome, and his wife was so pretty."

"Well?" I asked. "Kids have their own ways of seeing the world, and we mustn't hurt Alexandra's feelings. When she gets older, I'm afraid all of her little imaginary ways will give way to reality without our help. Let's let her enjoy her imaginary world while she can."

"She still freaks me out sometimes," Melissa muttered under her breath.

"Whatever," I said. "Just leave her alone."

Alexandra had very vivid dreams, too, which she loved to tell me about in sometimes patience-straining detail. They were mostly good dreams, but even the bad ones had happy endings. I suspected that Alexandra made them up, though, because she wanted everything in her world to have a happy ending.

I sat down on the bed with Alexandra. "What's the book you're reading tonight?"

"Alice in Wonderland," she replied. "Sometimes, I wish Alice never got near that rabbit hole. But then she never would have had an adventure."

"Well, don't you go looking for rabbit holes to fall into," I told her sternly.

Alexandra giggled. "Oh, Mom, my name isn't Alice. It could never happen to me." Her logic made me giggle, too. "I love you, Mommy," she said.

"And I love you, Alice," I teased.

Alexandra yawned. "I think I want to go to sleep. Where's Daddy? I want to kiss him good night."

"He went to the store," I lied. "I'll send him up to kiss you even if you are asleep."

"Okay," she agreed, burrowing down into her bed. "I always remember when he kisses me good night, even when I'm not awake, because I feel his lips on my cheek the next morning. His kiss stays warm."

"Is that right?" I smiled. I tucked her in and tiptoed out her door. Then, I heard the front door slam and hurried down to Steve. I was eager to find out if he had any news about what had happened to that little girl.

I gave Alexandra a quick kiss. "Daddy will be up in just a few minutes to kiss you good night."

"Okay," she mumbled, already half asleep.

I went downstairs to find Steve. He was slumped in a kitchen chair, his head in his hands.

"What's wrong?" I cried, afraid he had been in some kind of accident.

"It was our gas station. My hunch was right." Steve seemed to tremble all over. "It was Kaleigh Miller who disappeared," he said grimly.

At first I thought I had misunderstood him. "Kaleigh?" I repeated. "Our little Kaleigh? Hank and Audra's little girl? Oh, it can't be true. They are way too protective of her to let anything like that happen. Besides, Audra is pregnant!"

Steve gave me an odd look. "What has that got to do with anything, Annette? You're not making any sense."

I felt dizzy and ill, as if I were going to faint.

Steve glanced my way and immediately came to my side. He held me close. "Are you all right?" he asked worriedly.

His body felt warm and comforting next to mine. I held him to me and closed my eyes, hoping that, somehow, if I shut my eyes and held on tightly, when I opened them what I had just heard him say would not be true.

Steve went to the fridge and got a bottle of water. Twisting off the lid, he handed it to me. "Here, take a big drink of this," he said softly. "Do you want me to fix you a real drink? What can I do?"

I was trembling so hard that I couldn't think. I took a big drink and it was delicious. Then I got dizzy again and felt even more faint.

"Annette, let me get you into the couch. You need to lie down," Steve insisted.

I didn't protest as he carried me into the den and laid me down carefully on the couch. Steve sat down and put my head in his lap while he tenderly stroked my hair. His voice was gentle and calm, but even so, I knew he was fighting back his own emotions.

He explained that when he'd gotten to the store there had been a big crowd milling around, as well as emergency vehicles and personnel. He had spoken to some of the firemen that he knew. They'd told him that, apparently, the little girl had been looking at the candy while Hank, her father, had paid for his gas. When he turned around, she was gone. No one had seen her leave, and no one could remember seeing anyone suspicious in the store.

"It was busy, though." Steve sighed. "It could have been anyone."

"What was Hank thinking, letting a small child like that wander off?" I snapped. "I never did like him. He's always been so concerned about himself, and no one else. Poor Audra, with a new baby coming. What will she do? How can she stand it? Hank will be no help to her at all."

"Hey, hold on," Steve told me. "I know you don't like Hank, but he's all right. I know for sure that he loves Kaleigh. He talks about her all the time when I'm with him, and he seems very excited about the new baby."

"He wasn't paying attention!" I shouted, still wanting to blame Hank. I wanted to blame someone for the awful news that I still could not comprehend.

I could feel Steve's body slump down on the couch so I sat up to hold him for a while. "I'm sorry, honey," I whispered in his ear. "You must feel just awful, too. What are they going to do about finding her?"

"I don't know for sure. It's all just chaos at this point. But I think I'll go back down there, if you're okay here. I'd like to help them search for her. You should see Hank, Annette. He looks terrible."

"What about Audra?" I asked. "Should I call her? Should I go over there?"

Steve shook his head. "You aren't that close to her, Annette. I'm sure her mother and sisters are with her. They all live so close by. The last thing she needs tonight, I would guess, is a stream of people coming to her house."

"Oh, dear God," I whispered, holding my husband's hand. "Poor Audra. How will she bear it? She loves Kaleigh so much."

"And poor Hank," Steve added. "I can't even imagine how I would feel if I were in his place. I remember one time when we were camping, I lost sight of Melissa for about five minutes, and the panic was nearly lethal. I found her, of course, but before I did, I was sure that she was in the river."

"You never told me that," I said.

"I was ashamed," he admitted. "I can only imagine how poor Hank feels."

"I know what you mean." I nodded.

"I'm going back over there. Will you be all right? I'll call you from my cell phone and keep you up to date. Be sure the doors are all locked, and if you hear anything you call me, too."

I nodded again. Truthfully, I didn't want him to leave me, but I also knew that he had to go, because it was the right thing to do. "I'll be fine," I assured him. "Please don't forget to call me, though."

When he was gone I checked all the doors and windows, but I still didn't feel safe. Out there in that dark world I knew that there were people who were evil, and who would harm a child if given a chance.

I went upstairs and quietly opened the door to Melissa's room. She was fast asleep on top of her bed, still fully dressed, with her television still on.

I tiptoed to the closet and got a blanket from her closet. I covered her up, kissing her lightly on her forehead as I left the room.

When I went into Alexandra's room, I found her curled up in a ball, clutching her book in her arms as if it were a favorite doll. I covered her, too, kissed her warm little cheek, and closed my eyes in silent prayer that my girls would always be safe and happy.

I walked back downstairs, hating the quiet of the house without Steve in it, but comforted, too, by the fact that my girls were safe in their beds.

Steve came in the house quietly a few hours later. I was sitting on the couch, waiting for him. His face looked gray and angry. I stood up and met him before he could even sit down beside me on the couch.

"What happened? Did they find her?" I asked.

He shook his head and pushed past me. He sank onto his favorite chair, leaned his head back, and closed his eyes. "She's just vanished," he told me. "They decided to wait until dawn to start searching for her because it's so dark and wet outside."

"Where could she be?" I wailed, filled with true agony. "Don't you think she might have just wandered out of the store? She might be lost in the neighborhood. Why aren't they checking every house?"

"The police are doing that, but they don't want volunteers going door-to-door." Steve gave a huge, defeated-sounding sigh. "There are too many strange people in this crazy world."

He looked at me and saw the doubt in my eyes. "The police know what they're doing, Annette," he assured me.

"Well, what about that little girl who got grabbed and was found two years later, just three blocks from her home?" I reminded him.

"That was a custody battle. It was a whole different thing," Steve said. He stood up. "I'm not going to argue with you, Annette. I'm going to bed. And then, I'm getting up at dawn and I'm going out to search for that little girl."

I felt as if he had pushed me away. He'd treated me like one of the girls, when they got on his nerves. But I followed him upstairs, anyway. "What about Audra? Did you see her?"

"No, Annette," he said quietly. "Believe me, there's nothing you can do right now. Let's get some sleep."

"Forgive me for caring!" I snapped. But I followed him to bed and, when we were lying next to each other, I put my arms around him. "It just scares me, that's all."

Steve held me tightly to him, kissing my forehead. "It scares us all. Things like this aren't supposed to happen where we live. It's always somewhere else—someone else. But now it's here. We have to find her."

Despite our best intentions to get a good night's rest, neither

Steve nor I slept much at all that terrible night. I lay in bed, trying to be still and not bother Steve because I assumed he was sleeping. But I wanted to scream out in rage and fear at the very possibility that some monster might be lurking just outside our window, waiting to get one of our girls. Thoughts of Kaleigh tormented me. I kept conjuring up the awful images of what might be happening to that poor baby, that innocent child, right at that moment.

I finally slipped out of bed and walked barefoot down to my girls' rooms, just to check, just to be sure that they were all right. They were both sound asleep, oblivious to the awful world outside. If I could have, I knew, I would have kept them in the house with us forever. After that night, I didn't see how I could bear to have either one of them out of my sight.

Finally, I left Alexandra's room, softly shutting her door. As I turned, I saw a huge shadow coming toward me in the dimly lit hallway. I froze where I stood, but my hand never left the door to my child's room. Nothing was going to harm her, no matter who or what was in our house in the dark of the night.

"It's me," I heard Steve say as he pulled me toward him. "I'm so sorry. Did I frighten you?"

"Why didn't you say something?" I hissed. I was trembling all over. "I thought someone was after the children. What were you doing lurking about in the house, anyway? What's wrong with you, Steve? Don't you have any sense at all?"

Steve didn't say anything as he led me back to our room. He sat me down on the bed, then turned to me. "I was coming to look for you," he said angrily. "I didn't know where you were! I woke up and you were gone. I didn't know where you were. It frightened me."

I sat down onto the bed and started to cry. "I'm sorry, honey. I'm overreacting and I know it, but I just can't help it. I feel frantic and helpless. I don't want it to be true."

Steve got in bed beside me. He started to stroke my body, whispering that things would be all right. "We don't know for sure that she's being hurt," he told me. "We don't know for sure what happened. Let's just hang on to hope, and to each other. We have to try hard, Annette, because the kids are going to hear about this. We have to let them know that they're safe. We can't fall apart ourselves."

I pressed my body against his. "You are so wonderful, Steve." I sighed. "Of course, you're right."

When his touch became more ardent, more sexual, I shuddered with disgust and anger. I had never been so angry with him for simply showing me that he wanted me. That was the first time in our marriage that he actually repelled me. I jumped out of bed and stood there, shaking.

30

"What are you thinking?" I cried out. "How could you think of having sex when poor little Kaleigh may be going through the horrors that some man wants to inflict on her? What is wrong with men? When it comes to sex, does everything else just disappear? It's hideous and obscene. I wish every man would just be cursed with a lightning bolt so that their stupid sexual urges would vanish forever."

I knew as I said the words that I was making no sense, but it was impossible to stop. I wanted to hurt Steve. I want to hurt someone, because I was so scared.

Steve was silent for a moment. He seemed shocked. Finally, he got up and went into the bathroom. When he came out, I was back in bed, huddled as close to the edge and as far away from where he would lie down as possible. He came to my side, putting his arm around me to lift me into a sitting position.

"Here," he said. He handed me a pill and then held a glass of water to my lips.

I took the pill like a little child with no will and I sipped the water greedily. I smiled at him in the dark and touched his cheek. "One of your sleeping pills, right?" I asked quietly.

"Yes, you need it," he told me.

I didn't resist. The thoughts and the emotions that were tearing through me were so wild that I thought I might burst into pieces. "I'm sorry, Steve. I don't know why I said those things."

"It doesn't matter. Like the song says, they're only words." He got into bed beside me and held me until sleep enveloped me in a comforting darkness. Finally, I was in a safe place, where no thoughts of evil or danger existed.

I woke up before Steve or the girls the next morning. It was just barely light. I put on my robe and brushed my hair quickly. As I stared at my reflection in the mirror I thought of the awful things I had said to Steve the night before. I knew that I had said those words to him, not only because of my fears about Kaleigh, but because Steve had been unfaithful to me one time during our marriage. And, no matter how hard I'd tried, I'd never been able to get it out of my mind.

He'd told me that it had just "happened." She was the wife of one of his coworkers, and she'd come into the fire station a lot to show off her admittedly spectacular figure.

One afternoon when Steve was leaving work, his truck wouldn't start and she had offered him a ride home. They went to her house and made love. Steve was so ashamed of himself afterward that he told me about it as soon as he got home. I was stunned, shocked, and hurt. I wanted to hurt him as badly at that moment as he had hurt me.

After a few weeks of sullen silence, however, with Steve walking around the house like a mute outsider, I told him that because we had

31

kids, and because I respected our marriage vows, which he apparently did not, that I wanted to keep our marriage intact. We agreed to never mention the episode again, but I was never really the same after that incident. I heard that the woman he'd cheated with left her husband and left town, so I didn't worry that it would happen again—at least, not with her. But my trust in Steve had been broken and it would take time, I knew—maybe more time than my life would allow me— to really ever trust him fully again.

I went down to the kitchen and put on some coffee. Soon, I heard the familiar sounds of the family waking up. Melissa's music blasted through the walls of her room and I could hear Alexandra chattering away to one of her imaginary friends.

Steve came downstairs, looking fresh and clean from his shower. His eyes, though, were tired. "I'll just have coffee," he told me. "I want to start out early to help them organize the search team."

"Maybe they found her," I suggested hopefully, turning on the little television on the kitchen counter.

But the newscaster was saying that there was still no sign of Kaleigh, and no clues or witnesses. The chief of police was being interviewed and he was asked if the parents, Hank and Audra, were suspects in Kaleigh's disappearance.

"We are not ruling out anyone," the chief said solemnly.

"Oh, they can't be serious," I gasped.

"Don't get upset," Steve said, coming over and putting his arms around my shoulders. "They always say that. The investigation has just begun."

"But to even suggest that Hank or Audra would do anything to hurt Kaleigh," I stammered. Then I stopped in my tracks. "Maybe it was Hank," I heard myself say.

"Annette, don't say that," Steve chided me. "That's so unfair, and so unlike you."

I didn't answer him, not wanting an argument so early in the day. But in my mind, I was thinking that nobody ever really knew other people really well. Maybe Steve and I didn't know Hank at all. I refused to believe that Audra was involved in any way, however.

The girls came down to the kitchen. Melissa was muttering that she was absolutely not going to eat anything because she had just weighed herself and she had gained a pound.

Little Alexandra sat up to the table with her usual smile. "I'll have everything you've got, please," she announced sweetly.

Steve and I looked at each other and I nodded at him. It was my way of signaling to him that he should tell the girls the news before they'd heard it somewhere else.

32

Steve cleared his throat nervously. "We've had some bad news about little Kaleigh Miller," he began.

"I had a dream about her last night!" Alexandra told us, munching on a piece of buttery toast.

"Oh, you and your clueless dreams," Melissa muttered. "How can you tell your dreams from your reality, anyway? You live in a world of your own."

"What's a reality?" Alexandra asked, with a serious look.

"You are hopeless," Melissa replied. She sipped some orange juice and took a bite out of a piece of toast that I insisted she eat. "I have to go," she said. "Jocelyn's mom is picking us up today, and she always comes to my house first."

I gave Steve a stern look, knowing that he would rather not talk about Kaleigh if he could avoid it.

"Before you go anywhere," he said, "I want you both to listen to me. Kaleigh is missing. She went with her dad to the gas station last night, and she disappeared while he was paying his bill. That's all we know."

"Oh," Melissa breathed, sitting back down on her chair and clutching her backpack. "Little Kaleigh? She's so cute. Do you think she was kidnapped?"

"We don't know what happened," I said in a rush. "We just wanted you two to hear the news from us. Promise us that you won't listen to any gossip or wild talk. Nobody knows what happened to her."

"She has brown hair now," Alexandra said calmly.

We all stared at her. "No, honey, Kaleigh has blond hair. You know that. You play with her all the time. What makes you think her hair is brown?"

"I told you," she went on patiently, picking some crumbs from her plate. "I dreamed about her last night."

I realized that Alexandra was just too young to understand the implications of Kaleigh being gone, so I changed the subject. "Melissa, you'd better get going. And I have a million things to do, so I have to get busy, too. Alexandra, do you want to help me upstairs?"

She furrowed her brow as if she were thinking it over carefully. "No," she told me. "I want to play in my room for a while."

In a way, I was grateful that she was so happy on her own, entertaining herself with her imagination and her play. I didn't think I would have been able to maintain the usual happy conversation that the two of us shared on a normal day.

The next few days were an emotional nightmare. The search parties that Steve was involved with came up with nothing, and the police kept reporting that there had been no new breaks in the case. I didn't talk to the girls about Kaleigh any more often than necessary. Melissa asked about her a time or two, but she was too involved in her own teen melodramas to concentrate that much on anything else.

I kept thinking that I should call Audra, but then I would hesitate. The television news had been filming outside of their home. There were rows of vans from television stations outside, and reporters were standing around on her lawn and driveway. I thought about how terrible it must have been for her, to be invaded and watched by strangers who were only looking for news, or gossip. The whole thing made me shudder.

I decided to write Audra a note, simply stating that I was thinking of her, and to let me know if there was anything at all that I could do.

Alexandra didn't mention Kaleigh at all for about two weeks. Then one morning, when I was sorting laundry, she came into the laundry room.

"Mom, Kaleigh told me in my dream last night that she wants to come home now. She lives in a story in a purple birthday cake house with a piano and she says the cat lady who lives there won't let her come home. She told me to tell her mom and dad to come get her, please."

Her words sent a chill through me. I put down the laundry and took Alexandra by the hand. We went into the den and I sat down with her, holding her close. "Are you worried about Kaleigh?" I asked tenderly.

"Well, no," Alexandra murmured, looking at me with puzzled eyes. "She's not sick or anything. She just wants to come home."

"Honey, it was just a dream," I told her, holding her close. "We still don't know where Kaleigh is for sure, but I don't want you to worry."

Alexandra pulled away from me. "But, Mom," she argued. "I talked to her in my dream. She told me to tell her mom and dad. We'd better go to their house."

I tried to explain to Alexandra that we just couldn't go over there. At least, not until Kaleigh was found. As I spoke, she started to cry. It was so unlike her to argue with me. She was usually so happy and agreeable.

"We have to tell her mom and dad," she insisted. "Kaleigh wants me to tell them."

I decided that what we needed was a trip to the park and some ice cream. I was a little ashamed of myself for not talking to Alexandra more about Kaleigh. Suddenly, I realized just how traumatized she really was about her friend.

We went to the park and Alexandra hurried toward the duck pond. She loved feeding the ducks and watching the little babies

34

swim in rows after their mothers. I thought she was just fine, that all thoughts of Kaleigh were gone, but after about an hour, she came back over to the bench where I was sitting.

"Now, Mom, let's go tell Kaleigh's mom and dad where she is."

"I think I'd like some ice cream first," I said, thinking that would certainly get her mind off telling Kaleigh's parents about her dream.

I was surprised by the look of disappointment on her face. "Okay, Mom." She sighed. "If you really want ice cream, then we'll go. But then, can we please go tell Kaleigh's mom and dad where she is?"

I was starting to worry about Alexandra. I'd begun to think that maybe I should take her to a grief counselor. But I just smiled bravely.

"I just have to have some ice cream, that's all. We'll talk about Kaleigh later."

And so, we got our ice cream and Alexandra chattered on about all the things in her world that amazed and amused her. We were sitting outside on a bench by the ice cream store. When I reached over to wipe the drips of ice cream off her face, she gave me one of her glittering smiles.

"We'd better go now, Mom, and tell Kaleigh's mom where she is."

I looked at my innocent daughter's face and wanted to weep for the real world that one day she would have to face. But I wasn't ready yet for her to know how cruel people could be to one another. I took her little hands in mine.

"We can't go to see Kaleigh's mom and dad, honey. They're too sad about Kaleigh being gone. Even your story of your dream about her won't make them feel better. I wish it would, but it won't. It might even make them feel worse."

Tears pooled in Alexandra's eyes. "But, Mommy," she whimpered, "if we told them where Kaleigh is, they'd feel better and be happy again. I promised her in my dream that I would tell them."

"But it was just a dream, honey. It wasn't real," I insisted.

Alexandra jumped off the bench and stamped her foot in anger. "Yes, it was real!" she shouted at me. "Why can't you believe me? I believed Kaleigh."

"Alexandra, please, calm down," I told her, frightened by her anger. How was I to explain to her that dreams were fine, but reality was what we had to live with every day?

"Maybe, someday, when Kaleigh comes home, you can tell her and her parents about your dream. Won't that be fun? Won't she laugh when you tell her she had brown hair in your dream, and lived in a birthday cake house with a cat lady? She'll really like it that you thought she was living in a story, and that there was a piano in the house where she was staying."

35

Alexandra gave me a steady, thoughtful gaze. "What if they can't find her, though, without me telling them where she is?"

I nearly burst into tears as I looked at my sweet child's face. What was I to say to her? How could I tell her that, in my deepest heart, I doubted that Kaleigh was ever coming back? How could I explain to her that I was beginning to suspect, as so many others did, that Hank, her father, had had something to do with her disappearance?

"I bet she will come back, though," I said. I hated myself for misleading Alexandra, but I hoped that, just for now, she would forget about her dream and go on living in her own protected world.

"Well, if she doesn't come back soon, maybe in two hours, or three days," Alexandra persisted, "I think we'd better tell them where she is."

I knew that time was something Alexandra didn't have quite nailed down in her mind yet, so I agreed. "That's a good idea," I told her. "Let's wait a little while. Now, shall we go to the supermarket and get chicken for supper? You like chicken."

Alexandra nodded, but her face did not have its usual glow. She said very little while we shopped, which was unlike her. Normally, she loved the supermarket with all the people and the enticing displays. Everything fascinated Alexandra. She really seemed to love the world.

She didn't mention her dream again that day, but she ate very little supper. Steve was home for a few days off so I asked him if he would spend some time alone with Alexandra. I also suggested that, when he saw an opportunity to talk to her calmly about her dreams, he should do so.

"I don't know if I did a very good job of convincing her we can't go to Kaleigh's parents with her story," I said. "Maybe you could try, and don't let Melissa hear you. The last thing I want is for her to tease Alexandra about being 'weird,' or something equally mean."

Later, after being with Alexandra in her room, Steve came downstairs and sat beside me. "She said that she didn't want to talk about it anymore, and that she was going to wait a while for Kaleigh to come home. She said that if Kaleigh doesn't come home, you promised she could tell her parents then."

I shook my head. "I was a coward, I know. I just wanted to make her stop insisting that we go to Kaleigh's house. She's so little and trusting. I guess I've let her down, though. You know I can't ever take her over there."

"We'll work it out," Steve said gently. "We all do things sometimes to hurt the people we love most. And no matter how hard we try, sometimes there is no fixing a situation."

I looked my husband directly in the eyes. "A broken promise, a broken heart."

He nodded. "We all do it, Annette. We're all just hanging in there, trying our best. Alexandra is young, but she understands more than we think. She has a very tender heart, but she has a quick mind, too. She'll understand." His words sounded good, but his voice sounded unsure.

I kissed Steve. "I guess we ask more of kids than we expect of ourselves sometimes."

Steve didn't answer but, at that moment, something passed between us. It was a moment of understanding, and the beginning of my finally forgiving him for his betrayal.

Alexandra didn't talk about her dream for the next few days. I kept my fingers crossed that she had forgotten about it. Steve was home for his last day off on a sunny morning when the telephone rang. Alexandra was in the kitchen with Steve and she grabbed the phone before he could get it. It was a little game they always played together. Steve called it their "telephone tag" game.

I heard Alexandra greet the caller. "It's for you, Dad," she told him.

I was just dragging the vacuum cleaner out to the living room when Steve came rushing in, Alexandra close behind him.

"They found Kaleigh!" he shouted, picking me up and swinging me around. "They found her! They found her!"

Alexandra danced and twirled around the room. "You were right, Mom. They didn't even need my dream."

We turned on the television set and listened carefully, all three of us huddled together. A picture of Kaleigh came on the screen and Steve and I gasped as we saw her face surrounded by brown hair.

"See, she does have brown hair," Alexandra crowed. "I told you so."

Steve and I looked at one another in shock. "Let's listen, honey," I said as a chill shuddered through me. "Let's listen to the television." I wanted to divert her attention away from Kaleigh's hair so I could take it in myself.

We listened in speechless astonishment as we heard the story of Kaleigh and her captor. The Millers had taken a trip a few months before to a beach resort town. They had made friends with a lady who walked on the beach alone all the time. They called her the cat lady because she'd told them that she had twenty cats at home. She took a special liking for Kaleigh, the news reporter said, but the whole family had liked the strange woman. I watched as I heard Audra talking in an interview as she clutched Kaleigh to her.

"In retrospect," she said, "we should have known that there was something unnatural about her attachment and interest in Kaleigh."

Audra went on to explain about a dinner invitation they accepted

37

from the woman to her home. "It was a purple-tiered Victorian home, and Kaleigh remarked that it looked just like a birthday cake."

I looked at Steve as quickly he looked at me. Alexandra was enthralled with the television set, nodding her little head.

"Yes, yes, that's right," she whispered.

The interview continued as Audra went on to describe the home. "Inside, she had all kinds of cats. There were pictures all over her house, too, of the daughter she had years before. It was a little girl with brown hair, who looked very much like Kaleigh."

The reporter went on to explain that the lady had gotten the Millers' address before they'd left for home. Apparently, she came to town and watched for an opportunity to take Kaleigh home with her.

"Kaleigh knew her," Hank said in his interview. "She saw no harm in leaving with her."

Kaleigh was unharmed but happy to be home, the news reporter related. The woman who'd taken her had finally realized what a terrible thing she had done and brought Kaleigh back, right to her own front door. By then, the media trucks and cameras were long gone, and the police were working on the case at their headquarters.

"She's going to get the help she needs," Audra said, referring to the cat lady. "I am so grateful that she brought my baby home safe and unharmed."

Steve finally stood up and turned off the television. "How did you know all this, Alexandra?" he asked quietly. "Did you really dream about the birthday cake house and Kaleigh?"

"Yes, but I got some of it mixed-up, I think," Alexandra answered. "She wasn't living in a story at all, and there was no piano in the house." Alexandra sighed. "But when can I go see Kaleigh? I want to tell her about my dream."

We talked Alexandra into waiting for Kaleigh to be home a while before she told her about the dream, and she agreed without objection.

"I just want to show her my new books, anyway," she said.

Alexandra bounced out of the room, on her way to play outside in the lovely world she loved so much. A world, that despite a near tragedy, remained a place of joy and peace and safety,

Steve and I decided not to talk about Alexandra's dream to anyone. For one thing, we were afraid that the media might exploit Alexandra. And, for another, we didn't want to take the chance that people might think that we were trying to exploit our daughter. Our privacy and, more important, Alexandra's, was on the line. So long as Kaleigh was safe, we thought, there was no need to bring the dream to anyone's attention.

We have no answers to this day about our daughter's remarkable dream. She is a normal child in every way, even though she is gifted, still, with a bounty of imagination. It wasn't long before she forgot about the dream. She never even remembered to mention it to Kaleigh when she saw her about a month later.

Our family, neighborhood, and lives are back to normal now. But even so, I have noticed a certain air of caution in our community. No one I know takes safety for granted anymore, and we all watch our children with a more careful and cautious eye.

Alexandra developed a passion for art when she went to kindergarten. She draws wild, imaginative pictures which I sometimes study, almost guiltily, for any clues of the supernatural. So far, all I have seen are smiling trees and clouds shaped like kittens.

One night, several months later, as I sat beside her on her bed, Alexandra looked at me seriously. "Do you ever dream, Mommy?" she asked.

"Yes," I said, alarmed despite myself at her question. "Of course I do." I had an instinct to keep the conversation light. "Sometimes I dream that I have three little girls who are just like you."

Alexandra giggled. "Just don't go having a boy." She yawned. "I hate boys."

I smiled, but I shut my eyes at the same time in silent thanks. I was so grateful that she was normal and happy and, at least for the night, safe in a world that is sometimes dangerous, but sometimes as good as any dream could be.

THE END

SHOULD I SUE?
I'm traumatized by my job and
I don't know what to do!

I was thrilled when I was promoted to private secretary to Rupert Madden, senior partner at Madden & Carter Law Associates. I thought surely I'd found a job that I'd keep until retirement . . . but, when a new attorney joined the firm, my dream job quickly turned into a nightmare filled with overt sexual harassment and mental debasement.

Eli and I planned to get married just as soon as he completed his fourth and final year of veterinary college. He worked as a mechanic at a local garage during the day and attended college at night and on the weekends. It was a grueling schedule, and one that gave us little time to be together.

"All this will change soon, Rima. I promise," he said, pulling me into his arms one day and kissing me full on the mouth. "I'll have my degree in a few months and then we'll get married."

His hands felt warm on my back and I pressed my breasts into his chest. I loved the feel of his body nestled against mine. Plus, I loved the smell of him. He uses Walsted cologne and I could never get enough of its tangy fragrance. Truth is, I love everything about Eli Hoffman. Like his smile. He has a dimple in each cheek, and whenever he smiles at me, I feel weak in the knees. He has amazing blue eyes—the color of the sky when the sun is shining brightly. To top it off, he has dark-brown hair and a tall, thin body that looks great in everything he wears. He's my dream guy.

"I'm looking forward to being Mrs. Eli Hoffman," I told him, tipping my head for his kiss.

We'd begun to have sex, though we weren't married officially. It was just too darn hard to resist. They say that absence makes the heart grow fonder. Well, that may be so, but when two people love each other as deeply as Eli and I do, they give in to the yearnings of their bodies. But we hadn't, as yet, moved in together. I kept a small apartment on the west side of town and Eli lived above the local pizzeria. He often joked that it smelled better at his place, but that it was quieter at mine.

I'd managed to get a job at a law firm right out of high school. At first I was just doing routine office work, assisting Miss Jeffrey. But when she retired—finally—Mr. Madden asked me if I thought that I could do her job. I was stunned that he would even offer me the position, but I wasted little time in informing him that I was well aware of every duty Miss Jeffrey had handled, and that I thought I could do an equally good job. I'd been at the law firm for three years, and the whole time I'd hoped that one of the secretaries would retire so that I could have her position. But I'd truly never dreamed of becoming Mr. Madden's private secretary.

"How's your shorthand, Miss Simms?" he asked, his elderly face staring at me.

"Actually," I said, blushing slightly, "I'm quite good at taking dictation, Sir." I rushed over to my small desk in the office alcove and picked up a steno pad and a pen. "Would you like to dictate a letter, Sir?" I felt a little nervous as I stood there waiting with my pen poised at the ready.

He chuckled slightly, making his rotund body shake beneath his expensive Italian suit. Then he turned and led me into his private office. I followed with my fingers crossed, hoping that I could meet his standards. Despite the three years that I'd been at the firm, Mr. Madden still seemed indifferent in his mannerisms toward me. I worried over that sometimes. I'd even discussed the situation with Eli, but he told me that I was just imagining things and dismissed my fears.

As it turned out, my dictation skills impressed Mr. Madden, and he promoted me on the spot. I felt like leaning across his desk and kissing him on the cheek, but of course, I didn't. I rose politely and extended my hand, thanking him with all the dignity I could muster.

Two months later, Miss Jeffrey made her retirement official. We threw a little party for her. Everyone gave her little gifts and we had cake. The very next day I moved my things into her desk. It was all that I could do to contain my happiness, but Mr. Madden had a full calendar that day, so there was no room for any behavior other than total professionalism.

I settled into the job rather quickly, making myself fully aware of Mr. Madden's habits, likes, and dislikes. They weren't really that foreign to me since I'd observed Miss Jeffrey for three years. But now it was me who had to be responsible for every tiny assignment that he handed down.

I soon saw Miss Jeffrey's job in a totally different light. Mr. Madden had his demanding side—a side that I wasn't fully aware of before I became his private secretary.

He liked his coffee strong, black, and carried to him at precisely nine-fifteen in the morning—the usual time he arrived at the office. He had specific restaurants where he liked to eat lunch, and I was expected to make certain that there was a table waiting for him. I was expected to make dinner reservations for him whether he planned to eat with his wife or with clients. The job of private secretary required much more than taking dictation and keeping track of appointments.

"You seem distracted," Eli said to me one evening. "Is something wrong?"

I smiled at him and allowed him to pull me down on the couch beside him. I snuggled in his arms—a safe, warm place where there were no demands on me. "I'm just still trying to get accustomed to my new job," I said, not really wanting to talk about it.

"Is that Madden a tyrant?" he asked, chuckling slightly.

I shrugged my shoulders. "He's more like a demanding grandfather." I wrapped my arms around his neck and kissed him, hoping to end the speculation surrounding Mr. Madden.

"If you don't like the job, quit," Eli said, pulling away from me.

He had a rather disgruntled look on his face and I realized then that I should never have said anything about my trying to settle into my job.

"I mean it, Rima," he continued. "If you're unhappy working there—"

"No, I'm not," I cut him off. "Everything's fine. I just have to adjust to the new workload. And besides, the raise in pay is fantastic."

He pulled me into his arms again. "One day I'll be a real veterinarian who makes a lot of money, and I'll give you everything you want, babe. I promise. You won't ever have to work again. You can stay at home and have my babies." He pushed me to arm's length and locked gazes with me. "We are going to have kids right away, aren't we?"

I crinkled my nose at him. "Not right away, honey. I want to get used to being married for a little while first."

"We're not getting any younger," he cautioned with a laugh.

"Twenty-six and twenty-four aren't old!" I countered.

I was glad that it was the weekend and neither of us had to go to sleep to be rested for work the next morning. We made popcorn and watched an old Humphrey Bogart movie on TV. It was nice—just the two of us. I was really looking forward to marrying Eli. We enjoyed each other's company so much.

I got to the office at about eight-thirty on Monday and began preparing for the morning workload. Mr. Madden usually had a stream of people to meet with, and that day was no exception. He had back to back appointments all morning long, plus a court appearance in the afternoon. I carried the research data the paralegal had prepared into his office and positioned it on the corner of his big, mahogany desk just the way he'd instructed me to. Then I went to check on the coffeemaker in the outer office.

A few minutes later, Mr. Madden arrived with a younger man. I was a little surprised because he'd arrived earlier than usual, but what really took me by surprise was the introduction that followed.

"Rima, this is Kyle, my nephew," Mr. Madden informed me. He spoke as he walked, almost throwing his words over his shoulder as he proceeded into his office. "You'll be acting as his secretary as well as mine. Kyle is helping me on the Robbins case. Where's my coffee?"

I scurried about like a frightened mouse, rushing to pour his coffee and sputtering my sentences. I even asked if Mr. Kyle would like coffee as well. My nervousness drew a chuckle from the younger man as he trailed his uncle into his office.

After the coffee was served, the men shut the office door and I collapsed at my desk. Why did you act like such an idiot? I asked myself. Surely, Mr. Madden's early arrival hadn't thrown my schedule off that much.

As I tried to gather my senses, I realized that it wasn't Mr. Madden's early arrival or his demand for coffee that had flustered me. Instead, it was the assessing gaze from his young nephew, Kyle, that had upset my senses.

"He'll think I'm a total fool," I mumbled beneath my breath. I raked my fingers through my hair. Why was I so disturbed? The man had merely glanced in my direction.

The phone rang, interrupting my assessment of the situation. I transferred the call to Mr. Madden's office and placed the receiver back in its cradle just as the office door opened and Kyle strolled out. He headed to the coffeepot in the corner of the room. I busied myself assembling a stack of manila folders that I'd recently taken from the file cabinet.

Momentarily, I became aware of Kyle standing at the corner of my desk. Then, to add another unnerving surprise to my senses, he propped one hip on my desk. Raising his coffee cup, he took a sip and stared at me. It was then that I realized how keen his dark-brown eyes were and how handsome he was.

"We weren't properly introduced, I'm afraid," he said, keeping his voice low as though he didn't want his uncle to overhear. He held out his right hand to me and something quivered in the pit of my stomach. "Kyle Madden," he said, cocking an eyebrow at me.

I slid my right hand into his, warning myself not to make a mountain out of a molehill. "Rima Simms," I said, forcing a smile.

His hand tightened quickly around mine and shock waves skittered up my arm.

"It's nice to meet you, Rima," he said as he leaned toward me. "I like that red sweater you're wearing. Red is your color."

My cheeks flushed and I felt the hair on the back of my neck stand up in alarm. Why, I couldn't quite say.

I pulled my arm back, removing my hand from his grasp. It should've been his cue to rise from my desk, but he didn't budge. Instead, he continued to drink his coffee and look at me.

I've never thought of myself as beautiful; on the contrary, I think my face is too thin and I have too many freckles. My hair screams out to be styled in some other fashion than the shoulder-length bob I wear. And his compliment regarding my red sweater—well, I'm far from looking like one of those girls they used to call a "sweater babe."

"I'll be moving into the office across the foyer," he said, nodding his head in that direction. "And you'll be tending to me as well as my uncle."

He smiled as he spoke, like he was hinting at some sordid secret. I just sat there and stared at him, wondering what to make of it all. He took another sip of coffee and rose from my desk just as Mr. Madden opened the office door. In the back of my mind, I thought the timing was uncanny. Immediately, the atmosphere in the room changed to one of professionalism, and Kyle Madden acted like the cagey young attorney his uncle perceived him to be.

I watched the two men with reserved skepticism. Once they'd disappeared inside Mr. Madden's office again, I questioned my feelings. Had Kyle Madden just made a pass at me?

"That's silly," I mumbled out loud. "Absolutely silly."

Maybe I just think that because I find him so attractive, I told myself. Maybe I want to think that he finds me attractive, too.

I spent the next hour trying to figure things out only to wind up believing that I was imagining things. Why in the world would a man as handsome and professional as Kyle Madden be making passes at his uncle's secretary?

I didn't tell Eli about the newest addition to the law firm. Instead, I made a special dinner for the two of us and we ate it out on the small balcony off my living room. We chatted about Eli's classes while we ate, and then he had to hurry off to class while I spent the remainder of the evening in front of the TV.

Things were pretty quiet at work for the remainder of the week. Kyle Madden moved into the office across the foyer and he and his uncle spent most of the day discussing strategy for the Robbins case. Mr. Madden didn't usually handle murder cases, which the Robbins case was. Felix Robbins was accused of killing his wife. Since Mr. Madden has known Felix for most of his life, he agreed to defend him. Kyle, on the other hand, specialized in criminal law and was asked to lend a hand.

I'd taken several letters that morning and was busy transcribing them at my desk when Kyle suddenly appeared with a manila folder in hand.

"Rima," he said. "I need every scrap of info you have on the mortgage company where Felix Robbins worked."

"I believe Mr. Madden has all the information in his office," I said, pausing and looking at him. My senses were immediately jarred when I locked gazes with him. He had the darkest brown eyes I'd ever seen.

"I need you to check, to be sure," he continued.

I rose from my desk and crossed the room to the wall of file cabinets. I was absolutely certain that Mr. Madden had all the information in his office, but I couldn't refuse to check. After all, I was Kyle's secretary, too, for as long as he was at the firm.

I pulled one of the drawers open and began looking through the assortment of folders. Kyle crossed the room and stood beside me. I thought at first that he'd positioned himself so that he could look over my shoulder—he was well over six feet tall and quite well proportioned—but then he reached out his left arm and placed his hand on the top of the cabinet. His arm and chest were very near to my shoulders, and when I turned to inform him that there were no more folders pertaining to the Robbins case in the cabinet, I found myself inches from his face. My breath caught in my throat and I took an immediate step backward, only to find my backside pressing into his hip.

"Excuse me," I muttered, clearly flustered at my own carelessness.

His hand suddenly caught my left shoulder. That's keeping me from falling, I thought, but then he held it there long after I appeared steady on my feet. All the while my back and buttocks were nestled against his chest and hip.

"Careful," he said in a low, deep voice.

I drew in a deep breath and fought for a moment of sanity. I hadn't almost toppled over, as he would like for me to think, but rather he'd stood too close for me to easily move between him and the file cabinet.

"I'm fine. Thank you," I said. I immediately separated myself from the close quarters and returned to my desk.

"Make lunch reservations at Petit Maret," he instructed, staring at me.

There was a strange look in his brown eyes—one that would puzzle me throughout the day. It wasn't until I crawled into my bed that night that I came to a conclusion about Kyle Madden: He was, indeed, making sexual advances toward me.

The realization gave me cause to think. On the one hand, he was a very handsome man. But, on the other hand, I was in love with Eli. We were going to be married. Did I really want the attentions of another man? Did I have any desire to be with another man?

I had to admit that it was tempting. And the situation made me question my feelings for Eli. Was I really in love with him?

The Robbins case went to court the following day and I was relieved that Kyle and Mr. Madden were out of the office for a long time. It meant that my duties were lighter, though Mr. Madden had given me orders to revamp the filing system while he was in court. That itself was a mental challenge since each file had to be summarized before it could be placed correctly in the file cabinet.

It was Friday afternoon, and I was busy with a number of folders stacked on the floor when Kyle returned to the office unexpectedly. The men usually went straight from court to a local restaurant for dinner since court didn't recess before five o'clock. To say the least, I was surprised to see him. I scrambled up off the floor, straightening my skirt as I stood, and wishing that I hadn't kicked off my shoes before tackling the file folders. I was headed across the room to get my shoes when Kyle stepped directly in front of me.

"What's your hurry?" he asked, grabbing my left arm. In the next instant, he set his briefcase down and slipped his other arm around my waist.

I froze like a deer caught in the headlights of a car.

"What other duties do you perform for my uncle?" he asked.

I was immediately outraged—too mad to speak. I pushed roughly against Kyle's chest, feeling the solid, muscular wall beneath my palms.

"You seem incensed by my inquiry," he continued, smiling down at me. His dimpled cheeks suddenly lost their boyish appeal and I surmised that my suspicions about him had been correct all along.

"Suppose you add one little item for me to your list of secretarial duties," he continued. His hand moved so quickly that I was unable to prevent him from grabbing my left breast.

"I bet you wear lacy bras," he whispered.

"Get your hands off me!" I demanded, angrier than I'd ever been in my life. I pushed at his chest and wrenched my body from side to side, letting him know that I didn't like his treatment of me. He laughed at me, a low rumble in his throat that only served to reinforce my growing fears.

Then he released me just as quickly as he'd grabbed me, and it was all over. He didn't say anything else; he merely picked up his briefcase and strode into his office.

I was aghast at the man's audacity. Was this Jeckyll and Hyde who'd just joined the law firm? I stared after him with my jaw hanging open. Will people believe me if I tell them what just happened? Should I tell Mr. Madden? I foolishly wondered.

On the drive home I decided that I'd tell Eli what happened, but when I arrived at my apartment, there was a message on my answering machine from him. He couldn't make it to dinner because of an upcoming test. He needed to study. I realized then that I couldn't bother Eli with my problems at work. I'd have to handle things on my own.

The following Monday, Kyle came into the office early and summoned me to take dictation. I took my pad and went to his office, purposely leaving the door open when I entered. Well, that lasted for about as long as ice cubes in the desert. As soon as I'd taken a seat in front of his desk, he got up and closed the office door.

"We don't want to be disturbed," he said, smiling at me.

He began dictating a letter to an associate of Mr. Robbins's, leaning against his desk just in front of where I was sitting. While I wrote on my pad, I was aware of his masculine presence just inches away from my crossed legs, and I was completely surprised when he reached out and placed a hand atop my left knee.

"Mr. Madden," I began, trying to rise from the chair.

"Nice legs, Rima," he said. He slid his hand up my thigh despite my efforts to catch it. Then, to my horror, he rammed his fingers against my crotch!

"Stop it!" I bit out, anger flaring inside me. "You have no right to touch me!" I physically wrestled with him to get out of the chair.

"Do you like your job, Rima?" he asked, holding me against the chair. "Do you like your job?"

"Take your hands off of me!" I demanded again. I was shaking with fear, nearly in a panic.

"If you want to keep this little job, you're going to have to come across with more than your ability to take dictation and file data," he said. "I like my secretaries friendly. Do you know what I'm saying? Do you know what I mean by 'friendly'?"

"No," I said, hoping that he didn't mean having sex with him.

"No?" he said mockingly. "Then let me show you what I expect from you, Rima. First of all, I expect to touch you anywhere I get the urge to touch you. Secondly, I expect you to service me occasionally. In return, I'll let you keep your job."

I didn't have the words to describe how I felt at that moment. His words just kept going round and round in my head. Surely, I was trapped inside a nightmare, and at any moment I'd wake up to find myself safe in my own bed.

His hand was still between my legs. It was motionless, but there, nonetheless. I had both of my hands clamped around his wrist. My steno pad and pen lay strewn on the carpet beside the chair I was sitting in.

"Now be a good girl and turn loose my arm," he instructed.

47

I couldn't look at him. I was too ashamed of what he was threatening to do to me. I felt dirty and sordid.

"Rima," he said, his tone warning.

I loosened my grip on his wrist, and the muscles in my arms ached from trying to fight him off. I sat there humiliated while his fingers probed my crotch, and then to make matters worse, he pushed my skirt up so that he could look at me.

"That's a good girl," he whispered. "Tomorrow, don't wear underwear."

A chill surged through me. He means to have sex with me, I thought, hating the notion.

I could hear the telephone ringing at my desk, and I tried to explain to him that I had to go answer it. He laughed momentarily, but then he pulled his hands back and allowed me to get up. I literally ran from his office, my heart pounding in my chest. Tears filled my eyes as I tried to yank down my skirt.

I've got to tell Mr. Madden, I kept telling myself. I've got to make him aware of his nephew's actions. He'll fire him no doubt. He'll fire him outright!

A client was on the phone. He wanted to postpone his appointment until later in the week when Mr. Madden had some free time out of court. I made the necessary adjustment in the appointment book and slumped in my chair at my desk. A few minutes later, Kyle came into my office carrying my pad and pen.

"Have that letter done by the end of the day, will you, Rima? I'll sign it when I get out of court."

I was still too embarrassed and humiliated to look up at him. I just nodded my head and noticed that his voice was cordial, as though nothing in the world had just occurred between us.

I spent the remainder of the day trying to figure out what to do about Kyle Madden. I sure as heck didn't feel any attraction toward him. He was a sick man. He wanted to play sex games in the office. Well, I wasn't having any part of it!

Kyle returned to the office a few minutes before it was time to lock up. I'd typed the letter in triplicate and laid it on his desk for his signature, as he'd instructed. I gathered my purse and light jacket so that I'd be ready to leave for the day.

"Rima, this letter is wrong. There are a couple of mistakes that need correcting," he informed me, motioning for me to come into his office.

I was leery of going near him. I didn't want to experience another episode like the one earlier in the day.

"Come, Rima. Bring your pad."

Damn, I thought, putting aside my coat and purse. I had to force my feet to walk in his direction. I was clutching the pad and pen in my hand so tightly that I felt my knuckles begin to cramp.

He grinned broadly at me when I entered his office. He pushed back in his big, black-leather office chair and patted his lap.

"Just like in the movies, Rima. You sit on the boss's lap and take dictation," he said. He parted his knees and patted his left thigh.

"Sitting on your lap is not part of my job," I said, my voice quivering. "I'll take your dictation, but—"

"You have little to say about it, Rima," he informed me. "I'm your boss and we'll do things my way around here. Now, come here and sit on my lap."

I must've been out of my mind to obey him, but like a dolt, I walked around his desk and sat atop his left thigh. He began dictating his letter, and I was surprised that he didn't touch me. I took two pages of dictation and he announced that we were done for the day. I could go, and I could type the letters in the morning. I hurried out of his office as quickly as I could, only to meet Rupert Madden coming into the main foyer. It dawned on me then how Kyle had played me again. He'd known that his uncle would be coming back to the office, and he'd deliberately used those few minutes to humiliate me.

I thought really seriously about telling Eli about what Kyle was doing. In retrospect, I guess I was too ashamed to admit that I'd allowed the whole thing to happen. I should've stood up to Kyle at the first sign of harassment or gone straight to Mr. Madden and told him. But there was always the chance that Mr. Madden wouldn't have believed me, and in that case, I would've lost my job on top of everything else.

Eli and I met for pizza before he had to go to class. He looked haggard and in need of rest, so I abandoned all thoughts of asking him what I should do about the situation at work. I went back to my apartment feeling like the weight of the world was on my shoulders. I'd never been faced with a situation like the one I was immersed in at work.

Mr. Madden and Kyle were in court until mid-afternoon the following day. I was in the midst of a conversation with one of Mr. Madden's clients when he came through the door. I immediately transferred the call to his office and placed the phone back in its cradle. Kyle appeared in the office doorway, a look of complacency on his face.

"Bring your pad and come in, Rima," he said striding into his office.

I grimaced and reached for my pad just as Mr. Madden rang me on the intercom.

"Rima, when Kyle gets in, send him in to see me."

"Yes, Sir. He just arrived. I'll give him the message."

I was relieved to pass along the message that Mr. Madden wanted to speak to Kyle. At least for now, I was off the hook. I grabbed my purse and left the office, intent on taking a few minutes for myself. It wasn't often that I left the office during working hours. Sometimes I'd be sent to the post office, or, on one occasion, Mr. Madden had asked me to pick up his dry cleaning.

I rode the elevator down to the first floor of the building. Just as the doors slid open, Lindsay Burke, a young paralegal, rushed me back into the elevator, her hand on my arm in a tight grip. She poked the button to close the door and turned a wide-eyed face in my direction.

"I need to talk to you, Miss Simms," she began.

I could see that she was agitated about something, but I had no idea what kind of story she was about to relate.

"Something has to be done about Kyle Madden," she said. "Just yesterday, he caught me in the copy room and tried to force himself on me!"

I was shocked to hear her words, not because it was something more about Kyle Madden's actions, but because she was assuming that I could do something to make him stop.

"You, too!" I exclaimed letting her know that there were others without specifically revealing my predicament.

She looked stunned for a moment. "You know others who are having the same trouble with him? Well, I'm ready to go to Rupert Madden and rat him out." She bit on her bottom lip in uncertainty. "I'm just worried that he won't believe me because Kyle's his nephew."

"I know," I admitted.

"And I'd probably get fired, too."

"Yes, probably," I agreed. Clearly we had to come up with a solution before Kyle raped one or the both of us.

"I've got a good mind to hide a camera and catch him in the act," Lindsay said. "Mr. Madden would have to believe me then."

I went back to the office after my conversation with Lindsay. At least I wasn't the only one Kyle was harassing. The notion of hiding a camera and getting it on tape stuck in my mind. I decided on my way home that I'd browse through the local electronics store to see if I could make the idea into a reality.

I purchased a camera—a tiny little spy-cam. I hurried home to read all about it, but before I could get it out of the box, Eli appeared at my door.

"Can I crash here tonight? There's a damn party at the pizza parlor," he said, dropping his duffel bag inside the front door.

Any other time I would've been overjoyed that he wanted to spend the night, but he'd interrupted my plans to learn how to use the little camera, and I'd just spent a fortune on it.

He was quick to pick up on my mood. "What's wrong?" he asked, taking hold of my shoulders.

He peered down at me, those blue eyes boring into my green gaze as though trying to read my mind. I'm sorry, I can't tell you, I thought, fearing that he wouldn't understand. "Nothing's wrong," I lied. Then I felt terrible for not having told the truth. "Sure, you can stay the night. I love it when you stay with me!"

"You're not fooling me, Rima. I know when something's wrong. Now out with it."

"You're imagining things, Eli." I grabbed his hand and dragged him in the direction of my small kitchen. "You can help me cook dinner," I said, trying to take his mind off questioning me.

As it turned out, Eli didn't press me any further. But I noticed that he glanced at me all through the evening, wondering, perhaps, what I was hiding.

I never got the chance to read up on using the spy-cam, but I took it to work with me, anyway. They were scheduled to be in court all day, and I thought that maybe I'd have the opportunity to read up on it and find a good hiding place.

I had the office to myself all day until just about closing time. Luckily, both Maddens came into the office together, and Kyle acted like I was invisible. I knew for certain then that Rupert Madden didn't have any idea what his handsome nephew was like when he wasn't around. And, I knew that Rupert Madden wouldn't believe any stories about Kyle without proof positive.

I tucked the spy-cam between two books on the top shelf of a bookcase and aimed the lens at my desk. I had intentions of setting Kyle Madden up. Sooner or later, he'd catch the opportunity to harass me when his uncle wasn't around, and I'd get it on tape. Then I'd have evidence of sexual harassment that even his uncle would have to believe.

For two days everything was normal. Neither Madden appeared in the office without the other. But I couldn't say that everything was normal between Eli and me. Ever since the evening he'd suspected that I was keeping something from him, he'd been inquisitive and probing. Still, I remained silent. I loved him, but I wasn't sure how he'd react if I told him how Kyle Madden was harassing me at work. At least—and I thought about this fact often—Kyle confined his harassment to the office. God only knew what I'd do if he showed up at my apartment.

"Tell me what's been bothering you, Rima," Eli insisted.

He was on his way to class and had dropped by for the sole purpose of trying to pry my problem out of me. I held my ground, keeping it all inside. I had a plan—my spy-cam—but I couldn't divulge that to Eli, either.

He left, almost angry that I wouldn't confide in him. I cried myself to sleep because I was afraid to speak openly to Eli.

The following morning I went to work feeling very low. My life was on the verge of shambles, and it was all due to Kyle Madden and his continued harassment. I'd even thought about contacting Lindsay Burke and telling her about my plan so that she could get her own camera, but I didn't. I figured the fewer people who knew about my predicament, the better.

I carefully checked each Madden's appointments and noted that court wasn't on either agenda until after lunch. What if Kyle summoned me to his office and harassed me there, outside of the view of my little camera? I was too scared to hide the spy-cam in his office. I was afraid that he'd find it, though he really hadn't spent much time in his office since joining the firm. His chief reason for being there was aiding his uncle with the Robbins case.

I noticed that I was very nervous. I sat at my desk and went over my plan again. There was no way it could fail—unless Kyle discovered my camera hidden among the law books and suddenly started behaving himself or turned his lascivious attentions to someone else. I thought again about Lindsay Burke. Maybe there are others, I thought. And if so, perhaps when I expose Kyle, they'll come forward.

Kyle arrived at the office around ten, and while he went to deposit his briefcase in his office, I slipped over to the bookcase and turned on the spy-cam.

"Is my uncle in yet?"

I glanced at Kyle in the doorway of his office. He leaned against the doorjamb with his hands slipped inside the pockets of his slacks. He was a striking figure of a man, but I'd long ago overlooked his physical good looks. He was egotistical, cruel, and hated women, I felt.

"He's expected any time now," I replied, hoping that he'd take my words as a warning. My insides shook as though I were chilled with some horrid coldness. I wanted the whole thing to be over, but I was scared of having to go through the torture of catching it on tape.

Kyle pushed himself away from the doorjamb and came toward me, a condescending smile on his face. I slid into my desk chair. The telephone suddenly rang and I felt like I'd been given a reprieve from having to deal with Kyle.

Betty Stone was on the phone. She's an inquisitive, elderly

woman who seeks Rupert Madden's advice on just about everything in her life. She wanted an appointment and a dozen other things. I began checking Mr. Madden's schedule and making notes as she spoke.

Kyle came and stood beside my desk. I briefly glanced in his direction, but then it became necessary for me to stand in order to reach a file Mrs. Stone was questioning me about. As I tried to pay attention to what she was asking me on the phone, Kyle cunningly took advantage of the situation. He proceeded to sit down in my desk chair and I unintentionally sat on his lap!

I immediately jumped up when I saw what I'd done. I shot a hateful glare at Kyle and he laughed. He patted his right thigh and invited me to sit down. I threw the folder atop the desk and picked up the telephone cradle, distancing myself from Kyle. Then I hurried to explain to Mrs. Stone that I would have Mr. Madden return her call the second he came into the office and that I expected him at any moment. Kyle appeared to ignore my verbal warning. I hung up the phone and glared at him from across my desk.

He chuckled and rose from my chair. Then he came around to where I was standing. I made a move to get out of his reach, but he grabbed my left arm, yanking me against his chest.

"You act like you don't like my attention," he said in a growling tone.

"You know I don't like you harassing me," I said. "Now take your hands off of me!" I pushed at his chest, but my strength was no match for his. He held me easily, encircling my waist with his free arm. Then he placed both of his open palms on my buttocks and ground his abdomen against my belly. I felt the undeniable firmness of his erection!

"Turn me loose!" I shrieked, pushing my palms against his chest.

"You know you like it," he alleged. "I think it's time you and I got to know each other on an intimate level."

"I'll not be raped by you!" I yelled.

"Honey, it won't be rape," he said.

He started to kiss me then, lowering his head as though I would relent and offer my lips up, but I turned my head to the side, just in time to see the door open and Eli step inside.

"Eli!" I shrieked. "Eli!"

I'll never forget the look of hurt on Eli's face. He froze just inside the door, staring at me—at us—and then he turned and left, closing the door.

I began to struggle violently, desperate to get free of Kyle's hands, but Kyle seemed desperate to keep me pinned against his body.

"You don't really want to fight me, Rima," he warned, grabbing my shoulders and pushing me down on the desk.

All I could think of was that hurt look on Eli's face and how I wished I'd confided in him. But now it might be too late. He had no understanding of what he'd just seen and God only knew how I was going to rectify the situation.

Kyle leaned his upper body against mine, forcing me to lie back on my desk. The telephone clattered to the floor, and the Rolodex went reeling off the edge, too. Then I felt my skirt being pushed up and Kyle forced his way between my legs. He was going to rape me right there on my desk! Right in view of the lens of the spy-cam!

I fought Kyle with every ounce of strength I could summon. And then suddenly, whether miraculously or out of fear of reprisal, he stopped. He held very still, pinning my body beneath his.

As with his earlier attempts to harass me, I was fuming mad, and wanted no further contact with him. I scrambled across the desk on my back and heels until I literally fell to the floor. Then I got to my feet and ran out of the office.

My heart was pounding against my ribs. I thought I'd have a heart attack it was racing so violently. All I could think of was Eli. I had to find him. I had to tell him the truth about Kyle. I had to make him understand!

I hurried into the offices that housed the paralegal and law libraries to use the phone. But when I dialed Eli's apartment, he didn't answer. The phone wasn't a very good idea anyway, I decided. I had to speak with him in person. I had to look him in the eye and tell him everything that had been happening to me at work.

I decided to go to Eli's place of work, the garage, but I'd left my purse in the office. That meant that I didn't have car keys or money for a cab. I'd have to go back into the office and face Kyle to get my purse. I covered my face with my hands and cried. Everything seemed to have backfired.

I sought refuge in the women's bathroom and shut up in a stall for almost an hour while I settled my nerves and got straight what my next move would be. Luckily, I hadn't seen anyone in either the law library or the restroom, so I hadn't been asked why I was so upset.

I decided that I'd have to chance going back to the office to get my purse and the tape. In all the worry over Eli, I'd almost forgotten about my initial plan to film Kyle. I gathered my courage and walked back into the office, relieved to find it empty.

I went to the spy-cam immediately and pulled it from its hiding place. I planned to take it home and look at the tape before going to Mr. Madden's house. I'd let him see how his favorite nephew treated his coworkers.

I was exhausted when I got home, partly from worrying over

losing Eli and partly from the experience with Kyle. All I could think of was getting into the shower and washing myself clean. I felt soiled by Kyle's hands.

It was almost dark before I was able to console myself enough after what had happened. I removed the tape from the spy-cam, slipped it into the VCR, and sat down to watch it. At once my disgust was fully renewed. I picked up the phone and called Mr. Madden, announcing that I was on my way over to see him.

Anger fueled my actions after that. I marched right past Mr. Madden when he opened the door and demanded to know where his VCR was. Stone-faced, as usual, he led the way to an impressive, oak-paneled study where I proceeded to jam the tape inside the VCR and push the PLAY button. Then I turned on my heels and marched out of his house, too agitated to hang around and listen to any excuses he might make for his "special" nephew.

I drove to Eli's apartment, but he was out. In class no doubt. I went home. I didn't know what would happen next.

Eli's car was parked in the lot at my apartment building and I saw that he was sitting inside. I ran over to the car, wrenched open the passenger-side door, and bounded inside—straight into his open arms.

"I finally figured it out, Rima," he said, his arms tight around me. "All these weeks when you wouldn't talk to me."

"Oh, Eli. I'm sorry. I was afraid to tell you—"

"Because you didn't think I would understand. I know. I know. But, honey, I do understand. And I believe that you were innocent in the whole thing." He pulled in a deep breath and pushed me to arm's length. "I know there are guys out there who get their kicks out of harassing women they work with—just for the hell of it sometimes."

"Eli, I got it on tape—I got it on tape this time! He can't deny it. It's on tape and I just took it to Mr. Madden and showed him." I was crying by then and I wasn't sure why, except that I was relieved to have Eli back. "And there's another woman, a paralegal. He harassed her, too."

He silenced me then with a kiss. I was elated that the whole mess was behind me, and I promised myself then that I'd always confide in Eli—no matter what it was—because he truly loved me and somehow, he'd understand.

There was a message from Mr. Madden on my answering machine when Eli and I went up to my apartment. He apologized and promised me that he'd remove Kyle from the practice.

I took the rest of the week off. On Monday, when I stepped off the elevator into the foyer, I spied Lindsay Burke coming down the hall. She waved at me and picked up her pace.

"Did you hear?" she said, smiling brightly. "That bastard Kyle

55

Madden is out of here!"

I listened to Lindsay without revealing my experience with Kyle, and then wished her well before I proceeded to my office. Mr. Madden was sure to be in, and he'd want his morning coffee in a few minutes. Things were back to normal.

THE END

I MARRIED
A WOMAN HATER!
When his wife had left him, he'd
sworn never to love again. Could I
ever win his heart?

When Robert Parker asked me to be his wife I'd accepted, not because I expected to be happy with him, nor because Robert loved me—I knew he didn't—but because I had loved him all my life and would have died, I guess to make him happy. And, I'd really thought that if anyone on earth could make Robert happy—after what had happened to him—I could.

When Robert Parker asked me to be his wife I'd accepted, not because I expected to be happy with him, nor because Robert loved me—I knew he didn't—but because I had loved him all my life and would have died, I guess, to make him happy. And, I'd really thought that if anyone on earth could make Robert happy—after what had happened to him—I could.

You see, Robert's first wife, Allyson, whom he'd idolized, had run way one day with a handsome but good-for-nothing younger guy. She'd left Robert with a little four-year-old girl, Nicole, to raise. Before that, Robert had always been a happy man. He didn't drink or gamble, or need any of those things, and he'd just about worshiped his wife and child.

The man that Lola had run away with, Pete Stone, had worked for Robert at the mill. Robert had inherited the mill from his father, and did a nice business there. Pete had been his handyman, and Robert would about as soon have been suspicious of his own son, if he'd had one, as of Pete. Pete was nearly ten years younger than Robert and Allyson, who had been in the same class in high school.

Allyson's leaving him almost made a madman out of Robert. He'd vowed to kill them both. In fact, he'd spent days trying to track them down, but they had been too smart for him. No one ever did find out what had become of them.

My heart used to ache so badly for him when he tried to be father and mother both to his child. After Allyson left, his shoulders became bent, and his dear face looked drawn and haggard from the strain. I couldn't stand seeing him that way.

When Nicole was eleven she had a severe attack of scarlet fever, which left her sick for months. Robert never left her side. He turned his business over to his assistant and stayed at home with Nicole and nursed her until he was on the verge of a collapse himself. It was then that he came to me and asked me to marry him.

"Now, don't get me wrong, Sheryl," he said gruffly. "I'm not pretending to love you. I'll love no woman again. It's just that Nicole needs a—needs some one to look after her and I—well, I'm—" He stumbled to a confused stop.

"And you need a housekeeper?" I finished for him. "I understand, Robert, and my answer is yes."

When you loved a man as I loved Robert, nothing else mattered too much, not even the fact that he didn't love you.

We were married at the minister's house and I went home with Robert, and began my new life. I thought that all the love I had for him would make him love me eventually.

I loved poor little Nicole, too, and pitied her with all my heart. I wanted passionately to make up to her for her lonely, unhappy childhood. I supposes I made the mistake of being too good to her, too lenient with her, and spoiling her dreadfully. It was so easy to spoil the poor little frightened thing.

Right away, I put her on nourishing diet. I played with her and, as she grew better, allowed other children to come in and play with her, too—boys as well as girls. The boys stayed away at first, but I tempted them with cookies and lemonade, and I read adventure stories to all the children. The boys, especially, loved that.

When Robert learned about this, he was furious.

"You'll make her just like her mother, boy—crazy," he stormed.

Nicole grew prettier every year. And, when she was sixteen she was the image of her mother. She had her mother's mannerisms, too—her cute, silly little tricks. I knew it crucified Robert to see Allyson again in Nicole, and I would try harder than ever to be patient and brave.

Someday, she'll marry and go away, I thought, then Robert will change toward me, he'll have to. Oh, God, let him love me then!

I saw Nicole on the street one day with a couple of boys and she was acting so silly and unnatural that I was disgusted. She would push them away, then snuggle up to one or the other of them, and laugh and giggle until I wanted to shake her. I got home ahead of her and, when she arrived, I called her into my bedroom and tried to talk to her.

"Just act naturally with boys, dear," I said. "If you don't, they won't respect you and people will begin to talk about you."

The way she responded to my advice astounded me. She stamped her feet and told me to mind my own business.

"The only trouble with you is you're jealous!" she screamed. "You're crazy about my father and he doesn't care for you at all.

58

He's never loved any one but me and my pretty mother. And, because you're homely and can't win him like my mother did, you take your spite out on me because I look like her and can attract boys!"

Angry, I sent her to her room. A little while later, I had an idea. I went to Nicole's door and called her.

"What do you want?" she asked petulantly

"I want you—or I wouldn't have called," I replied, calmly but firmly.

She was so surprised that she opened the door right away. "First, Nicole," I said, "I want you to apologize to me for what you said to me. If you don't, I'm going to tell your father the whole thing."

"You wouldn't dare!" she said, almost under her breath. "You're afraid not to be nice to me because you think that by being nice to me you can win his love. But, you never can! He loves me—not you. I can make him do anything I say, and I'll make him send you away forever, if you don't watch your step!"

An hour before and I would have been terrified at the truth of her words. Now, I said sternly, "I'm giving you just one last chance to apologize for every word you've spoken to me today. And, unless you do, I'll go to your father and tell him exactly how silly you acted with those boys on the street today. He may send me away forever—as you say. But, that would be better than staying here to be treated like an underpaid servant instead of a wife and mother. It's true that I love your father, Nicole. I've always loved him, and always will, I guess. And it's also true that he doesn't love me. But, that doesn't seem to matter anymore. What matters now is that you must be taught some manners and some sense."

Nicole treated me differently after that. She did what I asked her to—but never a thing more.

Eventually, I could sense that something was very wrong with Nicole, and I became consumed with worry.

At first, she refused to say a word, but gradually I got the truth out of her. She was going to have a baby. Joe Mulligan was the father. He didn't know about it. She hadn't told him or anybody. She was afraid to. It had happened one night, two months earlier. She had slipped out of the house to meet him after her father and I were asleep. She didn't want to live and face the shame and her father's anger

"If you tell him, he'll kill me. You know he will, Aunt Sheryl. Oh, what can I do? What will I do? If you only hadn't interfered—"

"Hush!" I said sternly. "Two wrongs never make a right. And I won't tell your father—yet. I'll think of something."

My very soul inside of me seemed to be shuddering. I couldn't think or reason. I could only cringe against that awful thing. What would Robert say when he knew? What would he do? How had I

59

failed the child that had been put in my care? And then quite clearly, I knew what I had to do.

On that long ago day when Robert had demanded that she have no contact with boys, I should have faced him courageously and battled for Nicole's rights then. If she had gone around with boys as the other girls did, instead of having to sneak around, to pretend and lie, such a thing wouldn't have happened. If she could have invited Joe to the house honestly and honorably, she wouldn't have had to steal out in the middle of the night to meet him alone somewhere. Her home, which should be a girl's fortress, her protection, had been denied her. The thing which had happened was my fault—and Robert's—more than it was Nicole's and Joe's.

Only God knew the agony of my self—scorn, my remorse for my cowardliness, as I stood there looking down on the flushed tearstained face of that terrified child. I mustn't let her know how frightened I was.

"I'm going to Joe," I said as calmly as I was able to.

"No!" she screamed, sitting bolt upright and grabbing at me. "No, don't tell him. I'll die, if he knows. I can't face that."

"You've got to," I replied as calmly as I could. "Nicole, I've been a coward all my life. It never gets you anything. I'll see Joe's father. He's a good man. He'll see that his son does the right thing. You're only children, but if you're old enough for this, you're old enough for marriage."

"Marriage?" Nicole said in an awed whisper. "Do you think? Do you believe—" A little color had come back into her pale cheeks.

"I know," I assured her bravely. "Now you just undress and go back to bed and have a good sleep. I'll ask Joe's father to meet me somewhere. I'll fix everything. Don't worry, dear. Just be a brave girl and resolve to face things."

I helped her get her clothes off, then when she was tucked under the covers, I leaned down and kissed her. She put her arms around my neck and began to cry again.

"Oh, Aunt Sheryl, I'm so sorry, so ashamed. I've been so mean to you. I've been such a fool. Do you really think things can ever be right again, that Joe will—" She buried her face in my shoulder, and I let her cry.

I called Joe's father, asking him to meet me. How strange it was for me to be writing to Michael. Long ago he had been one of my admirers, one of those boys I could not love—because of Robert. Michael had married eventually, but his wife had died two years ago and so Joe was motherless just as Nicole was. He said that he would.

When Robert came home for supper I told him that Nicole was asleep, that she had gone to bed with a headache, which was partly me—she was still sleeping.

Robert went back to the mill as he did nearly every night. At a quarter to eight I put on. my things and started for the cemetery. I hadn't known where else to tell Michael to meet me. Down there, prying eyes wouldn't be watching us. I hesitated about waking Nicole and decided to let her sleep. Awake, she would only be in a nervous turmoil until I returned. I didn't expect to be gone for more than a few minutes.

I got there before Michael did and paced up and down by the cemetery gate, waiting for him. It was an eerie place to wait, but I was so upset about Nicole and so afraid that Michael wouldn't be reasonable that I didn't mind it much.

I heard a car coming down the lonely road and stepped behind a tree so I wouldn't be seen. How could I explain my presence at that dreary spot at such an hour? It was Michael, he had driven down.

I was shivering with the cold, or with nervousness, by that time, so Michael called out to me.

"Come, get in the car, Sheryl. We can talk here. It will be warmer than out there in the wind. Now, what in the world is wrong?" he asked anxiously as I climbed in beside him.

"Oh, Michael, it's so awful. I barely know how to tell you. It's— Joe and Nicole They— She's—" I burst into tears. I just couldn't put it in words to Michael.

Clumsily, Michael patted my hands. "Come, now, Sheryl," he said gruffly. "It can't be as bad as all that. What have those kids been up to? If they're in trouble of some kind, of course, we must get them out of it. What is it, trouble at school?"

When I finally managed to blurt out the dreadful truth, poor Michael was as heartsick as I over it.

"But, they're only kids," he kept repeating. "It doesn't seem possible. Are you sure? Joe's only a boy—a kid. What would his mother say? I'm glad she didn't live to see this day. Though, maybe if she had lived—Joe would have been different, and maybe this wouldn't have happened. I let him down somehow—I guess."

"That's the way I feel, too, Michael," I cried despairingly. "If I had been different with Nicole—if I had insisted that she meet boys normally, instead of always being so scared of what Robert would say and do. Oh, I've been afraid of Robert all my life. And, because of that fear, Nicole and all of us are suffering now. I've been a fool and a coward, God forgive me! Oh, Michael, I didn't know, I didn't realize—"

"Of course, you didn't, Sheryl," he tried to soothe me. "Here, wipe your eyes and calm down. We've got to plan what to do." He gave me a tissue.

Then I told him my plan—if we could get the children to elope, if Joe would be willing to marry Nicole—and they could leave town and be safely married by the time Robert caught up with them.

"Of course, that's the way out," Michael agreed.

"But if Joe won't—" I began.

"He will!" Michael replied grimly. "Why, I'll beat him within an inch of his life, if he even hesitates!"

"You can't handle things that way, Michael," I said sadly. "That's the way Robert has always reasoned. You can't make people decent—or anything else—by brute force. Oh, if Joe refuses—I think I'll die, Michael. I'm terrified of what Robert will do. He'll kill Nicole! After what Allyson did to him, this will be too much! He won't be sane. He'll commit some awful crime!" I burst into tears again. Michael put an arm about my shoulder.

"There, there, Sheryl, don't cry. It's a shame for you to be treated so badly. You always were too good for—"

"Oh, she was, was she?" a hoarse voice snarled, and I froze with horror as I saw Robert standing just outside the car, not three feet from Michael and me. Michael hastily drew his arm from around my shoulders.

"Get out of that car, you—" He called Michael a filthy name and grabbed him by the collar.

"Robert, you don't understand!" I screamed as Robert yanked the door open, pulled Michael out to the ground, and shook him as a terrier shakes a rat.

"I understand, all right," Robert bellowed. "Don't forget, I've gone through all this before! And you pretended that you were such a saint, so sweet and gentle!" he yelled at me. "I knew all the time that it was just a pose that you were just the same as her and all other women, a low-down, deceitful hussy, a—" He called me an unspeakable name.

"Shut up!" Michael ordered. "You can't call Sheryl a name like that while I'm alive, you dog! You aren't good enough to lick her boots. She came out here to plead for—"

"Michael, keep quiet!" I cried. "Don't say it, I beg of you—"

"So I can't call her names," Robert cut in. "Well, who's going to stop me?"

With all his strength, Michael struck him squarely in the mouth. Robert was taller than Michael and heavier, too. Michael's action had been suicide. With a roar like a bull, Robert struck him twice in the face. Michael went down like a log, hitting his head against the fender of the car as he fell.

I jumped out of the car, screaming. "Oh, you brute, you've killed him! You fool—you beast!" As I knelt beside Michael and lifted up his head, blood ran over my hand and arm. I knew that I would always feel that warm blood. It had turned me cold with horror.

"I hope I have killed him!" Robert yelled, as he jumped into his car and started the motor. "I ought to kill you as well as your lover, you whore!"

"Robert, come back here!" I screamed. "Don't you dare leave us. We've got to get him to a doctor! He can't die! You'll be a murderer."

Robert only laughed wildly. "Give your lover a kiss—that will bring him to. Don't ever come back to my house, you witch! Take your lover home and nurse him—" He drove away at a furious pace, leaving me there alone with Michael.

I didn't know how I got him into the car. I seemed to have a strength I had never before possessed. He was bleeding terribly. Blood was all over the front of my coat and my dress, and the car seat. I felt weak and sick. I was so afraid I'd faint before I got Michael to a doctor. As I drove over the rough road to Doctor Wilder's, I wondered what I had done in my life to deserve such a cruel break. There would be a scandal, and Michael's name would be linked with mine. I wondered frantically where Robert had gone—whether he knew about Nicole, and how he had found out about my meeting Michael.

Miraculously, Dr. Wilder was home. Between us, we carried Michael into his office.. He called his wife, who had been a nurse before her marriage. After a hurried examination he said, "I don't believe it's a fracture—just a scalp wound. He'll need stitches. Mrs. Parker, you'd better wait in the reception room."

I stumbled across the room and sank into a deep chair. "Thank God! Thank God!" I whispered to myself. "He isn't dead! He won't die!"

I was shaking violently, and everything in the room seemed to be whirling around and around. I knew there was something that I should be doing yet I couldn't seem to remember what. And then, all at once, I knew. Robert would go back to Nicole—maybe kill her. I reached unsteadily for the telephone and dialed Joe's number.

"Joe, Nicole is in awful trouble. Her father—go to her quickly—" I told him.

Everything turned black then. I heard a roaring noise, and then, I fainted.

When I came to, someone was holding me close, someone with Robert's voice was sobbing, actually sobbing.

"Oh, Sheryl, forgive me! Forgive me! I've been such a blind fool. I've been such an animal. Speak to me, darling!"

Of course, it was a dream. No one had Robert's voice but Robert himself. And, I knew that Robert would never talk to me like that! I was asleep and dreaming. It was a beautiful dream. I had had it before.

I was bracing myself against the shock and disappointment of the awakening, when I felt a mouth against my own. I felt hot tears on my face. I opened my eyes. It wasn't a dream at all. Robert was there! He was really there! He was crying and begging me to forgive him. He was saying that he loved me—had loved me for years, but had been too stubborn and bitter to admit it.

All the years of hell I had been through were worth suffering for the glory and joy of that moment.

"Oh, Robert," I cried, kissing his tear-filled eyes, his agonized face, his clumsy hands, which were caressing my cheeks.

As I wiped his tears away, I looked at him curiously. "But how did you discover your mistake? How did you find out that Michael and I were not—"

"Nicole told me everything," he replied, avoiding my eyes.

I struggled to a sitting position. "Then you know—" I gasped incredulously, "about her—and Joe?"

"Yes, I know," he said huskily. "When I got home from the cemetery, she was up and dressed. I told her that I'd found you and Michael together, and had ordered you never to come home again. I guess I carried on like a crazy man for a while. It made me want to commit murder when I thought of your loving Michael instead of me." He paused.

"Nicole got hysterical at the way I was acting and told me the truth about her and Joe. She said that you'd gone to try and fix things up for them by talking to Michael. I felt like I was just coming out of a bad dream, one that I'd been in for years. I hurried over here to tell you. I had to see you, to beg you to forgive me. Oh, Sheryl, can you ever forgive me for calling you those names?"

"Of course," I told him softly. "You weren't Robert then. You were a madman, crazed by jealousy and suspicion. But, Robert darling, you won't harm them?" I asked, scarcely daring to believe it yet.

"No, I'm not angry with them," he said slowly. "I can't understand it, really. Ordinarily, I would have been furious. But I was so scared about losing you, so sorry about being such a fool, that I didn't have time to get upset, I guess."

"Thank goodness for that!" I breathed, my heart swelling with gratitude. God had answered my prayer, not in the way I had expected, but he had answered it.

"Of course, I'm sorry and ashamed—about Nicole," he said huskily, "but I guess I had it coming. I always kept her away from boys. I know now that was wrong. When one of them started to make love to her, she wasn't used to it. He swept her off her feet, poor kid! We'll stand by her, won't we?"

He looked at me so sadly that I threw my arms around his neck and pulled his head close to my heart.

"Of course we will, Robert," I cried joyfully.

I thought of the day when Nicole had been so horrible to me—the day I had wanted to leave her and Robert. But, I hadn't. And from that very day, when I had learned courage as well as faith, Nicole had respected me. And long before that, Robert had loved me. Oh, it was too beautiful to be true!

When Michael regained consciousness, Robert shamefacedly apologized to him. And the doctor and his wife kept our secret.

When we got home that night a big surprise awaited Robert and me. Nicole had gone! We found a note from her. She and Joe had run away to the city, and were to be married the next day.

Robert hadn't told Nicole anything about his hurting Michael, so Joe didn't know his father had been hurt. He must have gone to Nicole right away after I'd called him, and they'd solved things together without the help of any of us.

Michael secured a job for Joe in the city and they have lived there ever since. They are doing well in spite of their youth and their mistake. They have a beautiful baby boy named for his two grandfathers, and Nicole is a wonderful wife and mother. I am sure that she's learned her lesson and will never follow in Allyson's footsteps.

Robert and I are very happy—much happier, I think, than if we had not gone through those years of stupid mistakes. Robert blames himself entirely for all of our unhappiness, but I know that I am to blame, too. It isn't enough to have faith and love—the love must be perfect enough to cast out fear. If I had done what was right and brave in the first place, instead of being so afraid of angering or offending the man I loved, how much better things might have been. Oh, well, there's no sense in useless regretting. We can only profit by our mistakes and try to get as much satisfaction and happiness as we can from each day that comes along.

Robert, who never used to go to church, goes regularly now, and teaches a Sunday school class. He seems to enjoy it more than anything he has ever done.

When he asked me one day how I had ever been able to stay with him so long and so loyally, when he'd treated me so boorishly, I told him the simple truth.

"Because I loved you, dear, and had faith."

"Faith?" he echoed curiously.

Yes," I explained. "I asked God to make you love me someday—then I had faith that He'd do it. That's all."

"Well, if faith will do that, it's good enough for me," he replied, and ever since then, he's been going to church with me. And, I think that when the whole world returns to an unquestioning, brave, simple faith, most of our deepest troubles will be over.

When Robert Parker asked me to be his wife I'd accepted, not because I expected to be happy with him, nor because Robert loved me—I knew he didn't—but because I had loved him all my life and would have died, I guess, to make him happy. And, I'd really thought that if anyone on earth could make Robert happy—after what had happened to him—I could.

You see, Robert's first wife, Allyson, whom he'd idolized, had run way one day with a handsome but good-for-nothing younger guy. She'd left Robert with a little four-year-old girl, Nicole, to raise. Before that, Robert had always been a happy man. He didn't drink or gamble, or need any of those things, and he'd just about worshiped his wife and child.

The man that Lola had run away with, Pete Stone, had worked for Robert at the mill. Robert had inherited the mill from his father, and did a nice business there. Pete had been his handyman, and Robert would about as soon have been suspicious of his own son, if he'd had one, as of Pete. Pete was nearly ten years younger than Robert and Allyson, who had been in the same class in high school.

Allyson's leaving him almost made a madman out of Robert. He'd vowed to kill them both. In fact, he'd spent days trying to track them down, but they had been too smart for him. No one ever did find out what had become of them. One young man came back to town from the Navy and said that he thought he'd seen them together in a city in Europe, but he wasn't sure.

No one in our town ever dared mention Allyson's name to Robert after that. He would go into a spell of such blind rage that he frightened everyone. For years, he lived alone with Nicole, except for an old woman who came once a week to clean the house for him. His temperament had changed, and he was jealous and suspicious of everyone. Furthermore, he wouldn't let Nicole out of his sight—for fear that someone would tell her about her mother, I supposed.

I had loved Robert with all my heart and soul ever since high school. I had been a junior when he and Allyson were seniors—but Robert had never thought of me in that way. Just as I could never see anyone else because of my secret love for Robert, so he never had eyes for any other girl because of his intense passion for Allyson.

She had been beautiful, and all the boys were crazy about her. My own features were very ordinary, and I hadn't had the bubbly personality and vivacity, the poise and self-confidence that Allyson had always had.

The year they finished high school, they were married. I'd almost died the day of the wedding. It was at the church that I attended, and just about everybody in town was invited. I pretended I was sick so I wouldn't have to go.

But, even though I wasn't at the church, I could see every move they made. I knew how lovely Allyson looked in her white satin dress and long white veil. I knew just how Robert was smiling at her and how proud he looked. I tortured myself all afternoon and cried my silly heart out, alone in my room

For awhile, they were very happy. Their little girl, Nicole, was born when they had been married about a year, and after that, Allyson took to running around with a pretty fast set of young, married women. They drank and played cards nearly every afternoon. Robert didn't like it, and they used to have violent arguments over it. Then, suddenly, Allyson seemed to sober up, and she stayed home more. That was when she got interested in Pete, but Robert never suspected that.

Everyone had begun to dislike Allyson for the way she was pulling the wool over Robert's eyes and, also, for the way that she neglected Nicole. No one but Robert was surprised when Allyson ran away.

My heart used to ache so badly for him when he tried to be father and mother both to his child. After Allyson left, his shoulders became bent, and his dear face looked drawn and haggard from the strain. I couldn't stand seeing him that way.

I used to make little dresses and sweaters for Nicole, and I'd send them over by Mrs. Svenson, old cleaning lady, because she was the only woman that Robert would allow in the house. He never knew where the little clothes came from. I supposed he'd thought that Mrs. Svenson had made them.

When Nicole started to attend school, Robert always drove her there and back. He didn't allow her to play with any of the children. It made me furious to see how the lonely little child was kept away from everyone. It wasn't human for a child not to have a single companion of her own age. Finally, I got up nerve enough to speak to Robert about it.

I stopped him on the street one day after he had taken Nicole to school.

"Robert," I began, "just because one person proved to be unworthy, there's no reason why you should hate everyone else and keep your child from having a normal life. You ought to he ashamed of yourself—taking your anger out on an innocent child. If you don't stop making her live your hermit's life, you'll be sorry someday. As soon as she gets old enough, she'll run away, too."

I hadn't intended to say quite so much, but when I'd gotten started, my feelings had sort of run away with me. I knew that he'd be angry, but I'd had no idea that he would carry on as he did. He cursed at me and told me to mind my own business. He said that he'd bring up his child any way he wanted to, without the help of any prying busybodies like me.

His words nearly broke my heart. I went home and cried all day, and half the night. After that, though, Robert would let some little girls come into the yard and play with Nicole—but only when he was right there to watch them. And he wouldn't let her even look at a boy. I believed that if a boy had come up to Nicole and started talking to her, Robert would have beaten him. Poor Robert—even when I was most disgusted with him, I was sorry for him, too.

Through all his years of trouble, I couldn't help remembering how I had felt on the day he'd married Allyson. Instead of being sensible and thinking: Well, Robert's married now. I might as well for-get him, I'd thought, instead, Someday he'll need me. I don't know when or why, but someday, I'm going to be able to help Robert. He's going to need me terribly.

I knew that it was silly to let a feeling like that keep me from marrying and having a life and some happiness of my own. But, I couldn't seem to overcome it. In my heart, I knew that Robert was going to need me someday—and, when he did, he wouldn't find me tied down by a marriage to someone else.

Call it foreboding, intuition, or what you like; it was there, and as strong as life itself.

He'll need me now, I kept thinking. He'll see it himself soon, and ask me to marry him. But, the years passed and Robert became more bitter and morose every year, it seemed that I was wrong.

When I saw him making the dreadful mistake of keeping Nicole away from any contact with boys, I longed to warn him that that was the very thing, which would make her boy-crazy when she grew older. And time proved that I was right.

When Nicole was eleven she had a severe attack of scarlet fever, which left her sick for months. Robert never left her side. He turned his business over to his assistant and stayed at home with Nicole and nursed her until he was on the verge of a collapse himself. It was then that he came to me and asked me to marry him.

"Now, don't get me wrong, Sheryl," he said gruffly. "I'm not pretending to love you. I'll love no woman again. It's just that Nicole needs a—needs some one to look after her and I—well, I'm—" He stumbled to a confused stop.

"And you need a housekeeper?" I finished for him. "I understand, Robert, and my answer is yes."

I said not a word about how much and how long I had loved him, and not a sentence about how I'd rather be his servant than any other man's wife. Just the simple word yes. But, in my heart I was saying: I'll marry you, Robert, and I'll be so good to you and to your child

68

that you'll have to fall in love with me.

When you loved a man as I loved Robert, nothing else mattered too much, not even the fact that he didn't love you.

Women were silly that way—but I believed that God had made us that way. And, God's work was good. They could call us silly, weak, spine-less creatures—to love a man and suffer any hardship, any indignity that he offered us. To keep on loving him through disloyalty, infidelity, cruelty, neglect. But I wondered if—in their secret hearts—they didn't admit that the thing that they called silly and weak was not, instead, the most beautiful, the strongest, truest, finest thing in the world?

We were married at the minister's house and I went home with Robert. Poor little Nicole lay weak and white on a couch beside the fire. The air in the room was stifling. Robert had been feeding her fried foods. She didn't like milk, so he'd never bought it for her. No wonder the child hadn't gotten better.

I was a born missionary, I supposed. Even if I had not loved Robert so dearly, my heart would have thrilled at the amount of good I knew I was going to be able to do in that neglected and dreary home. I felt that in no time at all, I would have Nicole rosy and well, and the tired, sad lines erased from Robert's face. That very first day, I longed to put my arms around his shoulders and say, "Cheer up, darling, your long years of trouble and loneliness are over. Everything is going to be all right. You see, Robert, I love you. I've always loved you. I know I can make you happy."

I often wondered if things might not have been a great deal different, if I had got up nerve enough to say those words that day.

But, I was afraid of offending Robert, afraid of alienating him, afraid of—oh, I didn't know what. I just didn't have the courage. I was afraid of a rebuff, afraid of frightening him away from me entirely, I guess. I should have remembered that "perfect love casts out fear."

I was unpacking my suitcases in Robert's room right after supper that night, when Robert came into it.

"You'll use the room right across the hall," he said in a strange, harsh voice. "I thought I made you under-stand this afternoon before we were married that this arrangement of ours is strictly a business affair. I don't love you! I'll never love you! I'll love no woman again." He went out without another word and left me standing there, my hand at my aching throat, my very heart turned to stone.

My outraged love seemed to be crying out, "Robert, Robert, you can't do this thing to me! You can't be so cruel, so inhuman, and so unjust! How can I make you love me, if you shut me out of your life entirely like this? I didn't know! I didn't under-stand! I thought you meant you weren't romantically in love with me—like you were with

Allyson. Oh, Robert, how could you? How could you?"

I didn't know how long I stood there, my hand at my throat, the tears running like rain down my cheeks. I only knew that, when I picked up my luggage and went to the room across the hall with it, I felt years and years older than I had a few moments before.

When I had closed the door of the empty, lonely room across the hall, I sank to my knees beside the bed.

"Oh, God, make him love me!" I pleaded. "I'll do anything, suffer anything, if you'll only make him love me at last. He's got to love me. I'll die if he doesn't. And he needs me so badly. Oh, please, Father, soften his hard, and bitter heart."

I rose from my knees believing with all my soul that God would answer my anguished prayer. Through all the days that followed, no matter how dark they were, I still believed it.

I loved poor little Nicole, too, and pitied her with all my heart. I wanted passionately to make up to her for her lonely, un-happy childhood. I suppose I made the mistake of being too good to her, too lenient with her, and spoiling her dreadfully. It was so easy to spoil the poor little frightened thing.

Right away, I put her on nourishing diet. I played with her and, as she grew better, allowed other children to come in and play with her, too—boys as well as girls. The boys stayed away at first, but I tempted them with cookies and lemonade, and I read adventure stories to all the children. The boys, especially, loved that.

When Robert learned about this, he was furious.

"You'll make her just like her mother, boy—crazy," he stormed.

I tried to explain that the only way to make a girl act normally around boys was to let her be with them as freely as with girls. But, he wouldn't see it my way.

"She has to see them at school—that's enough. They can't come here to the house. I won't allow it!"

So, at first, Nicole was shy and self—conscious with boys. Later, as she grew up, she became sly—which was to be expected, with her father feeling as he did. I should have had courage enough to face Robert and fight it out with him, but I was trying so desperately hard to win his love, I didn't want to anger or antagonize him.

When I learned that Nicole was walking home from school with one boy or another, leaving them a block away from the house, and coming the rest of the way alone, I wanted to tell her, "Honey, there's nothing wrong with walking home with a boy. Bring him home with you—don't be sneaky and sly about it."

I never dared say that, though, because of Robert's attitude. He was like a crazy man on the subject. So I made the ghastly mistake of pretending not to see, not to know. I never asked Nicole to help with the housework, either. That was another tragic mistake. I'd thought I was being good to her. I didn't dream that I was sowing the seed of future tragedy.

But, no matter how good I was to Nicole, no matter what a good wife I tried to be, Robert's attitude toward me never changed. It was a terrible thing to live in the same house with a man you loved with all your heart and soul—and never is able to touch anything except the outer shell of that man. Sometimes I would imagine a flicker of personal interest in Robert's eyes. Once I made the mistake of taking advantage of such an idea.

It was at the dinner table. I had cooked an especially nice meal, with apple pie, Robert's favorite dessert, to finish up with. He never told me that anything I cooked or baked was good, so I had to guess that he was pleased by the way he ate it. That night he asked for another cup of coffee.

"And, while you're up," he said gruffly, "you might get me another piece of that pie—if there's any extra."

"Yes, dear, there's plenty," I said, pleased that he wanted more. He frowned at my word of endearment, but I was bold that night. I knew that he had been terribly hurt by a woman—that he distrusted any display of affection. I also knew—or imagined—that he was as heart-hungry as I was for a little love or tenderness. And I knew that any such display would have to come from me. He was so firmly entrenched in that hard, outer shell of his that he would never come out of it voluntarily. At first, I had hoped he would, but I knew better by that time.

As I leaned over his shoulder to pour his coffee, such a wave of pity and tenderness for this unhappy man swept over me that I simply had to show it in some way. I put my hand on his shoulder and pressed hard.

"I'm glad you like my pie," I said softly. He recoiled from my caress as though it had been a blow.

"Don't try any of that soft stuff on me!" he hissed, his face an angry red, his eyes blazing. "It won't get you anything!"

It was all I could do to keep from crying out with pain at the cruelty and injustice of that remark. Nicole was watching me with a little half-sneer on her pretty mouth, so I braced my shoulders, and closed my teeth on the pain.

"I don't want anything!" I managed to say after I'd set the coffeepot back on the stove.

I should have told him then—what I told him years later. It would have been better for us both—and, for Nicole. But again, my cowardly fear of losing him forever held me back. Never again did I try any tenderness with him—never again did I try to touch him, although, sometimes, my fingers ached just to touch his hand or stroke his hair. That was usually after I had caught him off guard, somehow, and had seen—for a revealing second or so—the agony and bitterness in his eyes. If ever a man had tortured eyes, it was Robert. You could almost see a soul in deadly torment for a flashing moment before he regained control of himself again. I think it was knowing the hurt in those eyes of his that kept me in bondage to him for so long.

Nicole grew prettier every year. And, when she was sixteen she was the image of her mother. She had her mother's mannerisms, too—her cute, silly little tricks. I knew it crucified Robert to see Allyson again in Nicole, and I would try harder than ever to be patient and brave.

Someday, she'll marry and go away, I thought, then Robert will change toward me, he'll have to. Oh, God, let him love me then!

I saw Nicole on the street one day with a couple of boys and she was acting so silly and unnatural that I was disgusted. She would push them away, then snuggle up to one or the other of them, and laugh and giggle until I wanted to shake her. I got home ahead of her and, when she arrived, I called her into my bedroom and tried to talk to her.

"Just act naturally with boys, dear," I said. "If you don't, they won't respect you and people will begin to talk about you."

The way she responded to my advice astounded me. She stamped her feet and told me to mind my own business.

"The only trouble with you is you're jealous!" she screamed. "You're crazy about my father and he doesn't care for you at all. He's never loved any one but my pretty mother and me. And, because you're homely and can't win him like my mother did, you take your spite out on me because I look like her and can attract boys!"

I didn't reply. I couldn't. I motioned her out of the room, closed and locked the door, and fell on my knees beside the bed.

"Oh, God, I can't stand any more!" I sobbed. "I can't stay here and be insulted like that. I've given them all my love. I've worked night and day for them, and all I've got in return is ingratitude and abuse. I can't go on. I can't!"

And then, a still, small voice somewhere deep inside of me seemed to say: Yes, you can go on—you know you can! You can't quit now, when Nicole needs you most—when Robert needs you most. You know that if Nicole turns out badly it will break Robert's heart. You've got to stay and finish your work here. What if Robert doesn't love you? It isn't getting love that matters so much—it's giving love that matters! You've been trying to get love all these years as a reward for what you've done. Why not try just giving love, for its own sake, without any thought of reward? Wouldn't that be bigger—finer? Wouldn't your own inner assurance that you'd done the right thing be all the reward you needed?

72

I got up from my knees a different woman—a woman no longer afraid. Why, I wasn't even afraid of Robert! The fear that had held me in its dreadful bondage all those years was gone! I was through with it forever.

I had feared that Robert wouldn't love me—and, he didn't. In spite of my brave words about belief and faith, I had been a covert all the way through. But, faith wasn't enough—one must have courage, too. One doesn't win battles in life unless one deserved to win.

I knew that I hadn't deserved to win before that. I hadn't won their love and respect because I hadn't deserved it. One doesn't really deserve any thing but dirty boots—by being a doormat. I had invited their bad behavior and disrespect by suffering it in the first place. I simply wouldn't let either of them hurt or frighten me again.

I put on a fresh shirt and went out to start supper. I started to go down to the cellar for a jar of fruit when I had an idea. I went to Nicole's door and called her.

"What do you want?" she asked petulantly

"I want you—or I wouldn't have called," I replied, calmly but firmly. She was so surprised that she opened the door right away. "First, Nicole," I said, "I want you to apologize to me for what you said to me. If you don't, I'm going to tell your father the whole thing."

"You wouldn't dare!" she said, almost under her breath. "You're afraid not to be nice to me because you think that by being nice to me you can win his love. But, you never can! He loves me—not you. I can make him do anything I say, and I'll make him send you away forever, if you don't watch your step!"

An hour before and I would have been terrified at the truth of her words. Now, I said sternly, "I'm giving you just one last chance to apologize for every word you've spoken to me today. And, unless you do, I'll go to your father and tell him exactly how silly you acted with those boys on the street today. He may send me away forever—as you say. But, that would be better than staying here to be treated like an underpaid servant instead of a wife and mother. It's true that I love your father, Nicole. I've always loved him, and always will, I guess. And it's also true that he doesn't love me. But, that doesn't seem to matter anymore. What matters now is that you must be taught some manners and some sense."

For a long while, Nicole stared defiantly and sullenly at me, then she began speaking in a low voice. "I'm sorry, Aunt Sheryl. I guess I have been pretty mean to you."

Thank God! I thought. If I had taken this stand long ago, if I hadn't been so weak and cowardly, Nicole would be a different girl today. Aloud, I said, "Thank you. Now, Nicole, please run down cellar

73

and bring me up a can of cherries. And, after that, you can set the table," I added.

An angry flush stained her cheeks. "So that's the way you're going to act! The minute you get an inch you're going to take a mile!" she exclaimed. "Well, I'm not going—"

I didn't wait to hear anymore. I just went back out into the kitchen and started to slice potatoes. In a little while, Nicole did what I asked her to.

"Oh, why have I been such a fool for so long?" I asked myself impatiently. "Well, things will be different now."

Nicole treated me differently after that. She did what I asked her to—but never a thing more. And, I realized that it was only fear of what her father might do to her, if I told him about her behavior with those boys that was keeping her so docile. When I understood that she didn't really love me or want to help me, it hurt dreadfully for a while. Then I realized that I was to blame for that, too. You didn't win anyone's love or respect by making a slave of yourself for them. You didn't even prove your own love for them by acting that way.

Nicole began acting strangely—she stayed in her room a lot when she was home, and she seemed trying to avoid her father, and me too. I thought she was holding resentment for what I had said to her. I never dreamed the awful truth!

And then, one Saturday afternoon I went hurriedly into the bathroom for some cleaning powder I had left there and surprised Nicole in the act of putting a bottle to her lips. A bottle marked poison! I knocked the bottle from her lips before she had taken any. It fell against the tub and smashed into a hundred pieces. The poison spattered all over her dress and mine and on the rug by the tub.

"What are you doing?" I cried. "Are you crazy?"

Nicole ran into her room, screaming. "Yes, I'm crazy. You would be, too, if you were me. Why did you stop me? It would be all over in a few minutes. Now, Dad will kill me! He'll beat me! He'll torture me. Oh, how I hate you!"

She had thrown herself, sobbing wildly, on the bed. I went over and knelt beside her.

"Tell me, darling! I'll help you, what-ever it is," I pleaded.

At first, she refused to say a word, but gradually I got the truth out of her. She was going to have a baby. Joe Mulligan was the father. He didn't know about it. She hadn't told him or anybody. She was afraid to. It had happened one night, two months earlier. She had slipped out of the house to meet him after her father and I were asleep. She didn't want to live and face the shame and her father's anger

"If you tell him, he'll kill me. You know he will, Aunt Sheryl. Oh, what can I do? What will I do? If you only hadn't interfered—"

74

"Hush!" I said sternly. "Two wrongs never make a right. And I won't tell your father—yet. I'll think of something."

My very soul inside of me seemed to be shuddering. I couldn't think or reason. I could only cringe against that awful thing. What would Robert say when he knew? What would he do? How had I failed the child that had been put in my care? And then quite clearly, I knew what I had to do.

On that long ago day when Robert had demanded that she have no contact with boys, I should have faced him courageously and battled for Nicole's rights then. If she had gone around with boys as the other girls did, instead of having to sneak around, to pre-tend and lie, such a thing wouldn't have happened. If she could have invited Joe to the house honestly and honorably, she wouldn't have had to steal out in the middle of the night to meet him alone somewhere. Her home, which should be a girl's fortress, her protection, had been denied her. The thing, which had happened, was my fault—and Robert's—more than it was Nicole's and Joe's.

Only God knew the agony of my self—scorn, my remorse for my cowardliness, as I stood there looking down on the flushed tearstained face of that terrified child. I mustn't let her know how frightened I was. I must be calm, brave. Ha! That was a good joke! Brave, when it was too late. Fear swept me like a fever—that mental fear which was so much more terrible than physical fear. How could I face Robert and tell him such a dreadful thing? He would kill Nicole! If he would only kill me, instead. If I could only get her out of the way before I told him. Then his anger would be taken out on me. That was the answer.

"I'm going to Joe," I said as calmly as I was able to.

"No!" she screamed, sitting bolt up right and grabbing at me. "No, don't tell him. I'll die, if he knows. I can't face that."

"You've got to," I replied as calmly as I could. "Nicole, I've been a coward all my life. It never gets you anything. I'll see Joe's father. He's a good man. He'll see that his son does the right thing. You're only children, but if you're old enough for this, you're old enough for marriage."

"Marriage?" Nicole said in an awed whisper. "Do you think? Do you believe—" A little color had come back into her pale cheeks.

"I know," I assured her bravely. "Now you just undress and go back to bed and have a good sleep. I'll ask Joe's father to meet me somewhere. I'll fix everything. Don't worry, dear. Just be a brave girl and resolve to face things. You've done wrong, but you're going to forget all thoughts of dying. Why should you die and Joe go scot-free?"

I helped her get her clothes off, then when she was tucked under the covers, I leaned down and kissed her. She put her arms around my neck and began to cry again.

"Oh, Aunt Sheryl, I'm so sorry, so ashamed. I've been so mean to you. I've been such a fool. Do you really think things can ever be right again, that Joe will—" She buried her face in my shoulder, and I let her cry.

I called Joe's father, asking him to meet me. How strange it was for me to be writing to Michael. Long ago he had been one of my admirers, one of those boys I could not love—because of Robert. Michael had married eventually, but his wife had died two years ago and so Joe was motherless just as Nicole was. He said that he would.

When Robert came home for supper I told him that Nicole was asleep, that she had gone to bed with a headache, which was partly true—she was still sleeping.

Robert went back to the mill as he did nearly every night. At a quarter to eight I put on my things and started for the cemetery. I hadn't known where else to tell Michael to meet me. Down there, prying eyes wouldn't be watching us. I hesitated about waking Nicole and decided to let her sleep. Awake, she would only be in a nervous turmoil until I returned. I didn't expect to be gone for more than a few minutes.

I got there before Michael did and paced up and down by the cemetery gate, waiting for him. It was an eerie place to wait, but I was so upset about Nicole and so afraid that Michael wouldn't be reasonable that I didn't mind it much.

I wondered frantically if Michael would see things as I did— would agree that the children should marry at once, should elope be-fore Robert found out. I was terrified at the thought of what Robert might do, if Nicole— and Joe, too—were not out of his reach.

As I nervously walked up and down there by the old wrought-iron cemetery gate, for the first time since Nicole had told me the awful truth, I gave way to terror and despair. I had pretended to be calm for her sake. I had not allowed her to see how horrified I was at her attempted suicide. I had made believe that I was brave—that everything would turn out all right. Finally, I dared to give way to my real feelings, my agony of doubt and fear.

"Oh, God," I whispered, "Let Joe do the right thing! Let them get away before Robert learns the truth. Please, please, don't let Robert go crazy. Let something happen to make him see reason—"

Little did I know how God was going to answer my prayer? I felt a little better after I had prayed—as I always did It seemed that the few times in my life when things had gotten too terrible for me to handle, when I couldn't see any way out by my own best efforts and I asked God to settle it for me, He always did. Not in the way I have anticipated, perhaps, but in His own way.

I heard a car coming down the lonely road and stepped behind a tree so I wouldn't be seen. How could I explain my presence at that dreary spot at such an hour? It was Michael he had driven down.

I was shivering with the cold, or with nervousness, by that time, so Michael called out to me.

"Come, get in the car, Sheryl. We can talk here. It will be warmer than out there in the wind. Now what in the world is wrong?" he asked anxiously as I climbed in beside him.

"Oh, Michael, it's so awful. I barely know how to tell you. It's— Joe and Nicole They— She's—" I burst into tears. I just couldn't put it in words to Michael.

Clumsily, Michael patted my hands. "Come, now, Sheryl," he said gruffly. "It can't be as bad as all that. What have those kids been up to? If they're in trouble of some kind, of course, we must get them out of it. What is it, trouble at school?"

When I finally managed to blurt out the dreadful truth, poor Michael was as heartsick as I over it.

"But, they're only kids," he kept repeating. "It doesn't seem possible. Are you sure? Joe's only a boy—a kid. What would his mother say? I'm glad she didn't live to see this day. Though maybe if she had lived—Joe would have been different, and maybe this wouldn't have happened. I let him down some-how—I guess."

"That's the way I feel, too, Michael," I cried despairingly. "If I had been different with Nicole—if I had insisted that she meet boys normally instead of always being so scared of what Robert would say and do. Oh, I've been afraid of Robert all my life. And, because of that fear, Nicole and all of us are suffering now. I've been a fool and a coward, God forgive me! Oh, Michael, I didn't know, I didn't realize—"

"Of course, you didn't, Sheryl," he tried to soothe me. "Here, wipe your eyes and calm down. We've got to plan what to do." He gave me a tissue.

Then I told him my plan—if we could get the children to elope, if Joe would be willing to marry Nicole—and they could leave town and be safely married by the time Robert caught up with them.

"Of course, that's the way out," Michael agreed.

"But if Joe won't—" I began.

"He will!" Michael replied grimly. "Why, I'll beat him within an inch of his life, if he even hesitates!"

"You can't handle things that way, Michael," I said sadly. "That's the way Robert has always reasoned. You can't make people decent— or anything else—by brute force. Oh, if Joe refuses—I think I'll die, Michael. I'm terrified of what Robert will do. He'll kill Nicole! After what Allyson did to him, this will be too much! He won't be sane. He'll commit some awful crime!" I burst into tears again. Michael put an arm about my shoulder.

"There, there, Sheryl, don't cry. It's a shame for you to be treated so badly You always were too good for—"

"Oh, she was, was she?" a hoarse voice snarled, and I froze with horror as I saw Robert standing just outside the car, not three feet from Michael and me. Michael hastily drew his arm from around my shoulders.

"Get out of that car, you—" He called Michael a filthy name and grabbed him by the collar.

"Robert, you don't understand!" I screamed as Robert yanked the door open, pulled Michael out to the ground, and shook him as a terrier shakes a rat.

"I understand, all right," Robert bellowed. "Don't forget, I've gone through all this before! And you pretended that you were such a saint, so sweet and gentle!" he yelled at me. "I knew all the time that it was just a pose- that you were just the same as her and all other women, a low-down, deceitful hussy, a—" He called me an unspeakable name.

"Shut up!" Michael ordered. "You can't call Sheryl a name like that while I'm alive, you dog! You aren't good enough to lick her boots. She came out here to plead for—"

"Michael, keep quiet!" I cried. "Don't say it, I beg of you—"

"So I can't call her names," Robert cut in. "Well, who's going to stop me?"

With all his strength, Michael struck him squarely in the mouth. Robert was taller than Michael and heavier, too. Michael's action had been suicide. With a roar like a bull, Robert struck him twice in the face. Michael went down like a log, hitting his head against the fender of the car as he fell.

I jumped out of the car, screaming. "Oh, you brute, you've killed him! You fool—you beast!" As I knelt beside Michael and lifted up his head, blood ran over my hand and arm. I knew that I would always feel that warm blood. It had turned me cold with horror.

"I hope I have killed him!" Robert yelled, as he jumped into his car and started the motor. "I ought to kill you as well as your lover, you whore!"

"Robert, come back here!" I screamed. "Don't you dare leave us. We've got to get him to a doctor! He can't die! You'll be a murderer."

Robert only laughed wildly. "Give your lover a kiss—that will bring him to. Don't ever come back to my house, you with! Take your lover home and nurse him—" He drove away at a furious pace, leaving me there alone with Michael.

I didn't know how I got him into the car. I seemed to have a strength I had never before possessed. He was bleeding terribly. Blood was all over the front of my coat and my dress, and the car seat.

I felt weak and sick. I was so afraid I'd faint before I got Michael to a doctor. As I drove over the rough road to Doctor Wilder's, I wondered what I had done in my life to deserve such a cruel break. There would be a scandal, and Michael's name would be linked with mine. I wondered frantic-ally where Robert had gone—whether he knew about Nicole and Joe, and how he had found out about my meeting Michael.

MIRACULOUSLY, Doctor Wilder was home. Between us, we carried Michael into his office. He called his wife, who had been a nurse before her marriage. After a hurried examination he said, "I don't believe it's a fracture—just a scalp wound. He'll need stitches. Mrs. Parker, you'd better wait in the reception room."

I stumbled across the room and sank into a deep chair. "Thank God! Thank God!" I whispered to myself. "He isn't dead! He won't die!"

I was shaking violently, and everything in the room seemed to be whirling around and around. I knew there was something that I should be doing, yet I couldn't seem to remember what. And then, all at once, I knew. Robert would go back to Nicole—maybe kill her. I reached unsteadily for the telephone and dialed Joe's number.

"Joe, Nicole is in awful trouble. Her father—go to her quickly—" I told him.

Everything turned black then. I heard a roaring noise, and then, I fainted.

When I came to, some one was holding me close, someone with Robert's voice was sobbing, actually sobbing.

"Oh, Sheryl, forgive me! Forgive me! I've been such a blind fool. I've been such an animal. Speak to me, darling!"

Of course, it was a dream. No one had Robert's voice but Robert himself. And, I knew that Robert would never talk to me like that! I was asleep and dreaming. It was a beautiful dream. I had had it before.

I was bracing myself against the shock and disappointment of the awakening, when I felt a mouth against my own. I felt hot tears on my face. I opened my eyes. It wasn't a dream at all. Robert was there! He was really there! He was crying and begging me to forgive him. He was saying that he loved me—had loved me for years, but had been too stubborn and bitter to admit it.

All the years of hell I had been through were worth suffering for the glory and joy of that moment.

"Oh, Robert," I cried, kissing his tear-filled eyes, his agonized face, his clumsy hands, which were caressing my cheeks.

As I wiped his tears away, I looked at him curiously. "But how did you discover your mistake? How did you find out that Michael and I were not—"?

"Nicole told me everything," he replied, avoiding my eyes.

I struggled to a sitting position. "Then you know—" I gasped incredulously, "about her—and Joe?"

"Yes, I know," he said huskily. "When I got home from the cemetery, she was up and dressed. I told her that I'd found you and Michael together, and had ordered you never to come home again. I guess I carried on like a crazy man for a while. It made me want to commit murder when I thought of your loving Michael instead of me." He paused.

"Nicole got hysterical at the way I was acting and told me the truth about her and Joe. She said that you'd gone to try and fix things up for them by talking to Michael. I felt like I was just coming out of a bad dream, one that I'd been in for years. I hurried over here to tell you. I had to see you, to beg you to forgive me. Oh, Sheryl, can you ever forgive me for calling you those names?"

"Of course," I told him softly. "You weren't Robert then. You were a madman, crazed by jealousy and suspicion. But, Robert darling, you won't harm them?" I asked, scarcely daring to believe it yet.

"No, I'm not angry with them," he said slowly. "I can't understand it, really. Ordinarily, I would have been furious. But I was so scared about losing you, so sorry about being such a fool, that I didn't have time to get upset, I guess."

"Thank goodness for that!" I breathed, my heart swelling with gratitude. God had answered my prayer, not in the way I had expected, but he had answered it.

"Of course, I'm sorry and ashamed— about Nicole," he said huskily, "but I guess I had it coming. I always kept her away from boys. I know now that was wrong. When one of them started to make love to her, she wasn't used to it. He swept her off her feet, poor kid! We'll stand by her, won't we?"

He looked at me so sadly that I threw my arms around his neck and pulled his head close to my heart.

"Of course we will, Robert," I cried joyfully.

I thought of the day when Nicole had been so horrible to me— the day I had wanted to leave her and Robert. But, I hadn't. And from that very day, when I had learned courage as well as faith, Nicole had respected me. And long before that, Robert had loved me. Oh, it was too beautiful to be true!

When Michael regained consciousness, Robert shamefacedly apologized to him. And the doctor and his wife kept our secret.

When we got home that night a big surprise awaited Robert and me. Nicole had gone! We found a note from her. She and Joe had run away to the city, and were to be married the next day.

Robert hadn't told Nicole anything about his hurting Michael, so Joe didn't know his father had been hurt. He must have gone to Nicole right away after I'd called him, and they'd solved things together without the help of any of us.

Michael secured a job for Joe in the city and they have lived there ever since. They are doing well in spite of their youth and their mistake. They have a beautiful baby boy named for his two grandfathers, and Nicole is a wonderful wife and mother. I am sure that she's learned her lesson and will never follow in Allyson's footsteps.

Robert and I are very happy—much happier, I think, than if we had not gone through those years of stupid mistakes. Robert blames himself entirely for all of our un-happiness, but I know that I am to blame, too. It isn't enough to have faith and love—the love must be perfect enough to cast out fear. If I had done what was right and brave in the first place, instead of being so afraid of angering or offending the man I loved, how much better things might have been. Oh, well, there's no sense in useless regretting. We can only profit by our mistakes and try to get as much satisfaction and happiness as we can from each day that comes along.

Robert, who never used to go to church, goes regularly now, and teaches a Sunday school class. He seems to enjoy it more than anything he has ever done.

When he asked me one day how I had ever been able to stay with him so long and so loyally, when he'd treated me so boorishly, I told him the simple truth.

"Because I loved you, dear, and had faith."

"Faith?" he echoed curiously.

Yes," I explained. "I asked God to make you love me someday—then I had faith that He'd do it. That's all."

"Well, if faith will do that, it's good enough for me," he replied, and ever since then, he's been going to church with me. And, I think that when the whole world returns to an unquestioning, brave, simple faith, most of our deepest troubles will be over.

THE END

SO HOT FOR HIM
All the women wanted him—
lusted for his strong, hard body.
But I was the one who found ecstasy
in his arms every night

I heard Paul singing in the tub. There was no shower in our tiny apartment, so he was taking a bath. The sound of his voice brought a smile to my lips. All right, so it was a condescending smile, but it was also filled with fondness. So my husband wasn't the world's greatest singer? That didn't matter to me.

He bolted from the bathroom, wrapped in a towel. He grinned. "No good drooling, baby! I've got to be at the club in twenty minutes," he said playfully.

I smiled. "I'll suppress my lustful thoughts until you get home tonight," I told him.

"No, no!" he told me. "It will do me a world of good, having a hot woman in the front row gazing at me with adoration." Along with the words, he threw in a hug, taking seconds from his precious twenty minutes to give me a long, lingering kiss. When he released me, I caught my breath and nodded.

"Okay," I agreed.

"Great. See you in an hour or so. We can get something to eat after the show."

Listening to him sing later that evening, I thought of what I had been thinking, hearing him in the tub. He wasn't a great singer, I concluded as I gazed up at him adoringly, but when you watched him, it didn't seem to matter. If he didn't always do anything for the words of the song, he still managed to sell himself. Standing tall, swaying slightly to the music as he sang, smiling that slow, tantalizing smile, he completely captivated at least the female portion of the audience. If anyone knew what that smile could do to a woman, I did.

And then came the moment of the show that I loved, waited for, the reason I sat every night of his performance in that crowded room. The moment when he sang the quiet love song, just to me. It was if no one else in the room mattered, only Paul and me. I saw the smile at the corner of his lips as he signaled the pianist, and I knew even before I heard the first strains of the introduction that the song would be my favorite.

I could feel the envious glances of the women in the room as

Paul stood over my table, those intense eyes seeing only me as he sang. And I thought, for probably the millionth time in my life, that I was the luckiest girl on earth.

I still felt that way, at a little after one in the morning, as we were munching hamburgers in an all-night diner. Especially when he told me solemnly, "You owe me something, Marianne. For singing your song tonight, I mean."

"I'll try to think of some way to repay you."

"I'll try to help you," he added. "I always do my best thinking in bed. How about you?"

I felt the blood tingle inside me. Momentarily, I couldn't trust my voice. I merely nodded.

"Then let's get out of here," he suggested. "And get home to bed where can figure out, together, how you can pay me back."

We didn't make it home. Paul drove for a few blocks, but then, in a fit of impatience, he pulled the car over to the curb. Then I was in his arms, and he was smothering me with passionate, demanding kisses.

In the few minutes before his hands drove all other thoughts from my mind, I worried about being seen.

Yet I understood his urgency. Perhaps even more than my own. His evening had been made up of emotion. He sang love songs to me, and to other women. He swayed sensuously with the music. When it was over, he was bound to be keyed-up, ready to grab for release.

I was the lucky woman who could give him that release.

It lasted only a short time, that tempestuous, frantic clutching of bodies. I forgot about my fears of anyone seeing us, forgot everything except the soaring, wonderful fulfillment of belonging to him. Then his heavy breathing slowed and we held each other like two lost children.

I was glad that the next day was Sunday. I always looked forward to Sunday nights. That was the end of the weekend, the three-night stand that Paul had at the club. Starting Monday, we were average people again. I fixed dinner for my husband and greeted him at the door when he returned from his regular job at the music store.

That Sunday, Paul's accompanist, Mick, came to sit at my table before the show. "Did Paul tell you about the Water Club in Tannersville?" he asked.

"No," I replied.

As it turned out, Paul had been offered a gig at the Water Club. "Honey, he wants me for the whole week. And if they like me, the engagement could be unlimited! Do you know what that means? I could give up my job at the store and concentrate on singing!"

That was his dream. And it was coming true, while all I, his wife, could do was worry that following his dream would take my man away from me.

He also told me that he hadn't been able to bring Mick with him to the gig—the club had a house band.

"There's one other thing, honey," Paul said hesitantly.

"What is it?" I asked.

"At this stage of my career, the manager of the club, Ricky, thinks it would be better if it didn't get around that I was married." He paused. "He's got a few rooms above the club. He says I could stay there, and they could give me the big buildup. Promote me as a sex symbol, you know?"

His voice became pleading. "Honey, I'm twenty-three years old. If I'm going to start moving up, it has to be now, or it will be too late. I know how you feel, but it would only be for a while. I promise you. If I make it big there, I can do things on my own terms. And I know our anniversary is coming up. But I promise I'll be with you that night."

In spite of my misgivings, it didn't turn out to be so bad. Naturally, I couldn't drive to see Paul's show every night, since it was a two-hour drive and I would get home at three in the morning, but I went as often as I could. Our weekends became like honeymoons all over again, and as he had promised, Rob took me to a romantic inn for our anniversary

I met Mick one day, in the supermarket. He asked about Mick, and I told him how well he was doing.

He laughed bitterly. "He's a lucky guy. You do everything he wants, without question. He can do whatever he wants, with whoever he wants, and you're still here, waiting for him."

"We're married, Mick," I reminded him coldly. "And I trust my husband."

But he'd planted the seeds of suspicion in my mind. It wasn't my regular night to visit Paul during the week, but I needed him to convince me that what he was doing was for us. So I drove to the club.

And found my husband in the arms of another woman.

Well, not really. I could see that Paul was trying to get away from her. Gently, he was trying to disentangle himself from her, while she seemed determined to throw herself at him, kissing him passionately.

The relief in his eyes when he saw me was too obvious to be faked. There was no guilt at being caught—only gladness, and relief.

Ultimately, I knew that I could trust him. But I decided that I couldn't live the way we had been anymore. It was wrong for Paul and me to be married and living apart. It was living a lie, and I knew it.

That weekend, Paul was over the top. He'd been offered a chance to perform on a popular local television program. "Honey, do you know what this means?" he asked excitedly.

"That we can live together again?" I asked hopefully.

"Yes," he told me. "That's the first thing. I'm tired of lying. I want the world to know that I'm married to the woman I love!"

"That's good," I murmured happily. "Because I'd hate to have my baby while my husband is living like a single guy, and I'm a deserted woman."

Like a horror movie, in which the man turned slowly into a monster, I saw my husband's face fall. I had expected him to be as happy with my news as I had been—as happy as I had been with his news. Are you sure?" he asked shakily.

I nodded.

"Is it too late for an abortion?"

"I won't have an abortion, Paul," I said coldly. "I want our baby." "Honey, I want a family, too," he insisted. "But the next few months are crucial to my career. All I'm asking is that you give me a couple more years."

"No," I said. My voice sounded like it was coming from a long way away, and it was like I was in a dream. "I'm sorry," I whispered. "But you've asked me for my soul, and I can't give it to you."

It was the last bit of irony, I supposed, that while I was holding my baby in my arms for the first time, in my hospital room, I heard Paul's voice coming from the television set. Not on local television, but network television.

Mick had just left the room, so I could feed little Nicole, but he had been there as a friend, a stalwart arm to lean on while I was alone. I wasn't ready for anything else yet, and he knew it.

I watched as that slow smile crossed Paul's face on the TV screen, and my heart broke. Let him be a success, I prayed. He has nothing else.

He sang about love, but it didn't touch him. He'd loved me as much as he could love anyone. I had believed that during those hard months when I had been away from him. I could accept that, as well as the fact that I would probably always love him.

Yet so many things were more important to him. Success, adulation. My love hadn't been enough for him. He had needed more than I could give. I could love him, but I couldn't worship him forever.

I guess neither of us was as lucky as we thought we were. Unable to love, he's only half a man—and without him, I'm only half a woman.

THE END

MY HUBBY TURNED GAY ON LIVE TV!
A reader's ultimate heartbreak comes to pass on daytime television

"Listen to this—"

I looked up from cutting the too-brown edge off my toast and focused my attention on my best friend, Liz.

"Dr. Bill is going to be on our favorite daytime talk show next month." Liz tapped the newspaper article for emphasis.

This was our usual Saturday morning, "girls' day out," breakfast at Camille's and reading the paper, checking all the ads for the weekend sales. "Great," I said, going back to my toast. "But I thought you were looking for what Donovan's has on sale today."

Liz waved away my comment with one elegant flick of her hand as she leaned back in her chair. "I think the good doctor is so much more interesting than any ol' sale."

"Even a shoe sale?"

Liz pretended to think about it for a moment. "It's a tie," she said finally.

I couldn't help but laugh. Liz and I had been friends since the third grade, but she had been a shoe addict long before I met her. Well . . . we both liked shoes, but all that had changed when I'd had Caresse and Liz had married money. My best friend had turned into the glamour gal, and I'd turned into DeeDee, the mom next door who baked cookies.

"Dr. Bill," I mused, trying to remember where I'd heard the name before, and why it would seem so familiar to me.

"You know—the relationship counselor."

"Oh, yeah," I said, as an image of the extra-thin, extra-gray-haired man popped into my head. Dr. Bill was infamous in the tri-state area; he had a quick tongue to match his quick fame. Everyone who was anyone knew the man, if only for his sharp wit alone.

"I just love him," Liz was saying. "It won't be long before he goes national. I mean, the man deserves his own show. He's so . . . so—"

"Smart-mouthed?"

"Smart, period. He's a genius. A real genius."

"I guess," I mumbled. I didn't dislike the man, nor could I say—like the majority of people where we lived—that I liked him, either.

86

"I mean, you have to have been there in order to understand."

"There?"

"There," Liz repeated. "The big D."

I nodded with understanding. "No, I guess I haven't."

"Being divorced isn't so bad," Liz continued. "It's being alone that's the killer."

I laughed. Liz always cracked me up.

"Go ahead, Mrs. I've-Never-Even-Fought-With-My-Husband. It's easy to forget when you don't have the troubles."

"Be fair," I said, pushing my plate aside. "Dion and I have our problems."

"Sure," Liz returned. "I bet he does some really horrible things like leaving the toilet seat up and squeezing the toothpaste tube from the middle."

I frowned at her, but I'd learned a long time ago never to try to reason with Liz when she got in a "mood." "Actually," I started, then bit my lip. I didn't want to complain, especially when I really didn't have anything to complain about. It was just that sometimes. . . .

I mean, the fact that it seemed as if Dion was more my friend and less of a lover was trivial when compared to Liz's history of ex-husbands. But, hey, I figured—that's what happens when you've been married for fifteen years.

"So? Are you going to see Dr. Bill?"

Liz shook her head. "It's couples only. 'Rekindle the romance,' it says here."

Instantly, and against my will, my ears perked up. "Rekindle the romance?"

Liz pushed the paper across the table toward me. "Read for yourself."

I picked it up and scanned the announcement. Dr. Bill wants you! Now's the time to put the spark back into your romance! it proclaimed.

It took me only a couple of seconds to read the announcement, but those few words made me think. Maybe it was time to rekindle my romance with Dion. I mean, it wasn't bad being my husband's best friend. In fact, it was kind of nice—very nice. But every woman dreams of being swept off her feet.

"Why don't you and Dion go?" Liz suggested, looking for all the world like she'd just come up with the idea of the century.

"I don't know," I said, avoiding the truth that faced me.

The announcement mentioned a makeover, new clothes—the works. And as much as I hated to admit it, I had let myself go over the years. Oh, not badly. Just a little. Just enough. But it was hard to get up and get dressed every day when you're a stay-at-home mom.

"I'll think about it," I said finally, my mind already made up. I didn't need any old television show to help me rekindle my romance with my husband. I didn't need them to give me a makeover.

Besides, things like that just weren't important to Dion. Our marriage was based on love and understanding and friendship. We didn't need the traditional female trappings to validate our marriage.

Our relationship was perfect just the way it was.

By Saturday night, though, I simply couldn't erase the ad from my thoughts. Rekindle the romance seemed to play over and over again in my mind. I can't say why it haunted me; I don't know for certain. Maybe it was because I caught sight of myself in the mirror after dinner.

Caresse was upstairs in her room, working on her science project with Dion. He'd always helped her with her homework and such; it gave them quality time together. I usually did my best to stay out of their way; I felt it was the least I could do: give them that quality time with each other. After all, I'd gotten to spend so much more time with Caresse over the years. And every day, she seemed so much more like her father. Not just in her looks—the dark, silky hair and caramel-colored eyes, but in her mannerisms, as well: the way she tilted her head when she talked, the way she frowned when she read, and especially the way her eyes sparkled when she laughed.

So I stayed clear when they were working on one of their projects, but I never could resist the urge to peek in on them when they weren't aware. I loved to see them together like that—their dark heads so close together, so much alike. It filled my heart with joy, made me appreciate them both so much more. Made me realize just how lucky I am to have both of them in my life. How I would do everything in my power to keep them happy and safe and together with me.

That's what happened to me on this day after my breakfast with Liz. I peeked through the crack in the door, marveling at how wonderful and perfect they looked together—father and daughter—before heading down the hall to the master bedroom.

On the way, I caught sight of myself in the hallway mirror that Dion's mom had given us when we'd moved into our home. It was an oversized, gilded-framed glass bought as if to declare, "I'm proud of you." Dion's mother had a way of doing that—buying a present that somehow made more of a statement of love and support than any mere object could ever portray.

But on this night, it was my reflection that spoke to me. I passed myself, and then walked back to stare at the me I saw. I hardly recognized myself.

I had a mental image of me—of how I thought people saw me: young, glowing, silky hair, firm body, and bright smile. But the woman who stared back at me with my eyes was another person altogether.

Oh, I hadn't lost much of my firm, pre-baby body; I was lucky, in that aspect. But my pale brown hair seemed mousy, even drab, pulled back into a messy twist. I reached up and touched one of my cheeks; I hadn't worn makeup in years. Not that I had worn much before, but even a touch of mascara and a dab of lipstick might take away some of the sallow coloring in my face. And would it really hurt to do the whole shebang—blusher, eyeshadow, etc.? Liz did it every day—sometimes twice.

And my clothes. I'd used to dress with style. I'd worn the most fashionable outfits I could put together; I'd dressed every day to show the world that I had the trends nailed. Dion and I would go to the mall, scour the stores for the best deals on the best-looking ensembles we could find, and then we would dress up and go out on the town.

But we hadn't done that in . . . well, we hadn't done that since I'd become pregnant with Caresse.

And that was eleven years ago.

But what fun we'd used to have!

Don't get me wrong—I don't regret having Caresse—not even for a single minute. But she had certainly changed our lives drastically. For the better, overall, but there were some aspects where I knew we could use some help. Where I could use some help. After all, it was easy to see that the problem was mine, not Dion's. He got dressed every morning, still just as stylish as he'd been the day we met. I was the one who'd let myself go. And, I realized, I would have to be the one to get "me" back again.

And so I lifted my chin and walked with a new determination to our bedroom. I smiled to myself as the sound of Caresse's laughter floated into the room. And with that smile still on my lips, I filled the tub with hot water and lavender-scented bubbles. I undressed quickly and slid into the soapy water. Normally, I would have dawdled—taken my time and soaked, read, even dozed—but that night, I had a mission. It was time for me to become the woman Dion had married and make him fall in love with his wife all over again.

Half an hour later, I stood in front of the bedroom mirror and studied my reflection in the dim candlelight. Even if I said so myself, I looked good. Maybe not exactly like I had on the day I'd married Dion, but pretty darn close. I squinted and turned to the side to get a better look. The camisole and tap pants I'd found tucked into the back of my closet were champagne-colored and set off my complexion to perfection. I had curled my hair; I'd forgotten my hair could look so pretty. But it was my makeup that I was the most proud of. Even after all these years, I hadn't forgotten how to make my eyes look larger, my cheekbones higher, and my lips fuller. All in all, I looked like a woman about to seduce her man!

The scent from the lavender grains I'd used in my bath still hung in the air. I'd lit candles of the same scent and scattered them around the room; the flickering light they cast danced and jumped, casting romantic shadows on everything they touched. It was the perfect setting for the perfect rendezvous.

The door opened and I jumped, then spun around to face my husband. For some odd reason, I suddenly felt as if I'd done something wrong. I guess it had just been too long.

"Hi," I said, my voice quiet and breathy—like a phone-sex operator's. But, hey—that was good. Right?

"Hi, yourself," Dion returned, taking in the scene. "You look nice," he added.

"Thanks."

He stood there, just staring at me as if he'd never seen me before. I guess it had been way too long. The awkward moment seemed to last an hour. Oh, why hadn't I thought to chill some wine—or, at the very least—brought some into the bedroom with me? I certainly could've used the courage—and something to do with my hands.

I tucked a stray lock of hair behind my ear. "Did . . . Caresse get her homework done?"

Dion nodded, still standing in the same spot. His lack of action did nothing for my self-confidence. But this was my time, my chance to get my marriage back on track.

I took a deep breath. "Dion. . . ." I started toward him, taking small, almost hesitant, steps. "I thought we might—"

Dion cleared his throat before I could finish and sidestepped me. Without meeting my gaze, he headed for the master bath.

Before I knew what had happened, the door had closed behind him. I stared at the oak-finished wood for a moment, wondering what had gone awry.

O-kay. It was probably nothing. I'd just caught Dion by surprise. He probably wanted to freshen up, too.

After all, Dion had always been meticulous about his appearance and hygiene. And this evening was no exception. I heard the water start to run in the master bath, and I knew he was getting into the shower, just as I'd suspected. Ten minutes, tops, and he'd be out and we'd start rekindling the romance we'd once shared.

I checked in on Caresse and wished her sweet dreams, then waited for Dion to finish his shower. Nine-and-a-half minutes later, Dion stepped out from the bathroom smelling clean and dressed in both pieces of his navy-blue silk pajamas.

"Dion. . . ." I wasn't sure what I needed—or even wanted—to say.

90

But Dion just shook his head. "I'm sorry, DeeDee," he said. "Maybe some other time. Maybe tomorrow. I'm . . . tired." He lowered his head to mine and gave me an almost brotherly kiss on the cheek. "I was so busy with Caresse's homework, you know. . . ."

I nodded, unsure of what had just happened, but knowing all too well what he meant.

"You look beautiful," he whispered, brushing a gentle hand over my hair. "Really beautiful. Maybe tomorrow, baby."

I nodded once again. "Maybe," I repeated, realizing for the first time that my marriage was in more trouble than I had originally thought.

"Guess what?" I asked Dion at dinner the following week.

Caresse immediately perked up and abandoned the task of stirring around the food on her plate in favor of propping her chin in one hand. "What?"

"I was talking to your father," I said, hoping that neither one of them could hear the tremor in my voice. I don't know why I was so nervous; maybe it was because I'd accepted the producer's offer to appear on television and have my personal relationship examined and critiqued by an expert and all without even telling my husband that I'd even applied.

"What?" Dion asked, I'm sure just to humor me. He laid his fork down and gave me that look of his that said he knew I had something up my sleeve and it had better not be too bad.

"We're going to be on TV." I tried to make it sound like the best news he'd ever want to hear.

"We are?" Caresse exclaimed.

I shook my head. "No—we are." I pointed to myself, then Dion, and inwardly cringed at Caresse's crestfallen expression. Why hadn't I waited until we were alone before breaking the news to Dion?

Because whenever we're alone, one of us is asleep, and that's the whole reason for going on TV.

"We are?" Dion didn't sound nearly as excited as I'd hoped.

"You see. . . ." I started, still trying to keep the upbeat tone in my voice as I told him all about the scheduled program. "It's supposed to help us."

Caresse looked at each one of us in turn, a tight frown pulling at her brow. "You guys need help?"

"Caresse, go to your room," Dion commanded, his gaze never leaving mine.

"But—"

"Go to your room," he repeated.

"Yes, sir." She pushed herself back from the table and stood. She took her time; it was so obvious to me that she didn't want to leave. I couldn't blame her; she'd always been a sensitive child, keenly tuned into the emotions of those around her. And right then, the tension in our dining room was thick enough to cut with a knife.

"It's all right," I added with forced brightness. "You can come back down later and have your dessert. Go finish your homework first."

Once again, she looked from her dad to me. Then she nodded, a jerky little movement, and left the room.

With chagrin, I watched her go. She was my buffer. It's shameful, I know. But I had purposely chosen tonight's dinner to break the news to Dion. He was such a private person that I knew he wasn't going to instantly take to the idea of appearing on television. With Caresse around, I'd figured he wouldn't be able to instantly tell me no. But with her gone. . . .

"No," Dion said as soon as she was out of earshot. "I do not want to go on television."

"Oh, Dion. It's not about television; it's about us."

"And what's wrong with us?"

"Take a look at us, and then ask me that again. We're in a rut, Dion." I stood, trying to shake off my excess energy. "What happened to the DeeDee and Dion that we were back in college?"

"We turned into Dion and DeeDee and Caresse."

I shook my head. "It's not just that. Things are just . . . different."

"And?"

"And I think they could be better."

"DeeDee—"

"No," I said, my voice going from pleading to confident. "I signed us up for our own best interests. Both of ours. And Caresse's. I just want to make sure that we can always stay that way."

"Does this have anything to do with the other night?"

"Yes . . . no . . . I mean, it's not just that. They're going to give me a makeover and a whole, new wardrobe."

He shook his head sternly. "I just don't think it's a good idea."

"The wardrobe?"

"DeeDee, be serious!"

"I am serious." I resisted the urge to stomp my foot. "I want to look good for you. I want things to go back to how they were and I need some help!" My voice rose toward the end, enough so that when I stopped speaking, the silence that followed was almost deafening.

Dion sat there in our oh-so-quiet dining room and just stared at me for at least five full minutes.

"All right," he finally said softly. "I'll do it."

For the next two weeks, I put more effort into my marriage than I ever had. I knew that Dion had only agreed to appear on the show with me because it was what I wanted, so I scrubbed the bathroom tiles within an inch of their life. I cooked Dion's favorite dinners and breakfasts; I did everything I could to show him my appreciation. But it seemed like the more I did for him, the bigger the gap between us grew. Strange, I hadn't really noticed that space before. Maybe I'd been too busy with everything else, and maybe he'd been too busy at work. And then . . . BAM! All of a sudden, there it was: a Grand Canyon between two people who had once loved each other—two former soul mates.

It was this distance between Dion and me that made me even more determined to get my marriage—our marriage—back on track. I loved Dion. I had always loved Dion, and I didn't want us to become another divorce statistic. I didn't want Caresse to come from a broken home.

All of my contemplating should have shown me a few things. For, as much of everything that I didn't want, there were a few things that I did want. I did want to recover our marriage, to feel close to my husband again, to once again know that my family was secure. My doubts should have clued me in, though . . . there was much more to the troubles my marriage faced.

I'd always wondered why they called the off-screen waiting room the "green room." The walls were painted green, but I wasn't sure if they were covered with such a delicate shade of moss green because it was the green room, or if it was the green walls that gave the room its name.

"It's more of a sage," Dion corrected me.

I nodded. Dion had always had a better eye for color than I did. He'd picked out all of the shades and fabrics we'd used in our home. It was a beautiful showplace—to say the least.

"Jeter?" the backstage manager called from the doorway. "You're on next."

My palms were sweaty and my mouth went dry. Maybe this wasn't such a good idea, after all. I mean, how could a television show save my marriage?

I turned to look at Dion and he had "that" look on his face—the look that said: Don't even think about it. We've come this far. Now we're going to see this thing through.

He reached out a hand and wrapped his fingers around mine. "Smile," he whispered. "The whole state is watching."

I wished he hadn't said that. I wasn't used to being the center of attention. All of the reservations that Dion had voiced suddenly rose up inside of me. I stamped them back down. After all, we had come this far. And I wasn't doing this just for me; I was doing this for Caresse, for my family—for my whole world.

Suddenly, my courage was back. My knees grew stronger as we stepped up onto the stage and took our places. Someone came over and clipped microphones to our lapels, and then disappeared into the swarm of behind-the-scenes workers. Dion squeezed my fingers once again, and then we were on the air.

"Welcome back," the hostess said to the camera. "Today, we are talking with couples who want a fresh start to their love lives. We have our noted psychologist and relationship therapist here with us today to get these couples back on the right track.

"Joining us now is our third couple on today's show. Please welcome DeeDee and Dion Jeter."

I tried to hold my smile as the audience applauded. Although I knew my reasons for being there, it was still hard not to be just a little nervous.

"DeeDee, how long have you and Dion been married?" the doctor asked.

"Fifteen years."

"And tell everyone why you called and asked to be a part of today's show."

I opened my mouth, but then closed it again. Dion's fingers were still wrapped around mine, and courage flowed. Still, it was hard to say the words aloud—much harder than I had imagined. But I knew I had Dion and Caresse—our family—to think about. I knew I had to get my feelings out in the open so that we could keep it all together. And so I chanced a look at Dion.

"Take your time," the doctor gently added.

"Well, I guess it all started when I was pregnant with our daughter."

"Children are a challenging addition to any couple," the doctor agreed, nodding amiably.

I nodded. "Well, it just became so easy to let myself go. You know—not to worry so much about what I was wearing, or putting on makeup. I mean, there're only so many hours in a day, and Caresse—she's our daughter—she always seemed to take up so much of my time. Not that I minded," I clarified. "I love her, and what she's brought to our lives, very much."

"So, you had a baby and let yourself go," the doctor summarized.

"I didn't mean to," I said defensively. "It just, sort of . . . happened."

"And now you'd like this show to help you."

It sounded so simple—and stupid—when he put it like that. Like high school all over again. "My family means everything to me, Dr. Bill. I'll do anything to keep it together."

The doctor nodded. "It's obvious that your marriage has taken some hard knocks, DeeDee, or you wouldn't be here today. What makes you think we can help?"

I turned so briefly to look at Dion. He sat still and unmoving beside me. Stage fright, I thought. I couldn't blame him. Lord knows, he'd never really wanted to come on TV in the first place. "Well, Dion and I have always had a wonderful, loving relationship."

"But. . . ." the doctor prompted.

"But," I repeated, stalling, "but things definitely change after you have a child. And now . . . now I'd like to have things back the way they used to be. And have Caresse, too," I hastily added. I didn't want him, or anyone, to think that I even for one minute regretted my daughter. After all, Caresse was my heart.

"Dion, what do you have to say about all this?" Dr. Bill asked him.

Dion plucked at the creases in his slacks, a gesture I knew he only performed when he was extremely nervous. Suddenly, I felt all alone as he cleared his throat nervously. "I . . . uh . . . I love my wife. I love my family."

"And do you want things back the way they were before you had your daughter?"

"Yes . . . no—I mean, I love Caresse. She's my everything. If I had to pick between having my wife like she was and having Caresse, I'd choose Caresse every time."

I smiled at his words, but wished he were still holding my hand. He had let go of it.

"So, you feel that your wife has let herself go over the years," Dr. Bill supplied.

"I love my wife," Dion said simply.

"But. . . ." the doctor prodded once again.

Dion hesitated. "There was a time when she seemed to care more about the clothes that she wore and her hair."

"And her makeup?"

Dion nodded—reluctantly. I could tell that he didn't want to admit it, that he didn't want to say the words aloud—especially not on live television. "I love my wife," he repeated, almost like a mantra.

"But. . . ."

"But she's a beautiful person. And . . . and I wish she'd pay more attention to her appearance," he finished on a rush, as if saying the words quickly would help ease the stab they caused in my heart. Oh, I had known he felt that way, but it didn't lessen the pain any when he actually said it.

The doctor smiled. "Well, that's why we're here today, Dion."

The hostess turned to one of the many cameras. "Today, our crack team of designers, stylists, and makeup artists will transform

95

our harried housewives and mothers back into the dream girls they were years ago. Right after this break."

Live television is a little different from its taped counterpart, and we had a couple of minutes to spare between the breaks. I turned to Dion, suddenly regretting my insistence on bringing us to the show. "I'm sorry," I told him plaintively.

Dion pressed his lips together and merely nodded.

"I just thought it would help us, Dion. You understand."

Once again, my husband nodded. It felt like there were miles separating us.

"Then talk to me," I pleaded with him.

"What do you want me to say, Dee? That I like being here? That I like having everyone in the viewing area know that I want you to wear more makeup and take the time to make sure your socks match?"

"I—"

"You're my best friend, Dee," he continued. "I don't want to hurt or embarrass you, and I'm afraid that's going to happen here today."

I reached out a hand and trailed my fingers over the back of his knuckles. His fist was clenched so tightly that the skin had turned white. "That's not going to happen, Dion."

"I hope not," he muttered as the stage crew motioned to us that it was time to return to the air.

"We're back," our hostess said, introducing the doctor once again and telling the viewers who had just tuned in about the topic of the day.

"Our three couples are here with us now. We've been talking to DeeDee and Dion. In our last segment, Dion admitted that he wishes that DeeDee would take more time with her appearance, and DeeDee confirmed that since the birth of their daughter, she has let herself go."

"Now, Dion," Dr. Bill interjected, "your daughter, Caresse, is now ten years old. If you've been so unhappy for so long, why haven't you said anything to DeeDee about it before today?"

"She's my wife," Dion declared. "Not my slave. She's entitled to go around without makeup if she so chooses."

"But you're the one who has to deal with her looking distasteful every day. Can you tell me right now, Dion, that it doesn't bother you?"

"I've already said that it does." Impatience and a dash of something I couldn't name laced his voice. "And distasteful was your word, not mine."

"What about your sex life?"

Suddenly, it felt as if all of the air had been sucked out of the room. I'd known they would ask some tough questions, but I really didn't want to talk about our sex life—or lack thereof—on television.

96

"Uh—" Dion stuttered. I had a strong feeling he didn't want to talk about it, either. And what, exactly, was there to talk about? It had been so long since we had been intimate; we'd been so caught up in the day-to-day of living that we hadn't been living at all.

"Can you say that her appearance hasn't put a damper on your relations?"

"It hasn't," Dion stated emphatically and even though I was shocked by his response, I knew he was telling the truth. But if it wasn't my appearance that had put him off all of this time, then what was it?

"It doesn't bother you that she doesn't own a collection of Victoria's Secret for nighttime fun?"

"No."

"Or that she doesn't take the time to shave her legs every day?"

I couldn't help it—I slumped down in my seat, trying to make myself as small as possible. I felt like I was on trial. This was not what I'd had in mind when I'd signed us up to go on television. And, as bad as I felt for myself, I felt doubly so for Dion.

"No."

"Or that she doesn't take the time to put on makeup and pretty clothes when she knows she's going to be seeing you? That doesn't bother you?"

"No." Dion practically yelled the words, and for my polite, conservative husband, it was quite a show of emotion.

"Then what is it?" the doctor asked. "If it's not the lack of sexy underthings, then what has driven this wedge between the two of you?"

"I. . . ." Dion sputtered. Normally, he was so confident, so articulate. But that day on TV, he seemed unsure of himself, bumbling around like a blind man in the dark.

"Well, c'mon, Dion," the doctor encouraged. "This is your wife—the woman you've been married to for fifteen years. You've said that you love her. But she needs to know what it is that has you distanced from her. She deserves to know, Dion."

Still, Dion didn't answer.

"Tell her, Dion," Dr. Bill badgered, his voice growing louder. "Tell her now."

"I'm gay."

The words fell like a bomb in the studio. I heard the gasps of surprise, and the few snickers of embarrassment. Or maybe it was pity. Or out-and-out humor. Yes, that was it—

Maybe it was all a practical joke.

But things like that didn't happen on this show.

"Let's go to a commercial break," the hostess hurriedly said, but her words sounded like they were coming to me through a dense fog. My ears started to hum, and then ring, and for a full minute, I actually thought I was going to die.

I must have heard him wrong. Surely, that's all it was: a misunderstanding.

"Dion," I squeaked, somehow managing to focus my gaze on that man so dear to me.

"I'm sorry, Dee," he said, his voice thick with emotion. Tears brimmed in his eyes. "I've wanted to tell you for years. But not this way. Never like this."

So it's true, was all I could think. This man whom I've loved over half my life is a homosexual. He couldn't love me in return—not the same way that I loved him.

"I need some air," I choked, and fled from the stage.

Some angel must've been watching over me, directing me out of the strange building and into the blinding sunlight. Outside the studio, I gulped in as much air as I could, the words Dion had spoken playing over and over again inside my head:

I'm gay.

"DeeDee."

"Go away!" I cried, reeling around to face Dion, who'd immediately followed me outside. I couldn't bear to talk to him right then.

"Dee, please. Just hear me out."

"Go away!" I repeated, unable to even turn and look in his direction. I wasn't ready to talk, nor was I ready to listen, either.

And I didn't know if I ever would be.

That evening, I went home and started packing. Thankfully, Caresse had gone to stay with Dion's mom; I didn't want my packing to frighten her, and I desperately needed the time alone. I needed space; I needed room to bring things back into perspective, decide what I was going to do next.

"DeeDee."

The thick carpeting had muffled his footsteps, and now my husband stood in the doorway of the bedroom we'd shared for so many years.

"I . . . I need some time," I said, without looking directly at him. I hadn't been able to look him in the face since he'd dropped his surprise in my lap.

"Does that mean you're coming back?"

I stopped packing and stared down at the clothes I'd tossed into my suitcase. My shoulders slumped, and I felt as if I carried the weight of the entire world on them. "I just . . . I don't know. I just need some time."

I could almost hear Dion's nod. "Okay," he said. "But please remember that I'm here when you're ready to talk."

I spent my first night away from Dion at the Holiday Inn. I cried myself to sleep around four in the morning, feeling miserably sorry for myself. This was not the way my life was supposed to turn out. I couldn't help but think of Liz and her words of just a few weeks ago: How envious she had sounded of my relationship with Dion. But it had all been only a façade, a house of cards that had come down upon my head. It had been my idea to appear on television, and if I hadn't insisted, then my marriage would still be intact.

But at what price?

Dion was gay.

Nothing could change that, and whether he admitted it or not, it was a fact: My husband wasn't attracted to me; he probably didn't even really love me.

Maybe he never had.

I spent three days in that hotel. I called room service for the meals I tried to eat, never once leaving the room. I talked to Caresse every day; she couldn't grasp all the details of the problem, but she was old enough to understand that Mommy and Daddy had something important that they needed to work out.

"Are you and Daddy getting a divorce?"

Her candid question stunned me. "What do you know about divorce?" I asked her, trying to sound casual when I felt anything but.

"Weeelll. . . ." She drawled out the word, and I could see her in my mind's eye, twisting a silken lock of dark, dark hair around one finger as she formulated her answer. "Dena Simpson's parents got a divorce. Her dad moved up north and now Dena has to go and stay with him every vacation we get from school."

"Oh," I said, for lack of a good response. There were times when being a parent was almost too much responsibility on top of the drudgery of life. Right then was one of those times for me; I knew I should have been able to say something more appropriate, but all I could manage was, "Oh."

"Yeah. She wasn't able to join the cheering squad or play softball or anything on account of her dad. She has to go see him while the rest of us are here, practicing."

Suddenly, I was filled with guilt. I had been so selfish; I had only been thinking of myself, and not about how all of this was affecting Caresse.

"I wouldn't like it if I had to stop playing soccer because you and Dad got a divorce."

"Oh, honey," I said, fresh tears streaming down my cheeks. "That's not going to happen, sweetheart. No matter what happens between your father and me, you won't ever have to quit playing sports." It wasn't the reassurance she needed, but it was the best I could offer her right then.

"Do you promise?"

"I promise, Caresse," I told her. "I promise."

I went home that very afternoon. I left Caresse with Dion's mom just one more night so that Dion and I could talk without the fear of upsetting her any further. Because of Caresse, I needed to get things straight with Dion ASAP, even though I had no idea about exactly how things would turn out. As it was, I had no idea what I wanted to say, only that it had to be said.

Dion was waiting for me when I walked in the door. He stood when he heard me come into the living room, glass of wine in one hand. His stance was urgent, though his words were casual—a smooth surface covering the underlying turmoil of emotions we were both feeling.

"Can I get you a drink?" he offered politely.

I shook my head. "No . . . yes . . . I think so." I knew I needed a clear head, but I also needed the relative peace that a glass of wine would afford me.

It seemed like it took a week for Dion to pour me a healthy dose of vintage Chardonnay. He had an extensive collection of wines; he knew so much about them.

My hand shook, just slightly as I took a sip of the wine. Why hadn't I noticed? Because Dion had hid it so well? Or was it because I hadn't wanted to notice?

"I'm sorry," he said, and his eyes reflected his words. "I never meant to hurt you, you know. I would never hurt you on purpose."

I swallowed the lump that had formed in my throat. "I know," I whispered. And I did.

A tense silence stretched between us as I moved to sit on the sofa, perched on the edge of the cushions I used to comfortably lounge against.

"How long have you known?" I asked him. I'm not really sure why I asked, but it was something I felt I needed to know.

Dion shrugged, one shoulder barely lifting before it fell once again. "My whole life, I guess."

"Then everything we've had together is a sham."

"Everything we've had—have—together is beautiful."

I shook my head.

"DeeDee, please—"

"Please what? Please love you? I always have. Forgive you? You know I will."

"Trust me, then?"

"I don't know if I can."

100

"Oh, Dee." He moved to the space just in front of me and squatted down. He took the wineglass from my fingers and clasped my hands in his own. "I do love you, Dee. Ever since the first time I laid eyes on you, you've been the best friend I could ever have, and the best wife I could ever ask for. I've tried to be a good husband to you, Dee; you know I have."

I pulled my hands from his. "But you didn't want a wife, did you?"

Dion stood, his lips pressed into a thin, tight line. "Okay," he said, moving away from me to stand in front of the cold hearth. "I never asked to be this way, Dee. I denied it the entire time I was growing up. But even before then, I always knew I was different. I can't say how I could tell; I just could. And my father—"

I gasped. Up until this time, I hadn't even thought about how Dion's revelation had affected anyone but Caresse and me. I had kept myself sequestered in that hotel room, not realizing that others were hurting, as well. Dion's father was a Marine, a real man's man. I realized suddenly that the news must've hit him hard.

"I couldn't tell him," Dion finished.

"But he knows now."

Dion nodded.

"How . . . how did he take it?"

Dion grimaced. "As well as could be expected, I guess." He sighed. "I think he knew all along, but as long as I stayed in the closet, he could always deny it."

I nodded. I truly believe that was my unconscious theory, as well. Because, looking back, I realize now that Dion gave me plenty of clues over the years, little hints about himself that he couldn't hide.

"I'm sorry, Dion," I said, rising to stand beside him, one hand on his arm. "If I hadn't . . . I only wanted to . . . I mean, if I hadn't insisted that we go . . . then none of this would ever have happened."

"Stop it," Dion said. "It wasn't ideal, but I guess, sometimes, that's just the way life is."

And he was right. As sad and poignant as our dreams can sometimes be, this was certainly not how I'd expected my life might turn out. The irony of it all was the fact that the very solution I'd devised to cure my humdrum life had brought out secrets that I knew I'd trade back just to be able to live that boring life once again. I knew I'd rather have it as it had been, rather than how it was now. But learning secrets is often like losing your innocence: You can never go back again.

"I won't fight you," Dion was saying. "You can have the house. Everything. Whatever you want."

It took a couple of seconds for what he meant to sink in. "You want a divorce." I said the words, and they tasted bitter in my mouth.

"I want what's best for you and Caresse."

Oh, my God. Caresse.

Suddenly, all of the reasons why I didn't want to get divorced surfaced, with my daughter at the top of that very large heap. I looked at Dion, my gaze meeting his big, brown eyes. All of our years together rose up in my mind. All of the good times we'd had together. The family trip to Disneyland. Our trip for two to the Caymans. Even our many trips to the local zoo with Caresse. And I knew then that I didn't want it to end.

"I don't want a divorce," I whispered.

Dion stared at me for a full two minutes. "Are you serious?"

That's when the tears came streaming down my cheeks unheeded. "Very."

"Oh, God, Dee."

In an instant, he was on his knees in front of me. He gathered me into his arms and held me close like he used to. I knew then that I'd made the right decision; I'd made the only decision that was right for me, for Caresse, and for Dion.

I know it's unorthodox, but our family works for us. I no longer dream about being swept off my feet, but I don't mind, either. Not in light of everything that I do have. Dion is discreet, and so am I. We understand and respect each other's physical needs, even if we're not able to meet them. And so we give each other different things. We give each other family. We give each other constant, committed, unstrained companionship—someone to come home to, someone to share the events of the day with. Someone to love. Someone to grow old with.

After all, isn't that what family is really all about?

THE END

A GHOST SAVED MY LIFE
What happened to me is
nothing short of a miracle of faith

They say the only thing worse than losing your spouse is losing your child. Thank goodness, I haven't had to face that yet, and I hope I never will. Losing my husband, Ian, was bad enough. But they also say that the passage of time will ease the pain and the loneliness that follow such a loss. And I suppose they're right about that, too. Guilt and remorse, however, are deep and terrible emotions that seem to last forever.

I know it doesn't make much sense to keep blaming myself for Ian's death. But sometimes feelings don't make much sense. They just hang there before you, like the skull of a ghost, staring you in the face.

Hardly a day goes by that I don't think about Ian, and about the life we shared for nearly twelve years. We had everything. We shared love, hope, dreams, romance, friendship—all the things that make up a good marriage. And we had two beautiful children. Luckily, Savannah and Wyatt are still here with me. Beauty was still here, too, when Ian died.

What helped our eleven-year-old daughter, Savannah, through those difficult days was her strong belief in God. Savannah has always been our family's spiritual person. So when her daddy died, she had an unshakable conviction that he had gone straight to heaven. She was also convinced that one day, she would see him again. But she still missed him dearly, and she cried as much as I did.

To five-year-old Wyatt, his daddy's sickness was more confusing than anything else. He just couldn't understand why Ian couldn't play with him anymore. And even after the funeral, Wyatt couldn't understand why his daddy didn't come home from the hospital.

The third gift that my husband left behind was Beauty, the dog that Ian had brought home less than a month before the doctors found the cancer.

The instant I saw that little dog leaping out of Ian's arms and racing toward me like a long-lost friend, I knew she was a rare jewel. Even as a puppy, her energy was boundless, her personality adorable, and her loyalty absolute.

"What a beauty you are," I told her more than once during those first days. In fact, I probably told her that whenever she grinned up at me expectantly, her fluffy tail waggling furiously.

The puppy, whom we soon named "Beauty," settled happily into our home and into our hearts.

When we lost Ian in early June, Beauty became even more important to us. She missed Ian, too, of course. For days, she wandered all over the house looking for the man who had brought her home. And when the children and I cried about our crushing loss, Beauty cried, too, in her own way.

Her way was a sorrow-filled whine that made our tears flow even harder, especially when she snuggled against us and nuzzled our hands with her cold, wet nose. During those painful times I was certain that Beauty's sad eyes were also filled with tears.

But as it always does, the days and weeks continued to drag by. Yes, our life had been turned upside down, and it did have a huge, gaping hole in the middle of it. But gradually, painfully, the kids and I managed to bring the ragged edges of our world together again. Slowly, stitch by stitch, we managed to close the wound. We also started to fashion a new world, a world without the steady, rock-solid center that was Ian.

As best I could, I tried to take Ian's place. I tried to be that rock-solid center. And, sometimes, I was successful. I felt strong and confident, hopeful about the future.

At other times, I felt like a quivering mass of tears, unable to cope with anything. I tried to keep those fear-filled times to myself, and I was usually successful. But sometimes, late at night after the kids were sound asleep and the house was as still as a grave, I let the grief wash over me, like a cleansing flood.

On those bad nights, the bed I crawled into seemed so big and so empty, and I felt so utterly alone. The endless decisions that Ian always handled so easily had suddenly morphed themselves into enormous burdens that weighed me down.

The annoying little repairs, like the fan with the frayed cord, never got fixed. The endless responsibilities about the kids, about the bills, and about our home now pressed down heavily on my shoulders. All of a sudden, I was the one who had to guide our family into the future. And, on those bad nights, that future appeared to stretch out before me like a black, endless tunnel.

But even on the bad nights, Beauty was always there beside me, curled up on Ian's soft robe. Beauty's patience, her unconditional love, and her deep, sad eyes always brought me comfort. Then in the morning, when the sun crept warmly through the curtains again, it was Beauty's bouncy spirit and swishing tail that helped me face another day.

And so, day by day and night by night, we made it through that long and empty summer.

By August, Savannah's usual eagerness and impatience was slowly coming back. "Won't summer ever end?" she'd say with that cute little pout of hers. "I want to go back to school. I want to see my friends again."

"Three weeks," I would say, brushing her hair. Savannah's hair was the exact same color as Ian's. Savannah also had Ian's features. She looked so much like her daddy that sometimes, it made me cry.

The next time she asked me the same question I was able to give her the answer that she wanted to hear. "School is only two weeks away, Savannah. Try to be patient." Then, finally, I could announce: "Only one more week, Savannah. That's all."

Wyatt was getting excited about kindergarten, too. The previous year, he had gone to preschool every morning. He had loved his teacher, a sweet young woman named Meredith. He had loved his arts-and-crafts classes. He had loved his field trips to the library and to the museum. He was especially thrilled when Meredith took the whole class to the mall one morning. That field trip had included a concert by the mall's senior citizen band.

Wyatt strummed his plastic ukulele day and night after that. And the prospect of entering kindergarten filled him with delight.

"Why can't I go today?" That was his favorite question. A crinkled brow and a protruding lower lip always accompanied the question. It was Ian's crinkled brow and Ian's protruding lower lip.

"Because kindergarten doesn't start until the day after Labor Day," I explained patiently.

"But when's that?" Wyatt complained.

I wiggled my finger at him and winked. "Come with me," I told him.

We went to the big, bright calendar that hung in Wyatt's room.

"See," I said, sliding my fingers along the final weeks of August. "This is today. Here's the end of August. And here," I went on, flipping the page, "is Labor Day."

I poked my finger at the numbered square we had circled in red. "And this," I finished proudly, "will be your first day of kindergarten."

My new part-time data entry job at our town's largest car dealership also started the day after Labor Day. The monthly payments from Ian's life insurance policy covered most of the essentials, but I knew I'd need a weekly paycheck to help with everything else.

And so, by the end of August, we were all anxious to get our new life underway. "But in order to start things off properly," I announced to the children, "we must have an end-of-the-summer picnic."

Savannah and Wyatt cheered. They were, of course, remembering the many happy picnics we had shared with Ian.

"I vote for Oceanside Park!" Savannah cheered, pirouetting like a denim-clad ballerina.

"Me, too," Wyatt agreed. His spin was more like a whirling

dervish. It left him dizzy and staggering. He finally collapsed in a heap, laughing.

Beauty rushed to Wyatt's side and began to nuzzle his soft cheeks. The slathery swipes of Beauty's tongue, combined with a joyful tail wagging, made everyone laugh.

Oceanside Park had been our family's favorite picnic site for several years. With all the swings and seesaws, basketball hoops and softball fields, shuffleboard alleys and tennis courts, the park provided a physical outlet for almost anyone, regardless of age. A well-shaded picnic grove with plenty of tables made it especially popular with family groups like ours.

Labor Day, however, was a perennial favorite for late-summer outings. I knew the park would be swamped with people, especially since the county government had recently purchased a large parcel of land across the road from Oceanside Park. Everyone wanted to see where our higher taxes were going.

The new park addition, plus a perfect weather forecast, would, I knew, make the holiday crowd even bigger than usual. So I decided that the Saturday before Labor Day would probably be a better day for our picnic.

By nine o'clock we all piled into our dusty old car. By "all," I mean the kids, me, and Beauty, too. Luckily, part of Oceanside Park was considered a "paw park" where dogs could run free if they were properly supervised.

No problem there, I thought. Beauty had been with us to Oceanside Park many times and had always behaved like a lady. True, she loved to race around the park madly for the first few minutes. But she always wore herself out quickly and then trotted back to our table, where she flopped contentedly in the thick, shady grass for the rest of the afternoon.

As soon as I pulled into the parking area and turned off the engine, I sent Savannah and Beauty running to claim a picnic table. Even though it was still fairly early in the day, I knew there wouldn't be many tables left.

Happily, they found one that was about halfway between the rest rooms and the water fountains. The swings and seesaws were nearby, too.

Savannah beamed proudly as I piled some of our picnic supplies on the table. "How's this, Mom?" she asked. "Cool, huh?"

"Perfect," I told her, and gave her a big hug. "Why don't you guys take Beauty for a quick tour of the park? And keep your brother away from the highway, Savannah."

Savannah groaned. "Oh, Mom, I'm not a little kid, you know. I always make sure that Wyatt is safe."

While my two precious children and one precious pet romped around the park, I started to unpack our supplies. Going on a picnic had always been one of Ian's favorite ways to spend a Sunday afternoon. So I had the picnic packing down to a science.

But, even after I'd spread the tablecloth and unpacked the wicker hamper, I'd still had to make several trips to the car for the extra boxes, jugs of juice, and blankets. Nevertheless, I was proud of myself. I had everything set up and ready to go in less than ten minutes. While Beauty and the kids romped around, I sat at the picnic table and enjoyed one of my favorite past-times—people watching.

My eyes were soon drawn to a man who was just arriving and setting up his things at a nearby table. There were two children with him, too—a boy and a girl. They appeared to be about the same age as Savannah and Wyatt.

The man was attractive. His shoulders were broad, his hips narrow, and his legs looked sturdy and strong. He looked very athletic in his shorts, T-shirt, and glistening white running shoes.

When he saw me looking at him, he grinned and waved. "Hi!" he called. His smile was devastating. I could feel the heat instantly rush to my face. And then the guilt poured in.

Ian's been gone for less than three months and you're already ogling other men? I thought angrily.

"Beautiful day," the man added.

"Perfect," I replied, trying to beat back the guilt. Surely there was nothing wrong with simply being friendly.

"Your kids?" I asked casually as the two children started lifting soda cans and colorful snack bags out of cardboard boxes.

The man laughed and mussed the boy's hair. "Never saw them before," he teased. "I found them in the parking lot."

The boy squirmed out from under his father's hand. "Oh, Dad," he groaned.

I laughed, too, and waved vaguely toward the softball field. "Mine are out there somewhere taking our dog, Beauty, for a run."

I glanced over at the tennis courts and admired the attractive senior couple who appeared to be having a delightful time. I felt a twinge of envy and pain as I remembered the many times Ian and I had played tennis, before the kids had come along. There had never seemed to be any time for tennis after that.

"That's okay," Ian always used to say. "We'll have plenty of time for tennis when I retire."

"When you retire?" I'd always reply in mock horror. "That's more than thirty years away! Surely we'll be able to play a couple games of tennis before then."

But we never had. And now we never will, I thought.

I forced my eyes away from the tennis court and my mind away from self-pity. It's a beautiful day, I reminded myself. I have two beautiful children and a sweet and wonderful dog. I also have a life that is starting to move forward again.

I glanced at the softball field where a group of young girls appeared to be having batting practice. They were all wearing uniforms that had the name of a furniture store plastered across their backs in big letters. A female adult was shouting words of direction and encouragement.

When I glanced back at the man and his two children I wondered where his wife was. Maybe he's divorced, I thought, and just has the kids for the weekend. Or maybe his wife is working, or shopping, or cleaning the house. Maybe she'll come to the park later. A man who looks that good surely has a woman somewhere in his life.

A few minutes later, Savannah came running back to the table, followed by a puffing Wyatt. Both kids were red-faced and panting and appeared to be enjoying themselves immensely. Beauty, who was now wriggling happily around my feet, was also clearly delighted with how the day was going.

Savannah chattered away excitedly about the possibility of joining that very same softball team once school started. She gestured toward the adult who was working with the girls.

"She's the coach," she told me. "Her name is Linda and she's really nice. She told me she's looking for a few more girls for the team. Can I join, Mom, please? Can I?"

I smiled and pushed a strand of hair away from my daughter's flushed cheek. "I don't see why not," I said. "I loved to play softball when I was your age. I was even a pitcher."

Savannah's mouth dropped open. She looked at me strangely for a moment. Then she grinned. "You played softball?" she asked, totally shocked.

I shrugged. "Of course. I was very good at it, too. I was also one of the best hitters on our team."

When I glanced at Wyatt, he was also staring up at me with a gaping mouth and big eyes. It was obvious that neither Savannah nor Wyatt had ever even stopped to think that their mother was once a little girl herself—a little girl who played softball.

My children exchanged startled glances. "Wow," they said, almost in unison. They were clearly awestruck.

After a moment, Savannah continued. "Linda said she and the girls have to leave in a few minutes," she said hesitantly. "When they do, Mom, do you think you could show me how to hold the bat? And maybe pitch?"

"I'm sure I could," I told her. "If we had a bat. And a softball.

But we don't." I spread my hands helplessly.

I heard a voice behind me. "Excuse me."

When I turned around, the man with the two boys was holding an aluminum bat and a ball in one hand, a pair of baseball gloves in the other. He was grinning.

"I didn't mean to eavesdrop," he said pleasantly, "but I couldn't help overhearing your conversation about softball. My boys are crazy about the game." Tentatively, he held the bat, ball, and gloves out further. "Maybe your kids and my kids could start up a game together."

Savannah beamed expectantly. "Could we, Mom? That would be way cool."

I shrugged and returned the man's smile. "It's okay with me if it's okay with you."

The man handed the bat and gloves to his son and then tossed the ball to his daughter. "Here you go, guys. Andrew, why don't you give these kids a few pointers?" He turned back to me. "My son's getting to be a very good player. He's the captain of his team," he bragged.

Andrew grinned proudly and then waved to his sister. His wave also included Savannah and Wyatt. "Follow me," he told them. "I'll show you how to hit a homer every time."

Kicking up red clay dust, the four kids ran onto the field as the uniformed team ambled away toward a big bus in the parking lot. Andrew's father and I exchanged smiles.

"That should keep them busy for a few minutes," he said. Then he moved toward me and extended his hand. His smile brightened even more.

"By the way," he went on, "my name is Paul Haynes. That's my son, Andrew, of course. My daughter's name is Jenna."

His handshake felt warm and strong. His hand was so big it nearly swallowed my own.

I told him all of our names and then invited him to sit down at our table. I glanced at his left hand but saw no ring. "Is your wife coming later?" I asked.

Paul's smile dimmed a bit and he looked away, directing his eyes toward the kids. They were already trying on the baseball gloves and tossing the ball around. Beauty was hopping around awkwardly on her back legs. She was barking happily and trying to clamp her teeth into one of the bulky leather gloves.

"I lost my wife two years ago," Paul said quietly. A hint of bitterness crept into his voice. "Drunk driver." He scowled. "He got away without a scratch, of course. Erin died instantly."

Instinctively, my hand reached out and gently touched his wrist. "I'm so sorry," I murmured, feeling my own fresh pain spurt up again.

Paul looked back at me. His eyes were glistening. "Thanks," he said softly, his voice thick with emotion. He took a deep breath. "How about you? No father for those kids?"

I shook my head. Now it was my turn to glance toward the softball field. "Ian died in June," I explained slowly. "It was a particularly vicious form of cancer, so it happened very quickly. It was a devastating loss. For all of us."

I don't know where the next words came from, but they nearly caught in my throat. "Sometimes, I blame myself for Ian's death."

Paul stared at me for a long moment and then nodded somberly. "I'm sure you're not to blame, but I know what you mean. For quite a while after Erin's death I felt that, somehow, I should have done something to prevent it."

His words drifted away for a moment and then he sighed heavily. "The kids still miss their mother, of course," he went on. "And so do I."

We both grew quiet, each lost in our own memories. But it was a companionable kind of quietness—comforting, even. It was the kind of quiet Ian and I had often shared, after the kids had gone to bed. At times like that, you didn't have to say anything. Just being together was enough.

A few moments later, Paul seemed to rouse himself. He straightened his back and squared his shoulders. He was watching the kids again.

"You know," he said, changing the subject, "I'm glad the county finally decided to expand the park by buying that plot of land over there." His voice was firm again. He nodded past the field to a grove of trees some distance away. "But I don't like having a heavily traveled highway like that one cutting the park in half."

I followed his eyes to the constant stream of traffic that seemed to be whizzing by frantically between the field and the grove of trees. An incomplete segment of chain link fencing was the only thing separating the softball field from the edge of highway.

"It would have been nice if they'd finished putting up that fence before the holiday, don't you think?" I muttered sarcastically.

Paul laughed cynically. "That's the government for you. Always a day late and a few dollars short." He glanced at me. "I suppose you heard about the overhead walkway. It was supposed to run from this part of the park, up and over the highway, and then down again to that new section over there."

I nodded. "I saw the article in the paper. What happened? It sounded like a good idea."

"It was a great idea," Paul agreed. "But there was no money to back it up. So now we have half of a chain link fence separating all of us from the warp-speed maniacs who use that highway."

Paul glanced at me and grinned. His eyes were sparkling. "Sorry." He laughed. "Once I start grumbling about the government, there's no telling where I'll end up. So I'd better stop right now."

He grinned at me for a few seconds. "Hey, I've got an idea," he went on. "Why don't we join the kids? Maybe we could all play a little slow-pitch softball."

"That sounds like a wonderful idea," I agreed, accepting his hand as he helped me off the bench. I suddenly felt carefree—almost girlish. "I haven't hit a softball in years," I admitted. "I hope the kids don't mind us joining in."

It turned out that they didn't mind at all. In fact, Savannah and Wyatt continued to be amazed whenever I caught a grounder or slammed a two-bagger.

"Go for it, Mom!" Savannah yelled as I rounded third again and that time, headed for home. Naturally, Beauty was racing beside me, barking like crazy. Out of the corner of my eye, I could see the ball flying toward Paul, who was crouched over home plate. The ball and I almost got there at the same time. Unfortunately, the ball smacked into Paul's glove inches ahead of me. I tried to swerve around Paul but didn't quite make it.

With a shout and a grin, Paul reached out and tagged my left hip with his glove. "Out!" he cried happily as I went flashing by.

"Wait till next time," I warned as I circled back. "I'll knock one over the fence."

Paul's twinkling eyes moved down over me appreciatively as I headed back toward home plate. "You probably will." He laughed. "You're in pretty good shape for an old lady with two kids."

I laughed, too, as my eyes skidded across Paul's broad chest, muscular arms, and strong legs. "You don't look so bad yourself, Pops," I teased.

The good-natured bantering continued as Paul and his kids knocked in two runs and tied the score. We all agreed that my kids and I would have one last turn at batting. If the score remained tied, so be it. We'd end the game and turn our attention to hot dogs and sodas.

"But don't forget," I shouted as I hefted the bat one more time. "It ain't over till the fat lady sings. This time, I'll whack one clear across town."

With my kids cheering and Beauty barking happily, Paul's pitch sent the ball swooping toward me. The instant it left his hand I knew that this was the pitch that had my name written all over it.

With a joyful cry, I swung the bat with all my might. When the aluminum met the leather-covered ball there was a loud and very satisfying sound, and the ball took off like a rocket.

Beauty also took off like a rocket, racing after the high-flying spot of white. I took off for first base as fast as I could run, but I knew there was really no need to rush. The hit was a homer for sure. I knew it in my stomach.

Still, I kept my eye on the ball as I headed toward second base. Paul's eight-year-old daughter, Jenna, was also running as fast as she could toward left field. But I knew there was no chance of her catching the ball.

I started running, laughing and cheering all at the same time as I saw the ball veer slowly to the left. A second later it hit one of the tall light poles. With a loud clunk it careened off the pole and headed toward the half-finished chain link fence.

Beauty, her eyes still firmly fixed on the ball, tore after it, low to the ground. Her legs were a blur and for a second I thought she was going to run right into the fence. At the last possible instant, she swerved.

The laughter suddenly caught in my throat as Beauty streaked around the end of the fence. A second later my joy turned to stark, cold horror as I saw the ball arc downward. I staggered to a stop as the ball hit the ground and bounced wildly. A second later it leaped over the fence and rolled directly into the whizzing stream of cars.

"Beauty, no!" I screamed. "Come back!"

Suddenly, the kids were all screaming, too, trying to make Beauty stop. I vaguely heard Paul's powerful voice as well. We were all yelling as loud as we could. But it was too late. Either Beauty didn't hear us, or she was running too fast to stop.

Brakes shrieked, horns blew, and cars swerved wildly. A second later, I heard a thump and saw a bundle of fur flying through the air. The bundle bounced off another car and went cartwheeling into the ditch.

"No!" I screamed.

My heart was in my throat. Horror clouded my brain. I could barely breathe. But I was running as fast as I could.

Paul reached the highway before I did. More tires screeched, and more horns blew. I could hear a few angry curses as Paul maneuvered himself between the slowing cars. He was trying to direct traffic away from Beauty, who lay at the edge of the road.

One of the cars lurched to a stop some distance away. The driver leaped out of his car and came running back, his face twisted with fear and confusion. "I didn't see the dog," he was shouting as he ran. "I didn't see the dog at all!"

We all converged at the same time around the red-stained bundle of fur. Paul was already crouched by Beauty's side. I immediately fell to my knees, tears gushing from my eyes.

Oh, God, I prayed frantically. Please don't take Beauty. Please.

But the instant I saw the little twisted body I knew our precious Beauty wouldn't make it. As gently as I could, I cradled her head in my hands. I could see my own tears dropping onto her face as she looked up at me.

Her eyes were filled with fear and pain. They were also filled with confusion. And questions. "Why?" her heartbreaking eyes pleaded. "I trusted you. I loved you. Why did you let this happen to me?"

I buried my face in her fur and sobbed uncontrollably. Then I could feel firm hands pulling me back.

"We can't stay here," Paul said softly. "The traffic is too dangerous."

When I looked at Beauty's eyes again, the light had faded away. "No!" I sobbed. "Please, God, no!"

My precious, precious Beauty. She was one of Ian's last gifts to the kids and me. And now, suddenly, she was gone, too, just like Ian.

The driver of the car that had hit Beauty found a blanket in his trunk. Paul gently wrapped the shattered little body in the blanket while all of the kids watched, their faces white and rigid with shock.

Moments later, a police car with flashing lights pulled to the side of the road behind us. Then there was a policeman on the scene. He started questioning the driver of the car as Paul stood up slowly, holding Beauty in his arms. I slowly followed Paul as he started moving away from the highway.

The kids followed behind me. The shock and silence that had struck them dumb moments before now gave way to frightened wails and noisy tears. "We've got to get her to a doctor," one of them insisted between sobs. I think it was Paul's daughter, Jenna.

Sadly, numbly, I tried to gather all of the kids under my arms as we walked slowly back toward the picnic area. "It's too late for a doctor," I said wearily. "Beauty's gone."

I heard the shriek of my own daughter, Savannah, above the other cries. "No, Mommy!" she wailed. "She can't be."

"I'll put her in the car," Paul said softly to me. "Do you have the keys?"

Stunned, I looked around vaguely.

"Is that your purse over there?" Paul asked helpfully, nodding toward our picnic table.

"What?" I asked, utterly confused. "Oh. Yes. I think so." I tried to make my brain work. "The keys. Yes, you need the keys to open the trunk," I said.

After fumbling awkwardly for a few seconds, I finally managed to unlock the trunk of our car and let the lid glide upward. Gently, tenderly, Paul lifted the bloodstained bundle into the trunk. He hesitated, glancing toward the kids.

Savannah, now trying very hard to put up a brave front, was attempting to comfort the younger ones. With genuine kindness and conviction, Savannah was speaking to them.

"Beauty's in heaven now, Wyatt. He's with Jesus and Daddy. So we don't have to cry anymore." But the other kids continued to cry, anyway, and so did I.

"Maybe it would be better if I took Beauty with me," Paul suggested gently. "I could find her a resting place. Somewhere quiet and peaceful."

I shook my head firmly. "No. We have to take Beauty home. I'll find a place in the backyard." I gave Paul a quick hug. "Thanks so much for your help."

Paul's eyes searched mine. "Are you okay to drive?"

I nodded. "The tears have stopped for a while," I murmured numbly. "I'll be fine."

Paul's face was grim, his eyes sad. "Call me, okay?" He slid a wallet out of his back pocket and fished out a business card. "Here's my number," he said, handing it to me. "Home and office."

I glanced at the card and stuffed it into my purse. "Savannah?" I called. "Get Wyatt in the car and then come and help me gather up our picnic things."

In a stiff and pain-filled silence, Savannah and I quickly loaded everything onto the backseat next to Wyatt. Paul and his two children worked with us.

After we finished, Paul's children climbed somberly into their car. I looked at Paul and felt terrible. I could feel Savannah hovering in the background.

"If only I hadn't tried to show off," I said, my voice shaking with pain and regret. "If only I hadn't hit that ball so hard." I paused as a dreadful realization dawned on me. "Oh, Paul," I wept miserably. "It was the same with Ian. That was my fault, too. If only I had listened to him."

The tears filled my eyes as Paul took me into his arms. It was all I could do to keep from sobbing again like a child. After a moment, I pushed myself away from Paul's warm chest and slid behind the steering wheel. I closed the door and rolled down the window. Paul laid a hand on my arm.

"Call me," he said again, softly. "Okay?"

I nodded stiffly and started the engine.

The drive home seemed to take forever. The traffic was heavy nearly all the way. None of us said a word. The silence felt like a cold and heavy weight, pressing me down. It slowed my heart and dulled my brain.

That drive reminded me of another sad and lonely drive. During that one, however, I was not behind the steering wheel. I was sitting in the backseat of a limousine with Savannah and Wyatt, seeing the world through a stiff black veil. That was the day I buried Ian.

When we finally arrived home, Savannah and Wyatt carried the picnic supplies into the kitchen and piled them on the table. I searched the house for a casket of some sort, something in which to bury Beauty. The only thing I could find was an old cardboard box that had once held a VCR.

Then I went to my bedroom and found Ian's soft bathrobe. For a while after Ian died, I'd tried wearing the robe myself, but that was too painful. After that, I'd just left it hanging in the closet.

One day the robe had slipped from its wire hanger and fallen to the floor of the closet. When I'd found the robe, Beauty had already claimed it. She was curled up in the middle of it. She had looked up at me with her big, sad eyes. Despite the sadness, however, her eyes were also lit by a tiny spark of contentment.

That night and every night thereafter, I'd spread the robe at the foot of my bed and that's where Beauty had slept. So it only seemed right that Beauty should also sleep her final sleep, wrapped in Ian's robe.

As the children watched with stunned, glistening eyes, I carried Beauty's body to the bathroom and unwrapped it from the old stained blanket. Carefully, tenderly, I placed the crumpled body in the tub and gently washed it. Then I brushed the wet fur. Finally I wrapped our precious little friend in the soft robe. I placed the damp, heartbreaking bundle into the cardboard box and firmly closed the lid.

In a somber procession, I carried the box out to the backyard, followed by Savannah and Wyatt. The children were holding hands and crying quietly.

I gently laid the box on the ground under a young maple tree. It was the same tree that Ian had planted when we'd bought the house some years ago. I found a rusty shovel in the shed and quickly dug a deep hole in the shade of the maple.

Savannah, standing over the grave, somberly told God how lucky He was to be getting Beauty, and what a wonderful dog Beauty was. She also told God that she was sure her daddy would be delighted to see Beauty again.

After a brief benediction, Savannah unclasped a tiny silver cross she always wore around her neck. The cross had been a birthday gift from Ian. Savannah reached down into the grave and laid the cross on top of the box. I could barely see through the tears.

Wyatt watched his sister closely. Then he peeled off his favorite T-shirt. It was a shirt that Ian had given him.

Wyatt had to lie on his stomach in the fresh dirt in order to cover the cross and the box with his T-shirt.

Savannah suggested we all say a silent prayer. Then, after giving me a knowing look and a grim nod, she led her brother into the house while I closed the grave.

That was the second saddest day of my life.

Some people say that children adapt to the loss of a pet very quickly. And maybe some children do. Mine did not. Especially Wyatt.

For the longest time, he had nightmares nearly every night after Beauty died. Most of the nightmares were not about Beauty's death—but most of them were a result of Beauty's death. They had to be. I couldn't recall Wyatt ever having nightmares before Beauty died. And the nightmares went on for weeks, even after Wyatt started attending kindergarten.

He asked me many times why Beauty had to die. I never had a satisfactory reason. Finally, Savannah provided the best answer.

"Daddy was sad without Beauty," she told her brother. "Daddy missed her. So God decided that Beauty should go to heaven, too, to be with Daddy."

After the initial shock, Savannah seemed to adjust fairly quickly to Beauty's death. At least it seemed like that, for a while. Once again, her faith and her church activities carried her through another shock.

Slowly, however, I started to notice a change in Savannah. For instance, she started to get annoyed about little things—minor irritations and small disappointments. None of those things had ever bothered her before.

Soon her annoyance about life in general began to spread to her brother, and then to me. When I tried to brush her hair one morning like I always did before she left for school, Savannah pushed my hand away impatiently.

"I'll do it," she insisted, her voice stiff and cool. And she never let me brush her hair again.

Also, before Beauty died, Savannah used to come home from school and sit in the kitchen with me for at least a half hour. She would tell me all about her day.

Now, though, she went right to her room with barely a nod. And she'd stay there until I called her for supper. Then she'd trudge slowly down the steps. She'd wash her hands. She'd push the food around on her plate, hardly eating anything. Then she'd ask to be excused and trudge slowly back up to her room again.

Finally, after about two weeks of her increasing isolation, I sat Savannah down one afternoon while Wyatt was outside playing.

"Savannah," I began carefully, "I don't mean to pry, but it's obvious to me that something is very wrong. You seem irritated, annoyed, even angry all the time. You seem especially angry with me, and I don't know why."

Savannah glowered at me and then glared at the floor. I reached out to touch her hand but she jerked back as though I had just jabbed her with a needle.

"Maybe," I continued patiently, "if you told me what's troubling you, I could fix it, whatever it is, or change it."

Savannah glared at me. "Can you bring Beauty back from the dead?" she demanded.

My mouth dropped open in shock. "What?" I asked, confused.

"It's your fault that she's dead!" Savannah yelled. "It's your fault that Daddy's dead, too. I heard you talking to Paul at the park. The day Beauty died."

Savannah couldn't have shocked me more if she'd slapped my face. I stared at her, dumbfounded.

"What are you talking about?" I asked.

Savannah pushed back her chair violently. It toppled over behind her as she lurched to her feet. Her eyes were blazing with, what? Hatred?

My mind swirled crazily. "I don't understand," I stammered hesitantly.

Savannah was screaming. "You killed Beauty! You killed Daddy! You kill everything that I love. Because you hate me!"

Her screams turned into sobs as she whirled around and raced out of the kitchen. I could hear her footsteps pounding up the steps. Then I heard the slam of her bedroom door.

I stood there, frozen, rigid from shock, extremely cold and feeling very stupid.

Savannah barely spoke to me after that. But it was clear she had talked to Wyatt. Soon after she blew up at me, Wyatt began to change, too.

He got cranky and began whining at the slightest frustration. When I tried to reason with him he stomped away and pouted for hours. When I tried to chastise or correct him in any way, he'd throw a tantrum and hurl the same accusations that Savannah had used.

"You killed Beauty and Daddy!" he'd shout, his little face twisted with rage and pain. "I hate you!"

The stress at home quickly carried over to my job. I had always prided myself for my even temper and patience on the job, especially with impatient customers. But even I could see that I was becoming downright rude.

My boss, Hugh Granger, kept asking me what was wrong. Was I having personal problems? Were the kids sick? What was going on?

I wasn't exactly brusque with Hugh. After all, he was my boss and my job was in his hands. But I certainly let him know that my problems were my business. I also let him know that I preferred to keep my business to myself.

Hugh looked at me strangely and said nothing. But after that, he made sure that any conversations between the two of us were strictly work-related.

For a while after Beauty was killed, Paul called me several times a week, mainly to find out how the kids were doing.

"And how you're doing, too, of course," he'd add. I could picture the worried look in his eyes.

Then, as more months passed, he started asking me out to dinner, or to a movie. Once, on an unseasonably warm December day, he even suggested a picnic with the kids. He immediately realized his mistake and apologized profusely. Then he tried to modify the offer to a cookout at his place. But even that, I thought, was not such a good idea.

During those unsettled months, Paul and I did take in a movie every now and then, just the two of us. His sister, Anne, watched our kids. One night, he took me to one of the most exclusive and expensive restaurants in town. That's the night he first told me he loved me. He also hinted that he'd like our relationship to move on to another level.

I knew Paul that really cared about me. And I had to admit that I felt a strong attraction to him as well. But the last thing I needed just then was another complication in my life.

"Things are kind of rocky with the kids right now," I told Paul that night. "And I think any kind of major change would just make things worse."

"Maybe I could help you with the kids," he replied with a casual shrug. "I'm a father, too, you know. I know how the little angels can turn into little monsters, sometimes overnight."

I shook my head and extricated myself from his arms. "You don't understand, Paul," I said stiffly.

"But that's what I'm saying," Paul continued earnestly. "I want to understand. I want to help. I want to be part of your life." His eyes burned into mine. His warm strong hands clasped my upper arms. "All you have to do is let me in."

But I couldn't. I just couldn't.

To say my whole life had turned into a tumultuous whirlpool of emotion would probably be an understatement. It just seemed like everything was starting to fall apart. Whatever symptoms of stress each of my kids was having, I seemed to be having the same symptoms, all at the same time.

118

Like Wyatt, my sleep was shattered by nightmares. Like Savannah, I, too, had lost my appetite. And everything got on my nerves, too, now.

Often I was argumentative, bossy, remorseful, weepy, and defensive—all at the same time. I guess it wasn't surprising that my physical health began to deteriorate as rapidly as my mental health. So when Savannah brought a flu bug home from school it ran right through the house. It pummeled me worst of all.

With my runny nose, scratchy throat, hacking cough, and pounding headache, I quickly turned into a one-woman cold capsule commercial. But there was no time for convalescence. I simply had too much to do. I had let things slide for much too long, especially the housework.

Throughout our marriage, Ian and I had always done the housework together. There were no woman's job versus man's job. There were simply jobs that had to be done and we split them up. That way we finished everything in half the time.

When Ian died there was no one to help. So the housekeeping chores he and I used to do together every week, I now struggled to do every two weeks. Then three weeks would elapse between some of the chores.

For a short time Savannah tried to pitch in with the housework. But after Beauty died—and especially after she started blaming me for his death—she didn't want to help me do anything, no matter how much I nagged her.

At the same time, my own spirits were sagging badly. Because in a way, Savannah was right. In a way, it really was my fault that Beauty died. Beauty had depended on me to take care of him, to watch out for him. And I'd failed him. Just like I failed to take seriously Ian's complaints about not feeling well. So both deaths continued to gnaw at my heart and my brain.

I began to lose interest in everything, especially the housekeeping chores. It was all I could do to get the laundry done every week, never mind waxing the floors, shaking and vacuuming the rugs, or washing the windows.

All of a sudden, I looked around one Friday morning and realized I couldn't stand the accumulation of dust and clutter for another day. The fact that I'd just come down with the flu was no excuse. The whole house was a mess and I was the only one who could clean it up.

I reluctantly called Paul. "Do you think your sister could take my kids for the weekend?" I asked, stifling a sneeze. I'm sure I sounded very nasal.

"I'm sorry," Paul said, dashing my hopes, "but Anne and her son are visiting Mom and Dad this weekend. You sound terrible,

Elizabeth," he added sympathetically. "What's going on?"

"Nothing serious," I told him. "The kids brought a flu bug home from school. Now we all have it. Me worst of all."

Paul laughed. "I know. My kids have it, too. And I've been feeling a bit stuffy myself." He paused. "Is there some way that I can help you, Elizabeth?"

"Well, it's just that I was hoping to give our place a good housecleaning this weekend," I said hesitantly. "It's turning into a world-class mess and I thought I could get a lot more done if I didn't have the kids around."

Paul laughed. "I know what you mean. My guys know how to get underfoot, too, usually at the worst time." He thought for a moment. "I'll make you a deal, Elizabeth. I'll take care of your kids myself, from Friday night until Sunday afternoon. But only on one condition."

"Uh-oh," I teased. "I don't like the sound of that. What's the condition?"

"Simple," Paul assured me. "All you have to do is let me take you and your kids, plus me and my kids, out to dinner Sunday evening. What do you say?"

I laughed. "I'd say you'd be getting the short end of the stick."

"Oh, well." I could hear the smile in Paul's voice. "That's my final offer. Take it or leave it."

"I'll take it," I said quickly.

A sudden wave of gratitude, maybe even love, swept through me. "Oh, Paul," I gushed. "I don't know what I'd do without you." Tears burned my eyes.

Paul picked up Savannah right after she got home from school that Friday afternoon. Wyatt was waiting impatiently in the living room. Since the picnic, both of them had grown close to Paul's kids, Jenna and Andrew, so the thought of spending the whole weekend with them was a real treat. The fact that Paul had recently brought home an adorable fuzzy puppy made the weekend sound even more appealing.

As soon as the house was empty I popped another cold capsule into my mouth and swallowed another spoonful of cough syrup. After blowing my nose and gulping the last of my green tea, I felt almost ready to tear the house apart. Almost.

I looked around, sighed, and then resolutely rounded up the mop, waxer, vacuum cleaner, dust rags, and disinfectant. Then I simply jumped in with both feet.

Within minutes, my top was soaked with perspiration. For the past few days spring had descended with a vengeance and by six o'clock the house felt like an oven. I was reluctant to turn the air conditioner on that early in the year because I was looking forward to at least one more low electric bill. Instead, I carried my small oscillating fan with me, from room to room.

As I cleaned out the refrigerator, sprayed the oven, and scoured the sink, I began to think about Paul again. There was no doubt that he was a good and decent man, but was I ready for another relationship? After all, Ian hadn't been gone a year yet.

Savannah's accusations about Beauty and her daddy also slid through my mind again. As I scrubbed and dusted and fought with the grime, I tried to reason away the guilt and remorse that was still plaguing me.

It's just crazy to blame yourself for Ian's death, I thought as I plugged the frayed cord of the old rotating fan into the wall socket. I perched the fan on a stack of old newspapers and magazines and started to clean the pantry.

Once we found out about the cancer I had done everything I could think of to help my husband. Unfortunately, however, the symptoms had been there long before the diagnosis.

The tiredness, the weight loss, the unusual aches and pains— they had been about as clear as sunrise and yet, I hadn't seen them. Nor had Ian. We both assumed that his health problems were simply a matter of stress and overwork. We kept telling ourselves that as soon as he adjusted to his new job responsibilities, we would take a well-deserved vacation. Ian would rest up, regroup, and be ready for another assault.

Looking back even further, however, revealed another painful truth. Ian had been reluctant to accept the promotion in the first place. He had seen what the added pressure and responsibility had done to his best friend, Warren Turner.

Warren had gone into an emotional tailspin six months after he was promoted. He slid steadily into a serious depression, ended up in the hospital, and, eventually, had been forced to leave the company.

Ian and I had wondered if the same thing could happen to him. But with three kids, two cars, a hefty mortgage and the other monthly bills, Ian didn't think that he could refuse the extra money that went with the promotion. And there was no doubt that the increase in salary that went with the new job was very generous.

Then there were the extra benefits: Total-coverage health insurance for the whole family, a company car, two additional weeks of vacation every year, more life insurance, and a surprisingly good profit-sharing plan. The whole package was simply too good to turn down.

But the long hours, endless deadlines, and increasing pressure quickly started taking its toll on Ian as it had on Warren Turner.

Instead of coming home at five-thirty every night as he had

before, Ian started getting home at six-thirty, then seven-thirty. Sometimes he didn't get home until nine-thirty or ten.

An occasional hour or two at the office on Saturday mornings turned into a half a day, and then almost a full day. Sometimes even Ian's Sundays weren't completely free from work.

So I guess it wasn't surprising that the stress started piling up. But despite the strain and the pressure, Ian wasn't the kind of person who gave up easily. He was sure he could do the job, once he got through the difficult learning stage.

I tried to be as supportive as I could, in every way I could. And I, too, continued to believe that Ian could do the job. The word "failure" simply wasn't in his vocabulary.

But life has a way of throwing reality in your face every now and then. It came to us in the form of cancer. And the next thing I knew, my husband was gone. Now Beauty was gone, too.

The tears were starting to flow again as I sat at the kitchen table for another cup of green tea. The tears made my stuffy nose run even more. And that stirred up the cough again. So I gulped down another cold capsule and swallowed some more cough syrup.

I finally looked at the clock above the sink and gasped. No wonder I was feeling totally wiped out. It was nearly midnight!

With the cleaning supplies still scattered around the house I rinsed out my teacup and propped it in the strainer. After making sure all the doors were locked and the windows closed, I flicked off the lights, climbed the stairs, and wearily flopped into the bed. I was quickly submerged in a groggy, exhausted, dream-wracked sleep.

Later that night I started dreaming about a small dog that was running around our house barking frantically. I also saw a man who appeared to be saying something that I couldn't quite hear.

In the dream, I was looking out my bedroom window and the man was down on the sidewalk, looking up at me. His face was obscured by shadows and his voice was very soft. But I was certain his message was critical. I got very annoyed at the barking dog. The endless yapping was drowning out whatever the man was saying.

As I peered down at the man and the running dog I began to realize that they both looked vaguely familiar. I was sure I recognized them from somewhere and yet, something was wrong with how they looked. There was also a strange smell in the air. The odor seemed to be hanging around the man and the dog. It was like a noxious cloud that floated up to the window.

The odor was acrid and harsh. It burned my nose and made me cough. When I could no longer stand the smell I ran back away from the window and jumped into bed. I was coughing violently now.

Between coughs I realized the man's voice had gotten louder

and much closer. Half of his face, which had been hidden in shadows a moment before down in the street, now suddenly appeared at my bedroom door. The door was ajar and the face was lit by a glow that seemed to erupt behind him.

"Elizabeth," I heard the man say. His voice was gentle but firm. "Elizabeth, you must get up."

"No," I mumbled. "I'm too tired. Too tired." I closed my eyes as hard as I could, pinching them shut. But it didn't help. The light behind the man grew brighter still.

Then the door to my bedroom was abruptly flung inward. I heard the doorknob bang against the wall. At the same time, a bright orange light flooded my room. Like a searing searchlight, it swept across my bed and wavered along the walls.

I had never seen a light that bright. Even with my eyes shut tightly, I could see it. I could feel it as well. It seemed to be searing the back of my eyes.

The man's voice grew even louder, more forceful. "Elizabeth," he said again. "You must get up. Now!"

The frantic barking of the dog grew louder, too. The dog was in my room now, too, racing back and forth. Then I felt the dog leap onto my bed, barking hysterically.

Suddenly terrified, I pushed myself upright into a seated position. Cringing with fear I shoved myself back against the headboard. I pulled the sheet to my throat. I now knew for certain that I was awake. I had to be awake. Because the room was filling up with smoke and I could barely breath.

But, despite the smoke, the light grew brighter still. And the shadowy man was no longer hidden by shadows. His face was as clear as could be. And the shock of seeing that face—and recognizing it—was like a physical blow to my stomach.

"Ian?" I asked incredulously, struggling to breathe. "No, it can't be you. It can't!"

But there wasn't a doubt in my mind. It was Ian. He was standing in the doorway. He was coming toward the bed.

The intensity that had filled his eyes a moment before had lessened. He even smiled. "It's time to leave, Elizabeth," he said softly. His hand reached out, beckoning to me.

"What?" I asked, totally confused and awestruck.

Ian's hand beckoned slowly again, gently. It was as if his hand was being wafted back and forth by a light, delicate breeze.

The little dog was now standing squarely on the sheets near the foot of the bed. She was no longer barking.

"Beauty?" I asked hesitantly.

It didn't make any sense. And yet there she was, grinning at me.

Her tail was snapping back and forth, like a flag in a gale force wind.

Behind Beauty and beyond Ian the orange light was growing even more intense. It was flickering wildly now. It was also moving steadily closer. And I suddenly realized what was going on.

"Oh, my God!" I moaned. "The house is on fire!"

In an instant, Beauty had spun around, jumped down off the bed and sped away. Ian seemed to be moving backward with a floating kind of motion. It was almost as though the smoke and flames were carrying him away from me. And yet he was still smiling and his hand was still beckoning to me, urging me.

The smoke was searing my lungs as I hurled myself off the bed. In the wavering orange light I spotted my robe. It was still draped across the foot of the bed where I'd left it that morning. I whirled it on like a cape but couldn't find my slippers.

"You must hurry, Elizabeth," Ian said again.

By that point, my husband's voice was fading away, and so was he. He appeared to be melting into the flames and smoke. Only Beauty was still there, sharp and clear, racing wildly in and out of my room, barking crazily.

Coughing and half-blind from the smoke, I stumbled out of my room and into the hallway. When I looked down the stairs I could see the flames spreading across the living room wall. They were dancing like demons and the fire had already engulfed one of the drapes.

Beauty started hopping awkwardly down the steps. Every few feet she would glance back to make sure I was still coming. When I started down the steps after her I heard the scream of a siren, coming fast.

Coughing, stumbling, and bumping into furniture, I finally made my way through the smoke-filled living room toward the front door. I assumed the door would be open. It had to be. How else could Beauty have gotten into the house?

But the heavy front door was not open. It was securely locked. And the small safety chain I'd fastened before I went to bed still hung limply from the slider-slot.

As I struggled to disconnect the chain and twist the door's deadbolt knob, Beauty continued to bounce in the air around my legs, still barking wildly. The instant I ripped the door open she exploded onto the porch. Down the steps and across the lawn she flew like a streak.

The firemen were already racing around purposefully, pulling hoses, making connections, shouting orders. More fire trucks were screaming up the street. A cameraman from one of our local television stations had set up his camera near the sidewalk. He was filming the fire while a familiar-looking anchorman was talking excitedly into a microphone.

Beauty raced past the television camera and flew among the firefighters, barking merrily. For a few moments she seemed to be everywhere, making sure everyone understood the seriousness of the situation. Then she whirled around once more, looked directly at me, and took off like a shot.

I watched her bound over canvas hoses, swerve among the firemen, and then disappear between two parked fire trucks.

"Beauty!" I cried out. "Beauty!"

One of the firemen rushed over to me, dragging a heavy hose. "Ma'am?" he shouted above the din. "Are you all right?"

"My dog!" I cried, trying to make myself heard above the squealing sirens.

The fireman gaped at me, and then stared at the house. He shook his head grimly. "If your dog is in the house," he said, "I'm afraid there's nothing we can do."

"No!" I shouted back at him. "Beauty is not in the house. She was right here. You must have seen her. You practically stumbled over her."

Another fireman joined the first one. That one was carrying an axe in one hand and what looked like a small cell phone in his other hand.

"Hey, Ben, have you seen a dog?" He jerked his head toward me. "The lady said she lost him."

The other fireman shrugged and shook his head. His huge helmet shifted slightly. "I was one of the first guys here," he reported. "I didn't see any dog. Are you sure the dog got out of the house?"

"Of course I'm sure," I shouted. "She came out ahead of me. You must have seen her."

The two firemen looked at each other doubtfully and then back at me. "We both saw you running out of the house, ma'am," the first one said. "We didn't see a dog."

A muffled pop erupted behind me as something exploded in the house. The firemen cursed and then both of them started running toward the flames, one dragging the hose, the other one getting ready to wield his axe.

Flames were now streaking upward from the roof. Other flames were curling out of the windows, scorching walls. Window glass was popping and shattering from the heat. Paint was blistering, and beams were groaning. The whole house was a blazing inferno.

My heart sank as I suddenly realized there was absolutely no hope. In a few more minutes, and despite the valiant efforts of the firemen, my home and everything in it would simply be gone, reduced to a pile of smoking ash.

I sank to my knees and began to sob. I had never before felt so totally helpless. Minutes later, Paul was looking down at me, his eyes worried and deep.

"Are you all right?" he asked. His hand reached out and gently touched my face.

"What are you doing here?" I was confused for a moment.

"The kids and I were watching a late movie when the show was interrupted by a news bulletin. It was about the fire. Savannah recognized your house immediately. She wanted to come with me but I convinced her to stay with Jenna and the other kids."

Paul looked at me seriously again. He reached down and caressed my cheek. "Are you sure you're all right?"

I nodded stiffly and motioned toward the wall of flames that used to be our home. "It's gone," I said unsteadily. "Everything is gone."

Paul's expression was grim as helped me to my feet. He took me in his arms. "But you're safe," he reminded me. "And your kids are safe. That's all that really matters."

Paul was right, of course. And that became clearer during the next few weeks as I tried to get our life reorganized yet again. Paul and his sister, Anne, both asked the kids and me to stay with them, until we could move into our new home.

I wouldn't have felt right about living in Paul's house, but I did accept Anne's offer to live with her. And she couldn't have been a more gracious or a more helpful friend.

The man from the insurance agency was also helpful. He promised to get the ball rolling as quickly as possible, and he really did. In less than two weeks, the remains of our old house was bulldozed and trucked away. The ground was leveled off. And the foundation for our new house was nearly finished.

The fire inspector did a thorough investigation and came to the conclusion that the fire probably started in the pantry. That's when I remembered the fan with the frayed cord. I had forgotten to turn it off before I went to bed. When I told the fire inspector about the fan and the cord, he said they probably overheated. Sparks probably jumped to the stacks of old newspaper and magazines. From there the fire spread everywhere.

At first, I didn't tell the kids about seeing Beauty or their father that night. But I did tell Paul. He listened carefully and then was silent for a long time.

"I never used to believe in supernatural events, or in mystical, religious kinds of things. But when my wife died in that car crash, everything changed," he admitted. Paul's voice drifted away and his eyes began to glisten.

I reached out and touched his hand. "What happened?" I asked softly.

"For weeks after the accident," Paul began, touching his forehead wearily. "I was tortured by the thought that Erin had suffered terribly in the crash. One of the policemen told me that car was mangled so badly the firemen and paramedics worked for nearly an hour to get her out. But by the time they did, it was too late."

Paul shook his head, as though trying to banish the awful memories. "What made it even worse was that I was out of town when it happened, on a business trip. I didn't find out about the accident until the next day, when the police finally reached me by telephone."

Paul looked away, his face suddenly haggard and filled with pain. Tears glistened on his cheeks. "I used to go to the cemetery and sit for hours, telling Erin how sorry I felt for not being with her at the end."

When I tried to comfort him, Paul raised his hand to stop me. "But then, the strangest thing happened," he went on. His voice was edged with awe now. "Out of nowhere, a beautiful cat appeared, right there in the cemetery. It came over to the bench I was sitting on and looked up at me. Then it leaped into my lap, as light as a feather. After looking up at me once more it curled up in my lap, started to purr, and immediately fell asleep."

The tears were now flowing freely down Paul's cheek. They were welling up in my eyes, too.

Paul tried to wipe the tears away. When he glanced at me again his grin was slightly embarrassed but also very relieved.

"I know it sounds crazy," he told me, "but when that cat curled up in my lap and fell asleep, I knew in an instant that Erin was safe now, free from pain, and filled with peace. And that's how I felt, too," Paul said. "Peaceful. I had never known such peace before in my life."

I thought of Paul's words many times after that. And slowly the same peace he was feeling started to seep into my own heart and mind. Even now, months after the fire, I still don't know if the dog that saved my life was Beauty. I don't even know if the dog I saw that night was real.

Nor do I know for sure if I really saw Ian that night. Maybe he was just part of the dream I was having before the fire woke me up. Maybe Ian and Beauty were both simply part of the dream.

Or maybe they were real.

I do know one thing, however: I know that Beauty has forgiven me for what happened that day at the park. I know that Ian has forgiven me, too, for not being more concerned about his early symptoms. But I've learned something even more important from my experience.

When you sweep away everything else—the pain, the remorse, the guilt—nothing brings more peace than forgiveness. Especially when the one you forgive is yourself.

THE END

LAST DAYS WITH
MY DAUGHTER
A mother's heartbreaking good-bye

My story is one that no mother should ever have to tell. It's the story of a pain so unbearable that I had no will to survive. It's the story of grief so dark and overwhelming that I knew there was never going to be light, or laughter, or joy, again. It's the story of being forced to stare into the abyss, with no chance of going back. This is the story of how my little girl died.

Even before Emma was born, I loved her with all my heart. Scott and I had been married for six years and had almost given up on having a baby. Then there had been a missed period and my hopes began to soar. I kept it to myself, remembering two disappointments early in our marriage. Finally, after two more weeks, I bought a pregnancy test kit. It was positive.

My heartbeat accelerated with the actual possibility that Scott and I were going to have a child. Still, I was hesitant to tell him. What if the test was wrong?

Scott came from a big family of eight children and his five married siblings all had kids. He'd been so excited those times I was "late" early on in our marriage, certain that we would be the next to have a baby. Each time I'd had to disappoint him.

So even though I longed to share this news, waiting another week or two seemed best. I had no desire to build up my husband's hopes only to dash them again.

One week later, I felt as though I'd burst if I didn't tell him. Just to be sure, I took another pregnancy test. For the second time, it was positive. And that lovely early spring day, with birds singing and flowers budding all around, seemed the perfect time to tell him.

I went out on the back porch where Scott had just finished cleaning and hanging our porch swing. I'd wrapped the pregnancy test kit in fancy paper, topped with a huge ribbon. Barely able to wait another minute, I'd handed it to Scott without a word.

He looked at me quizzically. "A present for me? It's not my birthday, or our anniversary. Why a present today? Have I forgotten something?"

"Just open it," I said, trying to control my urge to jump up and down and shout the words out loud.

He unwrapped the box, then moved the tissue paper away from the plastic test kit.

"What the heck is this?" he asked, lifting it out of the tissue. Then the realization dawned in his eyes. We hadn't used one in a lot of years but he remembered. He looked at it, then at me. "It's positive."

I nodded as tears began to stream from my eyes. "You're going to be a daddy."

He whooped, picked me up, spun me around the porch then abruptly stopped. "Oh, gosh, I shouldn't be swinging you. Did I hurt you, Jennifer? Oh, what was I thinking?"

I laughed and kissed him. Then he took my hands in his and ever so gently led me to the swing. When we sat down, he brushed a kiss as soft as butterfly wings across my lips, then tenderly placed his hand on my still flat stomach. "He or she is in there, growing already, right?"

"Yes," I answered. "We're going to have a baby."

His eyes had a look of wonder that made me feel so precious. "And this time it's really going to happen," he murmured.

Nodding, I told him this was the second test I'd done because I wanted to be sure before telling him. "And I've already made an appointment with an obstetrician."

The next few days were exciting as we told family and friends. Since I was an only child, my parents were thrilled with the news that their first grandchild was on the way. Even my in-laws were excited to be having their eleventh grandchild. And Scott's siblings were happy to be adding a new member to the clan.

From the first day the doctor confirmed my pregnancy, until the actual day our baby was born, Scott and I vacillated between unbridled joy and irrational fear. We'd waited so long and combined with the joy of feeling that first flutter of life, there was an undercurrent of uncertainty, the possibility that something might go wrong.

But nothing went wrong. My pregnancy progressed without a hitch. I gained just the right amount of weight and the baby was active, yet slept enough to allow me to get my rest.

Scott and I took Lamaze classes to prepare for our baby's birth and we spent countless hours decorating a room for our own little prince or princess. We chose neutral colors, deciding not to ask the baby's sex at the two ultrasounds we had done. We were fascinated to see the child within me, a baby who came from our love.

"Look at that, Jennifer. It's the heart beating," Scott said, pointing to the spot the technician had shown him.

"The baby's got its foot in its mouth," the woman said, indicating the toes.

"Don't they usually suck their thumbs?" my husband asked.

"Often they do, but babies are inquisitive, even in the womb. This one is checking out its toes."

Scott and I watched each movement, entranced by the precious life inside me. "Oh, look!" he practically shouted. "The baby's smiling."

Sure enough the baby had turned, as though looking into the "camera" and smiled. The technician had seen it, too, and snapped a photo of that moment. The picture remained on our refrigerator until after our baby was born.

On that brilliant fall morning, the trees outside my hospital window glowed with dazzling shades of red and yellow. I remembered thinking what a glorious day it was for our child to be born.

Before long, Emma came into the world, waving her arms and screaming with a powerful set of vocal cords. She continued to cry as the doctor laid her on my belly. The sound truly was lovely, but I wanted to cuddle her so she wouldn't cry. Then Scott was cutting the cord and soon our daughter was in my arms. Still she cried, no matter how I hushed and cradled her.

"Good lungs," the doctor commented as the nurse went out to tell our parents their grandchild had arrived.

Scott had been snapping photos. He stopped and set the camera down, coming to kiss me again. "We have a daughter," he murmured, looking down at her with such love in his eyes. "Can I hold her?"

Nodding, I handed our squalling bundle of joy to my husband. "Come to Daddy," he said. As soon as he had her nestled in his arms, the most amazing thing happened. Our daughter stopped crying instantly and looked up at her daddy with eyes as expressive as his own. They remained connected that way for several seconds. It was almost like Emma was trying to figure out how she knew the man who held her so lovingly. Obviously she recognized her daddy's voice from the months he "talked" to her through my ever expanding tummy.

Our parents walked in at that moment. "Oh, look, Grandpa," Scott's mom said. "Your son has a baby in his arms." All four of them cooed over the baby, then Mom broke away to come and give me a kiss and hug. "She's the most beautiful baby I've ever seen, Jennifer," Mom said with tears in her eyes.

"Well, I thought so," I told her, "but figured I was prejudiced and you probably are, too."

"No, you're not," Scott's mom said as she came and kissed me. "We've had a lot of babies come into this family, Jennifer, and I'll deny it if you tell any of the other kids, but Emma truly is the most beautiful newborn I have ever seen."

"She's perfect," my dad said, coming over to kiss my cheek. Then it was Scott's dad coming over to thank me for giving him such a lovely new granddaughter.

Emma's birth day was a wondrous day, filled with love and family and balloons and flowers and parents who were overjoyed that she had finally arrived.

Every one of Scott's brothers and sisters, along with the spouses of the five who were married, filed through my hospital room that day, offering their love and congratulations. As an only child, I reveled in the joy of his big family. Emma had twelve aunts and uncles, each of them in love with her the minute she looked up at them with those big, bright eyes. Even my two youngest bothers-in-law, who were still in high school, were as enamored of their newest niece as their older siblings were. Emma was part of a very special family.

The next twelve months were filled with one joyful day after the next. Emma was not only beautiful, she was a good baby. After her squalling at birth, she rarely cried. And when she did it was for good reason. She was either hungry or wet and I soon learned to recognize her cries.

Scott and I found ourselves smiling at the darndest things. Even when she burped, it was reason to smile. And when she smiled at us, our hearts overflowed with happiness.

Of course, I shared more of those moments with Emma than Scott did because we'd decided while I was still in the hospital that I wouldn't go back to work. Scott told me he wanted me there for Emma and if we had to cut back on some things, it would be worth it. I wanted the same thing so there was no need for discussion. I'd be a stay-at-home mom. I knew how fortunate I was to be there with our daughter every day.

Through those first weeks and months of Emma's life, I couldn't get enough of looking at her. And she did the same. The one thing the entire family recognized about Emma was the intent way she gazed into your eyes. It was as though she wanted to communicate her feelings through them. They were so expressive, at times it felt like I was looking into the eyes of an adult, and I couldn't help wondering what she was thinking.

"I can't wait till you can talk," I'd say to her, knowing there would be some extraordinary conversations with this child of mine when she could put all that expression into her words as well as her eyes.

Even Scott's mom, who had ten other grandchildren, felt a special connection with Emma.

She and I were standing at the kitchen counter one day. I was making tea for us and my mother-in-law was getting the honey out of the cupboard. Emma was in her high chair contentedly chewing on a teething biscuit. She had been pretty intent on that biscuit until we sat down at the table with our teacups. Then she stopped chewing and looked at us, first at me, then at her grandmother. Emma stared at her for the longest time.

Finally, Scott's mom turned to me. "Jennifer, you know we have eleven grandchildren. Each is unique, but there's something truly special about your little Emma. Her eyes seem to be looking straight into my soul."

Nodding, I agreed. "I know. Scott and I have talked about that. It's as though she wants to see inside you. Such an intense gaze for such a little person."

My mother-in-law nodded. "Most of our grandkids would get really caught up in their toys or watching something on television, even when they were little, like Emma.

What we've noticed is how, no matter what she's doing, when someone walks into the room she turns away from the toys or television and looks right at that person. The depth of emotion I feel when she does that amazes me."

At that moment, Emma squealed with delight. It was as though she knew we were talking about her. And, naturally, we laughed along with her.

There were so many new things to be excited about during the first year of our daughter's life. Her first word was dramatic and thrilled Scott as she said "Da-da" before anything else. Probably because I talked to her all day long about her daddy.

The first tooth and the first time she sat up by herself were milestones to be recorded in her baby book. When she started propelling herself across the room with her feet and elbows we were almost as excited as she was. Then one day she pulled herself up on the edge of the sofa and looked back at me as though to say, "I did it, Mommy." She even repeated it for her daddy that night.

I thanked God and my husband every day for being able to be there with her for each of these wondrous achievements.

Of all the things that happened that first year, though, I think the biggest surprise was how quickly the year flew by.

Emma's first birthday party had to be the biggest party our neighborhood had ever seen.

It was another glorious autumn day, almost as perfect as the day she was born. We filled our house and yard and trees with balloons of every color. Emma had loved balloons from the first one she'd seen in my hospital room the day she was born. So, of course, her daddy made sure there were plenty for her party.

The entire family was there to celebrate our daughter's big day. Emma loved seeing everyone and giggled at all of her cousins who did their best to make her laugh. When it came time for the cake, she looked in awe at the flickering flame of the candle and then her eyes moved from one person to another as we all sang to her. It was an awesome celebration in honor of a full year with our adorable daughter.

Our second year with Emma brought even more achievements and I had to really hustle to keep up with her once she figured out how to walk. Oh, how exciting those first toddling steps were! And although she still "communicated" with her enormous eyes, the most exciting thing that second year were her precious words.

My dad was intent on getting her to say, "Grandpa," and he came over at least a day or two a week to work on it. "Say Grandpa, sweetheart," he'd coax. "Grandpa."

Her eyes would focus intently on his lips, then she'd look him in the eye as though to say she just couldn't do it yet.

One day, when Emma was just fourteen months old, my mom and dad came through the front door. Emma looked up, smiled and said, "Pa". My dad's face almost cracked from the huge smile that single word brought. It was a moment neither he nor I would ever forget.

We had our ups and downs of course, like anyone. Emma's first really bad cold with a high fever sent me into a panic. The pediatrician smiled as he must have smiled over mothers' worries for years. "She'll be fine. You're a good mother, Jennifer," he said, trying to reassure me.

And she was fine . . . that time.

After her first tumble outside on our driveway, I will never forget her looking up at me with such confusion in her eyes. By the time I got to her, she'd looked at her knee and started wailing. It was the first time she'd had a cut that bled and cleaning that scrape hurt me as much as it did her. She cried herself to sleep in my arms that day.

I knew she wasn't hurt badly but it seemed like she just couldn't understand what had happened. I remember whispering to her after she fell asleep that day: "You'll have lots more scrapes before you're married." It was something my mother had said to me when I had gotten hurt as a kid. Her words didn't really make me feel better but after a few years I knew what she meant. We all got scrapes and bruises and bumps in life and we got through them with the help of our mothers. But a time was coming when I wouldn't be able to help Emma.

We celebrated our daughter's second birthday with the family again and even more balloons that year since her daddy loved seeing her face light up with delight when she saw them. She'd bat them and hold the ribbons and squeal with delight.

Halloween that year was fun, too, as she loved, "dressing up" and could now toddle to our neighbors' doors and hold open her bag for treats. Not that she ate much candy, but she so enjoyed the jack o' lanterns on everyone's porches. She smiled and "talked" to each one of them.

Throughout those first two years of our daughter's life, people remained the most important thing to her. She would drop her toys when any of her aunts, uncles, cousins, or grandparents came through the door and run to them. If they picked her up, she'd pat their cheeks with both hands before giving them a kiss. Then she'd stop, even if it was for just a few seconds, and look into their eyes, as though to make sure everything was okay inside her favorite people, too. How I wish now that I had looked more closely to see if everything was okay inside of her.

Six months after her second birthday party, on a spring day as lovely as the day I chose to tell Scott I was pregnant, our world collapsed.

I'd gotten a couple flats of flowers to plant, along with some tomato plants because there was nothing like fresh summertime tomatoes. Mom came over to help me keep an eye on Emma. Our daughter now ran from one place to another so quickly I couldn't take time to sneeze without her taking off. She loved being outdoors but it was impossible to work on the garden and watch her, too.

The three of us were enjoying each other and the lovely spring weather when Emma started running across the yard. Mom took off after her. Emma slipped and slid right into a mud puddle that a spring rain had left in the middle of our yard.

I started to run, thinking she'd be scared by her fall, but Mom was already there and Emma was laughing. She laughed as she rubbed the mud on her cheeks and back into her hair and on her legs, like it was some wonderful lotion.

"A mud bath for Emma," Mom said, laughing.

"Guess she's going to get her bath early today," I added.

"Listen, Jennifer, you go ahead and finish up out here. I'll give her a bath."

"Are you sure, Mom? She can be a handful in the tub."

"I can manage just fine. You finish your planting."

About a half hour later, proud of what I'd accomplished, I headed inside to start dinner. I washed up at the kitchen sink then turned to go and look for Mom and Emma.

Mom was standing in the doorway, holding Emma. She just had a diaper on.

"Couldn't you find her clothes?" I asked.

Mom didn't say anything. She was looking at Emma and Emma was looking at her in that intent way she still had.

"Is something wrong, Mom?"

She smiled a half smile. "Probably nothing, but when this little one tried slipping away from me in the tub, she laid down on her belly. When I reached under to pick her up, I felt something, Jennifer. It feels like a lump, but not exactly. Don't know how to explain it. That's why I didn't dress her. Figured you could check it out for yourself."

The concern in Mom's voice was apparent. I went over to them. "Come here, you sweet thing," I said, taking her in my arms. I sat on a kitchen chair and gently pressed my fingers along her tummy. "I don't feel anything, Mom."

"I think it was the way she was lying. When I reached under her it was more noticeable."

Emma was staring into my eyes now and sensing some problem, she started to fuss. "Okay, sweet pea," I soothed. "Let's get you some clothes." Walking down the hall, I turned back to Mom. "I'll check her tonight when she's lying down in bed."

After dinner, Scott was playing with Emma while I did the dishes. I'd almost forgotten about my mother's concern until we were getting her ready for bed. When I laid her on her back to put her jammies on, I ran my hand down and across her stomach. My heart lurched. Mom was right. There was something. Not exactly a lump, though. It felt different, maybe flatter, rather than round like a ball as I'd been expecting.

"Scott, come check this out. Mom noticed it when she gave Emma a bath today. I never noticed it before."

By that time, Emma was ready to move on, but I coaxed her to lie still and Scott ran his hand over her stomach. The look on his face changed instantly. "What is it?" he asked.

"I have no idea. If it weren't for the way Mom picked her up out of the tub, we might never have noticed it."

"Did you call the pediatrician?"

"No. I couldn't feel it when she was sitting up. I told Mom I'd check her tonight. I just remembered."

"You call him first thing in the morning," he told me.

"I will, honey. You don't think it's anything serious, do you?"

He smiled but I could see it was a bit forced. "No. It's probably nothing. We'll just have the doctor check it out."

Dr. Connelly looked concerned as soon as he examined Emma. "There's definitely a mass here. I'm going to have you take Emma over to the hospital tomorrow." He wrote a name on a piece of note paper. "I'll tell them you're coming. You'll see Dr. Moore and he'll decide what, if any, tests need to be done."

His words shot a tremor of apprehension through my body.

"What do you think it is?" Scott asked.

"I really don't want to guess at this point. Let's wait and see what

Dr. Moore thinks and then we'll wait till we get the test results back."

I had a feeling he knew more than he was telling us. But I didn't push it and neither did Scott. Maybe we didn't want to hear any more.

That night we took more time putting our little one to bed. Scott read her an extra story and then I read her one, too. I didn't want to let go of her and found myself rocking her to sleep like I did when she was very small. I hadn't done it for a while but tonight it felt good to hold her, to look at her rosy cheeks and bright eyes. She didn't look sick. Emma couldn't be sick. She was normal and healthy.

I suddenly remembered that slide into the mud puddle. I hadn't told Scott about it the day before. "You should have seen her, Daddy. She was smearing mud on her cheeks and legs and in her hair like she was in a mud bath." I stopped suddenly overwhelmed with emotion. "Scott, what if something's wrong?"

"Don't think that way," he said. "Look at her. She's the picture of health. We'll get her checked and that will be it."

I slept restlessly that night, checking Emma each time I woke from a light sleep. Then I'd pray, right there in her room, looking down at her.

The next day we went into the pediatric wing of the hospital and handed the nurse the paper our pediatrician had given us. When we were shown into Dr. Moore's office, I tried to ignore the title on the door.

Scott glanced at me and I shook my head, pretending not to know what a pediatric oncologist was. I refused to think about it or why our doctor had sent us there.

After an examination and some blood work, which Emma was an angel for, the doctor sat down with us. He let Emma play with his stethoscope and smiled at her before beginning. "Mr. and Mrs. Miller, we're going to have to do more extensive tests. I suspect the mass we've felt is on her kidney. Are you familiar with ultrasound?"

"I had them when I was pregnant," I said, nodding.

"Right. Well this will be an abdominal ultrasound so we can get a better fix on this mass. She might need a CT scan and some X rays."

My heart was racing and I gripped Scott's hand, while still holding Emma on my lap.

Scott spoke first. "What happens after you do all these tests?"

"If the kidney is affected, we may have to do a biopsy or possibly surgery to remove the kidney."

"Surgery?" I wanted to shout but the word was barely a whisper. "She's only two years old."

"This type of tumor affects children in this age range, Mrs. Miller."

Scott was the first one to say the dreaded words. "Are we talking about cancer?"

136

The doctor nodded. "If my suspicions are correct, yes."

I felt the tears welling in my eyes and tried desperately to hold them back. I didn't want to frighten my baby. She was looking up at me with those eyes. I tried to smile. "It's okay, sweetheart," I said.

Scott had gone on asking questions but by then Emma was ready to get down and get moving. "Down, Mama," she said. I let her slide off my lap and walked behind her as she headed for a window, curiosity moving her forward.

Focusing on her pretty little face, I refused to listen to what Scott and the doctor were talking about.

Days later, I had to listen, though. The diagnosis was confirmed. The doctor had called it Wilms Tumor. The first step would be removal of the affected kidney. Only after the surgery would we know the extent of the cancer. Mom came with us that day and she took Emma out in the waiting room while the doctor talked to us. She was fighting back tears, too.

When the door closed behind her, I practically shouted: "How can a baby get cancer?"

"No one knows how or why," the doctor said. "But the statistics are there. One out of every three hundred and thirty kids will get some form of cancer by the time they're nineteen."

Statistics! He was quoting statistics, but this was about my baby, and she was not a statistic.

"She's not even three yet!" I cried, unable to hold back the tears. "Are you sure about this?"

"Yes," he answered simply. "But we won't know till the surgery if the cancer is contained or if there's any other involvement. Please let me emphasize that in most children the disease is localized and they have an excellent chance of a cure."

Relief flooded through me, like a cleansing rain after the heat of a summer day.

"Cure? You can cure my baby?"

Scott put his arm around me. "A cure is possible?"

"There's an excellent chance. Sixty percent of children with cancer survive. And as long as this is localized, Emma has a good chance of being in that percentage. Obviously, we haven't gone in yet so I can't make any promises. But hold onto the good thoughts. That will help to get you through no matter what happens."

Scott and I held each other that night after Emma had fallen asleep. We were holding onto those good thoughts. "She's going to be all right," Scott whispered. "She has to be."

Looking at our little girl asleep in her bed, I couldn't imagine life without her. Quickly I pushed that thought away. Emma would be fine. The doctor had told us that there was an excellent chance for a cure. That's what he'd said. That's what we'd told our parents and all the concerned family members who'd called. Several wanted to come over, but we asked to have this evening to ourselves, time with Emma.

"We'll need your support during and after her surgery," I'd told my mom and dad. And Scott had told his family members the same thing. They'd all promised to be there for us and we were grateful for their support and their prayers.

Scott and I prayed together that night, too. We prayed that Emma would be cured.

But she wasn't.

Those next few days are still a blur in my mind. Once the surgery was over, my only concern was caring for my baby and getting her through the post-surgical discomfort. That's what the nurses called it. But my baby was hurting. I knew her cries and those were cries of pain. They were able to help with medication, though, and soon she was smiling again. Such a happy little girl, despite being in a hospital and having all those strangers around.

The family helped by visiting and bringing her balloons. Each one that came into her room made her smile.

There had been talk of chemotherapy after the surgery and we were prepared for that, but when the pathology report came back and we'd talked to an entire team of specialists, the news was not good. Emma's cancer was not localized. Her lymph nodes were involved as well. "We'll want to treat her aggressively with chemotherapy and radiation," Dr. Moore said.

I heard his words but my mind refused to accept what he was saying. Scott was on one side of me, my dad on the other. Mom was crying and Scott's mother had gone out to the waiting room to tell the rest of the family.

"She can't die," I whispered, unable to stem the flow of tears down my cheeks.

"She's our baby and you can't let her die. Please," I begged. "Can't you do something?"

The oncologist took my hand in his. "Mrs. Miller, we will do everything in our power to save your little girl. With aggressive treatment there's always a chance of remission. You mustn't give up hope."

I clung to his hand that day and in the weeks that followed I clung to that hope.

Without our families and prayer, I'm not sure I could have gotten through the treatment. Thankfully, it was done on an outpatient basis. We were able to take her home after each treatment.

I'd hold her when she cried and sometimes I cried with her. The crying was almost easier than the times she'd just lay in my arms and look up at me with those beautiful eyes. Sometimes she'd ask me to read to her or to sing one of her favorite songs. Other times she was so worn out, she'd just stared up at me as though to say: "Why can't you help me, Mommy?"

Depending on where she fell asleep, there were nights I slept in her room and other nights I took her into our bed. Then Scott could put his arms around both of us and make me feel a little better.

My sweet little girl lost her soft hair, too. I was sitting with her one day, after her bath, which she still enjoyed, splashing and playing with her fish and ducks. I wrapped her up in a towel and was drying her when she reached up and ran her hand along my hair, then ran it over her bald head. She put her hands out and said, "All gone, Mama." Her eyes latched onto mine, but that time, there was something different there. She wasn't looking inside me. Emma was looking at me as though waiting for an answer to why her hair was gone.

The look in her eyes made me feel as though I'd betrayed her somehow. Like I'd made her go through all the things she'd had to endure in the past few months.

My heart ached for my baby and tears slipped from my eyes. Emma's hand came up and touched the wet spots on my cheeks. "Mommy hurt?" she asked, touching my stomach in the exact spot where her incision was.

I shook my head. "No, baby. Mommy's okay. Mommy doesn't hurt."

She smiled and snuggled up against me. In minutes, she was asleep. I got her pajamas on and laid her on our bed next to Scott. I needed us to all be together that night. I was so tired.

For a couple of months, things seemed better. Emma was almost like her old self.

She was thinner but now had about an inch or so of soft fuzz on her head. It was funny to see her sitting and watching her favorite television show, rubbing the downy soft growth.

Her team of doctors had told us remission was possible. We had reason to hope and we did.

We enjoyed taking our daughter to the zoo and to visit her cousins. She loved going over to "Pa's" and eating ice cream with my mom and dad. "We'll get you fattened up, angel," my mom told her, filling her bowl with her favorite chocolate ice cream.

Just as my mom and dad always had ice cream for Emma, Scott's parents always had a balloon on their porch so she'd see it when we pulled into their driveway. That always made her laugh.

Scott and I took our little girl to the local amusement park and rode with her on the merry-go-round. We went on picnics and to the lake where we rode paddle boats and laughed at her little girl giggles as she watched her daddy pedal furiously to keep the boat going. "Daddy go, go fast," she'd say, pointing to the other side of the lake, wanting to see the ducks. There were a batch of little ones and they followed their mother up on the shore. Emma "quacked" at them when we got closer and giggled when they seemed to answer her with their noisy quacking.

It was a good summer. Yet every night when I went to bed, I wondered if Emma would be with us the next summer.

During the first week of October, just a few days before her third birthday, Emma started coughing. When I took her temperature, I immediately called our pediatrician. We took her in and he gave us a couple of prescriptions and told us to call him in twenty-four hours if the temperature didn't go down.

She was so restless, whimpering in her bed. I sponged her off to cool her down, then took her in my arms and sat in the rocking chair we'd bought before she was born.

I held her all night long and when the first rays of dawn peeked through her window shade, her eyes opened. When she looked up at me, I thought my heart would break. The spark was gone from her eyes. She was listless and felt really hot. I called for Scott and asked him to call the doctor.

We were in the hospital in an hour. Emma was dehydrated and her fever was still raging. Pneumonia and other complications were ravaging her tiny body. Twenty-four hours later, she was on oxygen and so still.

I sat beside her bed, holding her hand, wishing it were me in that bed, instead of her. She'd barely begun to live and had so much potential.

Dr. Moore came in and checked her. He shook his head. "If we can't get this under control, there isn't much that we can do." He rubbed his forehead. "We've tried everything."

The defeat on his face told me more than I wanted to know. Emma wasn't going to make it. Our hope for her was fading.

"Can we take her home?" I asked, tears pooling in my eyes as Scott put his arm around me.

He sighed. "We can keep her more comfortable here, with the oxygen and medication."

I was torn between wanting her at home, but also wanting her to be free from pain.

The hospital was such a sterile-looking place, though. "Scott, we only brought her teddy with us. Could you go home and get her other stuffed animals? Let's try and make this place more friendly. Bring her music box, too, and anything else you think might make her smile again. I so want to see one more smile, Scott. Just one." I lost it then.

Unable to control the sobs, I stepped into the hall. Scott followed me. "No, Scott, go back in with Emma. Stay with her till I get this under control."

Minutes later, with a huge final sigh, I managed to stop the sobs that made my chest ache. I went back in the room and Scott took me in his arms. Our little girl looked lost in that bed. "Scott, she can't die like this. Please go and get her things. And tell your family and my mom and dad that they should come. Maybe take turns, work it out somehow."

Scott nodded. "I'll take care of everything. You take care of our little girl."

He was crying when he walked out of the room. I sat again and started to sing one of her favorite songs. "You are my sunshine, my only sunshine. You make me happy when skies are gray. You'll never know, dear, how much I love you. Please don't take my sunshine away." I barely got the last words out. How had we ever thought that it was a happy song?

I got as close as I could to my baby, holding her hand in one of mine and stroking her cheek with the other. "I'm here, baby. Mommy's here." I was so tired, I laid my head on the edge of the bed. Exhausted, I must have fallen asleep.

Hearing my mother's voice brought me out of a deep sleep.

"Oh, Jennifer, I'm sorry. I woke you."

"It's all right, Mom." I stood up to hug her and felt her tears on my cheek. Dad was right behind her and put his arms around both of us.

"Isn't there anything they can do?" he asked and I could see his eyes were red-rimmed from crying.

"They're keeping her comfortable, Dad. Why don't you sit down and talk to her? The nurses told me even though she appears to be unconscious, she may be able to hear."

So my dear, sweet father sat beside Emma. "Grandpa's here, sweetheart. I'm right here beside you."

Mom went and stood beside Dad. "Grandma's here, too, angel. I love you so much." Mom lost it and I ended up comforting her, doing my best not to fall apart again. I had to stay strong for Emma. If she woke up, I needed to be there for her.

Scott came into the room with a bag of stuffed animals and toys in one hand and a huge bunch of helium balloons in the other.

"Oh, Scott, she'll love the balloons," I said.

Right behind him came two of his brothers and their wives with more balloons. We hugged and they each went and kissed her and told her they loved her. The entire day was filled with family and hugs and prayers and more balloons. Everyone knew how much she loved them.

Scott begged me to go home and get some rest when everyone had finally left, but I couldn't leave. "I can't, Scott. If she opens her eyes, I have to be here."

"She may not, babe," he said softly.

"I know. But even if there's a chance."

He hugged me and kissed my cheek. "I'll go get us some coffee. It's going to be a long night."

"Scott, you could go home or at least go out and try and get some sleep on that couch in the waiting room."

"Nope. We're a family and family sticks together. I'll be right back."

Scott closed the door behind him, shutting out the hospital noises. Emma was so still. But she was surrounded by all her stuffed animals and didn't look quite so lost in that bed. Balloons of every color filled the room giving it a bit of added warmth.

I sat down again and started humming softly. When I'd come to the end of one song I'd tell Emma that I loved her, then start on another. I'd been gazing out the window as I hummed, watching the moon rise over a distant hill. When I looked back down at my baby, her eyes were open and she was watching me.

"Oh, baby, Mommy's here. Mommy loves you." She just kept looking at me. "I'm here, baby." I took her hand and stroked her cheek again.

"Juice. Want juice."

Her words were music to my ears. Minutes later after ringing the call button the nurse was there with apple juice and Emma drank every drop. Then she sighed and her eyes started to close.

"Oh, sweetheart, stay awake for another minute. Daddy will be right back. He'll want to see you."

She blinked, then looked across the room. "Balloons."

"Yes, all for you, Emma. Grandpa brought the one with the kitty and Grandma brought that one with the silly clown on it. Your cousins brought that big bunch over there and Daddy brought all the rest."

I turned back and she was looking at me again. There was just the hint of a smile on her face. Almost as though it was too much of an effort to smile. But her eyes held mine. "Emma loves Mommy."

Gently, I touched her cheeks, unbelievably moved by her words. "Mommy loves Emma, too."

The next instant she turned onto her side and slipped her hand around her favorite teddy bear, then gathered a stuffed rabbit Scott had bought her in her other arm. With a soft sigh she closed her eyes again. I didn't have the heart to try and keep her awake. She looked so terribly tired.

The nurse told me it was a good sign that she was awake and

actually drank the juice. "Never give up on that little one," she said. "I've seen miracles in this place."

When Scott came back he was thrilled to hear she'd been awake and at the same time sad that he'd missed talking to her. He hugged me and buried his face in my hair. "Now I understand why you don't want to leave. I'm so sorry I did."

"She'll wake up again. She will, Scott."

For two more days we waited but Emma didn't wake up again. Sometimes her eyes would flutter and we thought she was going to come out of it but it never happened.

The family continued to come and visit, to bring food, a change of clothes for Scott and me.

One of the nurses came in on that third night. "You have the support of a wonderful family," she said. "Doctors can only do so much in cases like Emma's but you always have prayer. I'm sure your family's praying. Keep on having faith. I'll pray, too," she added.

But our prayers didn't help Emma.

When I woke up that fourth morning in the hospital the sun was pouring into Emma's room. It was a spectacular autumn day, and the trees outside the windows glowed with brilliant autumn color.

All of our parents came in early that morning, hugging us and then sitting beside Emma, talking to her.

The days had all blended together for me and I didn't realize until family members started arriving with wrapped packages that it was Emma's birthday. She was three years old. Born in this same hospital on another sunshine bright autumn day. Last year on this day, we'd celebrated her second birthday. She was so alive, so excited by all the family gathered around her, singing and bringing gifts and her favorite balloons. Just one short year ago, Emma had a wonderfully bright future. Now she lay as still as death in a hospital room two floors above the maternity suite where she was born.

Dr. Moore's entrance broke through my thoughts. He seemed surprised to see all the people and gifts and even more balloons than usual.

"It's Emma's third birthday," Scott explained.

"Emma has quite a loving family," the doctor said. Then he asked if he could talk to Scott and me in the hall.

He had that somber look on his face that meant it was bad news. "You know we've been monitoring all of Emma's vital signs. This morning her blood pressure's dropped dangerously low and her heartbeat's erratic. I just want you to be prepared."

"No," I said, shaking my head. "She can't die on her birthday. Dear God, please don't let her die on her birthday."

The doctor took my hand. "Mrs. Miller, Emma is such a precious little girl. I would do anything to keep her alive longer. But there's nothing more we can do. You need to let your family know that it could be any time."

"Oh, no, Scott!" I cried. He held me while I sobbed. I couldn't believe it, even though we'd known she might die. All I could think of at that moment was the fact that I would never see her eyes again, those beautiful, expressive eyes. How could I live without ever seeing her look at me again?

I hadn't seen my dad come out and didn't know he was there until he spoke. "Has anyone considered organ donation if anything happens?" He choked out the words.

"Dad, I can't think of such a thing. Don't even ask me to." I turned to Scott, unable to hold back another round of weeping.

My father came and put his arms around Scott and me. "Jennifer, I don't want to upset you. But if Emma's death is inevitable, let's not allow it to be for nothing. She loves people, you know that. If she could help someone else live . . ." He couldn't finish, his voice cracked and then he just stood there holding onto us and cried.

Dr. Moore cleared his throat. "There is something you should know. In cases like Emma's, where the cancer has spread, we really can't use any of the vital organs."

Although I'd hated it when Dad mentioned donating Emma's organs, the doctor's words stunned me. I think, in the back of my mind, I'd always thought we could help someone else live if Emma had to die.

"She can't help anyone?" I asked.

"The only possibility, and we would have to run some tests first, would be the corneas. Since the cancer never spread to the brain, it's possible they could be used."

Scott and Dad and I all looked at each other. Without a word, we all knew exactly what the other was thinking. Emma's eyes, the part of her that touched so many in her short life, could be used to help someone else see again. The thought of it sent goose bumps through my body. We immediately agreed to allow the doctor to use Emma's corneas if at all possible.

When I'd cried to God earlier asking that Emma not die on her birthday, that prayer was answered. Emma took her last breath at twelve-ten a.m., ten minutes after her birthday was over.

Scott and I were beside her and her grandparents and two uncles were still there when the life went out of our precious child. We'd said our good-byes and told her we loved her long before midnight, knowing her breathing was labored and time was short.

Our prayer all through that long night was simply for her to have a peaceful death. I'd heard of dying patients gasping for their last breath and I couldn't bear the thought of Emma struggling like that. Blessedly, that prayer was also answered. Emma's final breath left her softly. She simply slipped quietly from life to death.

The next three days passed in a flurry of activity that left little time to mourn our loss. So much had to be done. The worst of it was picking out a casket and her clothes. I chose her pink dress with little flowers around the neckline. She'd worn it on Easter and loved those little flowers. "Pretty, Mommy," she'd said, looking in the mirror.

The decision to place her teddy bear, and the bunny she'd held that last conscious moment of her life, in the casket, broke my heart. I was torn between wanting her to have them and wanting to keep them myself. I wanted to sleep with them, to remember her arms around them, to smell her little girl smell on them. But in the end, I knew they were hers and should go with her.

At the funeral home, people were greeted not by the overwhelming scent of flowers that usually filled these places, but by colorful balloons. Emma had received countless "bouquets" of balloons. One of my dear friends told me she imagined balloons carrying Emma up to heaven. The image, though a pleasant one, made me cry.

There's no easy way to say good-bye to a child, especially such a young child. But that was all there was left to do. Our little girl's short life was over. All that was left to do was to put her body to rest.

Autumn leaves swirled around the gravesite, reminding me of Emma running through our yard the year before, trying to catch the leaves as they fell from the trees.

As our minister read the words of the twenty-third psalm, Scott was on one side of me and my mother on the other. Mom held my arm and Dad wrapped his arms around both of us from behind. He was trying to muffle his crying without much success.

Finally, the service was over. People began to move back to their cars. I couldn't go. How could I leave my baby there?

"Come on, honey," Scott said.

Mom started to turn but I didn't budge. "Jennifer, we have to go now," Mom said.

I shook my head, tears dripping onto my jacket. "I can't leave her, Mom. I can't leave my baby here."

Scott broke down then and Dad put his arm around Scott's shoulder, trying to comfort him.

Mom put her hand under my chin and turned my face toward hers. "She's not here, sweetheart. She always was my angel, now she's with all the angels in heaven. She's not here."

Mom's words helped me to ease away from the grave. I liked thinking of Emma in heaven with the angels, not there in the ground. Emma would like the angels.

The hardest thing in the days after the funeral was having nothing to do. Oh, I cooked for Scott and cleaned. But there was no one to read to, no one to play with. No one to sing to or to rock with. No one to hold my hand while we walked to the park. No one to take care of. No one to make me laugh.

Our families tried but no one could take away the awful emptiness inside me. A piece of my heart was missing and I couldn't imagine ever enjoying anything in this life without it.

I couldn't even bear to look at photos of Emma. They tore me up inside.

A little more than a month after Emma's death, shortly before Thanksgiving, I went out to our mailbox to get the mail. I shuffled through it and came across an envelope with an unfamiliar return address.

I opened the envelope and found a "thank you" card and a letter inside. When I began to read the letter my heart skipped a beat.

Dear Mr. & Mrs. Miller,

I've been told that it's not wise to contact your donor's family but I insisted on at least being able to send you this card of thanks. At this time of year when we are thankful for all we have received, I am having the best Thanksgiving of my life.

When I was only six years old, I lost my sight in an accident. And now, through your unselfish gift, I can see again. The world is a beautiful place, far more beautiful than I had remembered it as a child. It seems like so little to say thank you for this great gift of sight. And it feels somehow wrong to be this happy when I know you both are probably having the saddest Thanksgiving of your lives.

I was told my cornea came from a small child and my heart ached for both of you, knowing you must be missing your little one so much. Perhaps this letter will only add to your pain, but I pray that it doesn't. I pray that you'll know that each time I open my eyes in the morning and see the trees and the sky and the sun and my husband and children, I thank your child for this precious gift of sight. Now, I thank you, as well. Your child will live always in my heart and mind.

My husband and I tried to explain how I was able to see again to our four-year-old son. We told him that a little child like him got very sick and went to heaven with Jesus. He looked up at me and thought for a moment. "Mommy," he asked, "are you seeing with an angel's eyes?"

He was exactly right. I am seeing through the eyes of an angel and I pray you know the Lord and also know your little one is with Him. She is an angel now and will live in my heart until one day I meet her in heaven.

Thank you for this precious gift. Try not to be too sad on this

Thanksgiving holiday. I'm sure you are thankful for the time you had with your child, though it was short. Let the good memories remain in your hearts and do your best to allow those memories to ease the pain of those last sad days.

Thank you again for your angel's gift to me.

My tears spilled over long before I read the signature. I hadn't thought about the donated corneas for a long time. The act of donating them had been lost in my struggle to get through each day without Emma. Now this woman, by thanking us for the gift of eyesight, was giving us an even more precious gift.

I went and dug out a box of photos that I'd packed away in a drawer, unable to bear the pain when I looked at them. Now I rejoiced in the images, spreading them all around me as I sat on her bedroom floor.

In every one of those photos I found a memory, a good memory of precious times with our little girl. Memories I could always hold close to my heart until one day I, too, would see her again.

I picked up the last photo of Emma that we'd had taken at the mall. She had a beautiful smile on her face, but what caught my attention were those beautiful eyes of hers. Emma's eyes . . . an angel's eyes.

THE END

I FELL FOR
MY NOSY NEIGHBOR
I tried to shut out the world,
but he opened my heart

"I'm sorry, Mrs. Lewis, but I'm in the middle of sewing a slipcover and I just don't have time for coffee."

Mrs. Lewis is small, plump, and motherly looking, and she was giving me a motherly look just like my own mother used to. "Michaela, you spend too much time alone up here in this apartment. Why don't you take a break and come down to my kitchen and have coffee? The kids like your company and the slipcover will be waiting for you when you get back."

"Thanks, but I can't."

"See you later, then."

I saw the hurt in her eyes before she turned away and I wanted to call after her, "Mrs. Lewis, I've changed my mind. Is the offer still good?"

But I didn't.

I shut my apartment door and went back to my sewing machine.

But then I was restless. Instead of continuing to sew, I paced around the room and finally decided to make myself some coffee. Drinking coffee alone isn't the same as sharing a cup with someone, though, and my cozy apartment seemed so empty and lonely that I shivered. If Mom and Dad had been alive, I would've called them that night and said, "Please come and visit me. I'm here in the city in the middle of twenty thousand people and I'm dying of loneliness."

I think I made things worse for myself by choosing the apartment that I did. The Mortons own a huge, three-story Victorian house in a quiet neighborhood about five miles from downtown. The house has enough room for twice as many Mortons as there are. There's Mr. and Mrs. Morton—the mother and father—I didn't know their first names. The Morton kids are like stair steps: Vanessa, Angie, and Enid were in high school and junior high at the time; Scott worked part-time and went to the city university part-time; and Carl and Anthony were ten and twelve and heavy into baseball and football.

Everyone in the family had a bedroom of his or her own except for Mr. and Mrs. Morton, of course, and there's also a family room, a kitchen, a living room, a library, and a huge basement under the house. I knew because Mrs. Morton gave me a guided tour and told me all about her family when I rented the third floor apartment.

My place was on the third floor, but it wasn't your typical attic apartment. It used to be a ballroom and a servant's quarters in the old days when there were servants. When the Mortons bought the place they remodeled the third floor into an apartment. I just had a living room, kitchen, and bathroom—but they're elephant sized. My living room was really a living room and bedroom combined, and I could've fit a king-size bed in it instead of my sofa bed if I'd wanted to.

Besides my living room furniture, I had a room divider and a sofa bed, a chest of drawers, and a deep closet in my living room/bedroom. The kitchen would comfortably hold the dining room set that I hoped to own someday as well as my round, oak kitchen table, its chairs, and the matching sideboard that once belonged to Mom. I refinished them for her a few months before the accident. I even kept my rocking chair in the kitchen because its cheerful red-and-white checkered cushions fit in so well with the red-and-white checkered curtains that I'd made for the windows and the matching tablecloth on the table.

There was plenty of room for me to sit in the rocker on the braided rug and remember Mom and Dad and Bruce or listen to the family noises that sifted up through the downstairs ceiling. How I envied the Mortons for being such a big, happy family. They had each other and I didn't have anyone.

I moved to the city to escape my past. I grew up in a small town called Heartsville. We were a happy family: Mom, Dad, my brother, Bruce, and me. I didn't have any big ambitions other than marrying Frank, my high school sweetheart, and settling down in Heartsville. I wanted to always live near Mom and Dad so that they could enjoy their grandchildren. I wanted to be near them as long as they lived.

What I didn't know was how short their lives would be. The night of my graduation from high school we had a party at Kylie's Restaurant, a big place outside of town that had a hall that could hold all of our friends and relatives. It was quite a party and it had lasted until the wee hours of the morning. Frank and I decided to drive ahead in his car and Mom and Dad and Bruce followed us in the station wagon. It was loaded down with leftover food and some folding chairs that they had to return. They followed us, but they never made it home. A drunk driver crossed the centerline and hit them head on. There was hardly anything left of them to bury.

The hurt in my heart grew like the rotten spot in an apple. Instead of going on with my life, I stopped it cold. I cut Frank out like he was a bad spot in an apple, too. I left without even telling him good-bye and later Aunt Mabel wrote that he'd married Carol Avery, one of our high school classmates. I told myself that I didn't care—that loving just means hurting. I had to seal myself off so that I'd never be hurt again.

I'd been in the city for a year and I didn't know anyone except the Mortons. I tried not to get close to them, but they're such a nice family that it's hard not to like them. There's something special about Scott Morton, too. I like the way he smiles and the way he listens when his Mom talks to him like he really loves and respects her. I think a man who respects his mother is the right kind of man to love and marry. But I kept reminding myself that I couldn't get close to people because caring hurts too much, so I kept to myself. I filled in some of my time by using part of the salary that I made as a secretary in a small insurance office to buy old, painted-up furniture and refinish it. That took a lot of time because I did it the old-fashioned way.

My project at the time was an old chest of drawers that I'd bought at a rummage sale for twenty-five dollars. I brought it home and spent every night for a week sanding off the old varnish and layers of green paint that were on the outside. The sounds of my sanding, moving the chest, and moaning and groaning about the green paint must have carried downstairs because on Friday night there was a knock at my door.

"Now what? I've got enough trouble with this darn green paint!" I muttered.

Whoever it was knocked again.

"All right, all right," I yelled. "I'm coming."

I hurried to the door and threw it open. Scott Morton stood there, grinning down at me. "Uh, hi," I said.

"Hi yourself, Michaela." His warm brown eyes searched mine. "I heard a lot of commotion up here and I thought something might be wrong. Are you all right?" he asked.

"I'm fine. Sorry if I made too much noise."

He glanced around me at the chest of drawers. "Oh, you're refinishing it. Can I take a look?"

"I just started it," I said, stepping back to let him see my work.

He ran his fingers over the top of the chest that I had just sanded to a satiny-smooth finish. "You did a good job with that sandpaper," he said. "But I know something that takes paint off a lot quicker and easier."

My defenses snapped into place right away. Who does he think he is telling me how to refinish my chest? "What's that?" I muttered, not looking at him.

"It's called EZ-Strip. You just paint it on with a brush and it softens up all of the old paint without hurting the wood. Then all you do is take a scraper and scrape off all of the gunk. It's a good idea to spread newspapers around and wear old clothes, cause it's messy. But it works."

I was excited in spite of myself. "Hey, that sounds like a good thing to use. Sanding off the old finish takes a long time and I'm developing sander's elbow."

He smiled at me. Funny, I've never noticed how brown his eyes are until today, I thought.

"I'll tell you what," he said. "I've got a can of EZ-Strip downstairs because I refinished an old table for Mom. Why don't you come down with me and get it? Try it out and then tell me what you think."

"I can't—" I began.

But Scott wouldn't take no for an answer. He practically dragged me downstairs.

"Scott, we just can't barge in on your Mom like this. She's probably busy doing something in the house. I don't want her to think I'm a pest."

He smiled at me. It was a smile that made my heart flutter. "You could never be a pest," he said.

I didn't know what to say to that, so I just followed him. Mrs. Morton and the girls were all glad to see me. When Mrs. Morton found out that I was refinishing furniture she insisted on showing me the table that Scott had refinished for her. I ran my hands over its dark, gleaming surface.

"You did a beautiful job, Scott. I wish I could do as well," I said.

He smiled at me. "You will. It just takes practice and I can tell by looking at your work that you have the patience it takes to get the practice."

Mrs. Morton winked at me. "Scott's such a good boy. He'll make some lucky girl a wonderful husband."

Ten-year-old Anthony snickered. "Mom means you. She told Scott that he ought to go upstairs and meet you. Are you two going to get married?"

Scott turned beet red. "Anthony, will you dry up?"

All I could think about was making Scott feel better. Before I realized what I was saying, I told him something that I never intended to tell anyone. "Don't worry about it, Scott. My brother, Bruce, used to ask all of my dates when we were getting married and if he could come with us on our honeymoon. Then he'd tell them how ugly I look in the morning or show them my baby pictures."

"I didn't know that you have a brother," Mrs. Morton said. "You never talk about yourself, Michaela."

I was horrified. I'd managed to push thoughts of Bruce out of my mind for so long and then the memories came flooding back. Those memories made tears rush to my eyes and sobs catch in my throat.

"I've got to go," I choked. "Thanks for everything."

Mrs. Morton put her arm around me and I remember thinking

151

how much she was like Mom. "We didn't mean to make you feel bad, Michaela. Anthony was just kidding. He's always doing that."

Her sympathy finished me off. I ran out the door sobbing. Oh, God, I thought. Why did Mom and Dad and Bruce have to be snatched out of life so suddenly and violently? Why does life have to hurt so much?

Back inside my apartment, I threw myself on the couch and I couldn't stop crying. All of the months of pent-up grief were released in a flood of tears that left me limp and shaken. I was crying so hard that I didn't even hear the pounding on the door. The next thing I knew there was a hand on my shoulder. Scott was standing over me. He patted my shoulder. "We care about you, Michaela. Please, let us help. Come downstairs and have a cup of coffee with Mom and me."

"I can't," I sobbed.

"You can." Mrs. Morton's voice came from behind Scott's shoulder.

"I just need to be alone," I sobbed.

"Let us help, Michaela," Mrs. Morton said. "We all need each other, you know. No one can go through life totally alone."

"Oh, yes they can!" I said. "I can. That's the only way to keep from getting hurt."

"You're wrong, Michaela, and I hope you realize that before you're a lonely, bitter old lady. I'm going back downstairs now. If you need anything, call."

I heard Mrs. Morton go back downstairs, but Scott was still there, staring at me. I felt his eyes like a caress across my forehead.

"Whoever he was, he really hurt you, Michaela. I'm sorry. Won't you let me be your friend?"

"I don't need anybody," I said. "Go away."

"You know where I am if you change your mind," Scott said. He patted my shoulder.

I listened to his footsteps on the stairs and then silence surged around me again. You dummy, I told myself. Why don't you let him be your friend? And surely you don't have anything to fear from Mrs. Morton. But another part of me argued the opposite. No, you're too interested in that family. You care too much already. Do you want to get hurt again?

The next day at work I just couldn't concentrate on what I was doing. After I'd typed the same letter three times, Mr. Graham, my boss, said, "Michaela, you don't look well this morning. Why don't you take the rest of the day off? Go home and relax. You've earned a day off. You haven't missed a day in the year you've been with me."

It didn't take me too long to agree, and I felt a trickle of warmth at the concern in his eyes and voice.

First, I planned to sew some curtains for the living room when I got home, but then I looked at the chest of drawers standing there like an island in the middle of a sea of newspapers. I decided to do some more sanding. I wanted to go down and ask Scott for his EZ-Strip and apologize for being such a wet blanket. My feet turned toward the front door, but the withdrawn part of me with the high brick wall around my heart wouldn't let me. I picked up a piece of sandpaper and started sanding the chest. Then the telephone rang.

"Who could that be?" I asked out loud. No one ever called me. In fact, I'd been thinking about having my telephone taken out, I used it so seldom. It seemed to be an unnecessary expense. I picked up the receiver with trembling fingers. "Hello?"

"Michaela, this is Mr. Graham. I'm calling just to make sure that you're all right. I'm worried about you. You've been so pale and quiet lately. Is there anything I can do to help?"

I gulped. "I'm fine, Mr. Graham. Thank you for worrying, but I'm just fine."

"I have an invitation for you, Michaela. Mrs. Graham and I would like you to come over for dinner on Sunday if you're feeling better. We'd like you to meet our son, William, and see our new house. How about it?"

"Uh, thanks for the invitation, Mr. Graham, but I don't think so."

"If you change your mind, let me know. We'd really love to have you."

"Thanks, Mr. Graham. I'll see you tomorrow."

I kicked the table leg. Why do people have to care about me? I raged to myself. Don't they know that caring makes a person terribly vulnerable? I'd just picked up my sandpaper again when I heard a rap on my door. I opened it and Scott stood there smiling uncertainly.

"I brought you up the EZ-Strip," he said. "I thought you might need it today."

I stared at the EZ-Strip, refusing to meet his eyes. "Thanks. I will be able to use it."

He handed me the can and a paintbrush, and as he did, our hands brushed and I felt an electric spark leap between us. Instead of sending him back downstairs, I found myself stammering, "Won't you sit down and have some coffee? It's really nice of you to help me out."

"I like refinishing furniture, too," he said, smiling shyly at me. "Do you know it took me two months to do Mom's table?"

"It looks like an antique," I said. "It looks like she got it somewhere for hundreds of dollars."

He smiled. "She got it at a garage sale for thirty dollars. I just refinished it."

"You really did a good job," I told him.

153

He laughed. "Almost too good. Now she wants me to refinish her dining-room table. Do you know what that looks like?"

"Probably like it stood out in the rain for ten years," I said.

"I moved it down to the garage because she didn't want her dining room messed up." He looked around at my newspapers and sandpaper. "You sure keep your work area neat, Michaela."

"I just don't want to mess up your mother's floor and get into trouble with her," I said.

"Why don't you come down with me and take a look at my table? You could give me some pointers."

I found myself agreeing and we walked down the stairs to the basement together, still laughing and talking. He switched on the basement light. "It's over here," he said. "Be careful you don't fall."

He took my hand and led me through some stacks of boxes. I didn't even notice where we were going because all I could concentrate on was the touch of his fingers on mine. When we came to the table he let go of my hand and I felt cold and alone again. He switched on the overhead light and I gasped. The old table was only half refinished, but it already looked beautiful. I ran my hand over the silky smoothness of its top and smiled up at Scott. "You put a lot of work into this already," I said.

"Be careful that you don't get a splinter in your finger," he said. He gazed into my eyes and I couldn't look away. I was lost in the brown depths of his eyes, lost in their warmth. The next thing I knew his lips met mine and we were kissing with a passion that I didn't know I could feel. I don't know how long the kiss lasted, but it seemed like forever. Finally, I broke it off and ran upstairs.

"Michaela, wait!"

I heard him behind me and I ran up the stairs to get away from him, but he was too quick for me. He caught my shoulder when I was at the door of my apartment. He whirled me around to face him and took my hands.

"Michaela, I'm not sorry that I kissed you, but I'm sorry that you think it's so terrible. I'm sorry that you think I'm so terrible."

"I don't think you're terrible, Scott. Now, please, let me go in," I quavered. A hard knot in my heart was dissolving and I could barely keep myself from melting into his arms.

My embarrassment must've shown in my eyes because he dropped my hands and muttered, "I'm sorry I bothered you."

I watched him go down the stairs and I wanted to call him back so badly that I could feel my lips saying his name. But I didn't; I couldn't let him know that I cared.

The apartment I loved to be alone in so much was too quiet and empty when he left. You're being a dummy, I scolded myself. When will you start remembering that getting attached to someone spells trouble? Now get to work on your chest of drawers. That's one thing you can do without getting emotionally involved.

I brushed on the EZ-Strip. The directions said to let it set for ten minutes, so I watched a half-hour soap opera on TV just to give the stuff enough time to work. After I saw Paulina through her daily troubles, I took my scraper and started scraping the gook off the chest. "This stuff really works," I said to the empty room. "This old paint's coming off real easy—even the green coat."

I was so excited about how easy the job removing the paint was turning out to be that I stuck my face a little too close to the wood. The next thing I knew, I had a gob of EZ-Strip and paint in my left eye. The pain was horrible.

"It hurts," I moaned. "Mom, Dad, Bruce—help me! Help!" I screamed.

There was no answer. What was I going to do? Blindly, I stumbled to the phone. Mr. Graham would help me, but I couldn't see to dial the office number. Scott, maybe Scott would help me. No, I'd been so rude to Scott that he probably never wanted to speak to me again. The pain kept getting worse. I couldn't see at all. I felt my way along the wall to the front door. I flung it open and shouted down the stairs, "Scott, help me!"

There was no answer. There's never any answer when you desperately need help. You should know that by now, my cynical self said. Just take care of it yourself. Drive yourself to the emergency room at St. Joseph's. Another part of me said, You can't drive when you can't see. You need someone. You've got to give people a chance. You've got to let them know that you need help before you can expect them to do anything.

"Oh, it hurts," I moaned. "Scott, please help!" I grabbed the stair railing and eased myself slowly down, step by step. The burning had gone deeper into my eye. Am I going blind? Is that stuff eating away my eye? I wondered. My feet hit the bottom of the stairs with a thud. Slowly, I stumbled to the Morton's door. Would they want to help me? I pounded on their door. "Please, help me!"

I felt the door open and a figure stood in the doorway. I tried to see who it was, but I couldn't see out of my left eye at all and my right eye was clouded with tears of anguish and fear.

"Michaela, what's wrong?" Scott's voice was full of concern.

"I got some EZ-Strip in my eye and it hurts terribly. I know I'm bothering you, but please, help me."

I heard footsteps behind Scott and Mrs. Morton said, "Michaela, what happened?"

Scott put his arm around me. "She's hurt, Mom."

Scott led me to the kitchen and flooded my injured eye with cold water. "I'm sorry I was so rude," I sobbed. "I'll tell you why I acted like that if you want to know."

"Of course I want to know, but right now we have to take care of your eye, Michaela."

"Will I go blind, Scott? It hurts an awful lot."

"I won't let you go blind," he promised.

Mrs. Morton was back. "I called the emergency room at St. Joseph's Hospital. They're waiting for us. Let's go."

Before I knew what was happening, Scott picked me up in his arms. "We're on our way," he said.

Mrs. Morton patted my arm. "Don't worry, Michaela. Everything is going to be all right."

"I'm such a nuisance," I said. "I'm—"

"Michaela, shut up!" Scott murmured in my ear. "We care about you and you're not a nuisance. Quit worrying and concentrate on getting that eye back in shape."

I quit worrying and concentrated. With Scott and the rest of the Mortons rooting for me, what else could I do?

I was so lucky! The doctors cleaned all of the gook out of my eye and there isn't any permanent damage. I had to wear a patch for a few days, but that's all. And my boss, Mr. Graham, I mean, Tom, is a good friend of mine now and I often baby-sit for his son, William, when he and his wife go out.

I expected to see Scott the week after my accident, but it was Mrs. Morton who came upstairs every day to check on me and help me with my chores. I wanted to ask her about Scott, but I choked back my questions. After all, I had my pride. If he didn't want to see me, I wasn't going to throw myself at him. Then one night I was sitting watching a boring TV show around my patch when I heard a knock at the door.

"Come in, it's open," I said, marveling at how my attitude had changed in a just a week. Now I was glad to hear people knocking at my door.

"Michaela, how are you doing?"

My heart leaped. I'd been waiting especially for this person. "Scott, I've been waiting for you to come." I could feel myself blushing, but I didn't take it back. I really was glad to see him. He slid beside me on the couch.

"I would've come sooner, but I was making the arrangements."

"Arrangements for what?" I asked him.

"Arrangements for our shop in the basement. I already put the notice for the Grand Opening in our little Shopper and I've got a space cleared for your chest when you finish it. We can use that as a floor

156

model until we get some other pieces done."

"But Scott—" I started to say, but his lips came over mine and silenced me. In fact, as our kiss deepened, I forgot the questions that had been in my mind. Instead, I enjoyed the sensations sweeping over my body.

Scott wrapped his arms around me and pulled me close. "Michaela, I love you."

"Scott, how can you love me? We don't know each other very well."

"Now is the time to get better acquainted." He smoothed the hair back from my forehead and guided wisps of it away from my eye patch. "Besides, I know all I need to know. You're beautiful and sweet and smart and you want a big family."

"How did you know that?" I asked him, astonished.

"Because we're on the same wavelength, Michaela. Kiss me again and I'll show you what I mean."

I kissed him, and this time I saw fireworks and heard them, too. "Wow! I didn't know that kissing someone could be like this."

He cuddled my head on his shoulder. "Be careful of your patch."

"I think I'll take it off just for a minute," I said.

He nuzzled my cheek. "Why?"

"I want to find out if I see the same fireworks when you kiss me without the patch as I see with the patch."

Scott laughed and kissed me again. I watched the fireworks for the rest of the evening.

By the time Scott and I finished the chest of drawers and took it down to our shop, we'd decided to get married. Or, he says I decided. He says that he decided to marry me the first day he saw me. We decided to live up in my apartment for a while to be near his family and save some money.

Every once in a while, I go down to our shop and touch the chest of drawers that Scott and I refinished together. I marvel at the miracle of love and caring and how it helped bring other people into my life. And I wonder how I could've been so stupid for so long to shut out all of this love and happiness!

THE END

I GAVE UP MY
ONE TRUE LOVE

Can you believe that a man will give up someone whose love is as important to him as breathing? That he can say good-bye, knowing that never again will he hold a woman in his arms who truly needs him? Maybe you think that only happens to people in the movies or on TV, but I know it's possible. I know, because it happened to me. . . .

My story really starts the day Magda Mahmoud, my right-hand girl at the shop, announced she was quitting to get married.

"What!" I exclaimed, completely dumfounded. The Serendipity Boutique had become kind of a haven for me in the past eight years, an escape from the nothingness of my marriage, and it was mainly due to Mag's running the place so efficiently.

"Don't worry, boss," Mag kidded. "I'll be around for two more weeks to train a replacement." Then, taking another look at my crestfallen face, "I'll even hire my replacement, okay?"

"Sure, sure," I mumbled. Mag ran my small sportswear and lingerie shop so well that all I had to worry about was keeping the books and the buying. Now I'd have all the bothersome details piled on my shoulders again—no new girl could take over the way Mag had.

"Well, aren't you even going to congratulate me?" she prodded. "You didn't think I'd stay married to the store forever, did you?"

I laughed in spite of myself. That was another good thing about Mag—she could kid me out of my worries. Now she chattered on about her fiancé and wedding plans, and by the time we were ready to close up, I'd gotten over feeling so bad.

But when Mag came into the back office a few days later with the girl she'd hired, I nearly fell through the floor again.

Rabbit—rabbit was just the word to describe her. How could I say she wouldn't do, when Mag had assured me that out of all the girls the employment agency had sent, this Ivy Davison was the only one who seemed right for the job? To me, she didn't look right for anything—a skinny, tied-up-in-knots kind of kid who was dressed all wrong.

Mag went out to attend to a last-minute customer, and I asked the girl a couple of questions. She wasn't stupid, and once she was convinced I wouldn't bite, she raised her head, and I saw she had large, doe-like hazel eyes and a nice, though shaky, smile. Her voice was the kind Mag knew I liked—low, pleasant, clear. When I paused for a second in the middle of a sentence, the girl said abruptly, "Please don't let me take up your time. I—I guess I won't do."

That scared-rabbit expression annoyed me. "Pick up your head so I can get a good look, and let me make up my own mind, will you?" I snapped. "What are you so scared of?"

"You look so—so disappointed," the girl said breathlessly. "And, really the only other place I ever did any selling was in a bakery—and you don't have to sell there, you just wait on people."

I stared at her. "Don't you want the job?"

"Want it!" She went pink. Her hands fidgeted frantically with her handbag. "More than anything! But that's no reason you should—I mean. . . ." She turned gratefully as Mag came back and put a friendly arm over her thin shoulders.

"This kid really wants a job, boss," Mag said. "If you'd seen the other applicants they sent down—boy! They think they'll get paid for sitting out front doing their nails or something!" She patted the girl's shoulder reassuringly. "And don't forget, I'll be around for another week, breaking her in. You won't have a thing to worry about."

No, except wanting to burst into a rage every time I laid eyes on this mopey little mouse, I thought resignedly. But if Mag okayed her, I must be missing whatever she saw. I'd always trusted her judgment, and now I tried to sound convincing as I told them it was fine with me.

Later, to Mag alone, I mentioned that she might tell the girl to jazz herself up a bit. "After all, she's the front for a women's shop," I pointed out. "Why you ever picked such a drab little thing. . . ."

Magda's twinkling eyes brought a shamefaced grin from me. She patted my hand. "Now, you just forget the whole thing. I'll admit I felt sorry for her, but you'll see—she'll work out. She's got nothing else on her mind—no family, no boyfriends—nothing but the job."

That depressed me even more, but, as usual, Mag was right. During the next week I was hardly aware that Ivy was around. Thursday, our late night when I always helped out front, I realized that now Mag was merely helping Ivy. She'd gotten that girl to the point where she was really handling the whole counter, and knew where to lay her hand on every item of stock. My being there made her nervous, but she managed well just the same.

When we were closing up, I made a point of complimenting her, and then wished I'd kept my mouth shut—she got so flustered. I said in exasperation, "Look, you're doing a great job, but if you're going to jump like a rabbit every time someone talks to you—"

"It's not just someone. It's because you—you scare me."

"Oh, great." I locked the store door and dropped the key in my pocket, looking down at her uncertainly. Mag had hurried off to meet her Antonio and go furniture shopping, so there was nobody to help me talk to the kid. Suddenly, I realized that from Monday on, there'd be just the two of us anyway—I'd have to get along with her on my own. I saw the small hands fidgeting again. Why did she make me so darn nervous? Suddenly, I took her elbow, holding on even though she started violently.

"Look, I've got news for you. You scare me, too. Let's go get some coffee and see if we can't talk it out, huh? If we're going to work together. . . ."

She raised her eyes bravely. There were tears in them. Then she shrugged and let me lead her along the chilly street and down to Jerry's Coffee Shop. I steered her to a booth near the back and, by the time I'd ordered coffee and a sandwich for both of us, she was all right again—all right for her, that is. She apologized, then laughed and said, "Did you really say I made you nervous?"

"Yes, and I'll tell you why," I said crossly. "You make me feel— as if you're just waiting to be pushed around. It's all wrong. You're a young girl with your whole life ahead of you, healthy and strong. What keeps you from standing on your two feet and acting like a girl who knows where she's going?"

She laced her hands together nervously. "I guess I was born that way—and—and I never thought anybody'd hire me."

"Well, somebody did, so will you please quit acting as if you're taking up space on earth you're not entitled to?" I was annoyed, but it wasn't at the girl. It was at Mag for saddling me with her—who needed another problem, for Pete's sake! But then I made my voice softer. "I'm sorry. I've no business yelling at you." I smiled at her. "My plan was to convince you what a nice guy I really am, so you wouldn't jump every time I come near you."

She said shyly, "Thanks. Your coffee is getting cold," and I realized I'd been staring at her. A fringe of hair had fallen across her forehead, more flattering than the way she combed it on purpose, and the flush on her pale skin made her eyes look so enormous and clear, they seemed lit up from behind. She put down her sandwich then and smiled at me. "It's funny you should be sorry for talking to me like this. If you knew what it meant to have someone interested enough to bawl me out! My father used to do it but he was just—oh, bawling out the whole world, I guess. And my sister doesn't bother any more—I shouldn't be talking so much about myself."

But I urged her on, and she told me enough so I understood a little of what was behind that beaten surface. I suppose it was an ordinary enough story—coming from the poor section of town, a mother who worked herself to death, a father who drank more and more heavily and finally died of a heart attack. Ivy, fifteen then and still in high school, had moved up to her married sister Rosalie's home in the next county.

160

"Three of us in three little rooms was crowded enough," she said. "But now that little Adrian is big enough to be walking around—well, I've just got to get out. I just had to quit school so I could get a full-time job. It wasn't fair to Rosalie and my brother-in-law—even though they've been cool about it."

Privately, I thought Rosalie had been something less than "cool." Ivy didn't realize how often she'd unconsciously revealed Rosalie's constant disapproval. Rosalie always said she had no gumption; Rosalie always tried to get her to speak up for herself, but was the first to slap her down when she tried.

I felt I understood my scared-rabbit employee a little better when I dropped her off at the subway entrance a while later, and went on my own way home. But riding along the smooth highways to the suburbs, my own problems settled over me like a shroud. As usual, I wondered why I was bothering to go home at all. Not for Lorraine—my wife had been ignoring me for years. For the children? Fourteen-year-old Brendan and twelve-year-old Sheryl were as self-sufficient as their mother—she had seen to that.

I thought about Ivy Davison constantly that weekend. Maybe because Sheryl was around more than usual, getting over a virus, and Ivy's underdeveloped skinniness almost put her in the same age bracket as my robust, tall daughter—despite the fact Sheryl was a couple years older. But no two girls could have been more different otherwise. Sheryl was so self-assured I sometimes wondered if there'd be a boy who'd be just as confident. It was Lorraine who'd given her that. Lorraine, and the comfortable security that had surrounded her every day of her life.

At Sunday breakfast, I found myself, for the first time in months, coming out from behind the paper to look around at my family. I glanced at my wife's newly blonded hair, her careful makeup. Even at the breakfast table, she managed to look poised, with everything under control. Maybe Lorraine wasn't capable of love—it wasn't "manageable" enough. But that apart, she had other talents. From the looks of the house, the way we lived, anybody would put my income at almost double what it really was. Lorraine had always wanted to "live well," and she was doing it on a lot less than it took most people these days. Brendan and Sheryl couldn't have all the things their friends had—like expensive summer camps, birthday parties at clubs we couldn't belong to, a new car every year—yet their clothes, which cost a fraction of their friends', looked just as good. So did Lorraine's. Yes, she had a knack for it, and she had standards a man wanted for his kids. I caught back a sigh. If only she had something left for our marriage—for me.

Sheryl was the only one at home who showed the slightest

interest in my business. She remembered my saying Mag had left, and asked if the new girl was pretty.

"Far from it," I admitted. "In fact, if she doesn't perk herself up, I may not keep her. She's got to look good to sell lingerie—a woman's woman. You know?"

Sheryl nodded. "Well, maybe she'll get the message if you drop enough hints. She got any brains? A college graduate?"

I laughed. "Not even a high school graduate, baby."

My daughter was dumbfounded. "How can you not be a high school graduate? And what kind of career is a girl going to get without college?"

I tried to explain that everyone's circumstances were different, but it was almost funny how hard it was to convince Sheryl that there were girls who simply had to work if they wanted to eat. To her, a girl like Ivy was practically a delinquent, and to my own surprise, I ended up snapping at her. After she'd flounced out, I said irritably to Lorraine, "Sometimes she's got less common sense than a two-year-old. We're not millionaires. She must know a lot of people are poor. I don't think it's right for the kids to be so snobbish."

Lorraine flushed. "Oh, they know all they need to. I've told you before, Hugh, if you can't talk to the children without finding fault, just don't bother at all."

The familiar pain and resentment welled up in me. "I'd hardly call it 'finding fault,' trying to talk seriously to her once in a blue moon. Why can't things around here be more—more. . . ." Against her hard blue eyes, I gave up. Lorraine made me feel like a beggar, pleading for warmth and affection she just couldn't be bothered to give. I couldn't remember when I'd last held her in my arms. Why do we stay married? I wondered.

Now she said patiently, "Hugh, I don't want to quarrel. Why can't you just let well enough alone? The kids are fine. I'm fine, you're fine—why look for trouble?"

It was true enough for her. Amazing, but true. To me, what we had was a cardboard shell of a life, without warmth without love. But she had everything she needed: her own home, a husband, two nice children, enough money to manage with. Love between a man and woman—that was something she didn't even want. I gave up. How could we even talk to each other? What else was there to say?

Monday morning, I drove eagerly into town, so anxious to get away from home. My store, and the busy life I had in the city—that was really home to me. But it was like a douse of cold water to come face to face with Ivy, waiting at the store door to be let in. I looked at her, with her cheap hat squashed over her disarrayed hair, and I froze. What had made me think she might work out? How did she expect

162

to succeed in the business world when she went around looking like somebody's grandmother most of the time?

All morning, I avoided her as much as I could. I stayed in back, working on the books, till finally, at twelve, I left for a lunch date with a manufacturer.

Traveling uptown, I found myself eyeing all the young, pretty girls out on their lunch hours. Why can't Ivy look like that? I wondered angrily. A lot of them weren't much better-looking, either. It was the clothes, the way they fixed themselves—of course!

I hadn't been in the women's-wear business all these years without learning plenty about how women got to look the way they did. There were a thousand and one things a plain woman could do to transform herself in to a traffic-stopper. If I was going to keep that girl around, I had to do something about her. Why, under her very nose, right in my store, was stuff she could use, and on the street, there were plenty of other stores where I could get her a discount— shoes to replace the run-down loafers that seemed to be all she had, everything. Money? I'll advance it, I decided. I'll make her borrow it. I knew she wouldn't take it if I just handed it to her.

For a while there, I thought she wasn't going to take the money at all. I started out carefully, too carefully, trying to save her feelings— suggesting an advance on the basis that since she hadn't been working too long, she might be broke. She shook her head. "I don't need much," she assured me. "I can wait till payday to get the few little things I do want."

I groaned and gave up trying to be tactful. I just told her point-blank that she needed everything. I said if she didn't get some decent clothes and fix herself up, I just wouldn't be able to keep her. And then I stopped and waited.

After a stunned minute, she said, "I'm sorry. I thought I was doing—I mean, Mag said to iron my skirts, and always be neat, and I thought. . . ." Then she raised her head and looked me in the eye. "I'm not going to be stupid about this. If I need nicer things to keep on working here, then I've got to get them."

That evening, we walked down the street together, and I pointed out the places she could go to that weren't too expensive. I told her she could have sweaters and skirts and whatever else she could use from my place at cost. And we worked out a sort of loan system to come out of her weekly pay.

The new clothes did plenty for Ivy, but the real change in her came gradually. Once she looked better, it wasn't too long before she began to act more confident. She started standing straighter and walking prouder and looking people in the eye, and I guess it was then that I realized she was really lovely. And slowly, our relationship changed.

163

I gave Ivy a key, but I used to get in early myself, anyway, just for the kick it gave me to watch her come along the street, and see the way her eyes lit up when I said good morning. Her feelings were always so open on her small, fragile face, I thought of her as a delightful doll. She was such a sweet child, I loved doing things for her. As I would have loved doing things for Sheryl, if she'd have let me.

Then one afternoon, just before closing, I was back doing the books when I heard the rare sound of men's voices. I went out front and saw Ivy, flushed and bright-eyed, laughing with a couple of young men. Something sharp—surprise, resentment—flicked through me, even after I recognized one of them as the salesman who'd sold me our business machines. He was being transferred, and he'd come around to introduce his replacement, a good-looking young guy named Mathers.

Ivy went silent after I appeared. Two women customers came in, and I took the men out back with me, but not before I saw Ivy's face squeeze in fear. It was almost as though she had read my mind—had sensed my twinge of whatever it was when I saw her responding to those men. I didn't examine the feeling. I guess I was too scared. For a second, I'd seen her as a woman, pretty and attractive enough to catch any man's eye. And I didn't want to dwell on her that way.

That night was our late night, Thursday. We'd gotten into the habit of stopping off at Jerry's Coffee Shop together, before Ivy got her subway for home. The early spring air was fresh, and the street was jammed with couples coming in and out of the bars and movies, or just walking arm in arm. Other Thursdays, I hadn't given them—or us—much thought; I'd just found it comfortable to sit down for a few minutes with someone I could chat with.

But this night everything was wrong, like a picture hanging crooked. I was tongue-tied and depressed. The others hurrying along were couples—husbands and wives, girls and their dates. We didn't belong to any of it—to the lovely night or the laughing and kidding around. We didn't belong with each other.

When we got to Jerry's, I suddenly said, "Listen, I think I'll push along. You go ahead and have your coffee—I'll see you tomorrow."

She looked up at me sadly. "I knew you were mad about something. Were those guys making too much noise?"

"What am I, your warden?" I said hotly. "You've got a right to flirt with any guy you please!"

Her lips quivered. "Flirt with them? I was just—why, I wouldn't know how to flirt if I wanted to!" She clasped her hands in her familiar gesture. "You don't sound like yourself tonight."

I didn't feel like me. I felt all stirred-up and mixed-up, and something else besides—something that told me I should turn and

164

go right now. But instead, I took her elbow, and in silent agreement we walked on together, past Jerry's. At the crossing, my hand slipped down the thin arm and found hers, and her fingers turned into mine with such unthinking confidence that my heart skipped.

Ivy's hand trembled in mine. I didn't have to see her face to know that she was as excited as I was by the touch. And suddenly, I knew we had stepped into a new, wonderful world, strange to both of us, but magically inviting. So inviting that there could be no turning back any more.

Ivy stopped walking. "I'm scared," she said, not looking at me.

I held her arm closer—I was scared, too. "Will they worry if you get home later?" I asked. "I think we've got to talk."

"They won't worry, but maybe I should call up," she said uncertainly.

We went into a hotel lobby, and while she phoned her sister, I called home, too. Lorraine wasn't there. I just told Brendan I'd be held up in town for a while. He treated me as though I were a business client, calling to make an appointment.

The hotel had a small, dim bar that suddenly seemed very attractive. I guess Ivy had never been in a bar before, because her eyes were sparkling with excitement. We chose a small, isolated booth and, because she was under twenty-one, I ordered a Virgin Colada for her and a whiskey for me. Then, when the waiter had gone, it was possible for us to look at each other and admit that something shattering had happened.

"I feel so strange," Ivy said in a small, shaken voice. "How can I be sitting here like this, talking to you like this, when you're Mr. Drake, the man I work for—and yet how can I do anything else when I feel like this? It's so odd."

"Don't worry about it, Ivy." I covered her hand with mine. "It's never happened to me before, either—not like this. But one thing I know is that everything works itself out. Everything."

She shook her head. "How can this work out? Every time I see you—oh, ever since the first time!—my heart pounds so much I can hardly breathe. The only thing that made it better was that you didn't know. But now—how can I keep on working for you?"

I looked at her smooth, round forehead and the soft line of her chin, so young and lovely. My hand tightened hard on hers. Did she think for one minute I would let her go—send away the first real breath of life that had come into my dreary existence for years? "Do you want to leave?" I asked her. "Would you be happier if we cut it short now, before there's anything to cut short? You're terribly young, Ivy. There will be so many other men who'll want to—to look at you, and be with you."

Her eyes searched mine intently. I took her in my arms, held her close to me. "I've never known any other man," she whispered. "And—if you really want me with you, Hugh, that's what I want, too."

I drove Ivy home that night. I don't even know if I would have kissed her if she hadn't turned to me with her heart in her eyes just before she got out of the car. I reached for her, and she came willingly into my arms. Her mouth was soft and warm, her lips quivered against mine. I could feel her against me hours later.

From the beginning, there were no doubts in my mind that somehow I had to hold her again. I couldn't think of giving her up—I simply had no choice. From that night on, my whole existence had only one goal: to work out some way, without hurting Ivy or causing her trouble, for us to be together.

She never had found herself a place to live. We talked about it—we both realized she couldn't remain at Rosalie's if we were to see each other. I knew she'd have a hard time on what I paid her, but it took her a few weeks of looking before she realized it herself. It became my problem, and I solved it so easily you'd have thought the devil was on my side. I went around to an old building I'd lived in myself years before when I was single and I gave the superintendent enough money so that only three weeks later, Ivy was able to move into a one-room apartment she thought she could afford. She knew nothing about the palm-greasing I'd done and she accepted the raise I gave her, too, because I told her quite truthfully that I'd meant to give it to her anyway. She was still earning less than I'd paid Mag.

It was June when Ivy moved into the "apartment"—really a room with a sectioned-off kitchen and a tiny bathroom, but to her, it was more dazzling than a four-star hotel suite. It was furnished with broken-down equipment that I hated to look at, but she was so happy with it that after a while, I stopped noticing it, myself. And no matter how strange it sounds, it was more than a month before I stayed with her in that apartment. Not overnight. At first, I'd always go home, ready with a long string of explanations that Lorraine was perfectly willing to accept. I don't even know that she listened, particularly. She made it so easy for me to lie!

But still, eager as Ivy was for our love, I kept holding her off. I felt so responsible for her—she trusted me so completely. And I knew that once I loved Ivy and had her love, our lives would be changed beyond control.

"Why did you start all this if you didn't want to be with me?" Ivy asked one Friday night, near tears because I'd pushed away from her arms.

I knew why, but it was so hard to explain. "It's not because I want to leave, Ivy. But I—I'm trying to be sensible for us both. I know what you're going to mean to me if—we start. I don't want to hurt you."

"Oh, what's the good of so much thinking and worrying?" she wept. "I've made my choice, Hugh, or I wouldn't be here begging you now! I want to belong to you—I need you—I love you!" She sank down on the sofa and covered her eyes. "Why do I talk like that? You can't ever be really mine. I've no right to need you the way I do."

I silenced her with quick kisses. "You have every right, honey. Don't ever be sorry. We need each other, sweetheart." I wiped the tears that were rolling silently down her cheeks and kissed her where they fell. "Oh, Ivy," I groaned, "with you to love, I'll never be lonely again."

And I wasn't. Ivy loved me for myself, freely, openly. And she needed me. She was the only person in the world who leaned on me completely. And that night, when I couldn't make myself leave her, she came to me so eagerly that I felt reborn. Ivy took the tired, unhappy soul that had been me, and she put me back together again, gave me a new reason for living. I'd been provider, doormat, handyman, escort for so many years. With Ivy, I felt like a man!

And Ivy was a woman now. Sweet and gentle and capable of really loving a man. She was more of a woman at nineteen than my wife would ever be.

As the hot summer wore on, I was happier than I'd been in my whole life. In spite of the lies to Lorraine and the sneaking around, in spite of the few seconds of tension when I had to check my story to be sure it wouldn't be challenged—I felt a new joy in just getting up each morning. I invented a trade organization to account for two or three nights a month, and other things to serve as they occurred to me. And even though I was getting pressed pretty thin, financially, I urged Lorraine to take the kids away for a month that summer.

"Last year you insisted we couldn't afford it," she said suspiciously.

"Things are better this year. Besides, you can rent the Van Nortons' cottage for practically nothing. The kids will love it."

Lorraine's lips thinned bitterly. "They ought to see Europe." In other years, that remark had shriveled me, but this time I just got up, shrugged, and grinned down into her astonished face.

"Well, that's life!" I said cheerfully. "The kids might as well start learning that if you can't have the whole world, you might as well take what you can get."

"What's come over you?" She was puzzled by my new attitude. "All of a sudden you seem so—light-hearted, as if you'd just tossed off all your problems and don't care anymore."

"Maybe that's it. Maybe I just don't care anymore." I glanced out the window at the shimmering morning and thought how long it had been since I'd even noticed the small things in life. "Maybe I just got over caring. After all, what good did it do?"

A whole month of freedom! I was almost dazed. Did she suspect? Not Lorraine, I told myself. It was so long since she'd thought of me as a man, it would never enter her mind that another woman might want me.

It was a magical month. Neither Ivy nor I even noticed the boiling heat that everyone else complained about. We enjoyed each other's company in the store, business was good, everything was good. Just to walk through the hushed, hot streets, to shiver in air-conditioned restaurants, to go hand-in-hand through the iron gate of her building, up the cracked, broad steps and into the dim, shabby privacy of Ivy's apartment—it was like entering the promised land.

The only trouble was, it was too good. Spoiled by happiness that didn't have to be cut short in the middle of the night. Ivy forgot that it couldn't go on like this forever. I had to be the one to remind her, and it hurt her cruelly. Poor, sweet Ivy. Everything was so simple in her world. I hated to remind her of my wife and children because I loved her so much. Yet I couldn't pretend. I was married, and I couldn't ask Lorraine for a divorce. There was no love between us, but there were too many ties. I had to remind Ivy often and I knew it spoiled things for her.

"Look what I bought yesterday," she would gloat, showing me things like tablecloths or a new can-opener. She was so domestic, such a little homebody! I'd laugh. "I'm trying to learn to cook," she'd defend herself, blushing and laughing back. "Nobody ever taught me even how to set a table. I've got to learn sometime." Her face would get so serious, I'd want to cry with the sweetness of her.

I wanted Ivy to be happy, so I tried not to throw cold water on her homemaking efforts. In fact, though I was afraid of the importance of her home to her—she was doing it for me, and I could promise her no future—I loved the evenings we spent in her apartment best of all. We'd eat the dinner that Ivy cooked and afterward, completely sated and content, I'd collapse in the one big easy chair, Ivy at my feet like a beautiful, satisfied cat. We'd talk, or we'd be silent. We'd read the newspaper together. Those nights alone with Ivy became the reality of my life. They made me forget every past, ugly hour. It didn't matter that my wife hated me or my kids didn't need me. I had Ivy, young and sweet and beautiful.

The love that had changed Ivy from a hopeless, miserable, shabby waif had changed me, too. It was so long since things had been worth doing, since there had been anything for me to laugh about. Ivy made me feel life was a constant adventure, always exciting. She said I was the one who had done that for her, but that was only half of the truth.

It was a really enchanted August. I dutifully replied to letters from Lorraine, but I didn't lie awake nights, suffering over my lies. The last thing in the world I was doing was hurting her, or taking anything from her that she would miss or want.

It hurt, that first week Lorraine and the children were back, when I had to start the old routine all over again—snatching dinner and a few hours of the night with Ivy maybe twice a week, and then going "home." Ivy said nothing, but her glow faded, and during the day, her face drooped into sadness when she didn't know I could see her.

One Friday night, I recklessly phoned Lorraine and said I'd be home late. She didn't ask me why. She said it didn't matter, because she'd been invited to the Gossages' to play hearts, and I didn't care much for cards.

I took Ivy out to a wildly expensive place for dinner, and tried to forget that both of us were counting the hours. Finally, very timidly, she asked, "You couldn't possibly just—not go home, could you?" Then she bowed her head and half-whispered, "No, forget I said it. I've got no right."

It hurt. "You've got every right, damn it! Every real right! Oh, Ivy, I wish. . . ." I guess that was the first time I really thought of divorce.

Ivy seemed to sense it, too. She looked at me and shook her head. "I'll never ask anything, Hugh. You've already done so much for me—more than my mother did when she had me. Everything is because of you—the way I look, the way I feel, the way I can enjoy just being alive these days. If I had to die for it, I wouldn't ask another thing, not even an extra hour that might make it hard for you."

"But I want it!" I said fiercely. "Ivy, I'm wrong and I'm guilty as hell and she could tear me apart in court. But she knows in her own heart she's only been a wife on paper!"

"The children." Ivy moaned. "They need you. No child should ever think his father doesn't want him." A flash of remembered misery darkened her eyes. "You've done too much for me already, Hugh. I'm not asking anything more. Honest. Just remember I'm here whenever—whenever you want me."

But I wanted her always. I'd known it would be like this. You couldn't be starved for love as long as I'd been and then not lose your head when it came your way. Every time I saw Ivy, it was harder to leave her. And knowing that, except for work, there was nothing for her to do but wait for the next time we could be together—that made it harder still. I felt guilty for being her whole life, even though she kept saying before we found each other, she'd had nothing at all.

"You ought to have something else," I worried. "Things to do. Other friends." But she didn't want friends.

Finally, at my urging, she decided to go back to school, night school, and get the high school diploma she lacked. I would wait for Ivy outside the school building three nights a week, to drive her home. Most of the time, she came out alone. A couple of times, when she came out with a few fellow students, my eyes would quickly scan the group for males.

For a long time, I wouldn't admit even to myself what it did to me to see Ivy with another man. Even if he only said good night and turned down the street, I'd cringe. I could barely wait till she slipped in the car beside me and I could gather her in my arms and feel once more that she was mine. All that kept me from making a fool of myself was knowing how it would hurt her to see how possessive I'd become.

One night, though, it slipped out. Ivy had come out for the third time in a row with one particular man, a big-shouldered guy with a confident walk. As she got into the car and slipped her hand in mine I said, "He's getting to be a real admirer, isn't he?"

"Who?" Ivy asked. She followed my gaze. "Oh, him! He's my history teacher, Hugh. He—just happened to be leaving when I was."

"What about the other times? Did he 'just happen' to be leaving then, too?" Something, fear or bitterness or who knows what, forced the words out of me, even though I could see what they were doing to Ivy.

"I don't remember any other times." Her hand trembled on my sleeve. "What's the matter? Why are you like this? I don't say five words to anyone in my classes, women or men. Besides, Mr. Morrone's at least forty-five." She stopped, appalled. There was no need for me to point out that I was only four years younger.

Why was I like this? Because I must have realized, even then, that the dream was over. In August, when everything had been so smooth and simple, I had managed to kid myself, but not anymore. A man couldn't live two lives. He had to take the strain out on somebody. I'd tried desperately not to make that somebody Ivy, but now I'd started making even her working hours at the store more and more difficult. I wanted her to have a full life, other friends.

Yet when she fell into a lively conversation, even with a woman customer, I found myself listening from the back room, waiting to catch some accidental remark, some proof that she was growing bored or restless or envied the honest lives of other women. And when a man came in—a customer or a salesman, anybody at all—my reaction was so strong that it scared me. I wanted to rush out there and shout, "Leave her alone! She belongs to me!"

Christmas came and went . . . a lonely Christmas for Ivy, despite the tree and the presents I'd collected for weeks. And a time of such hypocrisy for me at home that at last I knew I just wasn't going to be able to stand it any longer. There was a big party at the Gossages', during which somebody suggested that we all go off on a New Year's weekend trip out to the end of the island, where the Van Nortons had their cottage.

Lorraine loved the country and I could see she was eager to go, but then she said quietly, "Better count us out. Hugh wouldn't be able to make it." She gave a frightened little smile and turned away. Suddenly I felt sorry for her.

"I'd like to go," I blurted out. "Why don't we work on it?" But I thought: Maybe I'd get the chance—to ask her for a divorce.

I hated telling Ivy I wouldn't be able to spend any part of the weekend with her, but I had to, of course. "Go see Rosalie," I urged. "As long as I know you're not down here alone. . . ."

She was quiet for a minute. Then she said timidly, "That teacher you didn't like —Mr. Morrone—he and his wife invited the class to a kind of open house on New Year's Day. Nothing fancy, only he said so many of the night students were from out of town and had no family or anything, they might be glad of some place. . . ." Her voice trailed off as she tried to judge my reaction. I don't think she knew my fists were clenched as I told her to go ahead and have a good time. I knew I had no right to keep her tied down any longer. I wasn't free, and I could see my demands had begun to cripple her. It couldn't go on. I had to do something!

In the end, we didn't go away anyway, because Brendan caught something and then Sheryl got sick, too. I stayed at home. Something began to puzzle me. Watching Lorraine, I could see she wasn't fussing with her appearance in her normal, careful way. She came downstairs to breakfast without makeup now, her hair loose and tied back with a scrunchie as she used to wear it in the old days. And strangely enough, she didn't look older, but younger. I couldn't help wondering what had come over her. There was so little for us to talk about that it was uncomfortable to be in a room together for any length of time. Lorraine kept urging me to go out for a walk.

"It's supposed to be a holiday weekend," she pointed out. "No use both of us just sitting around. Particularly when you've already sacrificed your plans."

My pulse leaped. "What does that mean?"

Lorraine walked to the window, adjusted the curtain, and then turned and gave me a long, level look. "I guess we both know what it means, Hugh, and that's the end of the whole subject, as far as I'm concerned. I just wanted you to know I've no objection to your making yourself as comfortable and cheerful as you can, under the circumstances."

171

"What the hell are you talking about?" I asked. "What circumstances?"

She shrugged. "Very simple. You're a married man with a wife and two children who happen to be at an age when they need you more than ever before, and you're going to stay that way."

In other words, she knew there was somebody else. And she was telling me before I asked that she would never give me a divorce.

"What made you marry me, Lorraine?" I asked. "Did you ever really love me?"

It was a long time since I'd seen her lose her poise, but now she went red and her voice wasn't steady. "If you can't remember the early days, why should I remind you? We've made our bed, Hugh, both of us. Now let's just carry on with our responsibilities and forget about how it might have been." She tied the belt of her robe more firmly around her waist. "If it's all the same to you, let's not talk about it anymore. There's no use making a lot of noise and upsetting the kids when it won't lead to anything."

She went out, and I was left hanging. Just hanging. I could have killed her, yet strangely, my anger wasn't entirely against her. Was it something I'd done that had begun to wreck our marriage? The months I'd been so absorbed and worried about the business that I had nothing to say to her when I staggered home and fell into bed? When I was constantly short-tempered from strain, never had time for anything but work and worry? I rubbed my forehead, but I couldn't remember too much about the times before I was certain the store wasn't going to fold up under me. Why hadn't Lorraine tried to tell me? How was a man to know, if he wasn't told?

No, she was just trying to make a case for herself, I decided bitterly. A real wife, a woman with an ounce of warmth and love to bring to marriage, would have understood and tried to help. She wouldn't have sulked like a hurt child, and then allowed the hurt to pile up into a wall of steely coldness that made it forever impossible for us to reach each other.

I started the New Year grimly. I had to find some way to free myself for Ivy. I'll force Lorraine to throw me out, I told myself. I'll humiliate her in front of the whole town. I'll bring Ivy to our home. But the crazy frustration always died right there. It wasn't just me or Lorraine or the kids. It was Ivy, too. And seeing her, small and eager and trying so hard to look happy behind the counter, I knew I couldn't do anything in the world that would hurt her or cause her shame.

Oh, yes, I felt protective and full of love for her, but it didn't stop me from making her life miserable. I went a little crazy when she returned to school after the holidays. It seemed to me she went to school more and more eagerly, as if she was grateful for the time away

172

from me. Five minutes before her classes were over, I'd be outside waiting—waiting not so much for Ivy as to satisfy myself that she would come hurrying out with no man beside her, nobody smiling down at her or looking as if he found her desirable. I had nightmares of anger and violence that terrified me. I started to take more and more advantage of the free ticket Lorraine had handed me at New Year's. She knew, didn't she?

And she didn't care, as long as I didn't make an open break. I stopped making my flimsy excuses. I just stayed out late. And yet instead of getting easier, the tension between Ivy and me grew worse. She always came to me warmly and forgivingly, our hours together. The love we gave each other was even deeper, if anything, and it was harder to tear myself away from her. Yet even if she gave me a sleepy smile of good night when I left, often as not I would see from her swollen eyes the next morning that she'd spent the rest of the night crying. A fine life for a nineteen-year-old girl! I began to feel as though a hundred stormy winds were ripping me apart. And Ivy's every smile, every loving touch, made me feel worse.

The beginning of the end came the day the cash register broke. On my way out to "the market," I told Ivy to call the company I'd bought it from; they could supply us with a fill-in machine while ours was being repaired. Then I left to order my summer stock. When I got back, there was a young man with Ivy. It was that Mathers, the salesman who serviced our machines. But there was nothing businesslike in the smile he was giving Ivy, or in the lively conversation I had interrupted. I zoomed through the store without saying a word, and went into the office.

And I listened, my hands balled into fists. Ashamed and humiliated, hating myself, wondering if this could be me, still I listened. I heard laughter and Ivy's voice, too low to catch the words, but Mathers' honest, boyish tones rang out clearly enough.

"Well, it's my quarter, so let me worry about it," I heard him say. "I'll call you and you can always say no, can't you?"

A wave of rage washed over me so fiercely, it left me sick. I wanted to push his face in. I strode over to the doorway of the shop. "I appreciate the service you're giving us, Mathers," I said sharply, "but don't let us monopolize your time."

Ivy went white, and her eyes pleaded with me. Mathers glanced from her to me and his friendly grin faded. "Sorry I've overstayed my welcome. See you, babe," he said, and was gone.

He'd called her "babe." "How many times has he seen you?" I asked in that same cold tone.

"Hugh—"

"Don't lie!" I shouted. My hands were shaking. I stuffed them

173

into my pockets. "Do you get some kind of kick of making a fool of me?"

"Stop. Please. You're scaring me." She was gripping the counter. "I've never laid eyes on him since that first day he came in with the other man." Ivy's beloved little face looked up at me pleadingly, without a trace of guilt.

I said quickly, "I'm sorry. I'm just so tired I guess I lost my head. I heard him call you babe and I couldn't stand it."

"He's just awfully breezy, Hugh, that's all. I—didn't encourage him." She let out a ragged breath. "It kills me when you're like this, honey. Please . . . there's no other man on earth but you, you know that."

Of course, I knew it. But I went home raging, helpless. What was the good of it when I couldn't be the only man for her legally and proudly, in front of the whole world? What did it leave for her?

I reached the lowest depth of self-hate that weekend by taking out my misery on Brendan, who had the misfortune to come sneaking in the back way at twelve-thirty while I was alone in the kitchen, downing a beer in the hope it would put me to sleep.

"I thought eleven was your curfew," I growled.

"Eleven-thirty on Saturdays." He was scared, but cocky. How big he was! I hadn't taken a good look at him in a long time. "Mom okayed it. I know I'm a little over tonight, but that's because—"

"A little over? Just a little hour, that's all." I stood up menacingly. "From now on, you make it on the dot, do you hear me? On the dot!"

He edged past me toward the door, still scared, but fighting to hide it. "Hey, it never bothered you before," he muttered as he disappeared up the stairs.

I buried my head in my hands. Taking it out on the boy—surely that was the rottenest thing yet! Okay, he was wrong—but after years of letting Lorraine run their lives, what sense did it make for me suddenly to start cracking the whip? And would I have come down on him so hard if I hadn't had to lash out at somebody? Next, it would be Ivy again. . . .

It was April once more, the same kind of spring that had been so wonderful the year before. But as everything freshened around me, it only made my wretchedness more acute. I couldn't even enjoy my time with Ivy anymore. There was only one answer, but I didn't have the courage to put it to her yet. Lorraine wouldn't release me; I couldn't walk out on her and the children. And I couldn't bear to go on demanding of Ivy, when I had nothing to offer her in return. The love we'd had would slowly turn to hate, fostered by the strain and stress of a relationship such as ours.

The final decision had to come soon. I knew it one evening, as

I watched Ivy cross the street on her way to the corner where she caught the bus for school. A man came up and spoke to her, and after a surprised instant, she stopped and they talked. It was Mathers. They seemed to be arguing in a friendly way; then after a moment, he took her elbow and led her up the street. My eyes were rooted on them. Had he been waiting for her? Had it been accidental? What did it matter? I thought in agony. If it wasn't him, sooner or later there'd be some other man. And then, when that day came and she knew she hated the ties that held us together, she'd hate me. I watched them together, Ivy and the young man. They were laughing, happy—young together. I had her love for fourteen months, but I was the outsider now, the jealous, pitiful old fool!

That night, I didn't pick her up at school. I walked around alone till I was ready to drop. At eleven, when I knew she'd be home, I went into a booth and called her.

"Oh, Hugh—where are you? I've been going crazy!"

"I'm tired, that's all. I just realized you might be worried, so I called."

"Worried? I thought you were in an accident or something!" She swallowed the rest of her sobs.

"I'm okay, darling. I'm going home. I'll see you tomorrow." I hung up.

That night was a sort of crisis, I think—like the turning point in a fever, when you sweat out the infection till you're limp and light-headed, but well again. At least my self-control came back. I'll always remember the next couple of weeks as a bonus of happiness I didn't deserve. Everything faded into the background except Ivy. The joy we gave each other was even greater than it had been the spring before. Night after night, I got home late. All I could think of was Ivy, seeing her every spare minute I had. We had a holiday coming up, a day away from the store. I told Lorraine I planned to take inventory that day, and arranged with Ivy to go on an all-day picnic to a quiet lake I knew about, where we'd gone before.

But something happened the day before the picnic. To this day, it doesn't make much sense. But to me then it spelled the end. The end of our love affair.

Early that morning, Mathers called Ivy to ask for a date. I heard her try to get out of it gracefully, without success. Then I heard her say hesitantly, "Maybe that's the best way to put it, Kit. Maybe I ought to tell you I am engaged."

I didn't have to hear any more. My heart ached for her. I wasn't even angry anymore. I just hurt all over, as though a giant weight was pressing inside me.

We were busy the rest of that day, and I was glad. I didn't want to talk to her. I picked Ivy up early the next morning, knowing what I had to say to her some time that day. I felt good as I led her down to the car, stowed our picnic lunch in the back. It was a pleasant, carefree drive to the lake.

That afternoon after we'd eaten, we lay side by side under a broad-branched tree by the quiet lake, and I gave Ivy back her freedom, her youth. "Ivy, we've come to the end of the line," I said. "From here on in it's all downhill, and I can't bear to see you hurt."

She started. "How can you say that, Hugh? After what we've meant to each other. After what you've done for me. Why, without you, I'd be nothing!"

"That's not so, Ivy. You don't need me now—I only get in your way." I watched anger flicker over her face, then fear, then I rushed on. "Oh, don't you see, honey? You've got to have a life of your own, decent, with a future! You've got to spread your wings! Whatever we gave each other was—oh, we both know what it was, but it couldn't last. It was the wrong time, the wrong place in our lives. Now we're only taking. At least—I'm the one that's taking, and I just can't go on. I'd end by hating both of us, because I hate myself and my own selfishness so much."

Ivy's lips trembled. "I love you. I can't see further ahead than that."

"That's why I have to see for both of us. Find what I see—it's no good, Ivy. I'll never stop loving you. But there are things, even wonderful things, that we just can't have if we don't get them at the right time. What we've had together was—well, like a bonus. An extra. If we tried to keep it, it would turn to ashes in our hands." I leaned over to her, touched her soft, slim arm.

"You go out and get your life, Ivy. Don't worry—you'll be all right. And I'll have more than I deserve. Not love, I don't even care about that anymore, because I'll have you to remember always. But I'll have the children to do for and at least I'll know I didn't just drop them by the wayside." I tried to smile, but my lips felt like dried wood. "You've made me very happy, Ivy. That's something we'll both always have."

"You're just saying words. I can't take them in," she said, sobbing. "But I'll try to remember, so when it stops hurting, I can think about it. If you're doing it, it must be right, Hugh."

I got up to go, and Ivy followed me wearily. The ride home was a silent one. Ivy sat close to me, and once her arm linked itself through mine, and I held it close to my body, its warmth steeling me for the bleakness I knew would follow.

When I pulled up in front of her building, I turned to look at her. Desire for her welled up in me, but I fought it. If I didn't make the break final now, it would be too late. "Good-bye, Ivy," I whispered. "I'll never stop loving you."

She broke into sobs and fled from the car as though I'd beaten her. I could see her body tremble as she ran through the iron gates. Let her go, I thought. She'll pull her way out, make a new life for herself. And someday she'll even be glad it ended this way.

That was the end. It's been a month since that day we were at the lake together. I found Ivy another job, and little by little, I've tried to pick up the broken pieces of my life. If Lorraine has noticed I'm home more, she hasn't said a word, but there's been a softness around her eyes when she looks at me I don't remember seeing there in a long time.

We pay for the things we do, the mistakes we make, and I'm paying for all of mine. I'm paying for my hours with Ivy in aching loneliness. I'm also paying for the part I never played in the raising of my children, because now I want their closeness, and I know I'll have to earn it, slowly, painfully. But yesterday, Brendan came to me for advice, and I take that as a sign of better things to come. At least I have this, I think, and maybe someday Sheryl will need me, too. At least I'll have my children. And I know Ivy will find her true happiness someday. That, too, keeps me going. People have made whole lives out of even less.

THE END

PLAIN JANE AND
THE HOLLYWOOD HOTTIE
My summer job changed everything!

I was always the girl that nobody noticed—plain to the point of being invisible with mousy hair, glasses, and I was shy to top it off. I kept to myself, enjoyed reading, and kept up on current events. I was a typical geeky girl—an observer of life more than a participant. Even my name was non-descript: Helen. That's why what happened to me was nothing short of miraculous.

It all started with a summer job a friend of my father's, Albert, had got- ten for me. I had just graduated from college and was living at home with no prospects for employment. As my parents had predicted, my double major in English and world studies hadn't resulted in any job offers.

The months stretched out in front of me, and though I'd grown used to my lonely way of life, I remember thinking that a change would be wel- come. I wasn't unhappy, but I wasn't really happy with my situation, either.

It seemed almost like a miracle the night my dad came to me with the job offer. I said yes almost before he finished explaining it to me. He was shocked. I never wanted to try anything new, and rarely wanted to do anything outside the house, but, what can I say—it was almost like I knew that taking this job would change my life.

Albert worked for the small town where we lived, and that summer, a big Hollywood movie was being shot just outside of town. Albert was the contact person for the production company and he needed an assistant to help cover the things that he didn't have time to deal with. He needed someone who was good with details and who he could count on—someone like me who wouldn't have any kind of personal agenda.

I knew nothing about the movie—not the plot, the stars— nothing. But I didn't really care. All I knew was that it was a job that I could do, and a job that I'd be good at. I had a real knack for details and organization. It was the one thing I knew about myself.

"When do I start?" I asked when Dad finished explaining the details to me.

He smiled at me. "You report to Albert's office in the morning, Helen. He'll get you started. I'm so glad you want to take it. I thought for sure that I'd have to talk you into it. This could be the start of something big for you."

I thought so, too.

I went to Albert's office excited, which is unlike me. He gave me the basic information about the movie, but it really didn't mean much to me. I didn't know anything about celebrities and hadn't seen a movie in years. I just wanted to work.

I dove into my first assignment enthusiastically. Albert gave me a few books to use as reference, but what he needed most was someone to do the legwork for him. I spent three days studying the books before I actually drove around and examined the layout of the town where I'd lived my entire life. I looked at it with new eyes, searching for the proper angles to complete the picture and the perfect backdrops for the script.

Once I knew what the movie was about and what the location shoots entailed, I was given my first official assignment. Albert gave me a list of locations that the production company was looking for and I drove around to see if I could find anything that would match up to the list.

I went to farms and fields and hiked across wide-open spaces at different times of the day to check the lighting at all hours. I took pictures and notes. I had several choices for each shot, and I did a thorough job of checking all the angles, as my reference books told me to do.

The whole town was talking about this movie. You couldn't go anywhere where people weren't talking about it, and most people in my small town knew that I had a job working on it. For once, people envied me when they saw me. It was a strange feeling, one that I'd never experienced before, and I didn't necessarily like it. I didn't like being the focus of other people's attention.

Now, don't get me wrong—it wasn't like I couldn't hold a conversation or anything like that. If someone sought out my opinion about something I had some knowledge of, I'd talk to them, but not many people sought me out.

I scouted the locations for many days before the production company arrived in town. The night before I was to meet with the producers, I sat down and organized my findings. I prepared a binder full of my scouting reports. I stayed up all night putting the requests together with the pictures that I'd taken and the written descriptions of everything I'd seen that I thought would work. I gave it to Albert in the morning and then waited for my next assignment. He told me that he couldn't give me anything to do until we met with the production people.

When the cast and crew for the movie hit town, it was like nothing I'd ever seen before. Most of the people in town were starstruck, but not me. I didn't really keep up with pop culture and I didn't even recognize the names of the big stars. But, the first time I laid eyes on the man playing the lead in what I by then knew was a romantic comedy, my heart skipped a beat.

Hunter Evans was the most attractive man I'd ever seen. He was tall, dark, and handsome—just what a big movie star ought to be. He had thick hair and beautiful eyes that were lined with dark lashes. His broad shoulders and boyish grin took my breath away. He seemed really kind, too—always making small talk with the extras and the people behind the scenes.

The woman playing opposite him was another story. She was a diva with a capital D—demanding and dramatic. Nothing was ever right for Kirstie Roberts, and she had a lot of demands. She had a whole group of people working for her who were almost as unpleasant as she was. Something went wrong with nearly every scene that she was in, and she'd either cry or scream at whomever was nearest. I was glad that I wouldn't really be working with her.

It was obvious from the start that they were a couple, though I didn't really know how happy they were. She was just as demanding of him as she was of everyone else. He spent half his time telling her that she really was a good actress, and the other half apologizing for her behavior to everyone on the set. I couldn't imagine what he saw in her.

The first time he spoke to me was the most exciting moment of my life. It was nothing more than an introduction; he was meeting everyone who was working on the film. But still, when he shook my hand and thanked me for all the work I was doing, I actually thought that I'd never wash that hand again.

It was so unlike me. I fantasized that he somehow would see the real me, not the shy woman behind the big glasses, but I knew the likelihood of that happening was next to nothing. I even spent my nights watching his old movies. I ordered all of them on the Internet so that no one in town would know about my fascination.

When filming started, my new assignment was to make sure that everything was at the location that needed to be there. I got the promotion because the production company had been so impressed by my scouting reports. The new assignment meant that I had to be there before everyone else and stay late at night to set up for the next day. I didn't mind it much, though, because it also meant that during the day, I didn't have much to do.

I set up a spot for myself in the dining tent. Every morning, I'd go through what needed to be done for the rest of the day, and then I'd read one of the ten newspapers that had been flown in. I was in heaven.

Once I'd read them, cover to cover, I'd pick up whatever book I was reading and start on that. Everyone knew where I was if there was a problem, but there seldom was. That summer, I was working on rereading all the great American authors.

One day I had my nose buried in my book when a man's voice interrupted my reading.

"Are you done with the papers?"

I nodded, barely looking up.

"What are you reading there?"

Annoyed, I closed the book. I looked up and my eyes met his. Once again, my heartbeat quickened.

"Hemingway," I stammered. I couldn't believe he was talking to me. "It's A Farewell to Arms."

"He's one of my favorite authors," Hunter said suavely. "Do you like it?"

"His descriptions are phenomenal, but sometimes it's a bit too masculine for me—all that war and bullfighting."

He laughed and then smiled—a smile that lit me from within. "That's exactly what I thought when I read it. A well-read woman is so interesting, I think." He picked up The New York Times from the table in front of me. "Well, I better get back to the set." He winked and walked away.

My face flushed. I was smart enough to know that he was just being kind, but my heart didn't seem to mind.

From that day on, I found reasons to be on the set. I'd linger after my job was done. Instead of reading the paper in the dining tent, I brought it or my book to the set and found an out-of-the-way chair to sit in. I always knew where Hunter was, and occasionally, he'd stop and ask what I was reading. Unfortunately, Kirstie seemed to have radar that went off anytime he talked to a woman. She'd appear out of nowhere, needing him desperately, and off he'd go. I couldn't figure out what he saw in her except for the fact that she was drop-dead gorgeous.

One evening, at the end of his shooting for the day, Hunter actually sat down and the two of us had a discussion about the upcoming presidential election. We were both for the same candidate, but we had differing opinions about just how he was going to get elected.

"No, you're wrong, he'll never get elected by riding the coattails of the party. He needs to let the people know who he is and what he stands for that's separate from them. No one in the real world trusts the straight party line," I said forcefully.

"But, if he does voice an opinion, and then doesn't follow through with it once he's elected, it hurts the party and we're right back where we started," Hunter countered. "And, by the way, I did live in the real world once." He smiled that sly grin of his, and for a minute, I forgot what we were talking about.

"It must take a lot for you to remember all those years ago." I laughed, but stopped when I saw how serious his expression was.

"Sometimes it feels like I was never even that person. Being famous has its perks, and I love what I do, but it's hard some days. Everyone handles you with kid gloves. There are times when I'd give it all up to live in the real world again," he admitted.

The sadness in his eyes went right to my heart and I wanted to reach out and touch his cheek, but I knew that he would never want a girl like me to do something like that.

"I guess I never really thought about it that way. It must be tough," I said sincerely.

He smiled again, "Listen to me. People should have my problems, right? God, it's been so long since I just talked to someone about anything that wasn't related to me or my career." He chuckled. "Thanks. You're a great listener, Helen." He touched my hand and I felt sparks run through both of us.

Kirstie's radar must have gone off because right then, the diva descended upon us.

"Darling! Here you are," she purred. "I've been looking everywhere for you. The press is waiting to hear how we feel about working together." She laid her hand possessively on his shoulder. "Our public awaits. Let's get you into the makeup trailer to fix your hair."

He stood, obviously reluctant. "It was really nice talking with you," he finally said to me with true regret in his eyes.

And then he was gone. She continued to hang on his arm and talk incessantly in his ear. "I. . . me. . . we. . . " I could catch only bits and pieces of it.

My heart really felt for the guy—he seemed truly unhappy, but yet he wasn't doing anything to change it. At least I was content with my quiet little life, as boring and unglamorous as it was.

The job and the challenges it presented were exciting to me. I loved the thrill of having the solution to a problem long before it was needed. I hoped when the movie wrapped that the people at the production company could find a place for me on their next location shoot. More than once, I was told that the shoot wouldn't be going nearly as well without me. I took solace in the fact that though I might not ever be able to make someone like Hunter fall in love with me, at least I'd found a career that I loved and was good at.

I immersed myself in moviemaking and tried to learn everything that I could about the process. But, try as I might, I couldn't help but look forward to the small amounts of time that Hunter and I would spend together. He seemed to be enjoying them, too, because he seemed to find more and more time to spend in my corner of the set. He'd stop by to trade political jabs or recommend a book to read. I fought the feelings I had for him, knowing that he'd never think of me like that, and tried to just enjoy the time I was spending with him. He was so interesting to talk to, and he really listened to what I had to say. I grilled him about the process of making movies, and he was happy to help me learn all that I could about it.

In fact, he was more than happy to help. I was beginning to think that he liked talking to me as much as I liked talking to him because of who I was—just an average person who would talk to him like he was the same. I could never tell him how I really felt. Instead, I would make do with the small parts of himself that he'd share with me.

I watched all his scenes; I noticed the way the light played across his face and the way he was able to express any emotion that was needed. He was an incredible actor. When the director said action, he was right on, and almost everyone on the set stopped to watch him work. It was amazing; he was amazing.

At the end of the day, I'd go into the trailer to watch the work they'd done, and I was shocked when people asked me what I thought. Without being aware of it, I'd become an integral part of making the movie. The director said that I had a natural eye for setting a scene. Even Hunter started to ask my opinion. I was flattered and glad because it gave me a legitimate reason to spend time with him, though almost every time, we were interrupted by Kirstie. I could tell more and more how unhappy Hunter was in the relationship.

On the last day of the shoot, I figured that I didn't have anything to lose by asking him what he saw in her. I was sure that we were good enough friends that I could ask.

Besides, he would soon be leaving and going back to his exciting life, and I'd probably be nothing more than a faint memory to him.

Kirstie had been particularly awful toward him, me, and everyone else on the set that day. Then she left to catch a flight back to Los Angeles to do some press for a movie she had coming out. Hunter was supposed to join her, but he had some scenes to re-shoot without her. That led to yet another tantrum, and then she was gone.

"You know, when we first got together she felt the same way I did. Both of us were just looking for some normalcy, but that was before Kirstie really hit it big. Then Conman came out. It was her breakthrough role, and ever since then, she's been like this—larger than life and demanding. When we're alone, she's a little better. She's just really insecure. She's sure that it's all going to go away one day." Hunter shrugged his broad shoulders and the brow above his eyes furrowed.

"I just think she might be part of your problem. It seems like she only wants to live in the world you so desperately want to escape."

"You know, you're probably right, but I could never break it off while we're in the middle of a movie. She'd fall apart, and I just couldn't do that to her." He sighed, resigned to his fate. There was still more work to do on the movie back in L.A.—voiceovers, and a few more re-shoots.

His scene was called and he turned and started to walk toward the set. Just then, he paused and turned back to me.

"If you can hang around till I'm done, I have a book back in my trailer that I want to give you," he said sweetly. "A thank you for all that you've done for me on this location."

"Sure, I can wait." I tried hard to keep my voice even and not betray the excitement that I was feeling.

"Great; I'll meet you at my trailer when I'm done, and maybe we can grab some dinner or something. It'll just be about four hours, I think."

I nodded, and he turned and went back to work.

I stood stunned where I was, hardly able to believe what had just happened. Then a voice behind me snapped me back to reality.

"You know, I've been on all his sets, and I've never seen him spend as much time with anyone as he has with you."

I turned to see the makeup woman, Layla, standing just outside her trailer. She was young and hip—everything I wasn't.

"Well, we're friends, I guess." I was unsure of what to say.

"Well, friend, why don't you come in here and we'll see if I can help you out some?" She pointed to the trailer behind her and I practically ran up the stairs.

My appearance had never bothered me. It suited my personality and allowed me to keep to myself. No one took a second glance, and that suited me just fine. But, for the first time in my life, I wanted to look attractive.

I sat down in her chair and she snapped a plastic cape over me. As it fell, she secured it behind my neck.

"Honey, when I'm through with you, your own mother won't recognize you."

Two hours later, she turned me around to look in the mirror. As I stared at my reflection, I knew that she was right: Gone was the straight, dirty-dishwater hair that I'd pulled back tightly into a ponytail at the nape of my neck. In its place was a head full of layered waves that fell just to my shoulders. She'd shaped my eyebrows and applied makeup, too. Not too much, which I was glad about—I didn't want to look like I was wearing a mask or something.

"Just enough to bring out your natural beauty," she said. I was shocked. I had never in my life thought of myself as beautiful. No one had ever told me that I was beautiful—besides my parents—but

184

they didn't really count. But Layla was right: I did look beautiful, and I couldn't believe that I was staring at my own reflection. I put my glasses back on to get a better look.

"Oh, Layla, I can't believe it." Tears formed in the corners of my eyes. "It's perfect."

"Not quite. I took the liberty of calling Dr. Long, the town ophthalmologist, and he's waiting at his office to give you some contacts. It's time for you to stop hiding behind those glasses." She smiled kindly. "Stop by the wardrobe department and pick out something to wear when you get back."

"Why are you doing all this for me?" I asked in disbelief.

"Two reasons, really. You've worked so hard, night and day— you're here when I get here in the morning, and you're still here when I leave at night. And I figured you could use a little pampering."

"I was just doing my job, the one I was paid to do," I protested. "Besides, I loved every minute of it."

"Well, then, let's just say that I like to bring out the potential I see in people."

I blushed. "What's the second reason?"

"Hunter," she said with a pleased smile. "Like I said before, I've never seen him spend so much time with someone on the set. Usually, he's in his trailer or propping up that girlfriend of his. But you had some sort of effect on him, and it really helped him on this shoot. He's a good guy and he deserves better than Kirstie."

I smiled. "Hunter doesn't think of me that way. We're friends— that's all there is to it."

"Well, I have a feeling that you'd like that to change. And when he gets a look at you now, I think he'll realize the same thing. Now get going. That doctor isn't going to wait forever."

I practically ran to my car. The magic of my makeover had made me believe that maybe she was right.

The trip to the doctor's office was quick, and I was surprised by how easy it was. The contacts were the finishing touch, and I was seeing my new self clearly. Layla was right—I'd been hiding behind them, but not anymore.

Even if Hunter didn't think of me in that special way, I was going to start a new life. This job had shown me what I wanted to do. But, I still held out hope that Layla was right about Hunter and me.

I had just enough time to scoot into the wardrobe trailer before I had to meet him. Layla had been there before me and she'd picked something out. It was perfect: a blue sweater that brought out my eyes and some brown suede pants that fit my slim hips like a glove. It was nothing that the old me would've worn, but that was the beauty of it; this was the new me, and for the first time in my life, I felt as though

I wanted everyone to look at me.

I walked across the set, enjoying thoroughly the heads that turned in my direction. Hunter was already there; the door to his trailer was open, and he was sitting just inside, talking to someone on the phone. I tapped on the door, my heart racing.

"Come in," he called, and I stepped up into the trailer and waited for him to finish talking.

"No, I can't come tonight—I just can't. No, it's nothing to do with you. Jeez, I just can't fly out tonight; I have something I need to do." He was silent for a moment. "You know what? That's fine with me. I can't take this anymore! I'll call you when I land and we'll finish this then." He snapped the phone closed.

"Hi," I said softly.

He looked up and the expression on his face told me that he liked my transformation.

"You look amazing." He stood and crossed the small trailer toward where I stood.

"Layla did this. She wanted to do something nice for me and I let her," I said in a rush. "She seemed to think that it would be doing something nice for you, too." I couldn't believe I was telling him that. The new me was definitely charging forward.

Hunter laughed and shook his head. "For a minute, I wasn't even sure that it was you."

"I'm not sure how to take that," I said, my voice wavering.

He stepped closer, reached out, and pulled me into his arms. I breathed deep, wanting to commit every second of that moment to memory: his musky smell, the look in those incredible eyes, and the sweet tone of his hushed voice.

"I swear, that Layla knows me better than I know myself sometimes." His breath was hot on my cheek. "But she was wrong about one thing."

"What was that?" I asked, raising my chin slightly. Our lips were just inches apart.

"I was planning on doing this even before Layla got a hold of you. I'd already fallen in love with the plain Helen." He leaned in and kissed me. Our bodies melted into one—his arms wrapped around my waist and mine around his neck. Then he paused and reached out to pull the door to his trailer closed.

"I think we should have some privacy." He smiled.

"But what about Kirstie?" I asked, afraid to let him hear the feelings my voice betrayed.

"Kirstie and I are going to be going our separate ways. Let's just say that our priorities aren't the same anymore."

"Oh, really?"

"She doesn't think that you moving with me to L.A. is a priority."
He smiled and pulled me close to him again. "See, spending time with
you has shown me that I can still be myself in this crazy world I live
in. I just have to find the right person to do it with. Will you come?"

"I'll have to check my calendar." I laughed. "I can't believe
this is happening to me. Someone like you with someone like me?" I
shook my head.

He put his finger on my lips to stop me. "Someone like you is
exactly what I need to finally be happy." Then he kissed me again,
and I knew from that moment on that I would finally be happy, too.

THE END

THE ABANDONED BABY
ON MY DOORSTEP
Why did he look so much
like my husband?

Sometime during the night, I awoke, startled, thinking that I'd heard the garage door creak. The garage was on the other side of the house from our bedroom. Alarm probed at my drowsiness. Was it a burglar?

Sometimes Darren forgot to take the keys out of the car and bring them into the house. A thief could start the car and back it out of the driveway and be gone before we could stop him. I thought I heard the door creak again very faintly, and I started to get out of bed. Beside me, Darren stirred.

"What's the matter?" he asked, in a surprisingly clear, wide-awake voice.

"Oh, are you awake?" I asked. "Did you hear it, too?"

"Hear what?"

"It sounded as if someone were opening the garage door." I made another move to get up.

"I'll take a look," he said quickly, and jumped out of bed. I heard the sound his bare feet made as he crossed the hall and went into Jimmy's room, which overlooked the garage. A minute later he returned.

"You must've been dreaming. The garage doors are shut and nobody's around."

Satisfied that I'd been mistaken, I drifted off to sleep.

The next morning was like every weekday morning. I had breakfast ready for Darren and myself and his lunch made by the time he came downstairs. He had to leave for his job by seven-fifteen to get there before eight. At seven-ten, he finished his second cup of coffee and stood up.

"Well, I'll run along," he said, just as he always did.

"Have a good day," I answered, just as I always did. He left and I went to the foot of the stairs and called up to my son.

"Jimmy! Time to get up!" I waited for our seven-year-old son's muffled, "All right," and went back to the kitchen. I cleared away the dishes, stacked them in the sink, and ran hot water over them. All the time, in the back of my mind, I was expecting something that didn't come, and it was as I turned the hot-water tap off that I knew what it was—the sight and sound of the car as Darren backed it along the driveway past the kitchen window.

Puzzled, I opened the door and leaned out, peering back at the garage. It was open, and the car was still inside. Darren had one of the car doors opened, and was bending forward so that his head and shoulders were out of sight. There was something so intent about his position that I felt a pang of alarm and remembered, for the first time since getting up, the noises I'd heard from the garage during the night.

"Darren, what is it?" I called, already halfway to the garage.

He straightened up. His face was expressionless. "Somebody seems to have left us a baby."

"A baby—" I rushed down the driveway and into the garage. Standing beside Darren, I saw a blanket-wrapped bundle on the seat of the car. An opening at one end of the well-wrapped bundle revealed a tiny face with closed eyes. I turned and gazed at Darren.

"Then there was somebody out here last night!" I exclaimed.

"I guess so. I didn't see anyone, though." He looked down at the baby again. "Hadn't we better do something?"

"Yes, I suppose—" I leaned into the car and picked up the baby. How light it was! From its weight, and from what I could see of its face, it couldn't be more than two or three weeks old. "Darren, who could have—" I began, and broke off, forgetting what I'd been going to say as the baby stirred and yawned and opened its eyes. They were the very color that Jimmy's had been before they'd turned.

"He's awake!" Darren said beside me.

"He?" I asked. "Maybe it's a she."

"Oh, that's right—maybe it is," he mumbled.

"How could anyone abandon a baby?" I said furiously. "Especially nowadays, when there are all sorts of adoption agencies, and people anxious to adopt children!"

"Maybe she—whoever it was, didn't want the baby to be adopted," Darren offered.

"She preferred to leave it in a stranger's garage?" I snapped. "Well, we can't just stand here looking at it. We'd better take it into the house and—and call the police."

"The police?" Darren asked sharply. "What for?"

I looked at him in surprise. "We have to report it, don't we? I think that's the law. And, anyway—" I stopped, puzzled by something I saw in his face. "You're not thinking we'd keep it, are you?" I asked slowly.

"Well—" Darren's eyes dropped to the baby's face. "We could think about it. I mean—we've only got Jimmy, and it doesn't look as if we'll ever have any more—"

An old pain awoke again in my heart. Having children was something Darren and I had stopped talking about four years ago, when our second child, a little girl, had been born and had lived only a few hours. We'd learned then that having any more children would be virtually impossible, or at least terribly risky.

"I don't know," I murmured. "But we'd have to notify the police, anyway. I'm sure of that, Darren."

The baby began to cry, and I went past Darren, out of the garage. "You're going to be awfully late to work," I told him.

"I don't think I'll go," he said.

"For heaven's sake, Darren!" I snapped, losing my patience. "There's no reason for you to stay home." Oh, I loved Darren, but loving him didn't blind me to his faults, and sometimes his dreamy, easygoing way of putting things off drove me crazy. I used to tell him, "If it wasn't for me prodding you all the time, Darren, you'd never get anywhere!" And it was true!

The last thing I wanted just then was to have Darren underfoot. Hurrying into the kitchen, I was thinking that the baby was probably crying because it was hungry, and I didn't have any bottles, nor any idea of what its formula might be. And there was Jimmy to be fed and sent to school, too. Jimmy was standing in the middle of the kitchen with his mouth open and eyes all round in amazement.

"What's that, Mom?" he demanded

"A baby that somebody left in our car!" I told him, sounding angry, I suppose, because I was so flustered. "And it's hungry and—" I stopped. My hand, curved around the bundle, had felt a hardness under the blanket. Quickly, I reached inside and brought out a bottle three-quarters full, with its nipple reversed inside the screw-on top.

"Well, thank goodness for this," I said. "Jimmy, put some water in a pan to heat, and put this bottle in the water. And Darren, please go to work. I'll be all right, really, and you know we can't afford for you to lose a day."

Darren, standing in the doorway, hesitated for a moment. Then, stubbornly, he turned to me. "No, I'm staying home. I found the baby, and if we're going to have policemen and reporters around here I'll answer the questions. Anyway, it'll need the two of us to decide what to do."

I stared at him, and then I gave an irritated shrug. "Well, I think you're being very silly," I said.

He didn't answer, just went past me into the front of the house where I heard him calling his boss to say he wouldn't be in that day.

I had always been the sort of person who instinctively resented anything unexpected, unplanned for. So, during the next half-hour, my nerves stretched tighter and tighter. Jimmy, entranced by the baby, seemed not even to hear me when I told him to pour some cereal and milk for himself. Both he and his father stood over me, watching while I gave the baby its bottle, with Jimmy asking an endless string

190

of excited questions: "Is it ours, Mom? Who do you suppose left it? Are we going to keep it?"

"No. I don't know. I don't think so," I answered absently. "I don't even know if we'd be allowed to keep it, Jimmy."

"Why not? We found it, didn't we? And finders keepers," Jimmy said with a seven-year-old's logic

"Not when it comes to babies," I said. "Darren, if you're not going to work, won't you at least see that Jimmy eats his breakfast and gets ready for school?"

"Sure," Darren answered. He fixed Jimmy's cereal. "Now, if you want us to keep the baby, you eat!"

The baby had finished the bottle. I lifted it, and laid it against my shoulder. "Darren," I said, "I don't think you ought to talk like that and get Jimmy any more excited than he already is. How can we possibly keep it?"

"Why not, Eva?" he asked anxiously. "He was left here. Wouldn't we have first crack at adopting him?"

"When we'd talked about adopting a baby before, you said you didn't want to," I reminded him.

Darren's eyes dropped, and a flush came into his cheeks. "Did I? Well, it's different having one left with you," he muttered.

I was silent for a moment, gazing at Darren. He seemed, just then like a stranger—a stranger with secrets. But that was silly. I knew Darren as well as I knew myself—better, perhaps, because his was a simple and uncomplicated nature. He was like Jimmy, intrigued by the idea of a baby coming to us so mysteriously. He hadn't stopped to think of the trouble and expense we'd run into if we kept it. Though, of course, it might be nice, I thought with a warm stirring of excitement in my heart.

"I expect he needs changing," I said briskly. Unconsciously, following Darren's example, I'd used the masculine pronoun. Laying the baby, still wrapped in the blanket, on the porcelain drainboard of the sink, I sent Jimmy for a clean dish towel to serve as a diaper. As I spread the edges of the diaper apart, a crumpled slip of paper appeared in the folds. I picked it up and read aloud the few lines scrawled in pencil:

"Please be good to my poor little boy. His formula is—"

Suddenly, I turned to my husband in desperation. "Darren, Jimmy's got to get to school! He'll be late now if he tries to walk. Won't you drive him?"

After they left, I changed the baby and wrapped him again in the blanket. Then, I put him on the living room couch to sleep, and put pillows all around him so he wouldn't roll off. Next, I snatched up the telephone and called the local police. A man answered and I poured out the story of finding a baby in our car. He said he'd get in touch with the appropriate agency and have them send somebody to our house.

I hung up and went to the couch. Bending over, I peered into the baby's sleeping face. There was something familiar about him. I straightened up with a start as I heard the back door open and close.

"Eva?" my husband asked tentatively.

"Yes—" I answered. "I called the police, Darren."

"Why the rush?" Darren asked, and I could see he was disturbed.

"I didn't see any point in waiting. I told you—" I began.

"Eva," he interrupted, "don't send him away!" There was a note of desperate, too desperate, entreaty in his voice. "We've got room here for another kid. And it'd be good for Jimmy."

"Why would it? We don't have so much. It seems to me that another child would only mean depriving Jimmy of things he could have if he was the only one."

"How can we turn our backs on a baby that was abandoned in our own home?" he asked.

I fell back a step from the urgency in his voice. My heart was beating so, it shook my entire body. "Why?" I whispered. "Why do you want to keep this baby so much, Darren?"

"I've told you! It's the only decent thing to do!" Something flickered, a shadow far back in what I'd always thought was the transparent honesty of his eyes. "Look, Eva," he said, "all the time we've been married, you've had your way about everything. Just this once, there's something that I want. Let me have it. You like children. I was watching your face while you gave him his bottle. You could learn to love him, just as much as you love Jimmy."

He was drowning me with words, using them to try and blot out the fear, the dreadful suspicion, that was growing in my heart. But words weren't what Darren used best. His hands were clever, not his tongue, and suddenly, everything he said sounded rehearsed—false. Only the pleading in his face was real. I was still shaking my head, helplessly, from side to side, trying to find a reason for Darren's odd behavior. Then Darren picked up the baby, and suddenly I knew! I knew why the baby looked familiar. He looked like Darren!

"He's yours," I gasped.

"No!" Darren shouted, but I knew he was lying. All at once, the things that had confused me were clear.

"Yes, he is! You heard the garage doors last night. You were awake, listening for the sound. You got out of bed to keep me from looking, and—and you lied to me about not seeing anyone. You knew the baby was there when you went to get into the car. You knew it was a boy, you kept calling it 'he.'" I stared at him, shocked.

192

"Eva," Darren said, putting the baby down and stepping toward me, arms outstretched. I whirled, shuddering, away from his touch and ran blindly up the stairs to our bedroom. I closed the door and stood with my back pressed against it and my hands covering my face.

"Oh, God," I moaned, "what's happened to us? Everything was all right this morning, and now this! What's happened to our marriage, our lives?"

Ten years—ten good years! Oh, we'd had our troubles: the loss of our second child, and the discovery that we could never have another; Darren's disastrous failure when he tried to go into business for himself—but they'd been the kind of troubles that you could meet with courage and hope. While this—Oh, Lord, why did this have to happen?

Darren and I had met at a party when I was twenty-two and he was twenty-four. I'd liked him from the start, and as we saw more of each other my liking changed into love—a tender, half-protective kind of love. He was shy and unsure of himself, but I had enough energy and ambition for two, and I was certain we'd make a great team. Well, it hadn't worked out quite the way I'd expected. I hadn't been able to supply Darren with the drive, the self-confidence that I had in such abundance. And yet, we'd been happy—until now.

Darren was a carpenter and I was a receptionist when we married. We'd bought an old house with our combined savings as a down payment. I'd kept my job and nights and weekends, we'd worked at remodeling and modernizing our house. I poured over homemaking magazine for ideas, and Darren's clever hands carried the ideas out. After two years, we sold the house at a nice profit.

But it was hard work, and constantly, I had to battle Darren's easygoing nature, his tendency to put off until tomorrow, next week, or next month, what should have been done right away. When the house was finished, he didn't want to sell it, although that had been our plan from the start, in order to have enough capital so that he could go into business for himself.

Our plan? Mine, really, for as always, I'd had to coax and argue and encourage him.

"We're doing all right," Darren would say, and I'd answer, "But we want to do better!"

And we could have done better. The proof of it was in the cabinet-making shop that Darren had started, which was still going and thriving under the man who'd bought it when Darren had failed.

At first, I used to tell myself it was my fault for keeping my job. If I'd been there in the shop, helping Darren, I'd have seen how things were going and might have been able to do something about it. But, I wasn't there, and I didn't find out, until it was too late, that he was allowing bills to go unpaid; that he was letting people talk him into giving them great reductions on his material—that he was losing money steadily.

No, I didn't know, so I continued to work, even until I was well along with Jimmy. Then, when I did quit, I stayed in the apartment we occupied above the shop, and by the time I became aware of the financial condition of the business, we'd lost it. That was the week before Jimmy was born. Darren hadn't told me the business was failing until it became necessary because he hadn't wanted to upset me. Poor Darren!

"Eva, I'm sorry," he kept saying. "I don't know how it happened. I guess I'm just not cut out to run my own business. I'm better off working for someone."

I'd always been grateful since then that I hadn't given way to the shock and anger that I'd felt. Instead, I'd comforted him. I'd told him that it didn't matter—we'd get along somehow—and I'd put my arms around him and held him close.

From that day on, I'd never reproached him for his failure. As soon as I was strong enough after Jimmy was born, we moved to a rented house near my parents. Mom agreed to take care of Jimmy during the day, and I got a job. With both of us working, we managed to pay off our debts, and when Mom and Dad decided to move to Arizona for Mom's health, we were able to take their house off their hands, with a down-payment and mortgage. The house was old and inconvenient, but we had no money to improve it. It took all we earned just to live, with an occasional small luxury, like the trip Jimmy and I had taken to visit my family last winter.

Last winter! I straightened up, thinking: Of course! That's when it had happened! Darren had been so generous. He'd been so supportive when I'd said that I'd missed my parents and wanted to bring my son to see them during his winter break. I'd been touched, grateful, and worried that he'd be lonely while Jimmy and I were gone. Lonely! That was funny, but there was no laughter in me anymore. At that time, if there was one thing I could have staked my life on, it was Darren's complete faithfulness to me. How wrong I'd been!

Darren seemed to be the same as ever when Jimmy and I had come home from our trip—quietly glad to see us, apparently, and letting me do most of the talking. Yes, he said, he'd gotten along all right. He told us that he'd eaten most of his meals out, seen a few movies, and gone to bed early. I'd suspected nothing.

And later, in the months that followed, there seemed to be no change in our pleasant, uneventful life. If he hadn't let the child be brought to our home, I'd never have known.

Thinking of the child, I felt a new wave of fury sweep over me.

194

How could he have dared bring him to my house, and try to palm him off on me as a genuine orphan—try to persuade me to keep him? Did he really believe I'd be so easily deceived? He must think I was a complete fool!

I heard a car stop outside, and a moment later, the doorbell rang. I took a deep breath, steadying myself for what was ahead. All my outraged pride, my humiliation, urged me to stay shut up in my room. But, I felt I couldn't do that. I had to go down there and make it plain from the start that we didn't want the baby and wouldn't consider keeping it.

Composing myself with a great effort, I went out into the hall. I heard a man's deep voice saying, "So, I hear somebody left a baby with you."

"Yes," Darren said. "Come on in."

Two men, one a policeman and the other in a business suit, carrying a camera, were in the living room when I came downstairs. So, the newspapers were after us already! How they'd love to know the real story! I let Darren tell them about finding the baby.

Then the reporter asked the question I'd been waiting for, and dreading. "Well, Mr. and Mrs. Morrisey, what now? Would you like to keep the baby, if you were granted the authority to do so?"

"No," I said quickly, before Darren had a chance to answer.

The doorbell rang again, and it was a young woman from Children's Services. That time, Darren was completely silent as I went over the story again for her benefit.

"I suppose you'll put him in a foster home?" I asked. Darren was silent.

"Why, yes," the woman said. "The only thing is—" She looked down at the note I'd found tucked into the baby's blanket, which I had given to her and the others to look at. "Has it occurred to you, Mrs. Morrisey, that the mother may not have wanted her child to be a ward of the state? She asks you in this note to take care of him—"

"She had no right to ask that!" My voice was too loud, too strained. "I'm certain she's an utter stranger to me," I added, more quietly.

"Well, we'll want a picture, anyway," the reporter told us. "If you'll just sit on the couch, Mrs. Morrisey, with the baby on your lap, and Mr. Morrisey, suppose you sit beside her."

"No," Darren said thickly. "I won't have our pictures plastered all over your paper!"

"Aw, come on, Mr. Morrisey," the reporter coaxed. "Makes a nice human-interest feature."

"No, I won't!" Darren took a step toward the reporter, his head lowered menacingly. "You've got no right to be in my house, anyway. I didn't call you!"

"Now, now," the policeman said, getting between Darren and

the reporter. "If you don't want your picture taken, no one will take it. I'll see to that, Mr. Morrisey. But, on the other hand, what harm would it do?"

"I don't want any pictures taken!" Darren's voice rose. All of them—the reporter and the policeman and the social worker—stared at him in amazement, unable to understand the reason for his outburst. I knew I had to do something to take their attention away from him, before they thought of the one possible reason—the right reason.

"My husband's camera-shy," I said, forcing a laugh. "I've never been able to get him to pose for photos. But you can take a picture of me with the baby, if you want to." I sat down and picked up the baby. I didn't want to touch him, but I realized that we had to behave as those people would normally expect us to.

Darren watchful stonily as I posed for the camera. Then at last it was over. The reporter and the policeman were ready to leave, and the social worker held out her arms. "I'll take the baby now."

"I'll get his bottle," I said, and went into the kitchen. From there, I heard Darren talking in a low voice.

"If we should change our mind and want him back—in the next few days, I mean—could we?"

"My name is Carla Grant. I'll give you my card. Of course, you understand we'd have to make all the routine investigations."

"What kind of investigations?" Darren asked.

"Oh, the sort of thing we do in any adoption case. We'd inspect your home, ask you for some references. We'd have to be certain both you and your wife wanted the child, and—"

"I see," Darren interrupted, sounding hopeless—and no wonder, because he must have known already that I would never permit that baby in my home—never.

I went back to the living room, and the woman turned to me. "I was just saying to Mr. Morrisey that if you should change your mind about keeping the baby—"

"Yes, I heard," I cut in, not even caring if I sounded rude. "But I'm quite sure that we won't. Thank you for everything."

So, she gathered the baby up and left. Neither Darren nor I spoke until the sound of her car had died away.

"Eva, please try to understand—" he began.

I supposed that deep down I had still kept a glimmer of hope that he might tell me I'd been mistaken when I'd accused him of being the child's father, and that he'd be able to make me believe him. Suddenly, I felt sharp disappointment, no less painful because there was so little reason for it.

"So, he is yours!" I cried. "You admit it?"

"Yes," he said wearily. "I guess it was crazy to try to fool you like that. But I thought. . . . Well, it doesn't matter what I thought."

"You thought you could get away with it!" I let my rage, my sense of having been betrayed, lash out at him. "Who is she?"

His head and shoulders sank in defeat. "Nobody you know. Just a—a woman that liked me. Eva, I don't blame you for being furious. I know I did a terrible thing, but at the time I never meant—"

"You know that you did a terrible thing! Well, isn't that nice!" I flared. "I suppose you think that makes everything all right!"

"Eva, please try to understand," he pleaded. "When you left, I—"

"When I left," I shouted hysterically, "you went out and—and had some fun. Only the baby came, and you had to do something about it!" I knew it couldn't have been as simple as that, but I was too furious to care.

Darren started to speak, and then he let the breath out of his lungs. "Maybe I'd better go to work," he said heavily. "Earn half a day's pay, anyway." He turned and went out, very quietly.

A moment later, the phone rang. It was Terri Carter, my neighbor across the street. She'd seen our visitors and wanted know if anything was wrong. So, I told her about the baby. Why not? It would be in the paper soon enough. From Terri, the story spread, and for the rest of the day, I was busy answering the phone or talking to women who came to the house. I was glad of that activity; it kept me from thinking too much. But, I thought enough. Several times, I had a crazy impulse to tell them the truth and beg for advice. But I was ashamed to expose my private tragedy to them. Besides, I knew that what I should do was something only I could decide.

When Jimmy came home from school and learned that the baby was gone, he was disappointed—he cried and cried. He was comforted a little when I told him the paper would have my picture in it.

Mechanically, I started preparing dinner at the usual time. It seemed incredible that we should still need to eat, that that night, we would lie down and close our eyes and perhaps even sleep, I thought dully. But one thing I knew—Darren and I would not share the same bed. Before he was due home, I got fresh sheets and made up the seldom-used bed in the guest room.

Darren came home at six o'clock, and when he'd washed up, we sat down to eat. Jimmy kept the meal from being a silent one. Sometimes I'd thought he'd chattered to much, but that night I was grateful for the sound of his sweet little voice. Afterward, Darren went outside and played ball with him while I cleared the table and washed the dishes. I was still in the kitchen when it got dark and they came in. I stayed there, finding little tasks to do that I could have put off, dreading the moment when Jimmy would be sent to bed and Darren and I would be alone.

At last, I could find nothing more to do in the kitchen. I sent Jimmy to bed. Then I stepped outside. I hadn't heard the house door open, but a few minutes later, I felt Darren standing behind me. I stiffened and took a step away.

"Eva," he said, "I suppose it's not much use saying this, but— I'm sorry. I didn't want you to know."

I laughed harshly. "I shouldn't think you would!"

"No man would, Eva, unless he wanted to hurt his wife. And you've got to believe this—I never wanted to hurt you. But I felt I owed something to the—the boy. I guess it was silly to think I could fool you, but I couldn't think of any other way."

"How about her?" I asked fiercely. "The mother? Couldn't she come up with a better idea—like keeping her own baby?"

"No," he said flatly. "Eva, I know how you feel, and I'd do anything if I could undo what I've done. And you've got to believe this, Eva, it only lasted while you were away. After you came back, I'd never have seen her again, except that she found out she was pregnant and asked me for help."

"What kind of help? Money?"

He was silent for a moment. "Yes, money!" he answered finally. "But I didn't have much to give." His voice broke. "The baby was a charity case, right from the start!"

In spite of my deep anger, I couldn't help recognizing his shame, but I couldn't pity him. "That's too bad," I said coldly. "But there shouldn't have been any baby at all. There wouldn't have been if you'd been—decent!"

"You're right," he said wearily. "I admit it. But what can I do about it now?" he asked helplessly. "Where do we go from here, Eva? How about you and me?"

"I don't know." I turned and started blindly toward the house. "I don't know," I repeated.

Darren stayed where he was, not following me. I went upstairs, into the guest room, and closed the door. I didn't lock it. I knew that Darren wouldn't disturb me, and the closed door would tell him where I was. After a while, I heard him come up and go into our room, and then, for long hours, there was only darkness and silence, except for the muffled sound of my sobs.

Where do we go from here? Darren had asked me. It was a question I didn't know how to answer. I shrank from the thought of divorce, or even of separation, with the explanations I'd have to make to Jimmy, my parents, and our friends. I didn't want them to know. I didn't want pity, curiosity, wagging tongues, and my privacy invaded. And yet, the alternative—going on as Darren's wife—seemed equally intolerable.

198

So, when morning came, I had made no decision. I got up, dressed, and made breakfast for Darren, and he ate it sitting alone and silent at the table. He left without saying a word. I called Jimmy and saw him off to school, brightly pretending that nothing was wrong, and knowing from the bewilderment in his eyes that he'd already sensed that something was very, very wrong.

All day, I went about the house, doing the things I had to do without thought or feeling for them.

That night, Darren and I talked to each other at the supper table, but only for Jimmy's sake, and what we said to each other was meaningless. That night, I slept in the guest room again. There, I thought, was the pattern of what our life might be—perhaps must be—from now on. Two people, living in the same house, tied together only by habit and a shared love for Jimmy. But could two people live out their existences like that—without love, without respect, or even affection?

The following day, Saturday, Darren worked. But Sunday he was home, and it seemed as though the day would never end. All the little pleasant things that usually happened on Sunday—sleeping a bit later than usual, having an unhurried breakfast with all three of us at the table, going to church and afterward driving to see Darren's parents— were nothing but routine now, and painful with a special kind of pain because once they had made us happy.

When we got home, I was exhausted from the strain of pretending, for my in-laws' benefit, that there was nothing wrong between Darren and me.

When I was saying good night to Jimmy in his room, he suddenly threw his arms around my neck and held me with a sort of desperation. "Mom," he said, almost whispering it against my ear, "why don't you and Dad still sleep in the same room?"

"Oh, we just thought we'd sleep better that way," I told him calmly.

He relaxed his grip around my neck, but still held me so he could look into my eyes. "Really, Mom?" he asked. "You still—you still like each other, don't you?"

"Oh, Jimmy, of course!" I lied, my heart bursting with pity for him.

"Well, I didn't know—" he said, still unconvinced. "Dad said you sent the baby back, and he didn't seem to like it much. I thought maybe he was mad at you about that."

"Mad at me!" The idea was so ridiculous that I wanted to break into angry laughter. But, of course, that would only confuse Jimmy more, so I said gently, "If he is, he'll get over it. We don't want any baby. We've got all the children we want right here."

199

I kissed him and went downstairs, frowning. Darren had had no right to tell Jimmy I'd sent the baby back; put all the blame on me.

The next morning, when Darren came downstairs for breakfast, I turned to him furiously. "You told Jimmy that I sent the baby away!"

"Yes," he said tonelessly. "He asked me if I didn't want it, and I said that I did, but that you didn't. That was the truth, wasn't it?"

"Yes, but—" My arms flew wide apart. "Darren, I'd like to forgive you—living like this isn't very pleasant for me, either—but you aren't giving me very much help!"

"I'm sorry, Eva. I want you to forgive me. I want that very much. And I also want to forgive you."

"What?" I cried shrilly. "What do you mean by that? What have you got to forgive me for?"

He got up. "I can't talk now, Eva. I've got to get to work," he said and went out the door.

I was shaking with fury, and yet a strange kind of fear was mixed with my anger. The fear of something unknown. But what could he possibly say that would prove I needed forgiveness? Nothing! For ten years, I had loved him loyally, devotedly. He had no excuse for what he'd done.

Don't think about it, I told myself. Don't get yourself more upset. And I tried not to, plunging into my Monday-morning washing. I was in the basement, just taking out the first load of wash when I heard the doorbell. I climbed the stairs and threw open the front door.

"Yes?" I said curtly to the woman standing there.

She was dressed in tight jeans and a sweater. Her face might have been pretty once, but now it was worn and tired looking, and she wore too much makeup. I supposed she was about forty. I couldn't imagine what she wanted.

"Mrs. Morrisey?" she asked in a rather husky voice. "I'm Carrie Summers." She saw that the name meant nothing to me, and added quietly, "I left my baby here last week."

"Oh!" My hand seemed to start closing the door of its own accord, but quickly, she put her own hand out and pressed against it to hold it open.

"Please!" she begged. "Don't send me away! I want—I've got to talk to you."

"There's nothing—" I began, but I knew I'd let her in. I had to know more about the woman who had conceived Darren's child. It wasn't possible, I thought. She was such a haggard creature, so much older than he—so cheap.

"Come in," I said stiffly.

She went past me and into the living room.

"What do you want?" I demanded.

She turned and looked at me, her eyes moving slowly across my face as if she were trying to find some hidden meaning there. "You look," she murmured slowly, "just the way I thought you would."

"I do?" I asked stupidly, before anger overwhelmed me again. "I asked you what you wanted here! What right—"

"Oh, I've got no right to be here at all," she interrupted with a little shake of her head. "I know that."

"Then you'd better get out."

"I will, but let me talk to you first, Mrs. Morrisey. I called Darren up at the place where he works to find out what had happened to the baby, and he told me how you felt. Let me tell you—I don't blame you for being angry with Darren, but you shouldn't be. He's a good man—the best man I ever knew."

"Then you've known some pretty bad ones," I spat cruelly.

She nodded in humble agreement. "I sure have. And I haven't been any angel myself. I wouldn't try to fool you about that. After all, well, I met Darren in a bar where I spend a good deal of my time."

"Where you—pick up men?" I asked.

She lifted her head quickly. "Not the way you mean," she insisted with a strange kind of pride. "I work for a living, Mrs. Morrisey. I'm a clerk in a store. It's a cheap store, but I earn regular wages. So, if I pick men up, it's not for money."

"That makes it all right, I suppose," I said contemptuously.

"No, I didn't say that. But I didn't come here to talk about myself, Mrs. Morrisey. I came to see if you wouldn't forgive Darren and—and think about keeping the baby. No, wait," she interrupted as she saw me starting to refuse. "I tell you, Darren's good. Just because he made one mistake—"

"It was a pretty big mistake," I said sarcastically. "You'll admit that, won't you? Or, don't you believe in the sacredness of marriage?"

She drew herself up, and answered with a shabby dignity. "Maybe I do, more than you think. But I know one thing: When a man like Darren—well, carries on with another woman, there's got to be a reason!"

Her words seemed to touch some raw, exposed nerve in me. "Reason!" I said loudly. "I'll tell you the reason—the only possible reason! I was away, and he thought he could get away with it!"

"That isn't true," she said steadily. "It might be for some men, but not for Darren. I don't know you, Mrs. Morrisey, but I know him, and I know that when he came to me it wasn't just because he wanted a woman and you didn't happen to be around. I gave him something you never did. I don't know what it was, but I do know it wasn't just sex."

My eyes fell before the challenge in hers. All at once I was remembering something—Darren's answer when I asked him who the woman was.

"Nobody much," he'd said. "Just a woman that—liked me." It hadn't occurred to me then that he'd meant anything special by that, but suddenly—I didn't want to think about that. I wanted to keep my anger and my scorn.

"If there's anything wrong with my marriage, I don't think it's your affair," I said bitingly.

"No," she admitted, "I guess it isn't." She was silent for a moment. "I told you, I came to ask if you wouldn't forgive Darren and think about keeping the baby. But I can see now he'd be better off in a foster home."

I stared at her, thinking at first that I hadn't understood. Then the hot blood rushed up into my face. "Are you trying to tell me I'm not good enough—"

"You'd never forget," she cut in. "You'd always remember how he came to be born, and that'd mean more to you than anything else—more than him being just a child that needed to be taken care of and loved. So, it wouldn't work out. Oh," she interrupted herself quickly, "I don't say that I blame you. Maybe if I was in your spot I'd be the same way. The only thing—" She hesitated, and a little smile came into her worn face, making it seem much younger, so I realized I must have been wrong by at least ten years when I first placed her age at forty.

"I guess," she said simply, "I had some kind of an idea you'd be a special kind of person because Darren's so special himself. I'm nothing. I couldn't bring up the boy if I kept him. And I don't expect anything from Darren for myself—ever. But I thought if you'd take him, then it wouldn't have been—" Suddenly, I saw tears in her eyes. "—such a waste to have him at all." She turned abruptly, and took a step toward the door. "I'll go now," she mumbled in a muffled voice.

"No! Wait!" The words burst from my lips. All at once, my anger had slipped away from me, and I knew I could never recapture it. My good, strong anger, giving me certainty and self-confidence, was gone, and suddenly I was groping in the dark. Yet, I knew the question I had to ask, if I could find the words for it

"The baby—" I began. "Why did you have it? I mean—if you've lived the way you say—" I stopped, swallowed painfully, and began again. "You must have known how not to have a child. Didn't you?"

"Yes," she said. "Sure, I knew."

"Then why?"

"I guess you know why," she told me. "Because I wanted to have it." She turned and faced me, tears streaming down her cheeks. "Feeling the way I did about Darren—liking him so much. All right, loving him, but he never knew it and never will. Anyway, I had some crazy idea I could straighten up and raise the kid myself. Live decently, stop drinking, and hanging around bars and—you know. I thought I'd move away, to some place I'd never been before, and take him along. But—" She tried to force her trembling lips into a smile. "—all the time, I was kidding myself. The last few months I was pregnant and couldn't go anyplace, I just about went crazy. So finally I had to admit it; I'm just not the type to bring up a kid. I'd make a mess of his life, the way I've made one of my own. So, Darren and I thought of bringing him here and leaving him. It was a crazy idea but we thought it might work. Only—it didn't. Sorry I bothered you, Mrs. Morrisey. I'm leaving town in a couple of days—figure it'd be better that way."

"I see," I said mechanically, hardly knowing what she'd told me. There was room in my mind for only one thing—the knowledge that this woman loved Darren. She loved him so much she had wanted to bear his child. She loved him too much to make any claims upon him at all. While I—I had every claim on him. Every legal claim. I was his wife, and any court in the land would say that he had grievously wronged me by committing adultery with another woman.

And he had wronged me! Darren knew that himself, and had tried to say that he was sorry. But I had closed my eyes and ears to his regrets—rejected them as being of no value. Had I, all these years of our marriage, closed my eyes and ears to other things?

"There's got to be a reason," the woman had said. And dimly, I saw what that reason might be.

There was a quality of bigness in that poorly dressed woman, and a quality of smallness in me. That was what she'd meant when she'd said, that, married to Darren, I should be "special." I wasn't special at all—and suddenly I wanted to be.

All of those thoughts passed through my mind in the second it took her to turn toward the door.

"Please," I said, "I'd like to change my mind and say I want the baby after all. Will you—let me?"

"Oh—" Her face grew radiant. "If you really want to—I'd be so glad!"

"I'll be good to him," I promised.

For a moment, our eyes held. Then she said softly, "I know you will. Thank you."

By evening, when Darren came home, I had talked to Miss Grant and told her that we wanted the baby back as soon as possible. She said she would start making the arrangements.

I didn't say anything to Darren until after Jimmy had gone to bed. Then, as we sat in the living room, I turned to him.

"Darren, you told me this morning you were trying to forgive me. No, wait—" I hurried on as he colored and started to say something. "I didn't know what you meant then. But, I do now. You see—she was here today."

Darren knew who I meant. "Carrie? Here?"

I nodded. "I'm glad she came, Darren. Oh, at first I was furious, and I told her to get out. But then we talked and I—I realized for the first time that if you'd had an affair with her, I must have been partly to blame. And I remembered something you'd said—that she liked you. Did you mean you think I don't?" I whispered.

"Oh, Eva, of course, I—" But he broke off. "No, I won't lie to you. I did mean something like that. I know I've been a disappointment to you. I failed miserably when I tried to go into business for myself. I don't make an awful lot of money, I don't have the ambition to. All I want is to do a day's work for a day's pay, and that's all I'll ever want. But you—"

"I've never complained, Darren," I said, but I knew the answer to that before he gave it to me.

"Not in so many words—no," he conceded. "But I know what you're thinking when you say something about the house being old, or our not having enough money to buy something or other. You're thinking that if I had more on the ball, if I'd made a go of that shop, things would be different. Somehow, when I'm around you I just don't—feel like I amount to much."

It seemed to me that no man had ever made a more terrible accusation against his wife. And yet, I knew in my heart it was true.

"And this other woman—this Carrie," I said, "she made you feel as if you amounted to something?"

"Yes! Oh—" He shook his head. "I didn't love her—not the way I love you. But I felt—comfortable with her, more like a person—I can't explain it."

"You explain it very well," I said sadly. "So, well, there's nothing I can say, only— Oh, Darren, I never meant to hurt you. I was thoughtless and stupid, but I've always loved you. I love you now—more than ever." I was crying, but I went on. "There's something else I have to tell you. I called and asked if we could have the baby back."

"You—" Darren stared at me in wide-eyed incredulous amazement. Then, slowly, wonder came into his face, and he left his chair and knelt on the floor beside my chair. "Eva," he whispered, holding my hands, "if you think you can love him—"

"I can. I know I can," I said, and I had never been more certain of anything.

We have Darren's other child now, and I do love him, in a very special way. For little Kyle is, to me, the living symbol of the one time

I was able to rise above pride, above thoughts of myself, my feelings, my desires. Because he was born, I learned that love, if it is real love, can accept faults as well as virtues in the beloved one. Oh, I'd told myself throughout my marriage that I'd accepted Darren's faults but I never had—not really. They were always in my thoughts, where he could—loving me—sense their presence and be deeply hurt. First, I had tried to change him and then, when the attempt had failed, I'd blamed him for the failure.

I do not blame him now, and I would not change him, even if I could. And that, I know at last, is true love.

THE END

www.ingramcontent.com/pod-product-compliance
Lightning Source LLC
Chambersburg PA
CBHW072057170626
46813CB00004B/1398